12 MINU

Dragon Leader felt muscles pulse and jump beneath his thighs as he turned his mount in the direction indicated by the swiftly moving misty patch on the magic detectors. Echeloned out below and behind him were the seven other dragons of his squadron.

"Time to intercept, 12 minutes," said a voice inside his skull. He did not reply.

One of his men waved and pointed below: silhouetted against the cloud tops were four dragons skulking north. He rose in his stirrups and looked behind him; the rest of his troop were waiting expectantly. He pointed downward and patted the top of his head in the time-honored signal to dive on the enemy.

He was well into his dive when suddenly the targets winged over and scattered into the clouds, almost as if they had been warned.

As if they had been warned . . . !

"Break! Break!" Dragon Leader screamed into his communications crystal. But it was already too late. The hurtling shapes were upon them.

RICK COOK

WIZARD'S BANE

BAEN

WIZARD'S BANE

Copyright © 1989 by Rick Cook

A Baen Books Original

Baen Publishing Enterprises
260 Fifth Avenue
New York, N.Y. 10001

First printing, February 1989
Second printing, January 1990

ISBN: 0-671-69803-6

Cover art by Alan Gutierrez

Printed in the United States of America

Distributed by
SIMON & SCHUSTER
1230 Avenue of the Americas
New York, N.Y. 10020

For Pati.
Who has her own
special brand of magic.

ONE

MEETING IN MIDSUMMER

It was a fine Mid-Summer's morning and Moira the hedge witch was out gathering herbs.

"Tansy to stop bleeding," she said to herself, examining the stand that grew on the bankside. Carefully she selected the largest, healthiest stems and, reciting the appropriate charm, she cut them off low with her silver knife. She inspected each stem closely before placing it in the straw basket beside her.

When she had finished, she brushed a strand of coppery hair from her green eyes and surveyed the forest with all her senses.

The day was sunny, the air was clear and the woods around her were calm and peaceful. The oaks and beeches spread their gray-green and green-gold leaves to the sun and breeze. In their branches birds sang and squirrels chattered as they dashed about on squirrelish errands. Their tiny minds were content, Moira saw. For them there was no danger on the Fringe of the Wild Wood, even on Mid-Summer's Day.

Moira knew better. Back in her village the fields were deserted and the animals locked in their barns. The villagers were huddled behind doors bolted with

1

iron, bound with ropes of straw and sealed with such charms as Moira could provide. Only a foolhardy person or one in great need would venture abroad on Mid-Summer's Day.

Moira was out for need, the needs of others. Mid-Summer's Day was pregnant with magic of all sorts, and herbs gathered by the light of the Mid-Summer sun were unusually potent. Her village would need the healing potions and the charms she could make from them.

That most of her fellow hedge witches were also behind bolted doors weighed not at all with her. Her duty was to help those who needed help, so she had taken her straw basket and consecrated silver knife and gone alone into the Fringe of the Wild Wood.

She was careful to stay in the quietest areas of the Fringe, however. She had planned her route days ago and she moved cautiously between her chosen stands of herbs. She probed the forest constantly, seeking the least sign of danger or heightened magic. There was need enough to draw her out this day, but no amount of need would make her careless.

Her next destination was a marshy corner of a nearby meadow where pink-flowered mallow grew in spiky profusion. It was barely half a mile by the road on whose bank she sat, but Moira would take a longer route. Between her and the meadow this road crossed another equally well-travelled lane. Moira had no intention of going near a crossroads on Mid-Summer's Day.

She was fully alert, so she was all the more startled when a dark shadow fell over her. Moira gasped and whirled to find herself facing a tall old man wearing a rough travelling cloak and leaning on a carved staff.

"Oh! Merry met, Lord," she scrambled up from the bank and dipped a curtsey. "You startled me."

"Merry met, child," the man responded, blinking at her with watery brown eyes. "Why it's the little hedge witch, Moira, isn't it?" He blinked again and stared down his aquiline nose. "Bless me!" he clucked. "How you have grown my girl. How you have grown."

Moira nodded respectfully and said nothing. Patrius was of the Mighty; perhaps the mightiest of the Mighty. It behooves one to be respectful no matter what style one of the Mighty chooses to take.

The wizard sighed. "But it's well met nonetheless. Yes, very well met. I have a little project afoot and perhaps you can help me with it."

"Of course Lord, if I can." She sighed to herself. It was never too healthy to become involved with the doings of the Mighty. Looking at Patrius she could see magic twist and shimmer around the old man like heatwaves rising from a hot iron stove.

"Well, actually it's not such a little project," he said confidingly. "A rather large one, in fact. Yes, quite large." He beamed at her. "Oh, but I'm sure you'll be able to handle it. You were always such an adept pupil."

In fact Moira had been so far from adept she had barely survived the months she had spent studying with the old wizard. She knew Patrius remembered that time perfectly. But if one of the Mighty asks for aid he or she can not be gainsaid.

"Lord," suggested Moira timidly, "might not one of your apprentices . . . ?"

"What? My apprentices, oh no, no, no. They don't know, you see. They can't know yet. Besides," he added as an afterthought, "they're all male."

"Yes, Lord," Moira said as if that explained everything.

The wizard straightened. "Now come along, child. The place is near and we haven't much time. And you must tell me how you have been getting along. It's been such an age since I saw you last. You never come to the Capital, you know," he added in mild reproach.

"For those of us who cannot walk the Wizard's Way it is a long journey, Lord."

"Ah yes, you're right, of course," the old man chuckled. "But tell me, how do things go on in your village?"

Moira warmed. Studying under Patrius had nearly killed her several times, but of all her teachers she liked him the best. His absentminded, grandfatherly manner might be assumed, but no one who knew him doubted his kindness. She remembered sitting in the wizard's study of an afternoon drinking mulled cider and talking of nothing that mattered while dust motes danced in the sunbeams.

If Patrius was perhaps not the mightiest of the Mighty, he was certainly the best, the nicest and far and away the most human of that fraternity of powerful wizards. Walking with him Moira felt warm and secure, as if she were out on a picnic with a favorite uncle instead of abroad on the Fringe of the Wild Wood on one of the most dangerous days of the year.

Patrius took her straight into the forest, ignoring the potential danger spots all around. At length they came to a grassy clearing marked only by a rock off to one side.

"Now my child," he said, easing himself down on the stone and resting his staff beside him, "you're probably wondering what I'm up to, eh?"

"Yes, Lord." Moira stood a respectful distance away.

"Oh, come here my girl," he motioned her over. "Come, come come. Be comfortable." Moira smiled and sat on the grass at his feet, spreading her skirt around her.

"To business then. I intend to perform a Great Summoning and I want your help."

Moira gasped. She had never seen even a Lesser Summoning, the materializing of a person or object from elsewhere in the World. It was solely the province of the Mighty and so fraught with danger that they did it rarely. A Great Summoning brought something from beyond the World and was far riskier. Of all the Mighty living, only Patrius, Bal-Simba and perhaps one or two others had ever participated in a Great Summoning.

"But Lord, you need several of the Mighty for that!"

Patrius frowned. "Do you presume to teach me magic, girl?"

"No, Lord," Moira dropped her eyes to the grass.

The wizard's face softened. "It is true that a Great Summoning is usually done by several of us acting in consort, but there is no need, really. Not if the place of Summoning is quiet."

So that was why Patrius had come to the Fringe, Moira thought. Here, away from the bustle and disturbance of competing magics, it would be easier for him to bend the fundamental forces of the World to his will.

"Isn't it dangerous, Lord?"

Patrius sighed, looking suddenly like a careworn old man rather than a mighty wizard or someone's grandfather.

"Yes Moira, it is. But sometimes the dangerous road is the safest." He shook his head. "These are evil times, child. As well you know."

"Yes, Lord," said Moira, with a sudden pang.

"Evil times," Patrius repeated. "Desperate times. They call for desperate measures.

"You know our plight, Moira. None know better than the hedge witches and the other lesser orders. We of the Mighty are isolated in our keeps and cities, but you have to deal with the World every day. The Wild Wood presses ever closer and to the south the Dark League waxes strong to make chaos of what little order there is in the World."

Moira's hand moved in a warding gesture at the mention of the League, but Patrius caught her wrist and shook his head.

"Softly, softly," he admonished. "We must do nothing to attract attention, eh?

"We need help, Moira," he went on. "The people

of the North need help badly and there are none in the World who can help us. So I must go beyond the World to find aid."

He sighed again. "It was a long search, my child, long and hard. But I have finally located someone of great power who can help us, both against the League and against the World. Now the time is ripe and I propose to Summon him."

"But won't this alien wizard be angry at being brought here so rudely?"

"I did not say he was a wizard," Patrius said with a little shake of his head. "No, I did not say that at all."

"Who but a wizard can deal in magic?"

"Who indeed?" Patrius responded. "Who indeed?"

It was Moira's turn to sigh, inwardly at least. Patrius had obviously told her as much of this mad venture as he intended to.

"What will you of me, Lord?" asked Moira.

"Just your aid as lector," the old Wizard said. "Your aid and a drop of your blood."

"Willingly, Lord." Moira was relieved it wasn't more. Often great spells required great sacrifices.

"Well then," said the Wizard, picking up his staff and rising. "Let us begin. You'll have to memorize the chant, of course."

Patrius cut a straight branch from a nearby tree, stripped it of its leaves and stuck it upright in the clearing. Its shadow stretched perhaps four handsbreadths from its base, shortening imperceptibly as the sun climbed higher.

"When the shadow disappears it will be time," he told her. "Now, here is what you must say . . . ."

The words Moira had to speak were simple, but they sent shivers down her spine. Patrius repeated them to her several times, speaking every other word on each repetition so magic would not be made prematurely. As a trained witch Moira easily put the words in the right order and fixed them in her mind.

While the hedge witch worked on the spells, Patrius walked the clearing, carefully aligning the positions where they both would stand and scratching runes into the earth.

Moira looked up from her memorization. "Lord," she said dubiously, "aren't you forgetting the pentagram?"

"Eh? No girl, I'm not forgetting. We only need a pentagram to contain the Summoned should it prove dangerous."

"And this one is not dangerous?" Moira frowned.

Patrius chuckled. "No, he is not dangerous."

Moira wanted to ask how someone could be powerful enough to aid the Mighty and still not be dangerous even when Summoned, but Patrius motioned her to silence, gestured her to her place and, as the stick's shadow shortened to nothing, began his part of the chant.

"*Aaagggh!*" William Irving Zumwalt growled at the screen. Without taking his eyes off the fragment of code, he grabbed the can of cola balanced precariously on the mound of printouts and hamburger wrappers littering his desk.

"Found something, Wiz?" his cubicle mate asked, looking up from his terminal.

"Only the bug that's been screwing up the sort module."

William Irving Zumwalt—Wiz to one and all—leaned back and took a healthy swig of cola. It was warm and flat from sitting for hours, but he barely noticed. "Here. Take a look at this."

Jerry Andrews shifted his whale-like bulk and swiveled his chair to look over Wiz's shoulder. "Yeah? So?"

Wiz ran a long, thin hand through his shock of dark hair. "Don't you see? This cretinous barfbag uses sizeof to return the size of the array."

"So how else do you get the size?"

"Right. But C doesn't have an array data type. When you call an array you're actually passing a pointer to the array. That works fine from the main program, but sometimes this thing uses sizeof from a subroutine. And guess what it gets then?"

Jerry clapped a meaty hand to his forehead. "The size of the pointer! Of course."

"Right," Wiz said smugly. "No matter how big the array, the damn code returns a value of two."

"Jeez," Jerry shook his head as he shifted his chair back to his desk. "How long will it take to fix it?"

Wiz drained his drink before answering. "Couple of hours, I guess. I'll have to run a bunch of tests to make sure nothing else is wrong." He stood up and stretched. "But first I'm going to get another Coke—if the damn machine isn't empty again. You want one?"

"Nah," Jerry said, typing rapidly and not looking up. "I'm probably gonna knock off in a few minutes."

"Okay," said Wiz and sauntered out the office door.

Save for the clicking of Jerry's keyboard and the hiss of the air conditioner the corridor was quiet. Wiz glanced at his watch and realized it was nearly five A.M. Not that it mattered much. Programmers set their own hours at ZetaSoft and that was one of the reasons Will Zumwalt was still with the company.

The drink machine was next to a side door and Wiz decided to step out for a breath of dawn air. He loved this time of day when everything was cool and quiet and even the air was still, waiting. *As long as I don't have to get up at this hour!* he thought as he pushed the door open.

The magical lines of force gathered and curled about the old wizard. They twisted and warped, clawing at the very fabric of the Universe and bending it to a new shape. Far to the South, across the Freshened Sea, a point of light appeared in the watery depths of an enormous copper bowl.

"A hit," proclaimed the watcher, a lean shaven-skull man in a brown robe.

"What is it?" asked Xind, Master of the Sea of Scrying. He descended heavily from his dais and waddled across the torch-lit chamber hewn of blackest basalt to peer over the acolyte's shoulder.

Looking deep into the murky water his eyes traced the map of the World in the lines cut deep into the bowl's bottom. There was indeed a spark there. Magic where no magic ought to be. Around the edge of the bowl the other three acolytes shifted nervously but kept their eyes fixed to their own sectors.

"I do not know, Master, but it's strong and growing stronger. It looks like a major spell."

Xind, sorcerer of the Third Circle as the Dark League counted such things, passed a fat hand over the water as if wiping away a smear. "Hmm, yes. Wait, there's something . . . By the heavens and hells! There are no wards. That's a great wizard without protection!" His head snapped up. "Let the word be passed quickly!" The gray-robed apprentice crouched at the foot of the dais jumped up and ran to do his bidding.

Xind stared back into the Sea of Scrying and his round, fat face creased into a particularly unattractive smile.

"Fool," he muttered to the spark in the bottom of the bowl.

The haze in the clearing turned from wispy gray to opaque white to rosy pink. It contracted and coalesced until it took the form of a dark red door with a silver knob, floating a yard off the meadow. The grass bent away from it in all directions as if pressed down by an invisible ball. Moira concentrated on her chanting and pushed harder with all the magic she possessed.

As if in slow motion the door opened and a man came through. He stepped out as if he expected solid ground and slowly toppled through when he found air. His eyes widened and his mouth formed a soundless O. Then everything was moving at normal speed and the man extended his arms.

Wiz took two steps and fell three feet onto grass in what should have been a level walk. He caught himself with his arms and then collapsed with his nose in the green grass, weak, sick and disoriented. The light was different, he was facing the wrong way and he was so dizzy he couldn't hold his head up. He squeezed his eyes shut and concentrated on keeping his stomach in its proper place. The grass tickled his nose and the blades poked at his tightly shut eyes, but he ignored them.

Patrius made a flicking gesture at the man and then returned to the business of completing the spell. Moira, absorbed in her chant, barely noticed the small drop of dark fluid fly from the Wizard's fingertips and strike the new arrival on the temple. It splattered, spread and sank into the flesh and hair, leaving no sign of its passing.

In the great, high-vaulted chantry of the Dark League, four black-robed wizards huddled about a glowing crystal. They murmured and moved like a flock of uneasy crows, all the while peering into the depths of the stone. Around them forces twisted and gathered.

The attack came with a rush of magic, dark and sour. Moira cried out in terror and gestured frantically but she was thrust aside ruthlessly as the bolt lanced into the clearing and struck Patrius full-on.

A crackling blue nimbus burst out around the old wizard. He raised his arms over his head as if to shield himself, but his clothes and beard burst into flame. In an instant he was a ghastly flaming scarecrow capering about the clearing and shrieking in mortal agony. He toppled over and the screams turned to a puling whimper. His flesh blackened and charred.

Finally there was nothing but a smoldering husk with knees and arms flexed up against the body. He was so badly burned that there wasn't even a smell in the air.

Moira cowered sobbing on the ground, the blazing after-image burning in her sight even through her eyelids. Wiz had gone flat on his face when the bolt hit.

All right, Wiz told himself. *Time to get up. On three. One, two* . . . He realized he wasn't going to make it, so he settled for rolling over on his back.

"Lord?" a small voice asked tentatively.

Wiz opened his eyes. Standing over him was the most beautiful girl he had ever seen. Her waist-length hair was the color of burnished copper. Her skin was pale and creamy under a dusting of freckles. Her eyes were deep sea green. She was wearing a long skirt of forest green in some rough-woven material and a white peasant blouse with a scoop neck. Wiz stared.

"Are you hurt, Lord?" the vision said in a lilting, musical voice. As she bent down to help Wiz up he was treated to a display of ample cleavage.

"N-n-n-no," Wiz managed to stammer, dizzy from the transformation and awed by her loveliness. He looked into her face. "You're beautiful," he said softly.

Moira saw the look in his eyes and swore under her breath. *Fortuna!* An infatuation spell! Patrius had bound this unknown wizard to her with an infatuation spell. Gently she helped the alien wizard to his feet and wondered if she should curtsey.

"How are you called, Lord?" Moira asked respectfully.

"Ah, Wiz. I'm Wiz Zumwalt, that is. Who are you?"

"I am called Moira, Lord, a hedge witch of this place." She ignored the discourtesy of his question. She reddened under his fixed gaze and wondered what to do next. She had already sent an urgent call for one of the Mighty to attend them, but even by the Wizard's Way that would take time. Wizards did not like to be bothered by idle chatter, but this one *stared* so.

"Lord, are you of the Mighty in your home?" she asked to make conversation.

"Say what?"

"Forgive me, Lord. The Mighty are the wizards of the first rank in our land."

"Wizards?" Between the transition and Moira, Wiz's brain wasn't working and he had never been much good at small talk with beautiful women.

"Magicians. Sorcerers," Moira said a little desperately. Wiz looked blank and a dreadful thought grew in the back of Moira's mind. "Forgive me Lord, but you *are* a wizard, are you not?"

"Huh. No, I'm not a wizard," Wiz said numbly, shaking his head to clear it.

Moira felt sick. This man was telling the truth! There was no sign or trace of magic about him, nothing save his odd clothing to distinguish him from any other mortal. She turned away from him and tears stung her eyes.

"Hey, what's wrong?" Wiz laid a hand on her shoulder.

"Everything," Moira sobbed. "You're not a wizard and Patrius is dead."

"Patrius . . . ?" Wiz trailed off. "Oh my God!" For the first time he saw the charred blackened corpse at the edge of the clearing.

"I'm sorry," he said. "Is there anything I can do?"

"Yes," Moira said fiercely. "You can help me bury him."

"If you value your life," the black robe hissed,

"keep your mouth shut and your eyes on the floor. Toth-Set-Ra has little patience with impertinence." Xind led the acolyte down the flagged corridor. Their sandals scuffed on the rough stone floor and guttering torches in iron brackets gave a dim and uncertain light to guide them.

The guards at the door were hobgoblins, creatures somewhat larger than men and nearly twice as broad and bulky. Their laced armor shone blackly by the torchlight and the honed edges of their halberds glinted evilly. At the approach of the wizards they snapped to attention.

"Two with news for the Dread Master," Xind said with considerably more assurance than he felt. "We are expected." The hobgoblins nodded. One reached behind to swing open the great oaken door.

Both wizard and acolyte prostrated themselves on the threshold.

"Rise," croaked a voice from within. "Rise and speak."

The room was dark but a balefire green light played round a high-backed chair and the figure hunched in it.

Shakily, the pair rose and moved toward the light.

The man in the chair was wizened and shrunk in on himself until he was more a mummy than a living man. But his eyes burned red in the black pits of his hairless skull and he moved with the easy grace of a serpent coiling to strike. The light seemed to come from within him, playing on the chair and the amethyst goblet in his hand. The reflected greenish glow made Xind's complexion appear even more unhealthy than usual.

"We have slain a wizard, Dread Master, one of the Mighty of the North."

"Yes," Toth-Set-Ra hissed. "It was Patrius. May his soul rot forever. And you destroyed him. How nice."

The novice started and opened his mouth to ask

how the wizard knew, but Xind trod on his foot in warning.

"He was performing a Great Summoning, Dread Master," Xind said, his head bowed respectfully.

"Indeed?" croaked Toth-Set-Ra. "Oh, indeed?" His reptilian gaze slid over his subordinates and settled back on the carved goblet. "And what was it that was Summoned?"

Xind licked his lips. "We do not know, Lord. The distance was too great and . . ."

"You do not know?" Toth-Set-Ra's voice grew harsher. "You disturb me with news I already know and you cannot tell me more than I can sense unaided?" His stare transfixed the black robe, steady, intent and pitiless. "What use are you, eh? Tell me why I shouldn't finish you now."

"Because you would lose our services," the acolyte said steadily. Xind blanched and trembled at the young man's audacity and Toth-Set-Ra shifted his baselisk stare to him. The acolyte stood with his eyes respectfully downcast but no hint of trepidation in his manner.

"Servants such as you I do not need," snapped the wizard. "Incompetents! Bunglers! Blind fools!" Without shifting his eyes, he threw the amethyst cup at them. It passed between the pair and shattered into priceless shards on the flags. Both men flinched away.

"Very well," he said finally. "Prove your worth. Find out what Patrius died to birth. If you are quick and if it is important I will give you your lives. If not, I have other uses for you."

The wizard sat glaring after them for several minutes. Finally he sealed the door with a gesture which raised a wall of blue fire across it. He went to a cabinet of age-blackened oak, opened it with curious and diverse gestures and removed an elaborately engraved box about the size of a man's head.

Carrying it gently he brought it back to the table. He set the box carefully in the center of the pentagram inlaid in silver in the dark onyx top and then, stepping back, made a gesture. The top flew open and a small red demon appeared in a puff of smoke. The demon flew toward him only to be brought up short by the pentagram. It dropped to its knees and pressed its clawed, misshapen hands against the invisible walls, seeking a way out.

"It is secure," croaked Toth-Set-Ra. "Now, by the spells which made you and the spells which bind you, I would have word of the world."

"There is pain and suffering," squeaked the demon. "There is mortal misery and unhappiness, and boredom and ennui among the non-mortal."

"Specifically!" snapped the wizard and the demon fell back gibbering under the lash of his voice.

"What you will, Dread Master. What you will of me?"

"The Wizard Patrius."

"Dead, Dread Master. Struck down unprotected by your servants as he strove to weave a powerful spell. The Mighty in the midst of the mighty laid low."

"The spell?"

"A Great Summoning, Master. A Great Summoning."

"His assistants?"

"None, Master. None save a hedge witch."

Toth-Set-Ra frowned.

"And the Summoned?"

"A man, Master, only a man."

"A magician? A wizard?"

"I see no magic, Master. Save the hedge witch's and Bal-Simba, who comes after Patrius's burning."

"And what is his virtue? What is the special thing which made Patrius summon this one?"

"I do not know, Master. I see no answer."

"Then look ahead," commanded Toth-Set-Ra. "Look to the future."

"Aiiii," gibbered the demon. "Aiiii, destruction for us all! Pain and fire and the fall of towers. Magic of the strangest sort loosed upon the land! A plague, a pox, the bane of all wizards!" He capered about the pentagram as if the table had become red hot.

"How?" snapped the wizard. "Is he a wizard, then?"

"No wizard, Master. Magic without magic. Magic complex and subtle and strange. A plague upon all wizards, a bane. A bane! Aiiii Good Master, let me leave him! Aiii!"

Toth-Set-Ra scowled. The demon was frightened! He knew from experience that it took a very great deal to frighten a demon and this one was so terrified it was almost incoherent.

"Leave then," he said and made the gesture of dismissal. The demon vanished in a puff of smoke and the lid of the box snapped down.

Toth-Set-Ra sat long scowling at the carven box while the heatless blue light from the flame at the door played across his leathery face and reflected from the sunken pits of his eyes. *A plague upon all wizards.* What could that be? And why would Patrius—may his soul rot!—risk his life to Summon such a one? The Northerners relied on magic fully as much as the League. Magic was as vital to life as air. More vital, he corrected himself. There were spells which allowed a man to live without air.

Might the demon have been mistaken? Toth-Set-Ra cocked his head to one side as he considered the notion. It was not unknown for demons to be wrong. They were, after all, no better than the spells that created them. But this scrying demon had never failed him. Not like this.

A trick by the Northerners? The scowl deepened. The wizard held out his hand to the side, fingers extended, and an amethyst goblet, twin to the one that lay in fragments on the floor, filled with wine from an unseen pitcher and flew to his clawlike grasp. Yes, it was possible the Northerners had staged the incident for the League's benefit, or even spoofed both the demon and the Sea of Scrying.

Toth-Set-Ra took a sip of the magically concocted vintage and shook his head. What possible advantage could the North have gained that was worth the death of their most powerful wizard?

Assuming Patrius *was* dead, of course. . . . Too many possibilities! He needed more information and quickly. He motioned toward the door and the curtain of fire vanished as suddenly as it had come. He struck a tiny gong and instantly one of his goblin guards was in the doorway.

"Atros to me," he commanded. "At once!" The guard bowed and vanished in a single movement and Toth-Set-Ra scowled into the bottom of his wine. He would have an answer. If it took every wizard, every spell and every creature at his command, he would have an answer. And quickly!

They raised a mound over Patrius where he lay. Moira set Wiz to finding rocks while she used her silver knife to cut the green sward into turfs. The profanation rendered the knife useless for magical purposes, but she didn't care. She placed the turfs about the charred hulk who had been the greatest and best of wizards. From time to time she stopped to wipe away her tears with the sleeve of her blouse, unmindful of the dirt that it left streaked upon her cheeks. There was no proper shroud to be had, so Moira covered Patrius's face with her apron, tucking it in carefully around the body and murmuring a goodbye before she gently laid the bright green sod over him. The tiny flowers nodding in the grass made a fitting funeral bouquet.

Finally, she and Wiz piled the stones over the turf. They stuck the charred stump of the old wizard's staff upright in the top of the cairn.

"Dread Master?" The bear-like form of Atros blocked the door. Where the League's greatest wizard affected the robe of an anchorite, his subordinate

wore a black bearskin, belted with studded leather
and pinned with an intricately worked and bejeweled
brooch. Toth-Set-Ra's pate was shaven and Atros
wore his thick, dark hair to his shoulders, held in
place with a golden filet. More, Atros was nearly as
large as the hobgoblins and Toth-Set-Ra was tiny.

In spite of the contrast there was no question as to
who held power.

"Patrius is dead," Toth-Set-Ra told his lieutenant
without preamble. Atros said nothing. His spies had
already told him that and he knew Toth-Set-Ra knew
it.

"He attempted a Great Summoning, or so I am
told, and he brought someone from outside the World.
A man."

Atros waited impassively.

"I want that man, Atros. I want him badly. See to
it."

"It will take resources . . ." the great bear trailed
off.

"You have them. Use them. Search the North.
Scour the Capital if you must. But bring me that
man!"

Atros bowed. "Thy will, Dread Master." And he
was gone, leaving Toth-Set-Ra to brood.

Out in the corridor it was Atros's turn to scowl.
The old crow had set him a pretty problem indeed!
According to his spies the Sea of Scrying had failed
to pick up any trace of the man. That scrying demon
Toth-Set-Ra was so proud of must have failed or he
would not have been given this mission—or the power
to command so much of what his master controlled.
Whoever he was, this man from without the World
must have a very powerful masking spell to so effectively cloak his magic.

Well, magic wasn't the only way to find someone.
That was the old crow's mistake, Atros thought. If he
couldn't do it by magic he didn't think he could do it
at all. But there were other ways. The Wild Wood

was alive with creatures who were either allies, could be bribed to help, who were controlled or who could be enticed into helping. In the lands of Men there were spies, human and non-human. There were the Shadow Warriors. And then there were the massive and mighty magics of the City of Night. Here was power indeed to turn on finding a lone man.

That was the crux of it, he thought to himself as he strode along the dank, unevenly-flagged corridor. All that power, but only until he found this man. Oh, he would find him, never fear. That would be the easy part. And there were other things that could be done with the power he had just been given. Perhaps even concocting a nice little surprise for that scrawny excuse for a sorcerer who sat in the room down the hall.

Atros was intelligent but he was no more subtle than the bear whose name he had taken. It never occurred to him to wonder if perhaps Toth-Set-Ra might have considered that possibility as well.

Moira knelt weeping over Patrius' grave. Wiz stood by feeling clumsy and awkward. She was so beautiful he wanted to take her into his arms and comfort her. But when he put a hand on her shoulder she jerked away. He felt like a total fool watching her cry, so he wandered around the edge of the clearing.

"Do not enter the woods," Moira said sharply through her tears. "It is not safe," she sniffed.

"You mean lions and tigers and bears?"

"And other things," Moira said grimly.

"You mean like . . . ULP!"

A huge black man stepped into the clearing directly in front of Wiz. He wore a leopard skin over his shoulders and a leather skirt around his huge middle. Around his neck was a necklace of bone with an eagle's skull as a pendant. In his right hand he carried an intricately carved staff nearly as tall as he was. He grinned and Wiz saw his teeth were filed to needle-sharp points.

He was so black his skin showed highlights of purple and he was the biggest man Wiz had ever seen. It wasn't just that he was more than six-and-a-half feet tall. His frame was huge, with shoulders twice as broad as a normal man's. He had a great black belly, arms thicker than Wiz's legs and legs like tree trunks.

Open-mouthed, Wiz backed away. Then Moira caught sight of him and let out a cry.

"Bal-Simba! Oh Lord, you came." She ran across the clearing to meet him, checked herself suddenly and dropped him a respectful curtsey. "I mean, merry met, Lord."

The black giant nodded genially. "Merry met, child." He looked over to the freshly-raised mound and his face darkened. "Though I see it is not so merry."

"No, Lord," Moira looked up at him. "Patrius is dead, slain by sorcery."

Bal-Simba closed his eyes and his face contorted. "Evil news indeed."

Moira's eyes filled with tears. "I tried, Lord. I tried, but I could not . . ." She broke down completely. "Oh, Lord, I am so sorry," she sobbed.

Bal-Simba put a meaty arm around her shoulders and held her close. "I know, child. I know. No one will blame you for there was nothing you could have done." Moira cried helplessly into his barrel chest. Wiz stood by, wishing he could help and feeling like a complete jerk.

"Now child," Bal-Simba said as her sobs subsided. "Tell me how this came to pass. We sensed a great disturbance even before you called."

Moira drew away from him and sniffed. "He performed a Great Summoning without wards," she said as she wiped her eyes. "Just as he completed the spell he was struck down."

"What did he Summon?"

"Him," said Moira accusingly.

The black wizard looked down on Wiz in a way that reminded Wiz uncomfortably of a cat watching a mouse.

"How are you called?" Bal-Simba asked.

"I'm Wiz. Wiz Zumwalt." He waved hesitantly. "Hi."

The black giant nodded. "You are a wizard then. Of what rank?"

"Well no, I'm not a wizard," Wiz explained. "Wiz is just a nickname. My real name's William Irving . . ." He stopped as Bal-Simba held up a hand.

"I did not ask you for your true name," he said sternly. "Never, *ever* tell anyone what you are truly named for that places you in the power of all who hear."

"You mean like knowing somebody's password? Ah, right."

"Like that," the wizard agreed. "I tell you again, Wiz. Never reveal your true name."

"Now," he went on in a somewhat gentler tone. "What is your special virtue?"

"Huh?"

"What is it that you do?"

"Oh, I'm a programmer. From Cupertino. Say, where are we, anyway?"

"We are in the North of World on the Fringe of the Wild Wood," Bal-Simba told him.

"Where's that in relation to California?"

"Far, far away I am afraid. You were Summoned from your own world to this one by he who is dead." He nodded in the direction of the freshly raised cairn.

"Oh," Wiz said blankly. "Okay." He paused. "Uh, how do I get back?"

"That may take some effort," Bal-Simba told him. The black giant suddenly became more intent.

"Again. What is your special virtue?"

"I told you, I'm a programmer. I work with computers."

"I do not think we have those here. What else do you do?"

"Well, ah. Nothing really. I just work with computers."

"Are you a warrior?"

"Huh? No!" Wiz was slightly shocked.

"Think," commanded Bal-Simba. "There must be something else."

"No, there really isn't," Wiz protested. "Well, I do watch a lot of old movies."

It was Bal-Simba's turn to look blank.

"That's all there is, honest." Wiz was facing the black wizard so he did not see Moira's face fall.

"There must be more here," said Bal-Simba. He paused for a minute.

"Now. I swear to you that I mean you no harm." He smote his breast over his heart. "I swear to you that I will neither willingly harm you nor allow you to come to harm." He struck his chest again. "That I may aid you, will you give me leave to look deeper into you?"

"Uh, yeah. Sure," Wiz said a little apprehensively.

"Then sit here where you may be more comfortable." Bal-Simba guided Wiz to the rock where Patrius had sat so recently. He reached into his pouch and drew out a small purple crystal. "Look at this." Wiz gazed at the tiny gem cupped in the great pink palm. "Look deeply. Fix your attention on it. Observe . . . observe."

Wiz's eyes glazed and his mouth went slack.

"To business then." Bal-Simba tucked the crystal back into his pouch and began the task of learning all he could about this visitor from so far away.

"Strange indeed," muttered Bal-Simba, turning from where Wiz dozed in a trance. "Very strange."

"How so, Lord?" Moira asked.

"There is no sign of magic."

"No magic! None at all?"

"None that I can detect. Despite his name, this Wiz is as lacking in manna as a newborn babe."

Moira crumpled. "Then it was all for nothing," she said bitterly. "Patrius died for nothing! Oh, Lord, I am so sorry."

"I do not know. There is something—strange—about him, but it is not magic."

"The effects of the Summoning?"

Bal-Simba frowned. "I do not think so. It goes beyond that, I believe." He kept silent for a moment.

"You say Patrius told you he was Summoning a wizard?" he asked at last.

"Yes, Lord." Then Moira stopped. "Well . . . not exactly."

"What then exactly?"

Moira screwed up her face in an effort to remember. "Patrius said he was Summoning someone who could help us against the League." She made the warding gesture. "Someone with great magical power. When I asked him if the man was a wizard he evaded the question. But," she added thoughtfully, "he never called him a wizard."

"But he did say that this man had great power?"

"Yes, Lord. He said he looked long and hard to find him."

"That I can believe," Bal-Simba said absentmindedly. "Searching beyond the World is long and hard indeed. Hmm . . . But he did not call him a wizard, you say?"

"No, Lord."

"Then what is he?"

"When I asked Patrius that he would not answer."

Bal-Simba's head sunk down on his chest.

"Lord," Moira interrupted timidly, "didn't Patrius tell the Council what he was doing?"

Bal-Simba grimaced. "Do you think we would have allowed this madness had we known? No, we knew Patrius was engaged in a great project of some sort, but he told no one, not even his apprentices, what he was about.

"He had spoken to me of the tide of our struggle with the Dark League and how it fared. He was not sanguine and I knew in a general way that he intended something beyond the common. But I had assumed he would lay the project before the Council when it came to fruition. I assumed rashly and it cost us dearly."

"But why, Lord? Why would he take such an awful risk?"

"Because with the League so strong not all of the Mighty together could have performed a Great Summoning."

He caught the look on Moira's face.

"You did not know that? Yes, it is true. All of us together are not enough to make magic of that sort against the League's opposition." He smiled ruefully. "Thus the Council wanes as the League grows greater."

"Then why . . . ?"

"Patrius obviously believed that by working alone and without the usual protections he might be able to complete the Summoning before the League realized what was happening. He was wrong and it cost him his life." He nodded toward Wiz. "Patrius risked his life to gain a man of great magical power. Instead he brought us someone who *seems* as common as dirt. It makes no sense."

Again the great Bal-Simba was silent, his head sunk down on his necklace in contemplation.

"What do you think of this?" he asked finally.

"Lord, I am not qualified to pass on the actions of the Mighty."

Bal-Simba waved that aside. "You were here. You saw. What do think?"

Moira took a deep breath. "I think Patrius made a mistake. I think he intended someone else and under the strain of the attack . . ." her green eyes misted and she swallowed hard as she relived those awful moments ". . . under the strain of the attack he Summoned the wrong person."

"Possible," Bal-Simba rumbled. "Just possible. But I wonder. Wizards who make mistakes do not live to become Mighty, still less as mighty as Patrius."

"Yes, Lord," said Moira meekly.

"I do not convince you, eh girl? Well, I am not sure I convince myself." He turned back and looked at Wiz, sitting dazed and uncomprehending on the stone. "In any event, the problem now is what to do with our visitor."

Moira snorted. "He is an expensive visitor, Lord. He cost us so much for so little."

"Perhaps, but we cannot leave him to wander. You can see for yourself that he is as helpless as a sparrow. Sparrow, hmm? A good world name for him, especially since the name he uses is too close to his true name. But no, he cannot be left to wander."

"Will you take him with you, Lord?"

Bal-Simba frowned. "That would not be wise, I think, and dangerous besides. The fewer who know of him the better. No, he needs to go someplace safe. A sanctuary with as little magic as possible. A place where he can remain while I consult the others of the Mighty."

"My village is . . ."

"Unsafe," the black giant said. "Already we are being probed. I suspect the League would like very much to get their hands on him."

"Would it matter so much? Since he has no magic, I mean."

"Hush, girl. You do not mean that."

Moira looked at Wiz with distaste but shook her head. Falling into the hands of the League was not a fate to be wished on anyone, even someone who had caused the death of Patrius.

"What then?"

"There is a place. A few days into the Wild Wood

where he could find sanctuary. A place of very little magic."

Moira's eyes lit and she opened her mouth but Bal-Simba motioned her to silence. "Best not say it. There might be others about to hear, eh? No, you will have to take him—there—and give him into the charge of the one who lives there."

"Me, Lord? But I have my work."

"I will see another is sent in your place. He must be guided and protected, do you not see?"

"But why me, Lord?"

Bal-Simba ticked off the reasons on his fingers. "First, you are here and already privy to this business. The less others know of it the better. Second, you know the way through the Wild Wood. Third, time is of the essence. This place grows increasingly dangerous. And fourth," he held up his pinky finger and his eyes twinkled, "he is in love with you."

Moira made a face. "An infatuation spell! But I am not in love with him."

"Nonetheless, he will follow at your heels like a puppy. No, you are the logical one to serve as the mother hen for our Sparrow."

"Forgive me, Lord, but I find his presence distasteful."

Bal-Simba sighed. "In this world, child, all of us must do things which are distasteful on occasion."

Moira bowed her head. "Yes, Lord." *But I don't have to like it!* she thought furiously.

"Very well, off with you then." He turned and gestured to Wiz. "Straight on and hurry." Wiz reeled and shook his head to clear it.

"I will need some things from the village, Lord."

"I will have someone meet you with food and your other needs at the bridge on the Forest Highway."

"Lord, cannot I at least go back to say goodbye? Just for a few minutes?"

Bal-Simba shook his head. "Too dangerous. Both for you and the villagers. No, you will have to move quickly and quietly and attract as little notice as possible."

"Yes, Lord," Moira sighed.

"Now go, girl, and quickly. I cannot shield this clearing for much longer. I will consult the Council and come to you at your destination."

Moira bowed her head. "Merry part, Lord."

"Merry meet again, Lady."

"Huh?" said Wiz groggily.

"Come on you," Moira said viciously and grabbed his hand. She jerked and Wiz staggered to his feet.

"Well move, clumsy. Come on!" and she strode off with a lovesick Wiz stumbling along in tow.

Bal-Simba watched the ill-assorted pair disappear down the forest path. Then he sat on the rock just vacated by Wiz and turned his attention to weaving masking spells to buy the travellers as much time as he possibly could.

TWO

PASSAGE IN PERIL

The afternoon was as fine as the morning, warm
and sunny with just a bit of a breeze to stir the leaves
and cool the traveller. The birds sang and the summer flowers perfumed the air. Here and there the
early blackberries showed dark on their canes.

Wiz was in no mood to appreciate any of it. Before
they had gone a mile he was huffing and blowing. In
two miles his T-shirt was soaked and beads of sweat
were running down his face, stinging his eyes and
dripping from the tip of his nose. Still Moira hurried
him along the twisting path, up wooded hills and
down through leafy vales, ignoring his discomfort.

Finally Wiz threw himself down on a grassy spot
in a clearing.

"No more," he gasped. "I've got to rest."

"Get out of the open, you crack-brained fool!" the
red-haired witch snapped. Wiz crawled to his feet,
staggered a few steps and collapsed against a treetrunk.

"Sorry," he panted. "I'm just not up to this. Got to
rest."

"And what do you think the League is doing
meantime?" Moira scolded. "Will they stop just
because you're too soft to go on?"

"League?" asked Wiz blankly.

"The ones who pursue us. Don't you listen to anything?"

"I don't hear anyone chasing us. Maybe we've lost them."

"Lost them? *Lost them!* What do you think this is? A game of hide-and-seek? You idiot, by the time they get close enough for us to hear it will be too late. Do you want to end up like Patrius?"

Wiz looked slightly green. "Patrius? The old man back there?"

Moira cast her eyes skyward. "Yes, Patrius. Now come on!"

But Wiz made no move. "I'm sorry," he gasped. "I can't. Go on without me. I'll be all right."

Moira glared down at him, hands on hips. "You'll be dead before nightfall."

"I'll be all right." Wiz insisted. "Just go on."

Moira softened slightly. He was a nuisance, but he was a human being and as near helpless as made no difference.

"Very well," she said, sitting down. "We rest."

Wiz leaned forward and sank his head between his knees. Moira ignored him and stared back the way they had come.

"That old man," Wiz said at last. "What killed him?"

"Magic," Moira said over her shoulder.

"No really, what killed him?"

"I told you, a spell."

Wiz eyed her. "You really believe that, don't you? I mean it's not just a phrase. You mean real magic."

Moira twisted to face Wiz. "Of course I mean magic. What did you think? A bolt of lightning just happened to strike him while he was Summoning you?"

"You're telling me there really is magic?"

Moira looked annoyed. "How do you think you got here?"

"Oh," said Wiz. "Yeah. Well look, this magic. Can it get me home?"

"Patrius might have been able to do that, but I cannot," she said angrily. She got to her feet. "Now come along. If you have breath enough to talk you have breath enough to walk."

By paths and game trails they pushed on through the forest. Twice more they stopped to rest when Wiz would go no further. Both times Moira fidgeted so impatiently that Wiz cut the stop short, barely getting his breath back. There were a thousand questions he wanted to ask, but Moira sternly forbade him to talk while they walked.

Once she stopped so suddenly that Wiz nearly trod on her skirt. She stared intently at a patch of woods before them. Besides a ring of bright orange mushrooms beside the trail, Wiz saw nothing unusual.

"This way," she whispered, grasping his arm and tugging him off the path. Carefully and on tiptoe, she led him well around that bit of forest, striking the trail again on the other side.

"What was the detour about?" Wiz asked at their next rest stop when he had breath enough to talk.

"The little folk danced there on last night to honor the Mid-Summer's Day. It is unchancy to go near such a place in the best of times and it would be very foolish to do so today."

"Oh come on! You mean you believe in fairies too?"

"I believe in what I see, Sparrow. I have seen those of Faerie."

"But dammit . . ." Moira cut him off with an imperious gesture.

"Do NOT curse, Sparrow. We do not need what that might attract!"

That made sense, Wiz admitted. If magic really worked—and there was the burned husk of a man lying under the sod back behind them to suggest that it did—then curses might work too. Come to that, if magic worked there was nothing so odd about fairies dancing in the moonlight. He shook his head.

"Why do you call me Sparrow?" he asked, feeling for safer ground.

"Because Bal-Simba called you so. You needed a name to use before the World."

"I've got a name," Wiz protested.

"Bal-Simba told you never to speak your true name to anyone," Moira told him. "So we needed something to call you."

"My friends just call me Wiz."

"I will call you Sparrow," Moira said firmly. "Now come along."

Again she set off in an effortless stride. Wiz came huffing along behind, glumy admiring the swing of her hips and the easy sway of her body. He was used to being treated with contempt by beautiful women, but he had never been this taken with a woman and that made it hurt worse than usual.

One thing you have to say about my luck, he thought. *It's consistent*.

Finally they topped a small rise and Wiz could see a road through the trees ahead. Off to the left he could hear the sound of running water. Moira crouched behind a bush and pulled Wiz roughly down beside her.

"This is the Forest Highway," Moira whispered. "It leads over the Blackstone Brook and on into the Wild Wood."

"Where we're going?" said Wiz, enjoying Moira's closeness and the smell of her hair. Instinctively he moved closer, but the hedge witch drew away.

"Yes, but not by the road. I am to meet someone here. You wait in the woods. Do not make a sound and do not show yourself." She pulled back and continued down the trail, leaving Wiz with the memory of her closeness.

In spite of its grandiose title, the Forest Highway was a weedgrown lane with the trees pressing in on either side. The Blackstone Brook was perhaps ten yards wide and ran swift, deep and dark as its name under a rough log bridge.

As Moira predicted, there was a man waiting under the trees by the roadside. He was tall, lean, long-faced and as brown as the rough homespun of his tunic and breeches. When Moira stepped out of the trees he touched his forehead respectfully.

"I brought the things, Lady."

"Thank you, Alber," Moira replied kindly.

"Lady, is it true you are leaving us?"

"For a time, Alber. A short time, I hope."

"We will miss you," he said sadly.

Moira smiled and embraced him. Watching from behind his bush Wiz felt a pang of jealously. "Oh, and I will miss you all as well. You have been like a family to me, the whole village." Then she smiled again. "But another will be along soon to take my place."

"It will not be the same, Lady," he said dejectedly. He turned and gestured to the small pile of objects under a bush by the roadside.

"The messenger said two packs. And two cloaks."

"Correct, Alber." Moira did not volunteer and he did not ask.

Quickly she began to sort through the items, checking them and re-stowing them into the packs.

"Shall I wait, Lady?"

"No." She smiled up at him. "Thank you again." The hedge witch made a sign with her right hand, first two fingers extended. "Go with my blessing. May your way home be short and safe and the journey uneventful."

"May you be safe as well, Lady." With that Alber turned and started down the road.

As soon as he had disappeared around a bend, Moira motioned Wiz out of hiding.

"A brave man," Moira said as she tied the drawstring on one of the packs and set it aside.

"Why?" asked Wiz, nettled. "For bringing us this stuff?"

"Don't sneer, Sparrow," she said sharply. "This 'stuff' will sustain us on our journey. Alber was willing to chance Mid-Summer's Day to see that we will eat and be warm in the Wild Wood."

"Nice of him. But brave?"

Moira finished loading the second pack and shook her head. "Sparrow, how did you survive so long?"

"I survived just fine up until this morning," Wiz retorted. "So what about Mid-Summer's Day?"

Moira sighed in exasperation. "Mid-Summer's Day is the longest day of the year. All magics associated with the sun and fire are at their most potent this day and magics of green and growing things are unusually potent as well.

"It is a day of power, Sparrow, and not a day for mortals to be about."

"We're out."

"Not by choice, Sparrow," Moira said grimly. "Now come." She slung a large leather pouch over her shoulder and shrugged one of the packs onto her back. Then she stood and watched as Wiz struggled into the other one. As soon as he was loaded, they started off across the bridge.

Well behind them, Alber stuck to the relative safety of the road. Thus he was easily seen by a soaring raven gyring and wheeling over the green and leafy land.

Alber saw the raven as it glided low over the road. He made a warding sign, for ravens are notoriously birds of ill omen, and hurried on his way.

Above him the raven cocked his glossy black head and considered. Like most of his kind he knew enough to count one and two and one person travelling alone was not what his master searched for. There were two, and the bird's keen eyes could see no sign of anyone else on the road.

But this was the only human he had seen today and this one was well away from the normal haunts of man. The raven was not intelligent, but he had been well schooled. With a hoarse caw he abandoned the search to his fellows and broke away to the south to report.

The forest deepened after Wiz and Moira passed over the river. They left the road around the first bend past the bridge and toiled up a winding game trail that ran to the top of a steep ridge. By the time they reached the top even Moira was breathing heavily. She motioned Wiz to rest and the pair sank down thankfully under the trees.

Through a gap Wiz could look ahead. The valley was a mass of green treetops. Beyond the valley lay another green ridge and beyond that another ridge and then yet another fading off into the blue distance. There was no sign of habitation or any hint of animal life. Only endless, limitless forest.

This was no second-growth woodland or a carefully managed preserve. The oaks and beeches around them had never been logged. The big ones had stood for centuries, accumulating mosses and lichen on their hoary trunks, growing close and thrusting high to form a thick canopy overhead. Here and there was an open patch where one of those forest giants had succumbed to age, rot or lightning and the successors crowding in had not yet filled the place. There were snags and fallen limbs everywhere, green with moss and spotted with bright clumps of fungus.

This is the forest primeval, Wiz thought and shivered slightly. He had never thought that trees could make him nervous, but these huge moss-grown boles pressed in on him from all sides, their leaves shutting off the sun and casting everything into a greenish gloom. The breeze soughing through the treetops sounded as if the forest was muttering to itself—or passing the news of invading strangers, like jungle drums.

"I see why they call it the Wild Wood," he said.

"This is not the Wild Wood," Moira told him. "We are still only on the Fringe of the Wild Wood."

"Does anyone live here?"

"None we would care to meet. Oh, a few cottagers and a small stead or two. But most who live on this side of the Blackstone have reason to shun their fellows. Or be shunned by them. We will best avoid company of any kind until we reach our destination."

"Where are we going anyway?" Wiz sidled closer to her.

"To a place of refuge. You need not know more. Now come. We have far to go."

It was late afternoon when they came over the second ridge and descended into another valley. Although the forest was as dense as ever, there was a water meadow through the center of this valley. The broad expanse of grass was a welcome sight to Wiz, oppressed as he was by the constant trees. Here and there trees hardly more than shrubs luxuriated in the warmth and openess. Also interspersed were small ponds and marshy patches marked by cattails, reeds and sweet blue iris.

They halted at the edge of the open and Moira surveyed the cloud-flecked sky uneasily.

"Nothing," she sighed. "Now listen, Sparrow. We cannot go around because there are bogs above and below. We must cross and do it quickly, lest we be seen. Once we start we must not stop." She looked him over critically. "We will rest now."

Moira knelt, scanning the meadow and the sky above it while Wiz caught his breath.

"Moira?"

"What?" She did not stop searching the meadow.

"We're being chased, right?"

"That is why we are running."

"Well then, can I ask a dumb question?"

"Of course," the hedge witch said in a tone that indicated he had been doing nothing else.

"Why are we being chased? What did we do?"

"*We* did nothing. It is *you* they want, Sparrow, and they want you because Patrius Summoned you at the cost of his own life."

"Yeah, but why?"

"We do not know that, Sparrow."

"Do they know?"

"I doubt it."

Wiz shifted slightly. "Well, if you don't know and they don't know then why the bloody—heck—are they chasing us?"

"They hope to learn from you what Patrius's aim was."

"But I don't know either!"

Moira snorted. "I doubt they will take your unconstrained word for that, Sparrow."

"Look, I don't want any part of this, okay? Can't we talk to them? Isn't there some way I can prove I don't know anything and then they can leave me alone?"

"Sparrow, listen to me," Moira turned to him. "The Dark League of the South is not interested in your innocence or guilt. The fact that Patrius Summoned you is enough to make them want you. Probably they want to squeeze you for the knowledge we both know you do not possess. Possibly they simply want you dead—or worse."

Moira laid her hand on his. "But either way, Sparrow," she said gravely, "if you are given a choice between the worst death you can imagine and falling alive into the hands of the League, do everything in your power to die."

Wiz dropped his eyes from her intense stare. "I get the picture."

"Good." She turned back to the clearing and checked the ground and sky again. "Then make ready.

We will not try to run because the ground is boggy, but walk quickly!"

Moira rose and moved into the clearing with Wiz on her heels. The thigh-high grass whisked against their legs as they walked and the soil squished beneath their feet. Unlike the forest, the meadow was rich with life. Insects buzzed and chirped, frogs croaked or plonked into puddles as they went by. Dragonflies flitted by and once a yellow-and-black butterfly circled their heads.

In spite of the sunshine and wildlife, Wiz wasn't cheered. Except for an occasional bush, the travellers were the tallest things in the meadow. He felt like a large and very conspicuous bug on a very flat rock, and the further they got from the suddenly friendly line of trees, the more nervous he became.

Moira was feeling it too. She pushed ahead faster, her head turning constantly. She dared not use active magic, but she listened as hard as she could for any sign of others' magic.

Suddenly Moira dropped in her tracks. She went down so quickly that Wiz thought she had tripped.

"*Get down!*" she hissed and Wiz sprawled in the wet dirt beside her.

"What?" Wiz whispered.

"Something in the air off to our left. No, don't look! The flash of your face might betray us." After a second she bobbed her head up for a quick look.

"Fortuna!" she breathed. It is searching the area. All right, see that tree ahead of us?" She nodded towards a big bush a few yards up the trail. "When I give the signal, *crawl* to it. Understand?" Again her head bobbed up. "*Now!*"

On hands and knees they crawled for what seemed to Wiz to be an eternity. He dared not raise his head, so all he saw was a narrow strip of wet black earth and green grass stems on each side. By the time he pulled up under the bush he was panting, and not entirely from exertion.

They dragged themselves back far under the over-hanging branches, heedless of the mud or the tiny crawling things in the litter of dead leaves. As soon as they were settled, Moira pulled her cloak off her pack and threw it over them, turning two people into one lumpy brown mass and leaving just a narrow crack to see out.

Even as frightened as he was, Wiz was exhilarated by Moira's closeness. Her warmth and the sweet, clean odor of her was wonderful and the danger added spice.

"What is it?" he whispered.

"Shhh."

Then a shadow passed over them and Wiz saw what they were hiding from.

The dragon glided noiselessly above the trail they had just left. Its hundred-foot batwings were stiff and unmoving as it let the warm air rising from the meadow bear it up. Its long flat tail twitched slightly as it steered its chosen course. The four legs with their great ripping talons were pressed close to its body and its sinuous neck was fully extended. It came so low and so close that Wiz could see the row of white fangs in its slightly open mouth.

Wiz's breath caught and he tried to sink into the dirt. Instinctively he grabbed Moira's hand and they clung together like frightened children while the nightmare beast swooped above the trees and turned to cross the meadow from another direction.

Clearly the monster had seen something on the water meadow. Again it glided across and again it flew directly over the bush where Wiz and Moira cowered. Wiz felt as if the dragon's gaze had stripped him naked.

Four times the dragon flew over the meadow and four times Wiz trembled and shrank under Moira's cloak. Finally it pulled up and disappeared over the trees.

For long minutes after Wiz and Moira lay huddled

and shaking. At last Moira threw the cloak back and sat up. Reluctantly, Wiz followed suit.

"Was that thing looking for us?" he breathed at last.

"Very likely," Moira said, scanning the skies warily.

"Are there more of them?"

"Dragons are usually solitary creatures and one so big would need a large hunting territory."

She frowned. "Still, I do not know of any like that who live nearby. Wild dragons make ill neighbors. It may be the one from the southern lake or it might be one of the ones who lair in the hills to the east. If it is coursing this far afield there may be others."

"Wonderful," Wiz muttered.

Moira sighed shakily. "I dislike playing hideabout with dragons, but we should be safe enough if we stay under the trees and are careful about crossing open spaces."

"Sounds good to me."

"There is risk, of course," Moira continued, half to herself. "The forested ways are not always the most free of magic. Besides, with the forest close around us we will not have as much warning of the approach of others."

"Others?"

"Trolls, wolves, evil men and others who do the League's work."

"Great," Wiz said.

Moira missed the irony entirely. "Not great, but our best chance, I think." She folded the cloak. "Now come. Quickly."

"Well?" Atros demanded.

"The searchers are out as you commanded, Master," said the new Master of the Sea of Scrying. "But so far nothing."

"With all the magic of the League you cannot find two insignificant mortals?" Atros rumbled.

The Master, only hours in his post, licked his lips

and tried not to look past Atros's shoulder at the place where a newly flayed skin hung, still oozing blood, on the stone wall of the chamber. The skin of a very fat man.

"It is not easy Master. Bal-Simba—cursed be his name!—has been casting confusion spells, muddying the trail at the beginning. The Council's Watchers are on the alert and we cannot penetrate too deeply nor see too clearly." He paused. "We do know he has not taken the Wizard's Way."

Atros rubbed his chin. Walking the Wizard's Way was the preferred method of travel for those who had the magical skill to use it. But it was also easy to detect anyone upon it. Perhaps this strange wizard preferred stealth to speed.

"And those already in the North," he asked, "behind the Watchers' shield of spells?"

"Our best servants are creatures of the dark. On Mid-Summer's Day their power is at its weakest. Our dragon allies and our others seek as best they can, but there is so much magic upon the land that it is hard to scan." He gestured into the Sea of Scrying. Atros looked and saw sparks and patches of magic everywhere.

"Someone mighty enough to be worth the risk of a wizard like Patrius must leave a track even through that," the giant magician objected.

The newly made black robe lowered his head. "We have found no sign, Master."

Atros bit his lip thoughtfully. It was possible for a magician to hide his presence through cloaking spells, but such spells usually betrayed that something was being hidden. Either the League's servants were unusually inept or this magician from beyond the World was extremely powerful. Someone that powerful might indeed tip the balance against the League.

Unless . . .

"Is there sign of aught unusual in the cities of the North?"

"Nothing, Master, save what you know. Nothing unusual anywhere in the North's territories."

"Then perhaps he whom we seek is not within the North's territories," Atros said suddenly. "Patrius performed his Great Summoning on the Fringe of the Wild Wood? Then search the Fringe most carefully. And extend your search into the Wild Wood itself."

"Thy Will, Master," said the Watcher. "But there is no sign of anything unusual on the Fringe. Besides, it will mean weakening our search of the North's lands."

"If he was in the North's lands we would have some sign ere now," Atros said. "Perhaps he goes another way to mislead us."

It was the Master's turn to rub his chin thoughtfully. "If he pushes into the Wild Wood he brings himself closer to our servants and his magic will stand out even more strongly against the non-human magics of that place."

"Only if he uses magic," Atros said. "If he weaves little or none he will be much harder to find, will he not?"

"What kind of wizard travels without magical protection?"

"A most powerful and dangerous one. So search carefully." Atros paused for a moment, looking down into the Sea once more.

"But our alien wizard will not find it so easy to shield his travelling companion," he said. "Tell your searchers to look carefully for sign of a hedge witch in the Wild Wood. That should stand out strongly enough."

They camped where dusk found them, spreading their cloaks against a fallen log. Moira would not allow a fire, so their dinner consisted of some bits of jerked meat and a handful of leathery dried fruit. Normally Wiz didn't eat red meat, but things were decidedly not normal and he gnawed gratefully on the pieces Moira placed in his hand.

As the twilight faded Moira took a stick and drew a design around them and their resting place.

"The circle will offer us some small protection," she told him. "Do not leave it tonight for anything."

"Not even for . . . ?"

"Not for anything," she repeated firmly.

Without another word Moira rolled herself in her cloak and turned away from Wiz. He sat with his back to the log staring up at the unfamiliar stars.

"This is soooo weird," Wiz said, more to himself than Moira.

"Sleeping outdoors is not what I am used to either," she said.

"No, I mean this whole business. Dragons. The magic and all. It's just not like anything I'm used to."

Moira rolled over to face him. "You mean you really do not have magic where you come from?"

"The closest I ever came to magic was working with Unix wizards," said Wiz.

"Eunuchs wizards? Did they do that to themselves to gain power?"

"Huh? No. Not Eunuchs, Unix. Spelled . . ." Wiz realized he couldn't spell the word. He recognized the shapes of the letters, but they twisted and crawled in his mind and no meaning attached to them. When he tried to sound the word out only runes appeared in his head.

"Never mind, but it's not that at all. It's an operating system."

"Operating system?" Moira said frowning.

"An operating system is a program which organizes the resources of a computer and virtualizes their interfaces," Wiz quoted.

"A computer? One who thinks?"

For the thousandth time in his life, Wiz wished he were better at making explanations. "Well, kind of. But it is a machine, not alive."

"A machine is some kind of non-living thing then. But this machine thinks?"

"Well, it doesn't really think. It follows pre-programmed instructions. The programmer can make it act like it is thinking."

"Is it a demon of some kind?"

"Uh, no. A demon's something else. It's a program that does something automatically when called. Unless of course it's a daemon, then it's active all the time."

Moira wrinkled her brow. "Let us go back a bit. What do you have to do with these creatures?"

"They're not creatures, really."

"These demons, then."

"I told you, they're not demons. A demon is something else."

"Never mind all that," Moira said impatiently. "Just tell me what you do."

"Well, I do a lot of things, but basically I'm a systems-level programmer. That means I write programs that help applications programs—those are the things people want done—to run."

"What is a program?"

Wiz sighed. "A program is a set of instructions that tells the computer what to do."

"You command these beings then?"

"I told you, they're not . . ."

"All right. These creatures, or not-demons or whatever they are. You command them?"

"Well, kind of."

"But you have no magic!"

Wiz grinned. "You don't need magic. Just training, skill, discipline and a mind that works in the right way."

"The qualities of a magician," Moira said firmly. "And with these qualities you master these—things."

"Well, you try to. Some days you get the bear and some days the bear gets you."

"There are bears involved too?"

"No, look, that's just an expression. What I mean is that sometimes it's easy to get the computer to do what you want and sometimes it isn't."

"Powerful entities are often hard to control," Moira nodded. "So you are the master of these—whatever they are."

"Well, not exactly the master. I work under a section chief, of course, and over him there's a department head. Then there's the DP Administrator . . ."

"These entities tell you what to do?"

"They aren't entities, they're people."

"But you do not master these, what did you call them?"

"The section chief, the department head . . ."

"No, I mean the other things, the non-living ones."

"Oh, the computers."

"You master the computers."

"Well, no. But I program them according to the tasks assigned me."

"So you are only a low-level servant," Moira concluded firmly.

"No, I'm not! It's an important job," Wiz said desperately.

"I'm sure it is," Moira said. "Even temple sweepers perform an important job."

"No, it's not like that at all! It's . . ." He realized it was hopeless. "Just forget it, okay? It was an important job and I was damn good at it."

"Do not curse, Sparrow," Moira snapped. "We are in enough danger as it is." With that she rolled over and settled down to sleep.

Wiz didn't follow suit. He sat there listening to the wind in the trees and the occasional cry of a night animal. Once he heard a wolf howl far off.

Damn!, he thought. *Here I am in the middle of a forest with a beautiful girl asleep at my side and I can't do anything about it. I didn't think it was supposed to work this way.*

Wiz had never read much fantasy, but he knew

that the hero was supposed to get the girl. But then he didn't feel very heroic. He was cold, uncomfortable and most of all, he just felt ineffectual. The same old klutzy Wiz.

And lonesome. Oh my God, was he lonesome! He missed his apartment, the traffic-clogged streets, the movies, the all-night pizza joint on the corner. With a great inrushing pang, he felt utterly lost.

He even missed the goddamn buggy text editor at work. *Do you realize there probably isn't a computer anywhere on this world?* he thought. *I have probably written my last program.*

That hurt worse than anything. All his life Wiz had only been good at one thing. When he discovered computers in high school, he found he was as good with them as he was bad with people. He had put his life into being the best ever with computers and if he hadn't been the best ever, he had certainly been damn good. Only a lack of money and fascination with immediate problems had kept him from going to grad school and getting the Ph.D. that would have led him to the top rank of computer scientists.

So here he was in a world where none of that meant diddly. What was he supposed to do with himself? He couldn't earn a living. He wasn't really strong enough for physical labor and the only thing he knew how to do was useless.

Goddamn that old wizard, anyway. Then he started guiltily remembering Moira's admonition against cursing. *I wonder if it matters if you just do it in your head?*

If he was big and strong it might have helped. But he was skinny and gangly. The only difference between him and the classic pencil-necked geek was that he didn't wear glasses.

Good thing too, he thought. *If I did, I'd probably have broken them by now.*

It wasn't fair. It just wasn't fair.

Somehow he got to sleep and dreamed uneasily of home and his beloved computers.

The next morning Wiz was sore all over. His legs ached from the unaccustomed exercise and the rest of him hurt from sleeping on the ground.

Moira was already up and seemingly none the worse for the night. Her copper hair was combed and hung down her back in a long braid. Her face was freshly scrubbed and she looked heart-stoppingly beautiful.

She was sitting cross-legged going through the contents of her worn leather shoulder bag. There was already a pile of things on the ground beside her.

"I do not think I can afford to keep all these," she said in response to his unasked question. "I will have to discard them carefully as we go."

"I'll carry them for you."

Moira snorted. "The problem is not weight, you idiot. Magic calls to magic and these things," she gestured, "are magical. The League may be able to find us through them."

She looked down at the small pile and sighed. "They cost much time and no little effort to gain. All are useful and in a way they are all parts of me. But," she added with forced cheerfulness, "better to discard them now than to have them lead the League to us."

"Uh, right."

Moira gathered the items back into her pouch. "I will dispose of them one at a time as we go along," she said standing up. "It will make them harder to find, I hope."

Wiz scrambled to his feet, feeling the kinks in his muscles stretch.

"We can make better time today," the hedge witch said. "Mid-Summer's Day is past and the magic will be less strong. We do not have to move quite so cautiously."

"Great," Wiz muttered, apalled at the prospect.

True to her word, Moira set an even faster pace for the day's journey. Wiz struggled to keep up, but he didn't do any better than he had the day before. Several times they had to stop while he rested and Moira fidgeted.

From time to time Moira would take something from her pouch. Sometimes she flung the object as far as she could into the woods. A couple of times she buried it carefully. Once she hid a folded bit of cloth in a hollow log and once she dropped a piece of carved wood into a swiftly running stream.

Wiz could see the effort it took her to discard each of those items but he said nothing. There was nothing he could say.

The forest was more open than it had been the day before. The trees were smaller here. They were just as thick where they grew, but they were interspersed with clearings. Once they passed the ruins of a rock wall, running crazily through the woods.

They kept to the forest and stayed as deep among the trees as possible. Occasionally they had to skirt an open space and it was near one such clearing that Moira stopped suddenly and sniffed.

"Do you smell it?" she asked.

Wiz sniffed. "Something burnt, I think."

"Come on," Moira said, forging ahead and breasting through the undergrowth.

They were in the clearing before they recognized it. One minute they were pushing through bushes and brambles and the next they were standing on the fringe of a meadow, looking at the smoldering remains of a homestead.

There had been at least three buildings, now all were charred ruins. The central one, obviously a house, had stone walls which stood blackened and roofless. The soot was heaviest above the door and window lintels and a few charcoaled beams still spanned the structure. Of the nearer, larger building, a planked barn, there was almost nothing left. On the other side of the house was a log building with part of one wall standing.

"Something else," Wiz said, sniffing again. "Burned meat, I think."

But Moira was already running across the meadow. Wiz cast a nervous eye to the clear blue sky, then shifted his pack and followed.

When he caught up with her, Moira was standing in the space between the remains of the house and the smoldering heap of ashes that had been the barn, casting this way and that.

"What about dragons?" Wiz asked, looking up.

Moira's suggestion on what to do with dragons was unladylike, probably impractical and almost certainly no fun at all.

"Did a dragon do this?" Wiz asked as they walked around the remains of the house.

"Probably not," Moira said distractedly. "Dragons might attack cattle in the fields or swine in their pen, but they seldom burn whole farms. This was done from the ground, I think."

"Well, then who?"

"Who is not important, Sparrow. The important thing is what happened to the people."

"I don't see anyone," Wiz said dubiously.

"They may all have escaped. But perhaps some are lying hurt nearby and in need of aid. I *wish* I had not been so quick to discard parts of my kit this morning."

"There doesn't seem to be anyone here."

"Then search more closely."

Moira didn't call out and Wiz didn't suggest it. He felt conspicuous enough as it was.

While Moira searched near the house and log building, Wiz wandered around the remains of the barn. The heaps of ashes were unusually high there and from the remains he guessed the barn had been full of hay when it went up. He wondered what had happened to the animals.

Wiz stumbled over something in the debris. He looked down and saw it was an arm, roasted golden crisp and then obviously gnawed. A child's arm. Wiz opened his mouth to scream and vomited instead.

"What is it?" Moira came rushing up as he heaved his guts out. "What did you . . . Oh." She stopped short as she saw what lay on the ground between them.

"Oh my God," he moaned, retching the last bit of liquid from his stomach. "Oh my God."

"Trolls," Moira said, her face white and drawn, her freckles standing out vividly against the suddenly pale skin. "They burned this place and put the flames to use."

"They ate them," Wiz said weakly. "They ate the people."

"Trolls are not choosy about their fare," Moira said looking out over the smoldering ruins.

"Hey! Do you think they're still around?"

"Possibly," Moira said abstractedly. "After a meal like this trolls would be disinclined to go far."

"Then let's get out of here before they come back for dessert."

"*No!*" Moira shouted. Wiz started and turned to see tears in her eyes. "We go nowhere until we bury these folk."

"But . . ."

"There was no one to do it for my family."

"Did your family end up . . . like that?" Wiz finally asked.

Moira's face clouded. "I do not know. We never found them."

"What happened?"

"It was a summer day, much like today only later in the year. I had gone into the wood to pick berries. I filled my apron with them that my mother might make preserves. My father had found a bee tree, you see.

"It took me all the afternoon to gather enough berries. I was away for hours. And when I returned . . . there was no one there.

"The door to the cottage stood open and the cream was still in the churn, but my parents and brother and sisters were gone. I looked and called and searched until after nightfall. For three days I looked, but I never found them."

"What happened to them?"

"I don't know. But there are worse things on the Fringe of the Wild Wood than being eaten by trolls."

Without thinking, Wiz clasped his arms around the hedge witch and hugged her to him. Without thinking she settled into his arms to be hugged and buried her head in his shoulder. They stood like that for a long minute and then Moira straightened suddenly and pulled away.

"Come on!" she said sharply. "Find something to dig with."

There was a charred spade leaning against the remains of the log building and Moira set Wiz to work digging a grave in what had been the kitchen garden. The tilled loam turned easily, but Wiz was red-faced and sweating before he had a hole large enough to suit Moira.

While he dug, Moira searched for pieces of bodies. Somewhere she found a smoke-stained old quilt to serve as a shroud. Wiz kept his head down and his back to her so he would not have to see what she was piling on the cloth spread among the heat-blasted cabbages.

With Wiz's help, she hauled the lumpy stinking burden to the hole and dumped it in. It weighed surprisingly little, Wiz thought.

They shoveled dirt onto the quilt as quickly as they could. Wiz wielded the spade uncomplainingly in spite of the aches in his arms and back and the blisters springing up on his hands.

"It will not stop wolves or others from digging down," Moira said frowning at their handiwork as Wiz scraped the last of the earth onto the mound. "It should be covered with stone that their rest may be more secure."

"You want rocks?" Wiz said warily.

She thought and then shook her head. "There is not time. We will leave them as they are and hope." Then she bowed her head and her lips moved as she recited a blessing over the pathetic mound of fresh earth. When that was done she turned abruptly and signaled Wiz to follow.

They hurried back to the shelter of the forest. For once Moira didn't have to urge Wiz on. He was more than eager to get away from that grisly farmstead and he was absolutely convinced of the reality of magic and their present danger.

"How did it go with the Council, Master?" Bal-Simba's apprentice asked as the giant wizard came into his study.

"Well enough, Arianne." He leaned his staff against the wall and loosened his leopard-skin cloak. "But it is very good to be away from them for a while." Bal-Simba settled into a carved chair with a sigh and leaned back.

The tower room was bright and sun-washed. The batik hangings spoke of animals, birds, flowers and cheerful things. The wide windows on both sides were thrown open and a soft summer breeze wafted through the room, stirring the hangings on the walls and ruffling the parchments on the large table in its center. Arianne, a tall thin woman with ash-blonde hair caught back in a single braid, brought him a cup of wine from the sideboard.

Bal-Simba drained the cup with another sigh and handed it back for a refill.

"Well, I have done all I can to protect our visitor. The Watchers are on the alert and they are confusing the search as best they may."

"And the other matter?" she asked, handing him a second cup of wine.

"The Council has not the faintest idea why Patrius brought this Sparrow among us." He shook his great head. "I had hoped that Patrius had confided in one of the Mighty, but it appears he did not. The Sparrow is as much a mystery to us as he is to the League."

"Why do you think Patrius Summoned this one?" Arianne asked.

"Our red-headed hedge witch thinks it was a mistake, that Patrius intended to Summon some great wizard, became confused under the attack and got this Wiz instead."

"And you, Lord?"

"I do not know. Certainly the Sparrow has no skill at magic, or ought else that I can find. But yet . . . Did I tell you that Patrius did not mark a pentagram to enclose the Summoned? That suggests he did not expect the Summoned to defend himself with magic."

Arianne frowned. "Which means that he either was certain the Summoned would not attack him or that he knew he had no magic. Yes. What did Patrius say to the hedge witch?"

"Apparently Patrius was being oracular. He said he sought help but when she asked him what kind he talked in riddles."

"That would be like Patrius," Arianne agreed. "He loved his little surprises."

"This surprise cost him his life, Lady."

They were silent as Bal-Simba finished the second cup of wine. Arianne moved to refill it, but Bal-Simba shook his head.

"Lord, there are certain aspects of this business I do not understand."

"You are not alone, Lady."

"I mean your actions."

"Ask then." Arianne was Bal-Simba's apprentice not only for her skill in magic but because, like Bal-Simba, she had considerable administrative ability. One day she would sit on the Council of the North.

"Why did you leave the pair of them on the Fringe with no protection?"

"I could not bring them here by the Wizard's Way, so I sent them to a place of safety. Why alone? Because two can go in stealth where an army may not tread. This Moira is no woods ranger, but she grew up on the Fringe and she has the reputation for a sturdy head on her shoulders."

"Where did you send them?"

"Heart's Ease," Bal-Simba told her.

Arianne looked hard at the huge map on the wall. "Lord, that is deep within the Wild Wood itself! You set them a dangerous course."

"But the safest available under the circumstances," Bal-Simba replied. "The League will be searching for a magician. This Sparrow has not the slightest magic. The League will expect him to come to the Capital, or at least to the civilized lands. Instead they go in the opposite direction. If we keep interfering with the League's searchers we can further confuse the League."

"We know the League is searching for them with every resource at their command." She smiled thinly. "Old Toth-Set-Ra must be stirred indeed to mount such an effort."

"When he realized Patrius had performed a Great Summoning, he decided that the Summoned was a weapon of some kind. He means to have it." Bal-Simba smiled. "Perfectly logical if you know how Toth-Set-Ra's mind works."

"And we bend our efforts to frustrating him. Lord, is this Sparrow really worth so much of our effort?"

Bal-Simba considered for a moment. "Probably

not. But while the League is engrossed in trying to find our Sparrow, they cannot make mischief elsewhere. That is worth some little effort on our part."

He stroked his eagle's skull pendant absently. "Besides, I think we owe this Sparrow something. He was snatched from his own world and dropped here by the efforts of one of the Mighty. It was no fault or choice of his own."

The blonde woman nodded. "But still, to send two people into the heart of the Wild Wood . . ."

"Would you have me bring them here by the Wizard's Way and all of us lost when the League saw and struck?" Bal-Simba said sharply. Arianne stiffened.

The wizard's face softened. "Forgive me, my Lady. You are right about the dangers and I am uneasy about our fugitives." He heaved a great gust of a sigh. "I gave them the best chance I could, now let us hope they can make good use of it."

She smiled and placed her hand on his shoulder. "Apologies are not needed, Lord. I understand." He smiled back and put his bearlike paw over her hand.

"There are so few unconstrained choices, Arianne. So very few choices left to us."

"We do the best we can, Lord."

Bal-Simba sighed again. "Aye. That at least we do."

Moira allowed them a fire that night, which was a mixed blessing for Wiz. It meant warmth and hot food, but he had to gather firewood, and the sticks and branches rubbed his blistered hands raw.

"Now what's your problem?" she asked when she saw him wince as he dropped a load of wood by the stone hearth.

"Nothing," Wiz said, blowing on his hands.

Moira scrambled up and took one of his hands in hers. "You're hurt," she said with real concern. "I'll attend to those once the food is started."

When she had the mixture of dried meat, fruit and

barley simmering in a small bronze pot, she pulled out her shoulder bag and motioned Wiz to sit down beside her in the firelight.

"You must not be used to work," she said as she rummaged in her kit.

"You don't get many blisters at a VT 220," he agreed.

Moira looked blank.

"It's a terminal. A, ah, thing that . . . oh, forget it."

Moira produced a tiny earthenware jar and smeared the raw and blistered places on Wiz's palms with the dark, pungent salve it contained.

"Your hands should be healed by morning," she told him, scraping salve from her finger back into the jar. "We should cover those, but I don't have anything to put over them."

"That's fine," Wiz said. "It doesn't hurt anymore. Whatever that stuff is, it works like a charm."

"Oh, it's not a charm," Moira said seriously. "Just a healing potion. With the proper charm I could heal your hands instantly, but that would take magic and it might attract attention." She moved away from him to check the contents of the pot.

"You're a magician, right?" he asked, trying to recapture the moment.

Moira shrugged. "In a small way. I am a hedge witch."

"That's interesting. What does a hedge witch do?"

"What do I do? Oh, herbs and simples. A little healing. Some weather magic. I try to warn of dangers, find lost objects and strayed animals." She lifted the pot off the fire and produced two wooden bowls and horn spoons from her pack.

"Eat now," she said. "You can use a spoon well enough even with your hands."

The mixture in the pot looked awful but tasted surprisingly good. The tartness of the fruit and the rich saltiness of the meat blended well with the bland barley.

"Is Bal-Simba a hedge witch too?"

Moira laughed, a delightful sound. "No, Bal-Simba is of the Mighty." Her face clouded. "Probably he is the Mightiest of the Mighty now that Patrius is dead." She returned to her eating.

"What do the Mighty do?" Wiz asked in an effort to keep the conversation going.

"They are our greatest wizards. They teach the other orders, they help wherever great magic is required, they study arcane lore and they try to protect us from the Dark League." She sighed. "These days mostly they try to protect us from the Dark League."

"Why aren't they protecting us then?"

Moira looked annoyed. "They are protecting us, Sparrow. Bal-Simba stayed behind to cast false trails to confuse the League's agents who sought to spy us out. The whole North is protected by the Watchers of the Council of the North who blunt the League's efforts to use their magic here. Even now the Watchers are doubtless holding off the League's efforts to search us out. Just because you cannot see the works of the Mighty, never doubt they protect you, Sparrow."

"Sorry."

"You should be sorry."

They sat in uncomfortable silence.

"What's magic like?" Wiz asked at last.

"Like?" Moira asked, puzzled. "It's not like anything. It simply *is*. Magic is the basic stuff of the World. We swim in a sea of magic like fish in the ocean."

"And you can make it work for you?"

"A magician can make magic work for himself or herself. But there are very few magicians. Perhaps one person in one hundred has any talent at all for magic and far, far fewer ever become truly skilled."

Wiz studied the effect of the firelight on her hair and eyes. "How do you learn to do magic?"

"You find a magician to take you as an apprentice. Then you study and practice and learn as much as you can. Eventually you either cannot learn more or you must travel to find a more advanced teacher."

"But there aren't schools or anything?"

Moira snorted. "Magic is a craft, Sparrow. It cannot be learned by rote like sums or the days of the week."

"How did you learn?"

"There was a hedge witch in the village that took me in after . . . after I left home. He taught me what he could. Then I traveled to the Capital and studied under some of the wizards there." She sighed. "I did not have talent of a high order so I became hedge witch for the village of Blackbrook Bend."

"So, how do you work magic?"

"First you must know what you are doing," Moira said. "Then you must perform the appropriate actions with the proper phrases. If you do it correctly and if you make no mistakes, then you make magic work for you."

Wiz gestured with the stick he had used to poke up the fire. "You mean if I wave a magic wand and say—uh—'bippity bobbity boo' then . . . ?"

A lance of flame shot from the smouldering end of the stick into the heart of the campfire. The blaze exploded in a ball of incandescent white and an evil orange column soared above the top of the trees. Wiz gasped for breath in the suffocating blast of heat. Through the haze and blinding glare he saw Moira, on her feet and gesturing frantically.

Suddenly it was quiet. The fire was a friendly little campfire again and the cool night air flowed into Wiz's lungs and soothed his scorched face. Moira stood across the fire from him, her hair singed, her cloak smouldering and her eyes blazing.

"Yes." She snapped. "That is *exactly* what I mean!"

"I'm sorry," Wiz stammered. "I didn't mean to . . ." Then his jaw dropped. "Hey, wait a minute. That was magic!"

"That was stupid," the hedge witch countered, beating out an ember on her cloak.

"No, I mean I worked magic," Wiz said eagerly. "That means I *am* a magician. Bal-Simba was wrong." He grinned and shook his head. "Son of a gun."

"What you are is an idiot," Moira snapped. "Any fool can work magic, and far too many fools do."

"But . . ."

"Didn't you listen to anything I just told you? Magic is all around us. It is easy to make. Any child can do it. If you are careless you can make it by accident as you just did."

"Well, if it's so easy to make . . ."

"Sparrow, easy to make and useful are *not* the same thing. To be useful magic must be controlled. Could you have stopped what you created just now? Of course not! If I had not been here you would have burned the forest down. A careless word, a thoughtless gesture and you loose magic on the world."

She stopped and looked around the clearing for signs of live coals. "And mark well, magic is not easy to learn. There are a hundred ways, perhaps a thousand of doing what you just did. And most of them are useless because they cannot be controlled. Without control magic is not just useless, it is hideously dangerous."

"But I still made magic," Wiz protested.

Moira snorted. "You made it once. By accident. What makes you think you could do it again?"

"What makes you think I couldn't?" Wiz countered, picking up the stick. "All I have to do is point at the fire and say . . ."

"*Don't*," Moira yelled. "Don't even *think* of trying it again."

Wiz lowered the stick and looked at her.

"Sparrow, heed me and heed me well. The chance

that you could do that again is almost nil. The essence of success in magic is to repeat absolutely everything with not the tiniest variation every single time you recite a spell."

She gestured at him. "Look at you. You have shifted your stance, you are holding the stick at a different angle, you are facing southeast instead of North, you are . . . oh, different in a dozen ways. Could you say those words with exactly the same inflection? Could you give your wrist exactly the twist you used in the gesture? Could you clench your left hand in exactly the same way?"

"Is all that important?"

"All that is *vital*," Moira told him. "All that and much more. The phase of the moon, the angle of the sun. The hour of the day or night. All enter into magic and all must be considered.

"No matter what you have been told, magical talent does not consist of some special affinity for magic, some supernatural gift. Magical ability is the ability to control what you produce. And that turns on noticing the tiniest detail of what is done and being able to repeat it flawlessly."

That makes a weird kind of sense, Wiz admitted to himself. *Like programming. There's no redundancy in the language and the tiniest mistake can have major consequences. Look at all the time I've spent going over code trying to find the missing semicolon at the end of a statement, or a couple of transposed letters.* It also meant he probably was a magical klutz. He was the kind of guy who walked into doors and spent five minutes hunting for his car every time he went to the mall.

"Wait a minute, though," Wiz said. "If all it takes is a good memory, why can't most people learn to do magic?"

Moira flicked a strand of coppery hair away from her face with an exasperated gesture. "A good memory is the least part of what we call the talent."

"Sure, but with practice . . ."

"Practice!" Moira snorted. "Perform a spell incorrectly and you may not get the opportunity to do it again.

"Look you, when those without the talent attempt a spell, one of three things will happen. The first, and far and away the most likely outcome is that nothing at all will happen. What comes out is so far removed from the true spell that it is completely void. That is the most favorable result because it does no harm and it discourages the practitioner.

"The second thing that can happen is that the spell goes awry, usually disastrously so." She smiled grimly. "Every village has its trove of stories of fools who sought to make magic and paid for their presumption. Some villages exist no longer because of such fools."

"The third thing is that the spell is successful. That happens perhaps once out of every thousand attempts." She frowned. "In some ways that is the worst. It encourages the fool to try again, often on a grander scale."

"So what you're saying is that it's easy to make magic by accident but hard to do on purpose."

"Say rather virtually impossible to do on purpose," Moira corrected. "Without the talent and proper training you cannot do it.

"But there is another level of complication beyond even that," Moira went on. "A magician must not only be able to recite spells successfully, he or she must thoroughly understand their effects and consequences—*all* their consequences." She settled by the fire and spread her cloak. "Do you know the tale of the Freshened Sea?"

Wiz shook his head.

"Then listen and learn.

"Long ago on a small island near the rim of the Southern Sea (for it was then so called) there lived a farmer named Einrich. His farm was small, but the soil was good and just over the horizon was the Eastern Shore where the people would pay good money for the fruits his island orchards produced. All he lacked was fresh water for his trees, for the rains are irregular there and he had but one tiny spring.

"Some years the rains were scant and so were his crops of apples and pears. Some years they came not at all and Einrich spent day after weary day carrying buckets of water so his trees would not perish.

"All around him was water, but he had not enough fresh to feed his groves. Daily he looked at the expanse of sea stretching away to the horizon on all sides and daily he cursed the lack.

"Now this Einrich, ill-fortune to him!, had some talent for magic. He dabbled in it, you see, and somehow he survived his dabblings. That gave him knowledge and a foolish pride in his own abilities.

"So Einrich conceived a plan to give him more water. He concocted and cast a spell to turn the water around his island fresh.

"He constructed a demon, bound it straitly, and ordered him to make fresh the water around his island."

"Wait a minute," Wiz said. "What do you mean he 'constructed' a demon?"

"Demons are the manifestations of spells, not natural creatures as the ignorant believe," Moira said. "They are the products of human or non-human magicians, although they may live long beyond their creators.

"To continue: In doing this, Einrich was foolhardy beyond belief. Great spells work against great forces and if they are not done properly the forces lash back. Einrich was not so fortunate as to die from the effects of his bungling. His house was blasted to ruin and a huge black burn still marks the place on the island, but he survived and the water around his island was turned to fresh.

"He spent all the long summer days working in his orchards while the fruit swelled and ripened on his trees. With plentiful water his fruit was the largest and finest ever. So when the time came he harvested all his boat could bear and set out for his markets on the east coast of the sea.

"He thought it odd that he saw no other vessels, for usually the waters inshore were the haunt of fishing vessels and merchantmen trading in the rich goods of the east. Einrich sailed on, finding nothing in the water save an occasional dead fish.

"When he sighted land his unease grew. For in place of the low green hills of the Eastern lands he saw cliffs of dazzling white. As he drew closer he realized that the familiar hills had turned white, so white the reflections almost blinded him.

"He sought the familiar harbors but he could not find them. All was buried under drifts of white, as if huge dunes of sand had devoured the land.

"And instead of the sweet scent of growing things, the land breeze brought him the odor of rotting fish. All along the shoreline were windrows of dead sea creatures. Here and there a starving seabird tore eagerly at the decaying flesh.

"Finally, Einrich put ashore in a cove. When he stepped from his boat he stepped onto a beach of salt.

"Einrich had bound his demon to its task, but he had not limited it. The whole of the Southern Sea had been turned fresh water. The fish within could not live in the fresh water, so they died.

"Worse, Einrich had not instructed the demon where to put the salt it winnowed. The creature simply dumped it on the nearest shoreline. In the space of a few days the greatest and most beautiful cities of the World disappeared under waves and rifts of salt. Their people perished or were doomed to roam the world as homeless wanderers—living testaments to the power of magic ill-used.

"And to this day the demon sits in the Freshened Sea, sifting salt from the water and dumping it on the land. The eastern shores are a desert of salt and the water is still fresh."

"What happened to Einrich?" Wiz asked, awed.

Moira smiled grimly. "A suitable punishment was arranged. If you travel to that cursed shore, and if you look long enough, you will find Einrich, ever hungry, ever thirsting and hard at work with a shovel, trying to shovel enough salt into the sea to render it salty again."

"Whew," Wiz breathed.

"The point, Sparrow, is that magic is not to be trifled with. Even successful magic can bring ruin in its wake and unsuccessful magic far outnumbers the successful."

"Could I have done something like that, by accident?"

"Unlikely," Moira sniffed. "You do not have a talent for magic and you have no training. You could easily kill yourself or burn down a forest, but you have not the ability to work great magic.

"The most dangerous magicians are the half-trained ones. Either the ones who are still being schooled or who think they are greater than they are. The evil they do often lives after them. They and the League, of course."

"What is this League, anyway? A bunch of black magicians?"

Moira frowned. "They are a dark league. Some of them are black, it is true. But so is Bal-Simba and many others of the North."

"No, I mean magicians who practice black magic. You know, evil spells and things like that."

"Evil magic depends partly on intent and partly on ignoring the consequences," Moira said. "Spells may help or harm but they are not of themselves good or evil."

"Not even a death spell?"

"Not if used to defend oneself, no. Such spells are dangerous and are best avoided, but they are not evil."

"All right, what separates you from this League?"

Moira was silent for a moment. "Responsibility," she said thoughtfully. "Magic is not evil in itself, but tends to affect many things at once. Often the unintended or unwanted effects of a spell are harmful. Like Einrich's means of getting water for his orchards."

"We called those side effects," Wiz said. "They're a pain in the neck in programming too."

"Be that as it may, the question a responsible magician must face is whether the goal is worth the consequences. All the consequences. Those who follow the Council of the North try to use magic in harmony with the World. Those of the League are not so bound."

Moira shifted and the fire caught and heightened the burnished copper highlights in her hair.

"Power is an easy prize for a magician, Sparrow—if you can stay alive and if you are not too nice about the consequences. The ones who join the League see power as an end to itself. They magic against the World and scheme and intrigue among themselves to get it."

Wiz nodded. "I've known hackers like that. They didn't care what they screwed up as long as they got what they wanted."

"It may be so on all the worlds," Moira sighed. "There are always those whose talent and ambition are unchecked by concern for others. If they have no magical talent they may become thieves, robbers and cheats. With talent they are likely to travel south and join with the Dark League."

"Why go south? Why not just stay here and make trouble?"

"Two reasons. First, the Council will not have them in the civilized lands. Second, they must still serve an apprenticeship no matter how much talent they have." She smiled tightly. "The tests for an apprentice are stringent and many of them are aimed at uncovering such people.

"Once they pass over the Freshened Sea they are beyond the Council's reach. They are free to work whatever magic they wish and that place shows the results. All of the Southern Shore is alight with mountains of fire and the earth trembles constantly from the League's magic. The land is so blasted that none can live there save by magic. The very World itself pays the price for the lusts of the League."

"Why put up with them at all? When we had problems like that we'd kick the troublemakers off the system. Or turn them over to the cops—ah, the authorities."

"You have an easier time than we do, Sparrow," Moira said ruefully. "There is no way to bar a magician from making magic, so we cannot 'kick them off the system.' As for the authorities, well, the Council exists in part to check the League but this is not a thing easily done.

"Individually the ones of the League are mighty sorcerers. Toth-Set-Ra, their present leader," Moira made a warding sign, "is the mightiest wizard in all the World."

"If he's so powerful how come he hasn't taken the North?"

"Because the League contains the seeds of its own destruction," Moira said. "To conquer the North, the League would have to act in careful concert. This they cannot do because of the rivalries within. The Mighty are more constrained than the sorcerers of the League and so perhaps not so powerful individually. But they work easily together and can defeat any of the League's efforts.

"The League is like the Phoenix which renews itself by regular immolation. When it is sundered by contention and many strive for the Dark Throne, then we of the North have a time of peace. When a strong leader emerges and brings most of the wizards of the South under his sway, the League harries the North and magics are loosed upon the land." Moira sighed. " 'Twas ever so. And now we live in a time when the League is united as never before.

"Toth-Set-Ra," again the warding sign, "is a mighty sorcerer, skilled in magic and cunning in lore. And it is our age's woe that he has especially powerful tools at his command."

"It doesn't sound very secure to me," Wiz said dubiously.

"Little in life is secure," Moira replied. "But we contrive." She rose and moved to the other side of the fire.

"And now let us see if we can get some sleep, Sparrow. Morning comes early and we still have far to go."

THREE

THE WATCHER AT THE WELL

The land was different here. The valleys were
narrower, the ridges more numerous and the slopes
steeper. But the trees were as tall and their leaves
shut out the sun as fully as they had in the flatter
country behind them.

The forest was making Wiz claustrophobic, but
since the water meadow open spaces didn't appeal to
him either.

They were following the valleys now, but Wiz
wasn't sure it was an improvement. Moira seemed to
become more nervous. When they walked they went
as fast, but Moira stopped more often to listen intently. She spoke seldom and only in whispers and
she glared fiercely at Wiz every time a branch cracked
under his feet.

Finally they came up a gentle rise and looked
down into a valley even steeper and narrower than
the ones around them. From the disturbance of the
treetops Wiz could make out the line of a road or a
stream running through its center.

Moira placed her enchanting head next to Wiz's,
so close he could count the freckles on her cheek and
inhale the fragrance of her hair.

"The Forest Road," Moira whispered nodding at the line. "We must follow its track."

"I thought we needed to stay under cover," Wiz whispered back dubiously.

"I said we would follow the road, not walk it. If we keep to the wood we should be all right." She grasped his wrist and squeezed hard. "But make no sound. This place is a natural funnel and if the League realizes we are bound into the Wild Wood, this is where they will set their traps."

Cautiously then went downhill until they struck a game trail that ran along the slope. As they moved with it, the land gradually grew steeper. Although he couldn't see, Wiz had the impression that the valley was narrowing as well.

"Hsst." Moira tugged at Wiz's sleeve. "Voices. Off the path." She looked left and right and then surprised Wiz by scrambling up the steep bank. They climbed like frightened squirrels until they were nearly thirty feet above the trail. They flattened themselves against the slope with a thin screen of bushes between them and the path below.

Two men came up the path. They were dressed in rough homespun. The taller one was lean and balding with a narrow rodent face and greasy stringy blond hair. The shorter one was also blond, but he was beefier, younger and his hair fuller. The tall one carried a machete-like sword that he swung idly with a practiced motion of the wrist. The other had a big knife or short sword thrust scabbardless through his belt. Wiz held his breath as they came close.

"What is it we're looking for anyway?" the younger man asked.

"Gold, me lad. Two bags of gold walking around in human skins." He swished the frond off a fern with a casual swing of his chopping sword. "There's a man and a woman as might be making for the Wild Wood and there's those who would pay steep for them."

Don't look up, Wiz prayed, *please don't look up!*

"What do they look like?" the young man asked as the pair passed the spot where Wiz and Moira lay.

"Like strangers, and strangers at the Gap are easy enough to find."

The man asked another question but they turned a corner in the path and the woods and distance made their speech unintelligible.

Wiz and Moira looked at each other.

"We don't have to ask who they're looking for, do we?" Wiz whispered.

Moira gestured him to silence and motioned for him to wait. He realized the pair who had just passed might be the vanguard of a larger party and clamped his mouth shut.

Minutes ticked by before Moira gestured him up and on. They climbed down from their perch and plunged downslope into the forest, breasting through thickets and thrusting past tangles of underbrush. The going was slower and noisier but somehow that seemed like a reasonable tradeoff.

At last Moira stopped them under a large clump of something multi-stemmed and leafy.

"Were those guys from the League?" Wiz asked in a whisper.

Moira shook her head. "Not they. They owe allegiance to naught but gold. There are robbers who haunt the Forest Road. Apparently the League offers rich reward for us and that has served to concentrate them."

"So what do we do now?"

"We must go on. The problem comes when we reach the Forest Gate ahead. That is a pass barely wider than the Forest Road itself. It marks the end of Fringe and the beginning of the Wild Wood and it will doubtless be guarded."

"Can we go around?"

Moira shook her head firmly. "We must go through the Gate itself."

"How do we get through?"

She smiled grimly. "Cautiously, Sparrow. Very cautiously indeed. Now move as quietly as you can, and no talking! That pair were not woodsmen, but a few of these rogues are skilled rangers indeed."

They went ahead even more slowly now. Wiz joined Moira in scanning the woods. After their encounter with the robbers the forest seemed even more oppressive. Every tree or bush became a potential hiding place until the woods seemed alive with bandits waiting to pounce. A burst of birdsong would make Wiz start and the scampering of a squirrel in a tree would reduce him to terror.

Finally Moira halted and pointed. Wiz followed her finger and saw the Forest Gate.

Ahead the canyon narrowed into a gorge. At the bottom it was only wide enough for the road and a rocky stream bed. The gray stone walls rose sheer for a hundred feet or more before the canyon widened out and the trees grew on the slope, which rose for hundreds of feet.

And the gate was guarded. Wiz saw four men on the road and one more sitting on the cliff edge. Their manner left no doubt there were more men on down the gorge or hidden by the trees.

"I don't suppose we could use magic to get through?" Wiz whispered.

Moira surveyed the scene and bit her lips. "It is a trap. Those men are out in the open in hope that we will try something like that. Make no doubt there are magicians waiting to pounce."

"What then?"

"We thread our way between them. I hope they are not too thick along the slopes. Now be quiet."

They were higher on the mountainside than the walls of the gorge, a good 200 feet above the place where the trees began. If most of the robbers were down on the road and there weren't too many sentinels on the heights and the robbers weren't too alert, they should be able to work their way along the slope without being seen.

And if frogs had wings they wouldn't bump their asses every time they took a step, Wiz thought sourly.

With agonizing caution they worked their way forward. In spite of their steepness the slopes were thickly wooded and well-grown with brush. Most of the time they could see only a few yards in any direction. Wiz kept his eyes on the ground, putting his feet down as carefully as he could. Every time he scuffed the leaves the sound rang in his ears. He was certain the noise they made echoed off the walls of the canyon. Every few yards they halted for a long minute to listen.

Luck seemed to be with them. It was a hard climb up to the slope from the road and few of the robbers were inclined to make it. Those that did were more interested in looking down the road than they were in checking the mountainside. Moving with exquisite care, Wiz and Moira passed the watchers, sometimes so close they could see them through the trees.

The mountainside grew steeper and the ground became more rocky. Trees were scarcer and the brush thicker. The terrain forced them closer and closer to the cliff edge. Below them they could see the gorge curve sharply in a hairpin bend and beyond that the land widened out again.

Finally, at the very point of the hairpin, the wood narrowed to a thin band. And at its narrowest point there was a man sitting on a rock.

He was at his ease, hands clasped around one knee and the other leg dangling. Like his fellows he was looking over the canyon. Obviously the last thing he expected was to find his quarry on the slopes. There was a leather patch over his right eye, the eye closest to Wiz and Moira.

But to get by him they would have to pass scant feet from him. *In the movies this is always where they jump the sentry,* Wiz thought. This wasn't a movie and Wiz wasn't a trained commando. The man was at least a head taller than he was and heavily muscled. He was wearing a broadsword, while their only weapon was Moira's eating knife. The last thing Wiz wanted to do was make like Bruce Lee.

Moira obviously agreed. Crouching low, she began to work her way forward, keeping as much brush as she could between her and the man on the rock. Crouching even lower, Wiz followed.

Moira was almost behind the man when Wiz stepped on a loose rock.

With a crunch and a clatter the stone went rolling down the slope, taking several others with it. The sentry's head whipped around and he saw Moira behind a bush not six feet from him.

"Hey!" he shouted and sprang to his feet, grabbing for his sword. Moira cringed and made ready to run.

Wiz stood up too. As the man took his first step toward Moira he literally blindsided him and shoved him with all his strength, away from his beloved and toward the cliff edge.

The man whooped, tottered on the brink and then went over the cliff backwards, screaming all the way down.

The scream was cut off by an enormous *splash* and a second later the gorge resounded with curses. When Wiz peeked over the edge he saw that the stream made a pool in the bend of the canyon and the man was in the middle of it, treading water and swearing at the top of his lungs.

A laughing voice called out to him.

"By the nine netherhells I was pushed! They're up there I tell you. Get after them!"

Again the laughing voice.

"Damn your mangy hide I am *not* drunk! There's someone up there and they're getting away."

"Better search along that cliff, lads," came a harsher, louder voice. "Who knows? There may actually be someone up there."

Wiz and Moira ducked in among the trees and ran for all they were worth, never slowing until they were past the Gate and out on the forest floor again.

There were no sounds of pursuit, but just to be safe Moira led them back and forth through the stream several times and doubled back on their trail twice. All the while she said nothing to Wiz and shushed him when he tried to speak.

By the time Moira was satisfied the sun was dipping toward the horizon. She paused as if considering, and abruptly she changed direction and started angling back almost the way they had come. Finally she struck a track like a sunken road and led Wiz up it.

The road was canopied over with trees and thickly covered with fallen leaves, but there was not so much as a blade of grass growing on it. Here and there were bare spots where he could see paving blocks of blue-gray marble dressed square and neatly fitted together. Occasionally there would be another stone sticking up to one side with a runic inscription on it.

Whatever this was, it wasn't the Forest Road. It was too wide and too well-built. More, there was a different—feel—about it, and Wiz wasn't sure he liked the feel at all.

They came over a crest and Wiz looked down on a ruin. Delicate fluted columns and graceful arches protruded here and there from the trees and bushes. Wiz could make out the remains of a wall of the same blue-gray marble running around the place.

It was big, Wiz saw as they trudged down the road toward the ruin. The wall had to enclose several hundred acres. It was hard to imagine what the ground plan could have been, but Wiz formed an impression of a palatial, spacious building that had stood in the midst of extensive gardens.

Moira turned off from the road before they got to what should have been the main gate and searched until she found a breach in the wall. Without a word to Wiz she scrambled over the broken stones and onto the grounds.

She led deeper into the ruin, passing dry fountains surmounted by statues weathered almost to shapelessness, elaborate porticos and paved courtyards which had apparently never been roofed. At last she found a spot that seemed to suit her.

"We will camp here."

"What was this place anyway?" Wiz asked, staring up at the ruined arches. The pillars were too tall and too thin and the arches themselves were too pointed. Like everything else about the ruin they were at once beautiful and unsettling.

"A castle," Moira said as she dropped her pack beside him. "They say it belonged to a wizard."

"I thought we were supposed to avoid magic."

"It was not my plan to come this way," the red-haired witch said tartly. "I hoped to be well beyond this part of the Wild Wood by nightfall, but we lost too much time playing hide and seek. This place still has the remnants of the owner's guard spells and they offer some protection. If it does not meet with your approval I am truly sorry."

"Hey, I didn't mean . . ."

"Oh, be quiet," Moira snapped and Wiz lapsed into abashed silence.

As the afternoon turned to twilight Moira sent Wiz to gather firewood. He came back with a good armload which she accepted wordlessly and with little grace. Then she set about kindling the fire. Wiz stood watching her.

"All right," he said grimly. "Let's have it."

"Have what?" She looked up as the fire sprang to life.

"Whatever's eating you. You've been mad ever since we got past the gate and I want to know why."

"Mad? Me? What have I to be angry about? Just

because your clumsiness nearly got us both killed, that is no reason for me to be angry."

"Okay, my foot slipped. I'm sorry, all right? And in case you hadn't noticed, I saved your bacon back there."

"And that makes it right?"

"It sure as hell makes it better."

"Sparrow, curing a disease is no excuse for causing it. If you had not been so lead-footed there would have been no need for rescue.

"Bal-Simba has given me the job of saving your worthless carcass. That would be dangerous enough if you were an adult. But you have the mind and manners of a child and that makes it ten times worse. If you do not feel I truly appreciate you, then, again, I am indeed sorry!"

"All right, that's it!" Wiz shouted and reached over to pick up his pack.

"Just what do you think you're doing?" Moira demanded.

"Leaving. You don't want me around? Fine! I'll make my own way."

"Don't be a bigger fool than you already are. You wouldn't last one day out there by yourself."

"Maybe not," Wiz said bitterly, "but it would be better than putting up with you. Lady, I'm sick of you and I'm sick of listening to you run me down. I'm outta here."

"And just where do you plan to go tonight?"

"I don't care. I'll find a place." He turned and stalked off.

"Sparrow! Wiz . . ." Moira dropped her arm. "All right, make a fool of yourself!" she yelled after him. "See if I care," she muttered as she settled on a log by the fire. *He'll be back as soon as he gets over this temper tantrum*, she thought. *Meanwhile he should be safe enough inside the walls. Oh Bal-Simba, such a task you have given me!*

By the light of the rising moon Wiz pushed his

way through the brush and weeds that choked the ruined courts and overgrown gardens.

Bitch! he thought. *Arrogant, insufferable goddamn bitch! I didn't ask for all this and I sure as hell didn't ask for her. She's done nothing but insult me since I met her. Well, to hell with that, Lady. And the hell with you too!*

He went on, stumbling occasionally over loose bits of marble, heedless of the branches that whipped at him. He'd find someplace to camp and then figure out what to do in the morning. It would probably be better to stay inside the walls tonight, he decided. That damn red-headed bitch was probably right about the protective spells and he had had a bellyful of magic already.

At the bottom of a ruined garden someone was playing a flute. The thin, plaintive music caught all the longing and unfulfilled dreams that ever were.

Guided by the bright moonlight, Wiz made his way among the overgrown bushes over the cracked flag path to the sound.

There was a pool there, rank with cattails and dark with lilypads. A broken marble bench lay beside it. On a dark rock overhanging the water sat the flute player, clad only in a pair of rough trousers with long hair down to his shoulders. Wiz listened until he reached the end of his song.

"That was beautiful," Wiz said involuntarily into the silence.

"Did you enjoy it, mortal?" the player asked. As he turned, Wiz realized his mistake.

It was man-sized and man-like, but it was not a man. The face was utterly inhuman with a broad flat nose and huge eyes with no trace of a pupil. The hair was a mane, starting low on the forehead and sweeping back to the shoulders. Large pointed ears peeked out of the mane on either side. The trousers were fur, fur that clad the body from the waist to the tiny hoofed feet.

"Uh, yes. I enjoyed it," said Wiz, startled by the creature's appearance.

"Oh, do not be afraid, mortal. I cannot harm you. I am bound to this well."

"You play beautifully."

"It is the song of heart's desire," said the creature.

Around the pool, frogs croaked and trilled in crescendo. There must be thousands of them, Wiz thought distractedly, but he could see none of them in the moonlight.

"When Ali Suliman held here . . . Did you know Ali Suliman?" the creature asked. "No? Before your time I fear. A most refined gentleman and a truly great sorcerer. Such a delightful sense of humor. Well, when Ali Suliman had this place things were much different. The palace was ablaze with light and filled with guests. Often Ali Suliman would bring his—special—guests to this pond to hear me play and to discourse with me."

The thing sighed gustily and shook its shaggy head. "All is changed, alas. Few mortals come here now and fewer still hear my music."

"I'm sorry," said Wiz, abstractedly.

The being waved its flute in a dismissing gesture.

"The music is not important. It is the desire it represents that matters. The longing, the yearning in the mortal breast." He gazed at Wiz with opalescent eyes. "I can fulfill that desire," it said with utter conviction. "I can give you the thing you want most. That is what matters."

The hair prickled on the back of Wiz's neck. The creature was so compelling that Wiz did not doubt for an instant that it could do what it said. In the back of his mind he knew he shouldn't be here listening to this, but the promise held him.

"Your heart's desire, mortal," the creature crooned. "Your heart's desire." The frogs croaked louder.

Wiz licked his lips. "How do I know you can deliver?" he asked.

"Oh, by magic" cackled the being, its pupilless eyes like opals in the moonlight. "By magic."

"What is my heart's desire?"

"Why a woman, mortal. A woman not far from this very place."

"What do you want in return?"

"Merely a game, mortal. It grows lonely here and time must be passed."

"What kind of game?"

"Why, any kind you choose. Would you have a race? Will you wrestle me?"

Neither one sounded like a good idea to Wiz. The furry haunches were powerfully muscled and the thing's chest was broad and deep.

"No, nothing physical."

"Then something magical?" The creature made a swipe with his hand and left a glittering trail through the night air.

"I—I don't practice magic," Wiz stammered.

The creature grinned disquietingly. "A pity. A true pity. Well then, what about a game of the mind? The riddle game? Yes, the riddle game."

Like a lot of programmers Wiz took inordinate pride in his problem-solving ability. He firmly believed that any riddle could be solved by a combination of logic and careful examination. Besides, by using truth tables it is possible to construct some mind-boggling riddles, and Wiz had a lot of experience with truth tables.

Wiz licked his lips and found they tasted metallic. The invisible frogs redoubled their croaking.

"All right. I'll play your riddle game. Who goes first?"

The thing on the rock chuckled, an eerie, burbling sound. "Oh, there is only one riddle in the riddle game, mortal. And I am the one who asks it."

"Oh." That wasn't the way the game was played as Wiz remembered it, but now he was committed. "Ask then."

The thing on the rock blew a thin airy phrase on its flute and began to sing:

Black as night, white as snow
Red as blood from the death-wound flow
Precious as gold
Worthless as dross
Cold beyond cold
Gained without loss
Higher and deeper and wider than all
At fingertips always, gone beyond call
What am I?

The frogs fell silent in chorus. Wiz racked his brains trying to come up with something that fit. *Precious as gold, worthless as dross . . .* Something that was valuable only to one person? *Gained without loss?* Wiz's mind ran itself in tight little circles as he tried to imagine what could possibly fit.

"The answer, mortal," the creature leaned forward, his yellow eyes glowing with unholy light. "I will have the answer or I will have thy soul."

"Give me a minute," Wiz muttered. "Just give me a minute, okay?"

"You do not have a minute, mortal, not even a second." The thing stretched its arms toward Wiz, its fingers spreading like talons. "Answer or you are mine, mortal. Now and forever!"

Panic crushed Wiz's chest. His mouth tasted like metal and his lips were dry. The thing's hypnotic eyes rooted him to the spot as firmly as one of the rushes. He could not run, he could not cry out. He could only tremble as the creature moved closer and closer in its mincing gait, hooves tapping on the rock.

"Leave him!" Moira's voice rang out. "You cannot have him."

The pressure released and with a great gasping sob

Wiz fell to the ground. He twisted his head and saw the hedge witch standing behind him.

"But he agreed," the creature howled, dancing up and down on the rock. "Of his own free will he agreed to the bargain!"

"The bargain is invalid. He is under an infatuation spell and has no free will on this."

Wiz simply gaped.

"He made a bargain. A bargain!"

"Trickster and cheat! There could be no bargain and well you know it. Now be off with you! Seek other prey."

Moira threw her arms wide and her cloak billowed behind her like wings in the moonlight. With an awful shriek the creature whirled and dove into the pond. The frogs cut off in mid-croak and waters parted soundlessly to receive him.

"Mortals, mortals, cursed mortals," the thing's words came faintly and wetly from the pool. "Doomed and dying mortals. One day soon the World will see no more of you. You will vanish like the dew on the grass. Doomed and dying mortals."

Wiz heard the words but he didn't look. He huddled in his cloak and dug his fingers into the sod as if he expected to be dragged into the pool at any second.

"Oh, get up," Moira said angrily. "It's gone and you're safe enough now.

"What in the World ever made you agree to play the riddle game with the likes of that?" she asked as Wiz picked himself up. "Don't you know you could never win?"

"He promised me my heart's desire," Wiz said numbly. "He said he could give it to me by magic."

"By magic!" Moira mocked. "You blithering, blundering fool, don't you know by now to stay away from magic? It's bad enough I have to leave people who need me to come on this idiot's errand, but I have to babysit you every second."

"I'm sorry," Wiz said.

"Sorry wouldn't have saved you if I had been a moment later. You blind fool!"

"Well, you said this place was safe," Wiz said sullenly.

"No, you ninny! I said the wards would keep out most of what was outside. They do nothing against things which are already within the grounds." She stopped, drew a deep breath and then let it out in a sigh.

"Listen to me. There is no place in the Wild Wood that is safe. Do you understand me? No place! You cannot let down your guard for even an instant and if you see or hear anything that even vaguely *hints* at magic, run from it! Don't investigate, don't stay around it, just get away and let me know."

"I'll try," Wiz said.

"You'll do more than try if you want to live to reach our destination. Now come with me." She turned on her heel and stalked away with Wiz following.

Moira fumed all the way back to camp. She was furious with Wiz and, she reluctantly admitted, furious with herself for letting him storm off. Her orders from Bal-Simba were to get him to a place of refuge and she had nearly failed because she let her dislike for him overmaster her judgment.

He has spirit, she admitted grudgingly, *even with that whipped-puppy air of his. Spell or no, he really would have gone off on his own.* Moira couldn't allow that. *I must be more civil to him.* The thought did absolutely nothing for her mood.

They ate dinner in uncomfortable silence. The food did little to lighten the atmosphere. The cakes were overbaked and the meat was almost raw on one side for lack of turning. The meal was over and they were settling down for the night before Wiz could summon up the courage to ask the question which had been gnawing at him ever since he recovered his wits.

"Moira, what did you mean when you said I was under a spell?" Wiz finally asked.

The hedge witch looked annoyed and uncomfortable. "Patrius placed you under an infatuation spell."

"Infatuation spell?" Wiz asked blankly.

"The spell that makes you love me," she said sharply.

"But I don't need a spell to love you," Wiz protested. "I just do."

"How do you think an infatuation spell works?" Moira snapped.

"But . . ."

"Oh, leave me alone and go to sleep!" She drew her cloak about her and rolled away from him.

FOUR

BEYOND THE FRINGE

Wiz woke from a dream of home to rain on his face.

Judging from the sodden state of the campfire, it had been raining for some time, but the water had only now filtered through the leaves of the tree they had slept under.

He sputtered, rolled over and wiped the water out of his eyes.

"Awake at last," Moira said. She was already up and had her pack on her back with her cloak on over everything. "Come on. We need to get going."

"I don't suppose there is any sense in suggesting we hole up someplace warm and dry?"

Moira cocked an eyebrow. "In the Wild Wood? Besides, we have a distance to travel."

Wiz pulled his cloak free of his pack. "How long is this likely to last?"

Moira studied the sky. "Not more than one day," she pronounced. "Summer storms are seldom longer than that."

"Great," Wiz grumbled.

"It will be uncomfortable," she agreed, "but it is a blessing too. The rain will deaden our trail to those things which track by scent." She looked up at the leaden lowering sky.

"Also, dragons do not like flying through rain."

"Thank heaven for small favors."

Their breakfast was a handful of dried fruit, devoured as they walked. They picked their way through a gap in the ruined wall and struck off into the forest.

It rained all day. Sometimes it was just a fine soft mist wafting from the lowering gray skies. Sometimes it pelted down in huge face-stinging drops. When it was at its worst they sought shelter under a tree or overhanging rock. Mostly it just rained and they just walked.

At first it wasn't too bad. The rain was depressing but their wool cloaks kept out the water and the footing was firm. However as the downpour continued, water seeped through the tightly woven cloaks and gradually soaked them to the skin. The ground squished beneath their feet. The carpet of wet leaves turned as slippery and treacherous as ice. Where there were no leaves there was mud, or wet grass nearly as slippery as the leaves.

At every low spot they splashed through puddles or forded little streamlets. Wiz's running shoes became soaked and squelched at every step. Moira's boots weren't much better.

Wiz lost all sense of time and direction. His entire world narrowed down to Moira's feet in front of him, the rasp of his breath and the chill trickle down his back. He plodded doggedly along, locked in his own little sphere of misery. Unbalanced by the weight of his pack, he slipped and fell repeatedly on the uneven ground.

Moira wasn't immune. She was also thoroughly soaked and she slipped and slid almost as much as he did. By the time they stopped for a mid-afternoon rest they were drenched and muddy from falling.

Unmindful of the soggy ground, they threw themselves down under a huge pine tree and sprawled back against the dripping trunk. For once Moira seemed as out of breath as Wiz.

Under other circumstances—say as a picture on someone's wall—the forest might have been beautiful. The big old trees towered around them, their leaves washed clean and brilliant green. The rain and mist added a soft gray backdrop and the landscape reminded Wiz of a Japanese garden. There was no sound but the gentle drip of water from the branches and, off in the distance, the rushing chuckle of a stream running over rocks.

Abstractly, Wiz could appreciate the beauty. But only very abstractly. Concretely, he was wet, chilled, miserable, exhausted and hungry.

"Fortuna!" Moira exclaimed. Wiz looked up and saw she had thrown back her cloak and pulled up her skirt, exposing her left leg and a considerable expanse of creamy thigh lightly dusted with freckles.

"Close your mouth and stop gaping," she said crossly. "I hurt my knee when I slipped crossing that last stream."

"How bad is it?" he asked as he scrambled over next to her.

Moira prodded the joint. "Bad enough. It is starting to swell."

"Does it hurt?"

"Of course it hurts!" she said in disgust. "But more importantly I will not be able to walk on it much longer."

"Maybe you should put some ice on it."

Moira glared at him.

"Sorry. I forgot."

"What I need is a healing poultice. I have the materials in my pouch, but they must be boiled and steeped." She looked around and sighed. "We are unlikely to find dry wood anywhere in the Wild Wood this day."

"There are ways of finding dry wood even in a rain."

Moira looked interested. "Do you know how?"

Wiz realized he hadn't the faintest idea. His apartment didn't even have a fireplace and his method of starting a barbeque involved liberal lashings of lighter fluid followed by the application of a propane torch.

"Well, no," he admitted. "But I know you can do it."

"That I know also," Moira snorted. "Were I a ranger or a woodsman I would doubtless know how it is done. But I am neither, nor are you."

"Can't you use magic?"

She shook her head. "I dare not. A spell to light wet wood is obvious and could well betray us. Besides, I threw away my fire lighter."

"What are you going to do?"

"I can walk for a while longer. As we came over the last rise I saw a clearing that looked man-made. We shall have to go in that direction and hope we can find someone who will grant us the use of his fire."

"That's dangerous."

"Less dangerous than using magic, if we are careful. We will approach cautiously and if aught seems amiss we will depart quietly. Now, give me your hand."

Wiz pulled the hedge witch to her feet and for a brief tingling instant their bodies touched down the whole length. Then Moira turned away and started off.

Mercifully, the going was easier in the new direction. There were no hills to climb and the rain gradually slacked off. Moira started to limp, but she refused Wiz's offer of assistance.

As afternoon faded to evening, they threaded their way through the dripping trees until at last Moira motioned Wiz to stop and eased forward carefully.

There, in a rude clearing hacked into the forest, stood a cottage. Some of the felled trees had gone to build the dwelling and some into the split rail fences around the field. Knee-high stumps still stood among the crops. The cottage was roofed with shingles and the chimney was stone. A thin curl of smoke hung low over the field. It was crude and spartan, but to Wiz it looked beautiful.

"Hallo the house!" Moira called without entering the clearing.

"Who calls?" came a man's voice from the cabin.

"Two travellers seeking a fire."

"Show yourselves then."

Moira limped into the clearing with Wiz following. Ostentatiously she reached up and threw back the hood of her cloak. She nudged Wiz and he did the same.

The householder stepped into the door of the cabin. He was a stocky middle-aged man with a full black beard shot with streaks of gray. Wiz noticed that one hand was out of sight, possibly holding a weapon.

"Advance then, the two of you," he called. Wiz and Moira picked their way across the field to the cabin door.

The man stood in the door, just inside the threshold. "I will not invite you in," he said stolidly. Moira nodded and stepped forward. He backed away to let her enter.

She turned and they both looked at Wiz, but neither Moira nor the householder bade him enter nor made any motion to him. They looked and Wiz looked. Finally he got tired of it and stepped inside.

"Welcome," said the peasant, smiling. "Welcome, Lady." He nodded to Wiz. "Sir."

The cottage was a single large room with a fireplace at one end. There was a ladder leading to the loft and at the loft trap Wiz saw three wide-eyed children peeking down.

The furniture was plain and obviously home-made, built to last rather than for comfort. A spinning wheel stood in the corner next to a bag of wool. The smell of smoke and wool oil filled the house.

"Seat yourselves, please." Their host gestured to a high-backed bench to one side of the fireplace.

"What was that all about?" Wiz asked as they sat down.

"What?"

"The business at the door."

"There are things which can take human form and deceive all save the most clever. But few of those can enter a house unbidden. In the Wild Wood only the foolish or very powerful invite a guest within."

"Umm," said Wiz.

The cottager settled himself on a similar bench across from them. "I am called Lothar," he said.

"I am called Moira, a hedge witch. He," she jerked a nod at Wiz, "is called Sparrow. We thank you for the use of your fire. I have injured my leg and wish to brew a healing poultice, if you will allow it. If you or any of yours have ills that I may treat I will be happy to do so."

"You're welcome to the fire, Lady, but none of us are in need of healing."

Moira looked skeptical but said nothing.

"You are also welcome to spend the night within if you so wish," Lothar said grandly.

"Thank you, Goodman. We would be most grateful."

Moira produced the small bronze kettle from her pack and Lothar called the children down from the loft. He sent the oldest, a boy of about ten, to fetch water. While Moira laid out her kit on the rough plank table the other two children, a boy and a girl about eight and six respectively, watched in awe.

When the water was fetched, Moira selected several leaves and roots from the packets in her pouch and put them to simmer over the fire. Meanwhile Lothar bustled about fixing a meal.

They dined on venison, tubers and vegetables and

Lothar served up a pitcher of beer to wash it down. It was a delicious change from trail food and Wiz wolfed down his portion.

As they ate the twilight deepened to night. The only light came from the fire crackling on the hearth. The smell of pine smoke filled the room. Outside the crickets began to sing.

After dinner they retired to the fireside. Although Lothar had said little while they were eating, he began to pump them for news as soon as they were seated. Since he was mostly concerned with happenings around his old village of Oakstorm Crossing, and since that village was fairly far from Moira's, there was little she could tell him. She answered as best she could and Wiz and the children listened.

"How fare you, Goodman?" Moira asked when she had run out of information.

Lothar smiled and Wiz saw two of his front teeth were missing. "Well enough, Lady. Well enough."

"You are far from neighbors here."

"Aye, but I've good land. And more for the clearing."

"Did you not have a farm where you were before?"

"Well, you know how it is on the Fringe. Farms are small and the soil is worn thin. It's hard to make a living in the best of times, and when the crops aren't good, well . . ." He shrugged his massive shoulders.

"My grandsire talked of this land," Lothar told them. "His father's father lived near here. So when things got bad in our village, we came here."

"It is dangerous to live this deep in the Wild Wood," Moira said noncommitally.

Lothar smiled. "Not if you keep your wits about you. "Oh, it was hard enough at first. Our first two crops failed in a row and the cattle were stolen. Then my wife died and my daughter had to look after the little ones. But we stuck it out and here we are." His

smile widened. "Secure on a farm the likes of which
I could never have had back on the Fringe."

Moira smiled back tightly and the tension grew
thick.

"It looks like a nice place," Wiz said.

"Wait another few years," Lothar told him. "Next
year I will clear more land and erect a proper barn.
Then we will expand the house and add storerooms.
Oh, my grandsire did not lie when he called this
land rich!"

"I wish you good fortune," Moira said neutrally.

"Thank you, Lady. But you can make good fortune. It takes hard work and planning, but if you
give it that, you will have all the good fortune you
could desire."

Moira looked uncomfortable, but she nodded as if
Lothar had said something wise.

"Well, it looks like you've done all right for yourself," Wiz said, trying to break the tension.

"Thank you sir. We have. It's not easy, running a
farm and raising four children without help, but it's a
good life none the less."

"Four children?" Wiz asked and then shut up when
he caught Moira's glare.

"There's my oldest daughter, Lya," Lothar said
hesitantly.

"She's gone to nurse an elf child," the youngest
child piped up. Her older brother poked her sharply
in the ribs and Moira and Lothar both looked
embarrassed.

"They offered us their protection," the man said
simply. "Since then things have been better."

Kar-Sher, late a brown robe of the League and
now the Master of the Sea of Scrying, hurried down
the corridor, his sandals padding softly on the uneven floor of black basalt. At every turning and each
intersection he paused to listen and peer around
corners.

It had all been so easy when Xind had done it, he thought as he strained to catch a sign that he might be followed. Now the North was stirred and the Watchers of the Council were blocking him at every turn. Clear sight of the North was hard to come by these days and the Dread Master grew ever more impatient. He wondered if he had been so wise to undermine Xind when he did.

Well, that is a deed done. It raised me high in the League and with a bit of fortune I may rise higher yet.

Satisfied there was no one behind him, he continued down the corridor. *I have power of my own now. I am no longer a brown robe, I am an ally to be courted.* A rough hand reached out of the darkness and clasped his shoulder in an iron grip. Kar-Sher jumped and squeaked.

"Quietly, you fool!" Atros whispered, dragging him back into a shadowed alcove.

"You, you startled me," he said looking up at the hulking form of the League's second most powerful wizard.

Atros grinned mirthlessly. "You should be more alert. Now, what have you?"

"Only this: The Dread Master . . ."

"The old crow," Atros interrupted.

"Eh?"

"He is an old crow. Soon to be no one's master, dread or otherwise. You should learn to call him so."

"Yes Master," said Kar-Sher. "Ah, as I said, the—old crow—stays close to the City. There is no sign of new magic further south."

"Cloaking spells?"

"They would show."

"Like the cloaking spell this new northern wizard shows?"

Kar-Sher made an annoyed gesture. "That is different. It would take a truly mighty wizard to cast a spell that effective."

"Toth-Set-Ra has that reputation."

"You don't think . . . ?"

"I think you should be very careful what you assume about the old crow. Now. Are you sure there is no sign of secret magic being made to the South?"

Kar-Sher considered and then shook his head. "Nothing at all."

"Well, then. Keep your watch." He turned to go, but Kar-Sher plucked at his cloak.

"Master, will we strike soon? The old crow grows impatient. I do not know how much longer I will hold my position."

Atros regarded him coldly. "The old crow is impatient for one thing only; this strange wizard. Events are already in motion to snare him. In a day or two that will be accomplished. Meanwhile it keeps our master occupied."

"What if he finds out about us?"

"He does not even suspect. Keep your wits about you a few days longer and you are safe. Now wait here until I am out of sight." Atros stepped out into the corridor and strode on.

Kar-Sher waited until he had his nerve back and started up the corridor in the opposite direction.

Neither of them had noticed the fat black spider hanging motionless in her web above their heads.

"So," hissed Toth-Set-Ra as he broke contact with his spy. "So indeed." He leaned back and rubbed his forehead. Peering through a spider's eyes was disorienting. His brain kept trying to merge eight images with apparatus designed for two.

A spider's eyesight might be poor, but there was nothing wrong with a spider's hearing. He had heard exactly what he expected to hear.

You run too fast, Atros. It is time you were taught another lesson. He extended his hand and an amethyst goblet flew to his grasp.

He expected Atros to connive against him, just as he had connived against the Council of the League to win his present power. It was his good fortune that Atros was nearly as clumsy a plotter as he was as a wizard. Powerful enough, perhaps, but lacking the finesse, the last measure of ability that raised a plotter or wizard to true greatness.

He sipped the wine and reflected on the best way to check his subordinate. *Someday soon, Atros, I will send Bale-Zur to you.* But not yet. One does not discard a tool merely because it is flawed. One uses it, preferably to destruction, while a new tool is forged.

Still, this tool was showing signs of blunting. In spite of all the power he had been given, Atros had still not brought him the alien wizard. Toth-Set-Ra rotated the goblet in his hand and frowned at the purple sparks that glinted off its facets. That wizard was the immediate problem, the unknown. Once he had been found and neutralized there would be time to deal with Atros.

A pity I cannot send Bale-Zur to that wizard. He could, of course. Bale-Zur could find and destroy any mortal whose true name had ever been spoken. Unlike other demons he did not need to know the true name of his quarry. It was sufficient that the true name had been spoken just once somewhere in the World.

It was that special power which had raised Toth-Set-Ra from a minor wizard to the leadership of the Dark League in a single blood-red night of slaughter. But Bale-Zur could only destroy. Toth-Set-Ra wanted to take alive this wizard whom Patrius had died for. He wanted to squeeze him, to wring the secrets of his foreign magic from him. Killing him was an option, but only a last resort.

Bale-Zur was almost as crude a tool as Atros, but both were useful. This other one now, this Kar-Sher,

was much less useful. Under his mastership the Sea
of Scrying had been useless in the search and all he
could do was whine about Northern interference with
his magic.

Yes, the wizard thought. *This one is eminently
dispensable*. He paused to admire the play of fire in
the goblet again. *But not yet. Not quite yet*.

In his own way Toth-Set-Ra was a frugal man. He
always wanted the maximum return from his actions.

They slept on straw ticks on the floor that night.
Lothar offered them his bed in the loft, but Moira
declined politely. Before retiring, she took the poultice, which had been simmering in the pot, wrapped
it in a clean cloth, and tied it about her knee. She
turned her back while she did so and Wiz tried not
to look.

By the next morning the swelling had vanished.
She did several deep knee bends and pronounced
herself healed.

"Lady, if we could get you back to my world, you
could make a fortune as a team doctor for the NFL,"
Wiz told her. She cocked an eyebrow but did not ask
for an explanation.

Lothar insisted on feeding them a breakfast of
flatbread, sausage and beer before they left. Both he
and Moira were obviously uncomfortable, but Moira
thanked him kindly and Lothar gave them some
dried fruit and parched grain to add to the supplies.

It had stopped raining and the sun was shining
brightly. As they left the clearing, Wiz noticed a
detail he had missed the night before. Four mounds
of earth, one large and three much smaller, neatly
laid out next to the cabin and enclosed by a rude rail
fence.

Moira saw him looking at the three small graves.
"They only count the children who live," she said.

Once out of the clearing, they angled away from

the path they had taken the day before. The woods were still sodden, but there were no rivulets to cross and, except in the shadiest places, things seemed to be drying rapidly.

Whether because the footing was still somewhat uncertain or to spare her knee, Moira did not walk as fast.

"What happened back there anyway?" Wiz asked when the clearing was lost from sight.

"What do you mean?"

"Between you and Lothar. Everything started out all right, then—boom—it was like you'd bumped into your ex at a cocktail party."

"My ex at a . . . ?"

"I mean you both got real cold and distant," he amended.

"Was it that obvious?" Moira sighed. "I tried to conceal it. He gave us shelter and aid when we needed it and that is no small thing in the Wild Wood. I should have tried harder to be gracious."

"Yeah, but why?"

"Because he is a fool!" Moira snapped. "There is no place in the Wild Wood for mortals, Sparrow. Only fools try to live here and they fail."

"I guess it was rough at first, but he seems to be doing all right now."

"Yes. Because he bartered away his daughter."

"What?"

"You heard the child. His daughter has been given to the elves in trade for the safety of his miserable farm!"

"He traded his daughter to the elves?"

"Life in the Wild Wood is hard for those who have little magic." She smiled a little bitterly. "Call it a 'fostering.' That puts a better face upon it."

"What did they want with her?"

"As the little one said. She is a nursemaid to an elven infant." Moira's face softened. "Elves seldom have young. That must have been an event beneath the Elf Hill."

"Wait a minute," Wiz protested. "She wasn't . . . ah, I mean she wasn't married when she went, was she?"

"You mean was she unspoiled? Probably. Elves prefer virgin's milk when they can get it."

"But how . . . ? Oh, magic. Never mind."

They walked on a bit in silence. "What a fate. Locked under a hill forever."

"It has its compensations. The elves are kind enough in their unhuman fashion. They do not mistreat their servants."

"But to spend your whole life like that!"

"No," Moira said. "Time passes oddly under the hill. Someday, when the elf child needs her no longer, she will emerge as young as when she went in." She sobered. "Of course that stead will likely long be dust by then and there will be none who know her. That is the cruelest fate."

"Yeah," Wiz said, thinking of the graves. "I'm not sure living in safety is worth what it cost Lothar."

"The price has only been partly paid." Moira made a face. "Wait. As the children grow up they will go one by one to drudge for the elves. Plague, murrain, raids by trolls or others. There will always be another need and Lothar will always return to the elf hill to seek aid."

Wiz was shocked. "Doesn't Lothar realize that?"

"Not he," she said contemptuously. "I have seen his kind before. He hopes long and hard that something will happen. Like most mortals he lives for today and puts off the reckoning as long as he may." She increased her pace.

"It is an old, old story, Sparrow. As farms get smaller and the soil wears out within the Fringe there have always been those who sought to go beyond it to carve out new homes. But the Wild Wood is not for mortals. It is a place full of magic, given to others, and mortals violate it at their peril."

"Well, why not? My whole country was a howling wilderness once and we settled it."

"Because the magic in the Wild Wood is too strong, Sparrow. Within the Fringe the hedge witches and other orders can stand between the World's magic and people. Beyond the Fringe there is too much powerful magic. If we were to make the attempt we would only be swept away and our people with us. Believe me Sparrow, it has been tried and it has never worked. The Fringe is the limit of lands where mortals can live."

"Umm," said Wiz again and shifted his pack.

"What did Lothar mean when he said his grandfather knew this place?" he said after they had walked a bit more.

Moira snorted. "He was probably making it up. I doubt his grandfather ever came within a week's journey of that stead."

"But men did live in the Wild Wood once, didn't they?"

"Parts of it, yes."

"Why did they leave?"

"Because they were fools like that man," Moira snapped. "Because they went where they should not and paid the penalty for it! Now save your breath for walking." She lengthened her stride and left him staring at her back.

They're being pushed back, Wiz thought as he struggled to keep up with the hedge witch. *This whole area was inhabited once and the people have been forced out.* The Wild Wood was creeping into the Fringe like the African desert creeps south in drought. And the results were the same. The people either moved or died.

Would the rains ever come to turn back the Wild Wood? Wiz wondered. Moira's reaction hinted she didn't think so. When magic became too strong, people could no longer co-exist with it and they had to leave. The part of the world where humans could live was shrinking under the pressure of magic.

Wiz shook his head. All his life he had been taught that wilderness needed protection from encroaching humans. Here the humans were the ones who needed protecting.

Wiz wondered if the trolls, elves and other magical creatures would establish preserves for humans. Somehow he didn't think so.

FIVE

NIGHT FLIGHT

"Have you found them then?" The balefire nimbus played about Toth-Set-Ra as he hunched in his high-backed chair.

Atros grinned. "We know roughly where they are. We have only to summon our creatures for the final search." He shook his great shaggy head. "We have been closing in on them for the last three days. They evaded our ambush at the Forest Gate and fought their way through to the Wild Wood. Then they camped for the night within the ruins of the Rose Palace of Ali Suliman," (while the search swept past them, Atros did not add). "We lost them somewhat in the next day's rain, but we have them generally located."

"How have they avoided you for so long?"

Atros shrugged. "Bal-Simba—blast his eyes—is a clever foe. His Watchers have been working hard to muddy our sight. The whole of the North is covered with blanking and false trails."

He hesitated. "There is another thing. The wizard has a most pussiant cloaking spell. We cannot find the least trace of his magic anywhere in the North."

"Indeed?" croaked Toth-Set-Ra. "Oh indeed? And the hedge witch?"

"That is the strangest thing of all. The hedge witch discarded most of her magical apparatus early on. Some trolls found parts of her magic kit strewn about." He neglected to mention that the trolls were sleeping off a feast and had not reported their finds for three days. That had cost the troll father his head. "Apparently the hedge witch is relying on the other one to protect her."

Toth-Set-Ra rubbed the line of his cheekbone with a leathery forefinger. "Strange," he agreed. "Either this one is a most powerful wizard or she is a most trusting witch."

"I would suggest he is a powerful wizard, Dread Master. Judging from their success at eluding us."

"But you have found them?"

"We have them penned in a small part of the forest. They are somewhat to the west of the elf duke's hold."

"But you have found them?" Toth-Set-Ra pressed.

Atros smiled. "Tonight, Lord. Since we cannot locate them by magic, we must search by eye and ear. I am flooding the area with our creatures and allies. At night they are at their most powerful." His smile grew broader. "Besides, what weary travellers can refrain from lighting a fire to cook their dinner and warm their bones? And a fire in the Wild Wood can be seen for a long way away."

Toth-Set-Ra looked unimpressed. "And if our Wizard chooses to use magic?"

"Our black robes will be watching, ready to pounce."

"*My* black robes," Toth-Set-Ra croaked softly. "They are mine and do not ever forget it."

We shall see, old crow, Atros thought. *After tonight we shall see.*

"In any event, it is results I want, not details. Bring me this strange wizard with the most perfect cloaking spell. And bring him to me alive, Atros. Do you understand? I want him alive."

"Thy will, Dread Master," said Atros and bowed out of his presence.

There were a few other details Atros forebore to mention. His searchers were mostly allies or those who wanted the reward promised. Worse, nearly half of the searchers were trolls. Trolls are none too bright and far too inclined to murder to be ideal for this task.

Beyond that, Atros knew he could not hold his army together much beyond one night. The creatures not sworn to the League were restless, chancy things who would not stay no matter how great the promised reward. Even the League's sworn servants could not stay long. Such a concentration would quickly attract the attention of the Council's Watchers.

Not that it mattered, Atros told himself. One night would be more than sufficient.

Where were they bound? he wondered. They seemed to have a destination. The elf duke's hill? That made no sense. Elves were badly disposed to mortals of all varieties. Besides, if they wanted shelter among the elves there were easier roads to take.

Whatever their destination, they would have to swing south shortly or they would blunder into the deadest dead zone in all the North, a place where the tiniest spark of magic would show instantly. By now Atros had a grudging respect for this alien wizard's masking spells, but no spell could be good enough to hide them in that.

Atros was well-satisfied as he went down the corridor. Not only did he have things well in hand for the capture of the strange wizard, but his other plans were well in hand besides.

Soon. Very soon.

"Where are we going anyway?" Wiz asked, sitting on a stump by the fire.

Moira looked up from stirring the porridge. "Someplace safe."

"You said that before."

"I prefer not to name it. There is always the chance of being overheard."

"Well, what's it like? A farm?"

Moira laughed. "No, it is a very special place hidden away in the Wild Wood. A place built like no other in the World."

"You make it sound wonderful."

"It is that."

"Have you ever been there before?"

"This deep in the Wild Wood? Not likely. I have heard of it, though."

"Right now anyplace that put a roof over our heads would be wonderful."

"Patience, Sparrow. We are perhaps a day or two from our destination."

"Then what happens?"

"Then you will be safe and I can return to my village."

"Oh."

"I have work to do, Sparrow. There are people who need me."

"Yeah, I guess so. Only . . ." Moira held up her hand to silence him.

"Wait," she said. "There is something . . ."

With a roar four trolls charged into the clearing. They were huge and foul-smelling, clad in skins and leathers and rags. One brandished a rusty two-handed sword in one hand and the others carried clubs.

A troll closed in on Moira, arms extended and fanged mouth agape. Wiz grabbed a faggot from the fire and charged. With a casual, backhanded swipe and without taking his eyes from his prize, the creature sent Wiz sprawling through the fire.

Wiz rolled out as the beast got a hand on Moira. Without thinking he reached back into the fire and grabbed a burning brand. He pointed it at the troll and yelled "bippity boppity boo."

The troll was unfazed but the tree behind it exploded into flame with a crackle and roar. The astonished troll weakened its grip and Moira twisted free.

"Moira! Run!" Wiz yelled and ducked under the grasping arms of another troll. He twisted about and pointed the stick at it.

"Bippity boppity boo!" he shouted and another tree blazed up. The troll cringed back.

Whirling in a circle, Wiz pointed the branch and yelled "BippityboppitybooBippityboppitybooBippityboppityboo." Trees all around the clearing turned to fiercely burning torches and the confused trolls cowered and whimpered in the ring of light and heat.

Wiz sprinted in the general direction Moira had taken. Behind him he could see the forms of the trolls black against the orange-yellow glow. The scent of burning pine filled his nostrils and he coughed from the smoke. One of the trolls groped after him. Wiz pointed the stick at a tree between them, shouted "Bippity boppity boo" and watched the tree turn to a lance of flame in the very face of the monster. Then he turned and ran as fast as he could.

As Wiz charged through the forest, a dim shape flitted from behind a tree into his path. He flinched until he saw it was Moira, her form distorted by her cloak. He clasped her hand and she gave a welcoming squeeze. His cloak was back in the clearing, he realized, as were both their packs. But Moira was safe and none of the rest mattered.

Behind them the reddish glow of the fires lightened the night. Also from behind them came a series of hooting roars.

"They hunt us," Moira whispered and released his hand. "Come quickly."

The forest sloped gently downhill and they followed the slope as best they could. Wiz silently blessed the open parklike nature of the Wild Wood here because they could move quickly and quietly through it.

Ahead he could hear the bubble and murmur of a

running stream. Behind him came the sounds of the
trolls. They seemed to have spread out along the
ridge and were casting back and forth, calling to each
other as they went. Once Wiz saw a misshapen form
silhouetted on the ridgeline by the faint fireglow. He
tried to shrink in on himself even though he knew
night and distance made him invisible.

They paused on the rocky stream bank while Moira
turned this way and that, seeking the best path.
There were boulders to serve as stepping stones, but
instead Moira led Wiz directly into the chill, swift
waters.

"The water will mask our scent," she explained
over stream's clamor, "and some things cannot cross
running water."

"You mean like trolls?"

"The trolls are the least of it," Moira said. "Listen."

Off in the distance came the sound of a horn and
again the hunting roar of trolls echoed through the
trees. *My God*, thought Wiz. *Is every nightmare in
creation after us?*

The water was not deep, but the current was swift
and the bottom rocky. By the time they left the
stream, some little distance above the place they had
entered, Wiz had fallen into holes twice and was
soaked from head to foot. Moira had lost her balance
once and was thoroughly wet down one side.

With Moira leading they sprinted over the wide
pebble beach and into the sheltering dark of the
trees. The forest was thicker here and the underbrush more profuse. Wiz and Moira crowded into it
and peered back the way they had come.

"Which way?" Wiz panted.

Moira cast about indecisively. "Ahh," she breathed
at last. "They throng to the south and east of us. To
the west and north are areas rich in magic."

"So we go west and north?" Wiz suggested.

Moira shook her head. "To enter a powerful area
with the hunt so close upon us would be our doom.

With magic all about us we would stand out like ants on a griddle."

"Lay low?"

Moira didn't answer. Which was answer enough.

"Can't you use magic to get us out of this?"

Moira snorted. "If I used magic they would sniff us out at once. We avoid them only because they cannot sense magic upon us."

A weird, warbling howl pierced the night, chilling Wiz's blood. Across the stream, a huge wolf-like shape loomed on the ridge, outlined by the rising moon. Even in the moonlight its eyes burned red. It was the epitome of all the wolf nightmares of Wiz's childhood.

"Dire Beast," Moira breathed. She squeezed Wiz's hand even tighter and they crept away, clinging to the shadow and thickets. Behind them the wolf creature howled again but made no move to follow.

Once away from the stream bank they ran. They scrambled up another ridge and half-ran half-slid into a valley. The woods were thicker and darker, but that was no comfort. Still the sounds of their hunters rang and the trees seemed to close in about them to the point of suffocation.

There were brambles to catch at clothing and rip the flesh. Once Wiz took a thorny branch full in the face and once they had to stop to disentangle Moira's cloak from a barbed bush. As they worked the fabric off the grasping thorns Wiz saw that Moira's hands had been cruelly lacerated by pushing through the spindly growth.

Finally, exhausted, Moira led Wiz into a thicket. There was a hollow in the center as if once long ago a tree had been uprooted there. Together they cowered and panted in the little crater beneath the bushes and listened to the sounds of pursuit echoing through the forest.

Dared they stay here? Wiz wanted to ask but he was afraid to make a sound. Besides, he didn't think

he would like the answer. Unbidden, Moira's words
on the first day came back to him. *If you have a
choice between the worst death you can imagine and
falling into the hands of the League, do everything in
your power to die.* Had they really come to that? he
thought, looking over at Moira.

Suddenly something hissed in Wiz's ear like a
disturbed snake. Wiz jumped.

"Hsst," came the sound again. "Hsst, Lady, over
here." He turned and stared but saw nothing. Then
part of the bush seemed to twist and coalesce and a
tiny man stood beckoning to them where a second
before there had been only moonlight and branches.
He was clad in a pointed cap, tunic and breeks with
pointed shoes. Wiz could not tell the color in the
dim light.

"Come this way. Quickly." The little being turned
and skipped through the undergrowth. Moira started
to follow but Wiz caught her arm. "Trap?" he panted.

Moira scowled and shook off his hand. She hurried
after the little man, who was dancing with impatience.

Wiz was half-blown when they started, but he
pushed ahead gamely. The trail led through glades
and over ridges until at last they arrived at the base
of a hill. As their guide approached, a rock rolled
away and pale golden light flooded out into the dark.

"Enter and be welcome," said a melodious male
voice from within.

Again Moira started forward and again Wiz caught
her arm.

"Didn't you tell me to avoid places like this?"

"Would you rather the trolls and Dire Beasts?" she
snapped. Wiz nodded and followed her into the hill.

"May there be peace upon you. May you leave the
woes of the World behind," the voice said, as if
reciting a formula.

"May there be confusion to our enemies and may
we return to the world we know," Moira said firmly
into the air.

"May it be so," responded the voice and their host seemed to step out of the wall of the tunnel to them.

He was tall, graceful and silver-haired. His eyes were so blue as to be almost purple and his skin was the color of milk. Wiz could see the blue veins underneath.

He wore a long tunic of scarlet, intricately worked, and a collar of beaten gold. His belt was dark leather decorated with bronze the length around.

"My Lady," he bowed to Moira. "My Lord," he nodded to Wiz.

"My Lord." Moira dropped a deep curtsey.

"My Lord," repeated Wiz and made a clumsy bow. He barely noticed that the rock had slid silently back across the entrance, sealing them within.

Their host regarded them serenely. "I am called Aelric. I am duke of this place and I bid you welcome here.

"We thank you for your hospitality, Lord," Moira said. "I am called Moira and this is one is called Sparrow."

Duke Aelric looked narrowly at Wiz. "Ahhh," he said simply, but with a world of meaning.

"You have heard of us then, Lord?"

"A mite." The elf duke made a languid gesture. "But there will be time for talk later. I hope you will do me the pleasure of dining with me this evening."

"We would be honored, Lord," Moira said.

"Let it be so then." Duke Aelric snapped his fingers and their guide capered out and bowed low to his master.

"Most dread Lord, most gracious Lady, if you will deign to follow me?" The little creature turned and moved down the tunnel. Duke Aelric touched his fingertips to his forehead and faded back into the rock. Wiz gaped until Moira jabbed him with her elbow. Then he followed her and their guide down the corridor.

Wiz's shoes squeaked on tesselated marble floors

inlaid in fantastic patterns. Over his head columns of scarlet and gold soared upward until lost in the gloom. Here and there an elaborately carved lantern cast a gentle yellow glow through its alabaster panes, making the light more mellow rather than brighter. Occasionally the glint of gold added accent and unostentatious richness to their surroundings.

They passed down stately corridors, through tapestry-hung halls and up sweeping curving staircases, yet they saw no one. Not even a faint, distant footstep or the furtive motion of a curtain dropping into place showed that there was anyone in the huge underground palace but themselves and their tiny guide.

At last they came to a massive door, twice their height and finely carved. The elf placed his hand on the intricately worked iron handle and pushed gently.

The door swung open to reveal a spacious, richly appointed room. It was more brightly lit than the rest of the palace and the carved and gilded lanterns along the walls cast a warm light on the furnishings of pale brown wood and heavy silken hangings the color of chrysoberyl. The ceiling was painted the blue of a summer sky and spangled with glittering golden stars. Lines of silver traced out the shape of unfamiliar constellations. The air was heavy with the scent of roses and lilies.

"My master bids you be comfortable," the elven major-domo squeaked. "There will be time to rest and bathe before dinner. My Lady's chamber is to the right," he swept a bow in that direction, "and my Lord's is to the left. Peace and repose be unto you." With that he bowed out.

"Wow," said Wiz as he looked around at the splendor. "This is really something."

"Elves contrive to live well," Moira said, laying her cloak onto an elegantly proportioned table and sinking down onto a silken cushion of the palest blue in the chair next to it.

"All right!" Wiz said and dropped onto a couch nearby.

Moira removed the ribbon from her hair and shook out her flaming locks. Wiz watched, enthralled.

"It was brave of you to save me from the trolls," she told him. "You gave me my life at the risk of yours and I thank you for it."

The words were sweet, but her tone was used to thank a stranger for a service. Moira was sincere and grateful, but that was all. She had been warmer to the man from the village, Wiz thought.

"It was nothing, Lady," he said uncomfortably.

"It was, and again I thank you."

Wiz did not reply. "Lady," he said finally, "may I ask you a question?"

"Since you must."

"I mean we won't be overheard or anything will we?"

"We will almost certainly be overheard, although mayhap Duke Aelric is too noble to pry into the affairs of his guests. Question if you must, but guard your tongue."

"Where is everyone? I mean, does Aelric live here all alone?"

Moira shrugged. "I doubt it, for elves are social creatures. But the place could be aswarm with elven folk and we might see none. All elves have the trick of not being seen when it pleases them."

"Why did Aelric help us? Are the elves allied against the League?"

Again the shrug. "Allied against the League? No. Elves ally with none and barely notice what mortals do to each other. His Grace acted for his own reasons and those are beyond conjecture. Barring war or murder, elves are deathless and they fill their years with contests and rivalries among themselves. They play deep and subtle games with their own kind and meddle seldom in the affairs of mortals. Perhaps we are part of such a game."

"Well, as long as he's willing to put us up, we can be whumpuses for all I care."

"What's a whumpus?"

"An imaginary animal." Wiz lay back on the couch and started to put his feet up before looking at his muddy shoes and thinking better of it. "Now what?"

"Now we had best make ready for dinner." Moira rose from the chair. "That is your room, I believe."

The bedroom managed to be magnificent, simple and cozy all at once. The canopied bed was made of some rich dark wood crafted in sleek, almost modern, lines and polished until it glowed a warm reddish brown. The sheets were tan and the thick comforter was a pale russet. The lighting was soft and indirect, brighter than the twilight the elves seemed to prefer but not as bright as the sitting room. The bed looked so inviting Wiz nearly sank down onto it, but he knew if he got that comfortable he'd never be ready for dinner. He had a strong feeling it would not do to keep Aelric waiting.

The bath beyond was walled in pink-veined marble set with gold. In the center of the room was a sunken tub of steaming water, fragrant with herbs.

Wiz moved toward it, pulling at his shirt.

He had the shirt over his head when soft warm hands touched his bare back.

"Hey!" Wiz tried to turn, but the hands restrained him gently and helped him get the shirt off. With his head free, Wiz turned, but the room was empty.

"What is this?"

The only answer was a very feminine giggle as someone started to undo his belt. He looked down and saw nothing, yet his belt was unhooked and fingers began to unzip his fly. Instinctively he reached down to knock the invisible hands away, but he met only air. Again someone or something giggled.

Oh well, Wiz thought and submitted.

Once his unseen companion had undressed him,

he stepped into the just-too-warm water and sighed luxuriously.

Wiz was expertly soaped, scrubbed and rinsed. The water that came off him was black with dirt, but the water in the tub remained so clear he could see his toes.

Clean and glowing, he was assisted from the tub and rubbed down with towels he could not see. It felt like there were two or three pairs of hands working on him at once. *Either there's a whole harem in here or she doesn't look anything like what I imagined,* Wiz thought.

His clothes were gone, but when he reentered the bedroom new clothes were laid out for him, a shirt with enormous puffed sleeves, a russet doublet several shades darker than the bedspread and a pair of tight buckskin breeches. Soft calf-high boots of ox-blood leather completed the outfit.

This time there were no invisible hands to help him so Wiz dressed himself, struggling with the unfamiliar fastenings.

Not bad, he thought, surveying the result in a full-length mirror. He looked like a real swashbuckler, lean rather than skinny.

Moira was waiting for him when he emerged. If Wiz look good in his borrowed clothes, Moira was breathtaking. She wore a gown of emerald green velvet, cut low and caught tight at the waist, with full-length sleeves that flared sharply from elbow to wrist. Her hair was a flaming mane about her face, held in place with silver pins set with opals. Wiz could only stare.

"Do you like it?" she asked somewhat shyly. "I've never had a dress like this."

"It's gorgeous," said Wiz when he finally got his lower jaw under control. "You're gorgeous."

"Thank you, Sparrow," she dropped him a mock curtsey. Then she became serious. "Now watch yourself. Be respectful and above all, be courteous. Elves

place great store on courtesy and there are very few
mortals who have shared Duke Aelric's table."

Wiz nodded dumbly and moved toward her. She
moved away with fluid grace.

"Shall we go?"

"Is it time?"

Moira only smiled and opened the door. Their
guide was waiting for them. He bowed so low his
forehead almost touched the floor and led them off.

Again their way took them down empty corridors
and magnificent halls, all bathed in the soft dim
light. At length the little man brought them down a
stair as subtly curved and carefully proportioned as
a sea shell, to a great bronze door. The door swung
open at their approach. The creature bowed to the
floor and motioned them within.

Their host awaited them inside the door.

"My Lady. My Lord." He had changed his red
tunic for a tight-fitting outfit of silver-gray velvet.
Silver glinted at his neck and wrists and a silver band
set with a fiery blue opal held back his white hair.
He was fully as magnificent as he had been when
they first saw him, but now the effect was less bar-
baric, more civilized.

He bowed to them and Wiz bowed back as best he
could. Then the duke took Moira's arm in his and led
them to the table.

The odd half-light made it impossible for Wiz to
judge the size of the room. The far walls were lost in
the dimness, but Wiz didn't feel dwarfed. The floor
was elaborately patterned marquetry and the table
was draped in snow-white linen. Softly glowing balls
of light hung above the table. They danced gently in
an unfelt breeze and the ripple and play of the light
was like candlelight on the table and diners.

Invisible pipers played a high reedy tune in the
background, at once medieval and modern, like soft
progressive jazz performed on recorders.

The duke seated Wiz on his left and Moira on his right.

"You seemed to have created an uncommon stir among the mortals," Aelric observed to Moira as they sat down.

"It was not intentional, Lord."

"And you were the object of a Grand Summoning," he said to Wiz.

"Yes, Lord. Uh, it wasn't my idea."

"No doubt," Aelric said equitably.

The elf duke was a perfect host, charming, gracious and witty. He made Moira laugh and dimple without arousing more than a twinge of jealousy in Wiz and contrived to make Wiz feel more at ease than he had since he arrived on this world. Only once did Moira bring the talk back to the circumstances which led them beneath the elf hill this night.

"Lord, why did you aid us?"

Aelric smiled, just a hint of a smile. "Let us say we find your pursuers an annoyance. Trolls and such like are uneasy neighbors and were they to find that which they seek they might be encouraged to tarry."

"We thank you for your service."

"The pleasure was mine, Lady," he said with an easy smile and again changed the subject.

For all his charm, Wiz could not warm to their host. There was malice there, Wiz thought, as he listened to the flow of the elf duke's talk. The casual malice of a cat with a mouse. There was alien, and underneath it was boredom. Would it be boring to live forever? Yes, in the end it would be, no matter how rich, how powerful or how skilled you were.

The food was rich and varied. The portions were small but there were many dishes and each plate was brought forth as carefully arranged as if by a master designer. Most of it was unidentifiable but it was all delicious.

Once Wiz had been taken to one of the fanciest

restaurants in San Francisco as part of a dog-and-pony show for a client. The meal had been very much like this. Excellent food, beautifully presented in magnificent surroundings. Except this was better on all counts.

The girl who served them was human. Wiz wondered if she was Lothar's daughter. But she was so quick and efficient and so quiet and downcast she was gone before he could ask the question. Probably not a good thing to ask anyway, he decided uncomfortably.

They had gone through a half a dozen courses of meats, vegetables, sweets and savories when the duke reached out to lay a gentle hand on Moira's wrist, interrupting the story she was telling.

Aelric frowned. "Your pardon Lady, Lord. But it seems we have a caller asking for you."

Wiz froze, his spoon halfway to his mouth.

Aelric listened and then said into the air. "You may speak."

A hazy shimmering began to congeal in the center of the hall but the elf prince raised his hand. "I said you may speak. None enters here unbidden." The half-shadow dissipated until only a little shimmer remained.

"You have two mortals here," wailed a voice, high, thin and reedy with all the despair in the universe.

"What is within this hill is not the business of outsiders."

"You have two mortals," the voice repeated. "We want them."

"Your wants are no concern of mine," Aelric said in a bored tone. "Now speak on matters of interest or begone."

"My master will reward you well," crooned the voice.

The elf duke cocked his head and arched his brows. "It might be of interest to know what your master has that he possibly believes I should want. But not tonight. Say you further?"

"My master offers double what the Council offers for the mortals."

Aelric frowned. "I have no part in mortal quarrels," he said sharply. "What I do, I do because it pleases me and for no other reason. Those who are here stay here and those outside stay outside."

"My master is powerful," the voice wailed. "He is powerful and determined. Give us the mortals."

"Your master is a mortal," Aelric responded. "That is limit enough on his power."

"Will you duel him by magic?" the voice asked.

"Perhaps some other time. Now I am at meat. And you grow tedious."

The voice changed. It deepened and became louder. "GIVE THEM TO US," it roared. "GIVE THEM OR WE SHALL KICK THIS HILL DOWN ABOUT YOUR EARS."

Aelric yawned elaborately. "Tedious indeed," he said. "Now be off with you." He lifted a hand languidly and gestured.

"GIVE US the mortaaalllls. . . ." the voice lessened and died like a train whistle down a tunnel.

Aelric turned to Wiz and Moira and smiled sweetly. "Uncouth creatures. Now, you were saying?"

"Forgive me, Lord," Wiz broke in, "but aren't you afraid he will do something?"

Aelric gave Wiz a look that froze his bones and cleaved his tongue to the roof of his mouth.

"Forgive him, Lord," said Moira quickly. "He is from far away and is unused to our ways. Please forgive him," she begged. "Please."

Aelric cocked his head and stared at Wiz. "Far away indeed, Lady. Very well, but teach him manners." Then his expression softened.

"Know, infant, that this place has stood for aeon and on. It was builded by magic on a foundation of magic and it would take more magic than a mortal could learn in a puny lifetime to touch it or any of mine."

"Yes, Lord," said Wiz, very subdued.

The rest of the dinner passed off without incident. Aelric was again the gracious host, diverting and ever attentive to his guests' needs. By the time the last sweets had been removed with nuts in golden bowls and the wine brought forth in crystal flagons, Wiz was almost relaxed.

Almost. He regarded the elf prince in the same light as a friendly lion—magnificent, unsettling and not at all someone you wanted to spend time with.

At last Moira yawned delicately behind her hand and Aelric took that as a sign that the dinner was over.

"I should not keep you," he said with a charming smile. "You have had a long day already and several—interesting—days before that. May you rest well."

"Thank you, Lord." Moira returned the smile. "And thank you again for your hospitality." She extended her hand and the elf lord raised it to his lips.

"You are more than welcome. Thank you for gracing my table." He turned to Wiz. "And thank you, Lord. It was a privilege to meet someone from so far away."

Wiz bowed as best he could.

"You do not know why you were Summoned then?" Aelric said suddenly.

"Beg pardon?" Wiz asked, confused by this turn of the conversation. "Ah, no Lord."

"Well then," said Duke Aelric with an odd, cold smile. "It will be interesting to see what becomes of you, Sparrow."

"Thank you, Lord," Wiz replied, not sure whether he should be thanking the elf or not.

"Then will we see you again, Lord?" Moira asked.

"I doubt it," Duke Aelric said. "But it will be interesting nonetheless." Again the alien smile, like a rather sleepy cat examining a newly discovered plaything.

"Lady, do you suppose he knows something about

me?" Wiz asked as soon as they were back in their rooms.

"He knew who we were," Moira said, yawning and stretching in a way that made her dress swell alarmingly and Wiz's heart nearly stop.

"I mean do you think he knows why Patrius brought me here?"

"Who knows what an elf knows?"

"Shouldn't we ask him?"

"Sparrow, if he knew and if he wanted us to know, he would tell us. It might be he was making sport of us. Elves are prone to such tricks. But I do know this. If he did not tell us there is no point in asking him."

"But . . ."

"But I am going to bed," Moira said firmly. "You may sit up and attempt to fathom the unfathomable if you wish."

Wiz watched the door to Moira's room close after her and then turned toward his room. He dropped his clothes on a chair in the corner and headed groggily for his own bed.

I wonder if he really does know. Or if he's just playing head games, Wiz thought dreamily as he drifted off to sleep.

In the morning there were fresh packs in the main room. The clothes they had worn into the hill were waiting for them with all traces of travel stain gone. Somehow they had even restored the nap to the suede on Wiz's running shoes. Moira's cloak was clean and patched so expertly there was no sign it had ever been rent and tattered. There was a new cloak hanging next to Wiz's pack to replace the one he had lost.

Sitting on the table was a round loaf of rich brown bread, still warm from the oven, a slab of pale yellow cheese, a pitcher of foaming brown ale and a bowl of white onions.

"It appears we are to break our fast alone this morning," Moira said, pulling her chair closer to the table. She poured herself a tankard of ale and used her knife to hack off a chunk of cheese and a thick slice of bread. With the knife point she speared one of the onions and took a healthy bite.

Although the idea of beer and onions for breakfast made Wiz a little queasy, he followed suit. In spite of his misgivings the combination was delicious. The cheese was sharp and tangy, the onions were mild and sweet and the ale refreshingly astringent on his tongue.

"Doesn't time run differently in these places?" Wiz asked Moira around a mouthful of bread and cheese.

"Not if the elf lord does not will it so," she said. "He promised me when we entered that it would not."

"So that's what that greeting was all about!"

"Just so. Albeit we had little enough choice should he have decided to make centuries pass like minutes."

"I take it we're going on this morning?"

"I doubt Duke Aelric's hospitality holds for more than a single night," said Moira, appropriating the heel of the loaf. "Besides, the sooner we reach our destination the better." She looked at the bread and sighed. "I wish we could carry bread like this on our journey. It is unusually good."

"It's baked by elves," Wiz said smiling.

"Their servants morelike. What's so funny?"

"Never mind," Wiz chuckled. "I'm not even going to try to explain it to you." Then he turned serious. "What are the chances someone is going to be waiting for us outside?"

"Small enough. Oh, they may watch the door we entered like cats at a mouse hole. But I do not think we will go out that same way. Not only time but space runs strangely in places the elves make their own."

Wiz picked up the last crumb of cheese and popped it into his mouth. He let it melt away on his tongue savoring the bite and flavor. "Well, when do we leave?"

"As soon as we gather our things," said Moira. She stood up from the table and fastened her cloak at her pale freckled throat with the turquoise and silver clasp. Wiz followed suit, throwing his cloak over his back.

"Don't we need to ring for someone to show us out?"

"I doubt it," said Moira as she reached for the door handle. "If a guide is needed one will be waiting when we open the door."

The door swung outward at her touch and brilliant morning sunlight flooded in. Instead of a marble corridor lined with travertine pillars the door opened into a sunny forest glade. An orange and brown butterfly flitted lazily above the deep green grass that ran to their threshold.

Moira looked over at Wiz, smiled slightly and shrugged. Wiz shrugged back. Then they adjusted their packs and set out under the warm morning sun.

SIX

HEART'S EASE

The morning was bright and sunny. Instead of dark and sinister, the Wild Wood was fresh and green. There was almost nothing among the trees and ferns to remind them of the night before.

Their path led out of the glade and back up the heavily wooded hill above the door. There was no hint or scent of danger, but still they moved along quickly.

They climbed a series of forested ridges, each looking down on the tops of the trees in the valley below. At the top of the third ridge, Moira scanned the valley while Wiz sat puffing on a rocky outcrop.

"There!" the hedge witch said, pointing. Below and off to one side a square stone tower stood rough and grey above the trees of the forest. About its base clustered outbuildings enclosed by a stockade of peeled logs.

"Heart's Ease," said Moira. "Our journey's end." She shifted her pack as Wiz struggled to his feet and they headed off down the path.

"Will we be safe here?" Wiz asked as the trail flattened out in the valley and he found he had breath for more than walking.

"In daylight nothing dare come close," Moira told him. "Anything magic here would be immediately known to the Watchers. There are non-magic agents, of course, human and such, but . . ." she shrugged. "We are as safe here as anywhere."

"Thank God!" Wiz said fervently.

Moira frowned. "Do not be so free with names of power."

"I'm sorry," Wiz said contritely.

The forest enclosed them until they were almost on top of the castle. The trees were as huge and hoary as anywhere in the Wild Wood, but they didn't seem as threatening here.

"It feels friendly," Wiz said wonderingly, aware for the first time how opressive the Wild Wood had been even at its most benign.

"It is friendlier," Moira agreed. "The forest folk hereabouts are kindly disposed toward the inhabitants of Heart's Ease. They watch over the place and those who live there." She shifted her pack with a swell and jiggle in her blouse that made Wiz's heart catch. "Besides, this is a quiet zone. There is almost no magic here, for good or ill."

Atros returned to his sleeping chamber fuming. It had been a long, frustrating evening. *Damn those elves and their impudence!* They had spirited his quarry out from his very grasp, humilated him in front of the entire League and ruined his plans. His impromptu army disintegrated once they knew the elf duke guested the two they sought.

So they had been making for the elf hill after all, the wizard thought as he stripped off his bearskin cloak by the light of a single lamp glowing magically in one corner. He did not understand it and he was too tired to really think upon it. Perhaps the one who had been Summoned was some strange kind of elf and not a man at all? True, Toth-Set-Ra's scrying demon had called the Summoned a man, but demons could be wrong.

Too many possibilities, he thought as he pulled his silken tunic over his head. *For now sleep and in the morning* . . . He moved toward the great canopied bed and then stopped. There was something, or someone, making an untidy lump under the sheets. He stepped back cautiously and possessed himself of his staff. He muttered a protective spell and then moved to the bed again. Reaching out with his staff, he flipped back the fine woolen coverlet and recoiled at what lay beneath.

There on the gore-clotted sheets was a thing which had once been a man. His back was broken, his ribs were smashed, his arms and legs dislocated and cruelly contorted, and his head lay at an impossible angle. But worse, he had no skin. He had been so expertly flayed that even his nose remained in place. His pallid eyeballs stared up at the ceiling and his ivory white teeth seemed to smile out of the mass of bloody tissue that had been a face.

Even in its present state, Atros had no difficulty identifying the body as Kar-Sher, Keeper of the Sea of Scrying.

"Do you like my little present, Atros?" hissed a familiar, hateful voice. The dark-haired giant started and looked around. In the shadows behind the feebly glowing lamp a face took shape. The face of Toth-Set-Ra.

"I told one I know what he was called," the wizard's voice went on, soft and full of menace. "Not his true name, Atros, just what he was called. And you see the result."

The old wizard cackled. "Oh, I did take his skin afterwards. I needed it, you see. It is amazing what you can do with the skin of a wizard, even a wizard who set himself so much above his station. A wizard who was such an inexpert plotter as this one."

Atros looked around wildly, swinging his staff this way and that to try to ward off an attack.

"I tell you again Atros, the League is mine!" The skull-face image said. "You, all of you, exist to serve me. And serve me you shall—one way or the other. Meditate upon that, Atros. Meditate upon it while you sleep."

The image winked out, leaving Atros alone in the chamber cold and shaking. Did the old crow mean to spare his life? Or was this just some torture designed to shake his will before he too was killed?

Atros spent the rest of the night in sleepless suspense and confusion. Plots to replace Toth-Set-Ra were very far from his mind.

A woman waited to greet them at the stockade gate. She was beautiful, tall and stately as a ship under sail. She was not young, yet not as old as her long white hair proclaimed. As Wiz got closer he saw that the lines around her eyes and mouth were those of one who had lived hard, not long.

She wore a long gown of midnight blue velvet, caught with a silver cord at her waist. The dagged sleeves of her dress fitted her upper arms tightly and swept halfway to the ground at her wrists.

Her right hand rested on the shoulder of a bent, manlike creature with a long sharp nose and huge hairy ears. He was as ugly as she was beautiful, but the contrast was not incongruous.

"Merry met and well come," she said in a voice like ringing silver. "I am Shiara, the mistress of this place, and Heart's Ease is your home for as long as you care to stay."

"Thank you, Lady," said Moira, curtseying. Wiz hastened to bow.

"Not 'lady,' " the woman told her. "Just plain Shiara."

"Not plain either," said Wiz, moved by her beauty.

Shiara smiled but did not look in his direction. *She's blind!*, he realized.

"Your companion is gallant," Shiara said to Moira.

"He has his moments," Moira sniffed.

"You are called Sparrow, are you not?"

"Yes, Lady. Ah, yes Shiara."

"Well, merry met at Heart's Ease, Sparrow," the lady said. "You must both be tired. Ugo will show you to your rooms."

The ugly little creature sniffed and shuffled through the stockade gate without a backwards glance.

The ground within covered perhaps two acres. There were six or eight small buildings, huts and storehouses and a large garden laid out behind. Attached to the base of the stone tower was a large building, also of peeled logs, roofed with shingles and chinked with moss.

"Is she a wizardess?" Wiz whispered to Moira as they came up the flagstone walkway.

"She was of the Mighty," Moira said and motioned him to silence.

Ugo led them into the building and Wiz saw it was a single large room, a great hall with a huge smoke-blackened fireplace in one side and a table big enough to seat twenty people down the center. In spite of its rude exterior, the hall was richly furnished with heavy velvet drapes on the walls and massively carved furniture placed carefully about. The whole effect reminded Wiz of a picture he had seen once of J.P. Morgan's hunting lodge.

Ugo took them down the hall without pausing and through a low stone door into the tower proper. There was a narrow stair twisting off to the right and climbing so steeply Wiz was afraid he would lose his balance. At the second floor landing Ugo opened a door for Moira and bowed her through. Wiz started to follow but Ugo blocked him with a rough hairy arm.

"Lady's room," he said gruffly. "Come." He led Wiz on up the stairs to the very top of the tower.

"Your room," Ugo grumbled as he opened the door.

The room was small and simply furnished with a narrow rope bed, a table and single chair. But there was a fire laid in the fireplace and a basin and pitcher of steaming water sat on the table. The bed was covered with a bright counterpane and a snow-white towel lay beside the basin. Against one wall, next to the fireplace, stood a full-length mirror.

"Dinner at sun's setting," the goblin told him. "Do not be late."

Dinner was simple but savory. Most of the dishes were vegetables and tubers from the castle garden, with wild mushrooms from the forest and forest fruits for dessert. There was very little meat, which suited Wiz.

"Moira has been telling me of your travels," Shiara said. She held a knife in one hand and extended the other hand, palm down and fingertips spread, over the table, finding her plate by the heat from the food.

"It was quite a trip," Wiz said. "Lady," he added hastily as Moira frowned.

"I understand you rescued Moira when you were beset by trolls."

"Well, kinda. Mostly she rescued me."

"Still, from what Moira tells me it was a bravely done deed." She smiled slightly. "Though perhaps charging a troll with a stick is not the wisest move."

"Thank you, Lady," said Wiz, ignoring the second sentence. "Uh, Lady, do you know if they are still looking for us?"

Shiara turned serious. "Somewhat, I understand. Although your guesting the night in an elf hill seems to have thrown them off the scent and dampened the ardor of many of the League's allies. There are few who would willingly try conclusions with any of the elven kind, much less an elf duke."

"Then are they likely to find us here?"

She considered. "Perchance. But in this quiet place it would be hard. We do not use magic at Heart's

Ease, so they cannot find you directly. There is little magic here to reflect off us and show us those with the Sight. No, Sparrow, if they find you at all it will be by accident.

"Besides," she continued, "finding you and getting here are very different things. In a quiet zone such as this any attempt at magic would be seen instantly by the Watchers and countered. We are a hundred leagues or more from the shores of the Freshened Sea so they cannot come at us overland. The forest creatures are our friends, so they would find it difficult to sneak close.

"All things considered we are safe enough."

"That's a relief."

"Just do not get careless," Moira said sharply.

"True," their blind hostess said. "Safety is at best relative and we are deep in the Wild Wood. Do not wander off, and leave things you do not understand strictly alone."

There was silence for a bit while they ate.

"Lady, what do we do now?" Wiz asked at last.

"You remain here as my guests while the Mighty consider your situation."

"And Moira?" Wiz asked, dreading the answer.

"I am to remain as well," said the red-haired witch, in a tone that showed she didn't like it. "In their wisdom the Mighty have decreed that even here you need a keeper." She grimaced. "And I am chosen for the task."

"You don't have to stay on my account," Wiz protested.

"I stay because the Mighty would have it so."

"Peace, peace," said Shiara. "Lady, I think your quarrel is with those not present, not the Sparrow."

"True, Lady," Moira said contritely. She turned to Wiz. "I am sorry I spoke so."

They contrived to get through the rest of dinner without snapping at each other.

* * *

At first Wiz simply luxuriated in life at Heart's Ease. He had a bed to sleep in, a roof over his head, no one was chasing him and, best of all, he didn't have to walk all day.

But that palled quickly. There was nothing for him to do. Moira made herself useful, cooking and helping to clean, but Wiz had no domestic skills.

"Is there anything I can do?" he asked Ugo one day as the goblin was sweeping out the great hall.

"Do?" Ugo grunted.

"To help."

Ugo bent to his sweeping. "Don't need help. Take care of Lady by myself."

It wasn't that he was interested in doing housework, Wiz admitted to himself; he was bored and he felt completely useless.

He wandered out into the garden where Moira was on her hands and knees weeding an herb border.

"Can I help?"

Moira looked up and did not rise.

"How?" she asked suspiciously.

Wiz spread his arms. "I just want to make myself useful."

Moira snorted skeptically, as if she felt his offer was a ruse to get close to her. Since that was partially true, Wiz reddened.

"Very well, weed that section over there." She nodded her head toward a part of the border on the other side of the garden.

The border contained tall fennel plants, their feathery pale green foliage smelling strongly of licorice. Sprouting thickly around them were broad-leafed seedlings, each with two or three yellow-green leaves.

Even though the smell of licorice made Wiz slightly nauseous, he set to work with a will, pulling up the tiny plants without damaging the fennel. The summer sun beat strongly on his back and before he had weeded five feet he was sweating heavily. The border was wide and he had to reach to get the weeds at the far side. In ten feet his shoulders were twinging from the reaching and by the time he had done twenty feet his back was sore as well. He took to stopping frequently to rest his aching muscles—and to watch Moira at work on the other side of the garden.

Moira worked steadily and mechanically, flicking the weeds out of the bed with a practiced twist of her wrist. Her long red hair hung down beside her face and every so often she would reach up and brush it out of the way, but she never broke the rhythm of her work. There was a smudge of dirt on her cheek and her skirt and blouse were grimed and stained, but she still took Wiz's breath away.

At last Wiz reached the end of the fennel and went to Moira for further instructions.

"It took you long enough," she said as he approached.

"There were a lot of weeds," said Wiz, bending over backwards in an effort to get the kinks out of his back. "I don't think that patch had been weeded in some time."

Moira looked up at him sharply. "I weeded it myself not three days ago."

"Well, weeds must come up quickly here. They were all over the place."

Moira got to her feet and went over to examine Wiz's handywork. At the sight of the clean bare earth under the fennel plants she sucked in her breath and clenched her teeth.

"What's wrong?"

"Those," she said pointing to Wiz's piles of "weeds," "were lettuces. They were planted there so the fennel could shade them." She sighed and stooped to gather the wilted plants into her apron. "I hope you like salad, Sparrow, because there is going to be a lot of it tonight."

"I'm sorry," he mumbled.

"It is not your fault, Sparrow," she said in a resigned voice. "I should have known better than to trust you with such a task."

That made Wiz feel even worse.

"Go back inside. I will finish up here."

"Lady, I'm really sorry."

"I know you are, Sparrow. Now go."

Finally, by appealing to Shiara, Wiz got a regular job. Under a shed roof against the palisade was a woodpile and next to the woodpile stood an old tree stump with an axe in it. Wiz's job was to chop firewood for Heart's Ease.

The axe was shaped like a giant tomahawk with no poll and a perfectly round straight haft. The design made it hard to handle and it took Wiz two or three hours a day to chop enough wood for the hearths and kitchen fires. He didn't see how Ugo had been able to get the wood chopped with all his other work. *Except*, Wiz thought glumly, *he's probably a lot more efficient at it, than I am*.

The goblin servant came by the wood pile several times to check Wiz's progress and sniffed disapprovingly at what he saw. He also very ostentatiously examined the axe for damage each time and strictly forbade Wiz to sharpen it.

Worse than the boredom, Moira avoided him. She wasn't obvious about it and she was always distantly polite when they met, but she contrived to spend as little time in his company as she could. Wiz took to standing on the battlements of the keep and watching her as she worked in the garden far below. From the occasional glance she threw his way he knew she saw him, but she never asked him to stop.

He had been closer to her when they were on the run, Wiz thought miserably. About the only time he could count on seeing her was when they sat down to dinner.

But the worst thing of all was that there were no computers. Because of the magical changes that let him speak the local language, Wiz couldn't even

write out programs. He took to running over algorithms mentally, or sitting and sorting piles of things
algorithmatically. At night his dreams of Moira alternated with dreams of working at a keyboard again and
watching the glowing golden lines of ASCII characters march across the screen.

One morning Moira found him sitting at the table
in the hall practicing with broomstraws.

"What are you doing, Sparrow?" she asked, eyeing
the row of different length straws on the table before
him.

"I'm working a variation on the shell sort."

"Those aren't shells," Moira pointed out.

"No, the algorithm—the method—was named for
the man who invented it. His name was Shell."

"Is this magic?" she demanded.

"No. It's just a procedure for sorting things. You
see, you set up two empty piles . . ."

"How can piles be empty?"

"Well, actually you establish storage space for two
empty piles. Then you . . ."

"Wait a minute. Why don't you just put things in
order?"

"This is a way of putting them in order."

"You don't need two piles to lay out straws in
order."

"No, look. Suppose you needed to tell someone to
lay out straws in order."

"Then I would just tell them to lay them out in
order. I don't need two piles for that either."

"Yeah, but suppose the person didn't know how to
order something."

"Sparrow, I don't think *anyone* is that stupid."

"Well, just suppose, okay?"

She sighed. "All right, I am working with someone
who is very stupid. Now what?"

"Well, you want a method, a recipe, that you can
give this person that will let them sort things no

matter how many there are to be sorted. It should be simple, fast and infallible.

"Now suppose the person who is going to be doing the sorting can compare straws and say that one is longer than another one, okay?"

"Hold on," Moira cut in. "You want to do this as quickly as possible, correct?"

"Right."

"And your very-stupid person can tell when one straw is longer than another one, correct?"

"Right."

"Then why not just lay the straws down on the table one by one and put them in the right order as you do so? Look at the straws and put each one in its proper place."

"Because you can't always do that," Wiz said a little desperately. "You can only compare one pair of straws at a time."

"That's stupid! You can see all the straws on the table can't you?"

"You just don't understand," Wiz said despairingly.

"You're right," the red-headed hedge witch agreed. "I don't understand why a grown man would waste his time on this foolishness. Or why you would want to sort straws at all." With that she turned away and went about her business.

"It's not foolishness," Wiz said to her back. "It's . . ." *Oh hell, maybe it is foolishness here.* He slumped back in the chair. After all, what good is an algorithm without a computer to execute it on?

But dammit, these people were so damn literal-minded! It wasn't that Moira didn't understand the algorithm—although that was a big part of it, he admitted. To Moira the method was just a way to sort straws. She didn't seem to generalize, to see the universality of the technique.

Come to that, most of the people here didn't generalize the way he did. They didn't think mathematically and they almost never went looking for underlying common factors or processes. This is what it must have been like back in the Middle Ages, before the rise of mathematics revolutionized Western thought.

Well, he thought, looking around the great hall with its fireplace and tapestries, *this isn't exactly Cupertino. This is the Middle Ages, pretty much.*

So here I am, a Connecticut Yankee in King Arthur's Court. Full of all kinds of modern knowledge. And that and a quarter—or whatever they use here for quarters—will get me a cup of coffee—or whatever they drink here for coffee.

If he had been a civil engineer or something he could have put his knowledge to use. He might at least have shown people how to build better bridges or catapults or whatever. But he wasn't even a hardware type. Strictly software. And the only thing his knowledge was good for was sorting straws.

With a digusted motion Wiz swept the half-sorted straws onto the floor. He dragged the heavy carved chair from the table to a place by the window and sat with his feet propped on the window ledge staring out.

Back home he could look out over the freeway and housetops to rolling golden hills marked with dark slashes where clumps of oaks and eucalyptus grew. Here all he could see was trees and off in the distance mountains covered with more trees. He missed that combination of open vistas and people close by. He even missed the rivers of automobiles that poured down the freeway.

He did a quick calculation and realized they were coming down to the wire on the project at work. Probably cursing him for disappearing at a critical point. *I wonder who they got to replace me?* The thought of a stranger working at his terminal, rearranging his carefully piled stacks of printouts made him ache. He got up and started to pace the length of the hall.

He had left half a box of fried chicken in his desk

drawer, he remembered. *Will they find that before it starts to stink up the office? And what about my apartment? The rent should be due by now. The bills will be piling up in the mailbox. How do they handle stuff like that when someone disappears?* Wiz didn't have a cat because the apartment didn't allow pets. For the first time he was glad of it. *At least there was no one who was really dependent on me.*

Ugo came in with a load of wood for the evening's fire. As he dropped it by the fireplace, he saw the chair against the window.

"You move?" he demanded.

"Yes."

He scowled and pointed at the chair. "Do not move things. It would confuse the Lady." He shifted it back to its place by the table.

"I'm sorry," Wiz said contritely.

"Do not move things," the goblin said sternly and continued on his way.

"Damn!" Wiz said to the empty air.

"Do not curse, Sparrow."

Wiz turned and saw Moira had come back into the hall.

"Sorry," he muttered.

"Is something wrong?"

"No, just a little homesick."

"I am sorry, Sparrow. I, too, wish to go home."

"At least you can get there from here," he said sullenly.

Moira compressed her lips. "Not while the Mighty bid me here to watch over you."

"You don't do much watching. The only time I see you is at meals."

"Oh? Do you feel the need for a nursemaid, Sparrow?"

"I'm in love with you. I want to be close to you. Is that so hard to understand?"

Moira dropped her eyes. "That was none of my doing."

"All right, you don't love me," Wiz said bitterly. "Then take this damn spell off me!"

"Do not use language like that," Moira said sharply.

"Sorry," Wiz snapped, "but that's what it is."

The red-headed witch sighed. "Sparrow, if I had my way you never would have been bound to me in the first place. If it were in my power to remove the spell I would do so in an instant. But I cannot.

"*I* did not put the spell on you, Patrius did. It is not an infatuation spell I know and I do not have the faintest idea how to release you. Bal-Simba or one of the other Mighty could perhaps remove it. When Bal-Simba comes here I will ask him to take the spell off. More, I will *beg* him to take it off."

She softened. "I am sorry, Sparrow, but that is the best that I can do."

"Great," Wiz said. "In the meantime I've got a case of terminal puppy love combined with the moby hots for you. I've got to live under the same roof with you and have nothing to do with you. Da . . . darnit, before this happened you weren't even my type! I liked willowly brunettes."

Moira reddened. "I suppose you think this is easy for me! To have you trailing after me like a puppy dog, or a bull and me a cow in season? To have to stay here when there are people elsewhere who need me? To have to tiptoe around avoiding you for both our sakes? *Do you think I enjoy any of it?*" she shouted, her freckles vivid against her flushed skin, her bosom heaving and her green eyes flashing like emeralds in candlelight. Wiz could only stare, but Moira didn't notice.

"Sparrow, believe me when I tell you I want nothing so much as to be rid of you and gone from this place." She turned on her heel and slammed out the door.

"*Damn* that old wizard anyway!" Wiz said viciously in his teeth. Then he went off to the woodpile to turn logs into kindling.

Moira didn't exactly apologize and neither did Wiz. But the outburst seemed to clear the air slightly and for a while things at Heart's Ease were a little less strained.

Other than that, life went on as before. Wiz chopped wood and moped about, Moira stayed out of his way, Shiara was as beautiful and gracious as ever and Ugo grumbled.

In addition to cutting firewood and sighing after Moira, Wiz did try to learn more about his new world and his new home.

"Ugo, why is Heart's Ease so special?" Wiz asked one morning when the little wood goblin came out to the wood pile to collect his work.

"Because the Lady live here," said Ugo in a tone that indicated only an idiot would ask such a question.

Wiz put the axe down and wiped his brow. "I mean besides that. Moira said there was something about the way it was built."

"No magic," Ugo told him. "Every stone raised by hand. Every board and beam felled by axe and shaped by adze. All joined with pegs and nails. No magic anywhere in the building."

"Why not?"

"The Lady does not like magic," the goblin servant said, gathering in an armload of wood. "It hurts her now." With that he turned away to his duties.

Pumping Ugo for information was never very satisfactory, Wiz thought as he washed and changed for dinner. *But then damn little around here is.*

Wiz pulled a clean shirt out of his chest and paused in front of the mirror before putting it on. The days at the woodpile had put muscle on his frame and the sun had darkened his normally pasty torso. He still wasn't going to win any bodybuilding contests, but he had to admit he looked a lot better than he normally did.

"Pretty good for someone who's totally useless," he told himself.

"Are you sure?" the mirror asked soundlessly.

Wiz jumped and gasped. Then he stared. The mirror was angled so it did not catch the full brightness of the sun. Its surface was dark and cloudy as always.

"Are you sure you're so useless?" the mirror repeated. The words formed in Wiz's mind.

"Well, yeah I'm sure," Wiz said aloud.

"You shouldn't be," the mirror said. "You were brought from a long way at the cost of a man's life. There are a lot of people who are looking very hard for you. I'd say that makes you pretty important."

Great! Wiz thought. *Now I'm getting a pep talk from a Goddamn mirror.*

"You need it from someone, bub. You've been sulking like a twelve-year-old ever since you got to Heart's Ease. You need to pull out of it."

"What's the use? I don't fit in here and I never will."

"With that attitude you're damn straight you never will," the mirror told him. "This isn't the first time you've been a fish out of water. You're the guy who spent two years doing software maintenance in a COBOL shop and managed to fit in pretty well."

"Well yeah, but that was different."

"Not that different. Wiz, old son, you've never exactly been a fount of social graces, but you've always gotten by. And you have never, *never*, given up before."

"So I should beat my head against a stone wall?"

"How do you know it's a stone wall? Face it, you haven't tried all that hard. There's got to be something here for you. All you have to do is find it."

"I'm not so sure."

"Patrius was. He must have had a reason to bring you here."

"Moira says Patrius made a mistake."

"Moira may be beautiful, but she's not always right."

"Well . . ."

"Moira is a consideration, though. If you were someone here, it might change her attitude."

"If you're going to offer to play me a game, I refuse," Wiz told the mirror.

"No offer," the mirror told him. "Only the observation."

"Okay, but what could make me special here?"

The mirror was silent.

"Well?" Wiz demanded.

"I don't know the answer to that."

"Great. Then why the hell bring it up?"

"Because you have two choices," the mirror bored on inexorably. "You can believe you will never amount to anything here, never fit in, and dissolve in your own bile. Or you can believe you have a place here and try to find it. Which do you prefer?"

"All right. But how? What do I have to do?"

"You'll think of something," the mirror told him.

"You'll think of something," Wiz mimicked. "Thanks a lot!"

"Sparrow?" Wiz turned and there was Shiara standing in the open door."

"Who are you talking to?" she asked. Wiz flushed and opened his mouth to deny it. Then he changed his mind. After all, magic worked here.

"I was talking to the mirror, Lady."

Shiara frowned. "The mirror?"

"Well, it talked to me first," he said defensively.

Frowning, the mistress of Heart's Ease swept into the room, her long black gown swishing on the uneven floor. "This mirror?" she asked, putting out a hand to brush her fingertips across its silvery surface.

"Yes, Lady. That mirror."

Shiara smiled and shook her head.

"I'm sorry, Lady, I know you don't allow magic in the castle, but . . ."

"Sparrow, I think you have been brooding overmuch," Shiara told him gently.

"Lady?"

"There is no magic here. This is an ordinary mirror."

"No magic?" Wiz repeated dumbly.

"No magic at all. Just a mirror."

Wiz felt himself turning crimson to his hair roots. "But it talked to me! I heard it."

"It talked to you or you talked to you?" she asked gently. "Sometimes it is easier to hear things about ourselves if they appear to come from outside us."

Wiz looked back at the mirror, but the mirror remained mute.

Late one afternoon Wiz happened to pass Moira in the great hall.

"Moira," he asked, as she went by with a nod, "what happened to Shiara?"

The hedge witch stopped. "Eh?"

"She was a wizardess, wasn't she? But Ugo told me magic hurts her."

"It does. To be in the presence of even tiny magics causes her pain. That is why she lives here in the quietest of the Quiet Zones in a keep built without the least magic."

"How?"

"By carpenters, masons and other workers who built without magic. Isn't that the way you build things in your world?"

"No, I mean how did it happen to her?"

Moira hesitated. "She lost her sight, her magic and her love all in one day. It is a famous tale, but of course you would never have heard it." She sighed. "Shiara the Silver they called her. With her warrior lover, Cormac the Gold, she ranged the World recovering dangerous magical objects that they might be held safely in the Council's vaults.

Not only was she of the Mighty, but she was a picklock of unusual skill. No matter what wards and traps protected a thing, she could penetrate them. No matter how fierce the guards set over a thing,

Cormac could defeat them. With him to guard her back, she removed magic from the grasp of the League itself."

"What happened?"

"We went to the well once too often," Shiara said drily from the doorway.

They both whirled and blushed. "Your pardon, Lady," Moira stammered. "I did not know . . ."

"Granted willingly." Shiara swept into the hall, moving unerringly to them. "So you have not heard my story, Sparrow?"

"No, Lady. I'm sorry. I didn't mean to talk about you behind your back."

"There is no need to be sorry." Her mouth quirked up at the corner. "The bards sing the tale in every tavern in the North, I understand. The price of fame is having your story told over and over by strangers."

"I'm sorry," Wiz said again.

"Perhaps you would like to hear the story as it happened?"

"We do not wish to pain you, Lady." Moira said.

Shiara chuckled, a harsh, brittle sound. "My child, the pain is in the loss. There is little enough pain in the telling." She seated herself in her chair by the fireplace. "Sometimes it even helps to repeat it."

Moira sat down on the bench. "Then yes, Lady, we would like to hear the story, if you do not mind."

"I've never heard it, Lady," Wiz said, sitting down as close to Moira as he could without being too obvious about it. Moira shifted slightly but did not get up.

"Well then," Shiara smoothed out the folds in her skirt and settled back. "We were powerful in those days," she said reminiscently. "My hair was white, even then and Cormac, ah, Cormac's hair was as yellow as fine gold."

"And he was strong," Moira put in breathlessly. "The strongest man who ever lived and the best, bravest swordsman in all the North."

"Not as strong as the storytellers say," Shiara said. "But yes, he was strong."

"And handsome? As handsome as they say?"

Shiara smiled. "No one could be that handsome. But he was handsome. I called him my Sun, you know."

Ugo entered unnoticed with a bundle of wood and set about kindling a fire.

SEVEN

SHIARA'S STORY

Shiara sensed the boy and girl looking up at her. *Young*, Shiara thought, *so very young. Convinced the world is full of hope and possibilities and so blind to the truth*. She felt the warmth of the fire on her face and turned her head to spread the heat. Then she sighed and began the old, old tale.

"Once upon a time, there was a thief who loved a rogue . . .

Cormac, tall and strong with his corn-ripe hair caught back by a simple leather filet. He had doffed his leather breeks and linen shirt and stood only in his loin cloth. The fire turned his tan skin ruddy and highlighted the planes and hollows of his muscles. The scars stood out vividly on his torso and legs.

"Well, Light. Do we know what the thing is?"

Shiara shook her head and the motion made her tresses ripple. The highlights in her hair danced from the flames and the motion.

"Only that it is powerful—and evil. An evil that can shake the World."

"Mmmfph," Cormac grunted and turned back to his sword. Again he checked the leather cords on the

141

hilt, running his fingers over them for any sign of looseness or slickness that might make the sword slip in his hand. "And it lies above us, you say?"

Shiara nodded. "In a cave well above the tree line this thing sleeps." She bit her lip. "It sleeps uneasily and I do not like to think what it might become when it awakens."

"And we must either possess it or destroy it." He shook his head. "It's an awful way to make a living, Light."

"Terrible for two such honest tradesfolk," she agreed, falling into the well-worn game.

The thief had been very, very good. With skill, cunning, carefully arrayed magic and a good element of luck he had managed to penetrate the crypt beneath the Capital where the most dangerous treasures of the Council were stored.

In the end it had not been the council that had caught him. When the vault's magic detectors screamed and guards and wizards came rushing to investigate, they found the thief already dead, his throat torn out by the guardian the original owner had set upon the thing he had come to steal.

The object of the daring raid had been a chest imprisoning a demon of the sixth order, a thing powerful enough but not so unusual as to attract the close scrutiny of the Mighty. The real treasure was in the hidden drawer in the bottom of the chest. What the compartment contained was well worth scrutiny.

"I had heard of the thieving of course," Cormac told her as they toiled up the steep trail toward the foreboding summit, "but I had not known what was in the compartment."

"A parchment," Shiara said. "A map and a note that a very old and very great treasure of magic lay somewhere in a cave near the top of this mountain."

"So we come hotfoot deep into the Wild Wood to stir up something which has lain undisturbed for aeon and on," Cormac said. "Better, I think, to leave it lie. Sufficient unto the day are the evils thereof, Light."

Shiara smiled thinly. "This evil's day has come it seems. Someone knew of the map and we have strong reason to believe that that someone now knows at least generally what the map had to say. We think someone was looking through the eyes of our thief when he died."

Cormac grunted. "So it is a race then." He looked up at the summit with its wreath of grey-black clouds.

"A race," Shiara agreed. "Although we may have lost already."

"You sense something?"

"No, but I can use my head as well as my magic. Whoever sent that thief had more time to prepare than we did. If the League knew generally what was on that parchment they could easily have been ready to move."

"So that is why we were sent upon the Wizard's Way. I mislike this, Light. If the League are ahead of us it means a meeting battle. Those are always chancy and I have the feeling we would be out-numbered."

"I doubt any of the factions of the League Council would be left out of such an enterprise, so I cannot argue with you. But what would you? There were no others in the Capital fit for such a mission and we dared not delay." She looked up the trail. "We can only hope we are in time."

As they worked their way up the steep slopes the forest changed around them. The great oaks and beeches gave way to pines and firs and thick green rhododendrons. Here and there outcrops of dark rock poked through the thinning soil, more and more of it as they climbed.

The air changed about them as well, growing cooler and dank with the glacier's breath. There was a dampness in the air that hinted fog and even in full daylight the mists moved the horizons closer. The mountain loomed over them and they had to crane their necks further and further back to see the snow-clad summit.

They were almost to the treeline when Cormac pulled even with Shiara and spoke quietly in her ear. "We are being followed I think."

Not by look or action did Shiara show she had heard. "How many?"

Cormac shook his head. "Not many. Not creatures born to the woods either."

"The League? The ones who set the thief?"

"Possibly."

Shiara stopped and closed her eyes. With intangible eyes and ears she searched for signs of magic about them. She did not dare risk active magic so close to something so powerful.

"Ahhh," she breathed at last. "The League indeed. But one man only. Luck may be with us, my Sun. I think this is a private quest, not an expedition sent by the League Council."

"You know this man?"

"He is called Toth-Ra, a minor wizard."

"Is he dangerous?"

"Like an adder. Small and puffed with malice."

"And we seek a dragon yonder." Cormac jerked his head toward the snow-covered heights. "Well, Light, what say you?"

"I say leave him for now. He cannot do us much harm and I will need everything I have for what lies above."

Well behind the pair Toth-Ra toiled up the slope. He puffed as he came and stopped to rest frequently—both because he was unused to exertion and because he did not want to tread too closely on the heels of the two Northerners ahead of him.

A pretty train this, he thought, *like ants following a scent trail*.

Even further above, he knew, was the party sent by the League to obtain the treasures of the mountain. A group of black robes and apprentices, carefully balanced to represent each faction of the League council. After them the two from the Council of the North. And finally, himself, representing naught but his own interests.

Like a jackal following lions. He smiled sourly. *Well enough. For when lions fight, jackals win.*

Toth-Ra had little doubt these lions would fight. Even without the Northerners, the very richness of what lay above guaranteed that.

And if perchance he was wrong? If the fragile coalition that governed the League could hold together under the pressure of the indescribable wealth and power from this hoard? Well, there would still be crumbs for a clever jackal to gather.

With his face set in an unaccustomed smile, Toth-Ra continued his climb.

Shiara and Cormac were almost to the tree line when they heard a noise. The trail paralleled a cliff here and a thin moan came from a clump of bushes off the trail on the cliff side.

Cormac drew his sword, but Shiara moved instinctively to the sound of a creature in pain. She thrust though the narrow band of bushes that lay between them and the cliff face.

"Cormac, come here."

As Cormac breasted through the brush he saw a twisted shape like a small man lying on the rocks. Obviously it had fallen from the cliff above them.

"It's a wood goblin," Cormac said, looking over it. "Leave the poor creature."

Shiara shook her head. "He has a soul and so deserves succor."

"Have we time to do this?"

She looked up at him. "Have we time not to?"

Gently she moved the twisted broken body off

the blood-smeared rocks and placed it carefully on a patch of grass. Quickly the wizardess spread out a collection of healing implements and set to work.

Shiara labored over the chance-found creature as if it were one of her own. She chanted and muttered, made passes with her silver wand and sprinkled the body with herbs and powders.

As Cormac watched the wounds scabbed over and began to close. The twisted limbs straightened and the bones within them knit. The little creature's breathing slowed and became more regular. At last it relaxed and began to snore sonorously.

"Now what?" Cormac asked as Shiara turned away from the sleeping goblin.

"He needs rest and a chance to rebuild his strength. In another day or two he will be fine, but now . . ."

"We do not have a day or two to give over to nursing him. Have you forgotten what brought us here?"

"No, I have not forgotten. But he," she nodded to the creature, "will be awake soon and we can ask where his tribe is. I will have to rest a bit in any case." She finished packing her kit and sat down heavily beside her patient.

It was less than an hour later that the wood goblin stirred, moaned and opened his eyes. He started and tried to rise at the sight of the two humans, but Shiara placed a hand on his shoulder.

"Rest now," she told him. "We are friends." The goblin looked dubious but settled back. "I am Shiara and this is Cormac. What is your name?"

"Ugo. Me Ugo." The goblin's speech was creaky and slurred but he was understandable.

"Does your tribe live nearby?" Shiara asked.

"Tribe all dead," the little goblin said sadly. "Ugo all alone."

Cormac grunted in sympathy. Unlike their larger cousins the hobgoblins, wood goblins lived in closely knit groups. A wood goblin whose tribe had perished had little to live for and scant chance of surviving.

"I am sorry," Shiara said. "Now rest here for a while and you will feel better." She rose and signaled Cormac that she was ready to move on.

"Wait, Lady," cried Ugo. The little creature scrambled painfully up and knelt in front of her. "Take me with you. I serve you, Lady," the goblin pleaded. "Let me stay and serve you."

Cormac looked at Shiara. The last thing they needed was a servant of any sort, much less an ailing wood goblin. But refusing would surely doom him. Without a substitute for his tribe the little creature had no will to live.

Shiara reached down and put a hand on the goblin's head. "Very well, Ugo. We accept your service." His ugly face glowed and he looked up adoringly at Shiara.

"Here is your first task, Ugo, and it is an important one. We go to the top of this mountain on a mission from the Council of the North. If we are not back in three sunsets," she held up three fingers for emphasis, "you must make your way to the Fringe and contact the Council. Tell them we have failed and others must be sent to complete the business. Do you understand?"

"Yes, Lady. Wait three sunsets. If you not back, go tell Council."

"Then wait for us here, Ugo. Do not follow. Rest and stay out of sight. We should be back in three days and if not, the message must reach the Council."

"Yes, Lady. Ugo wait."

"Do you really think the wight can get through the Wild Wood if something happens to us?" Cormac asked once they were out of earshot.

Shiara shrugged. "Probably not. But it gives him a reason to live and a sense of his own worth. We will be done in less than three days."

"Much less, I hope," said Cormac, scowling at the mountain jutting above them.

*   *   *

Evening found them above the tree line, halfway across a jumbled field of boulders. There was no snow but the air was cold and the wind keen and sharp. They used the faggots they had gathered on their climb through the forest to build a fire in a place where two great boulders leaned together and provided shelter from the winds.

"Our follower?"

"Camped down in the trees. He apparently plans to gain the summit in a single push tomorrow."

"By which time, luck willing, we will have completed our business and be away."

"Luck willing," Shiara agreed.

Their evening meal was barley porridge flavored with dried meat. It was quickly eaten, but neither made a move to bed down. Instead they sat, staring into the fire and enjoying the warmth reflecting off the boulders.

"Light, would you have chosen this life," Cormac asked her. "Could you have chosen freely, I mean?"

Shiara stared into the flames. "I do not know," she said at last. "Being a wizardess is not a free choice. You are born gifted and you try to build your life around it." She lifted her head and looked at him. "And you? Did you choose freely?"

He laughed easily. "Oh, aye. Even as a child I had a taste for trouble. Mine was a free choice." He sobered. "As freely as any man can choose, at least. I had no hand for farming and I did not want to starve."

"Do you regret it?"

Cormac shook his head. "We've had a good run, lass. We've had some fine times and our fame will live after us. But there are times I miss the things I have not had."

"A home?" she asked with a little smile. "And children?"

"The rest, aye. And children, perhaps. I was an only child you know. My line dies with me."

Shiara laid her fingertips on his shoulder. "That could still be," she said softly.

"Perhaps. But I'm an old horse to break. I suppose it's a matter of making choices and then regretting that in making them we give up other things." He picked up a stick and poked the fire with it idly. "I chose the sword road because it promised honor and fame. I have had all that, so I cannot complain of a bargain unfulfilled."

"Did duty have no role in your choosing?"

Cormac grinned. "Oh, a mite. But I remember the day you came to the parade ground seeking a guardsman to cover your back while you burgled some trinkety bit of magic. I saw you and decided none other would be your quest companion." He shook his head. "There were one or two others who were minded to volunteer, but I convinced them otherwise."

"So you presented yourself to me the next day with knuckles bloody." Shiara smiled at the memory. "But was it only my beauty?"

"Well, I always have been a frippery fellow, Light. With never your fine, serious purpose."

"Mock me if you will, but we do important work." She sighed. "I do not know what I would have chosen had I been free to choose. But I had a talent for this and a head for the proper sort of spells. The job needed doing, desperately, so here I am."

"And you regret it?"

Shiara shook her head and the ends of her silvery hair danced in the firelight. "No. My bargain has been fulfilled as well." She smiled at him. "I have had all that and love as well."

Cormac reached over and squeezed her hand. "We've had more luck than any two mortals deserve, Light."

Shiara stared into the fire. "It cannot last, you know."

Cormac's brows arched. "A premonition?"

"A thought, rather. It is risky work we do and soon or late it will catch up with us."

A ghost of a cloud crossed Cormac's brow. "Mayhap," he said easily. "Or mayhap we will both die peacefully in bed." He leered at her. "The same bed, I hope." Shiara reached out and drew him to her.

They made love, desperately and with a bittersweet passion, as if their coupling could erase the whole World and any thought of the morrow.

They found the cave less than three hours after they broke camp the next morning. Above the boulder field ran a steep canyon, cleaving its way toward the mountain's top. There was a rushing glacial stream, chill and sharp, down the canyon, making the dark rocks slippery and hard to climb.

They came around a twist in the canyon and saw the cave mouth halfway up the cliff. There was a boulder-strewn ledge leading up from the canyon floor, making a natural pathway. The cave entrance itself was dark, jagged and about as inviting as the mouth of Hell.

"Wait," hissed Shiara and put her hand on Cormac's bicep. She pointed a little downslope from the mouth of the cave.

There was a flash of white against the dark rock, like the branches of a dead and barkless tree. Cormac squinted and caught his breath. They were bones, not branches and from their shape and size they could only be the bones of one thing.

"A dragon," Cormac said quietly. "A dragon died here, and not a small one, either."

"Dragons prefer caves as lairs," Shiara said. "It would appear that this one chose the wrong resting place."

"It did not die naturally." Cormac pointed with his blade. "Look at the way the ribs are smashed. But what could do that to a grown dragon?"

"The sort of creature which would be set to guard a great treasure," Shiara said gravely.

"And you think it is still there, Light?"

"A thing which could slay a dragon would not be expected to have a short life."

Cormac scanned the ledge and the cave mouth again. "There are no other bones. Surely other things would have tried to lair here from time to time."

"Perhaps they did not arouse the guardian. Dragons are more intelligent than most animals. And greedier than most men. Or perhaps whatever is within is careful to dispose of its refuse so as not to warn others."

"Hmm. A pretty problem then." Cormac backed warily out of sight of the cave mouth and settled on a rock. "Do you sense magic?"

Shiara wrinkled her nose. "Like smoke in a hut in wintertime. It is everywhere and strong. There is a blocking spell to confine the emanations, but this near I can feel it pressing. Whatever is within that mountain is powerful indeed." She shivered. "And malign!"

"But you cannot tell me what guards that door?"

"If I had to guess I would say a demon. But it would be only a guess."

"So what now?"

"Now," Shiara said, bending to her kit, "we need a stalking horse. Something to enter the cave in our stead and see what lies within." She looked up at him. "Plug your ears."

Cormac clapped hands to his ears while Shiara drew from her bag a gnarled brown root no longer than the length of her index finger. Looking more closely Cormac could see that the root was bifurcated and vaguely man-shaped.

Shiara blew upon the root and spoke softly to it. Instantly the valley was filled with a hideous inhuman screaming. The root writhed and screamed in Shiara's grasp until she completed the spell. Then she stood up and threw the root to the ground.

Cormac blinked. Standing before him was himself,

an exact duplicate down to the scars on his arms and the creases in his worn leather swordbelt.

"How do you like our stalking horse?"

"A mandrake image." Cormac walked around the figure and nodded approvingly. "Lady, you outdo yourself."

"Let us hope the guard at that gate finds it satisfactory," Shiara said. She leaned close and whispered in the ear of the homunculus. Wordlessly the thing turned and strode up the path toward the cave.

"It even has my walk," Cormac said as the thing climbed to the cave mouth.

"It is your true double."

The homunculus went fearlessly to the cave mouth and stepped in without breaking stride. Shiara and Cormac held their breaths for three long heartbeats. Then there was a terrible bellowing roar from the cave and the sounds of swift combat. They saw movement in the darkness and then a tiny brown thing came flying out of the cave to bounce off the opposite wall of the valley.

"A demon in truth!" Cormac breathed. "How do you slay such a one?"

"With a more powerful demon," Shiara said, still transfixed by what they had seen.

"You don't have one of those in that bag of yours do you, Light?"

"Not likely. But if it cannot be slain, then perhaps it can be immobilized." She set down her bag and rummaged around in it. "First we must know more about it."

"You're not going to send another homunculus of me into that, are you? It does me no good to see myself slain."

"That was the only mandrake root I had. But let us see what happens with something different."

With her silver wand she sketched a quick design in the dirt and spoke a single phrase. Now another warrior stood before them, a tall lean man with dark hair, a lantern jaw and icy blue eyes. He was dressed in a mail hauberk and carried a two-handed sword over his shoulder.

"Donal to the flesh!" Cormac laughed. "He looks as if he just stepped off the drill ground at the Capital."

"No flesh, just an illusion. Now let us see what the demon makes of this one." She spoke to the thing and without a word it turned and started up the ledge.

At the mouth of the cave the false Donal halted and bellowed out a challenge that made the valley ring. There was no response. It approached the entrance and thrust over the threshold with its great sword. Again nothing. Finally it strode boldly into the cavern calling insults to whatever was within.

Once more Cormac and Shiara held their breaths. But this time there was no sound of battle from the cave.

After a minute the illusion returned to the cave mouth and waved to them.

"It didn't go for it."

"But that does not make sense," Shiara protested. "The illusion was indistinguishable from the homunculus."

"Not to the demon," Cormac observed.

"Yes, but I don't see why the demon would attack a homunculus and a dragon but not an illusion. It doesn't . . ." she stopped short. "Fortuna, a true name! The homunculus had a true name but the illusion did not." She turned to Cormac with her sapphire eyes wide. "That thing can sense a being's true name!"

"Dragons don't have true names," Cormac protested.

"Adult dragons do. Oh, not juveniles such as our cavalry ride, but when a dragon becomes a full adult it acquires a true name. The homunculus had a true name just as any demon does. That is how you control them. But the illusion did not."

Cormac eyed the cave mouth. "A very pretty problem then."

"Worse than that," Shiara said. "The demon did not know the true name of homunculus and I doubt the dragon stopped for conversation before entering the cave. Yet the demon killed them both."

"Meaning what?"

"Meaning it distinguishes beings with true names from beings without them. But that it does not have to *know* a thing's true name to find it and kill it. It is enough that a thing has a true name."

Cormac gave a low whistle. "No wonder it is tied so tight to that cave. With that power it could seek out and destroy anyone in the World. Light, do you suppose the demon itself is the treasure?"

"I doubt it. I think the demon merely guards the treasure."

"It must be treasure indeed to have such a guardian."

"Aye," Shiara said, studying the cave mouth. "Well, we will learn little more sitting here. I think it is time to take a closer look."

"Tread softly, Light."

She turned to smile at him. "I will, my Sun."

The pair approached the cave mouth cautiously. Cormac had his broadsword out and Shiara held her silver wand before her like a torch.

As they came closer Shiara stopped and pointed to a line carved in the living rock across the front of the cave.

"The ward line. The demon cannot cross it."

"Are you certain?"

"Certain enough. Give me a torch."

Cormac reached into his pack and pulled out one of the pine torches Shiara had prepared. The wizardess tapped the end with her wand and it burst into flame. Shiara drew back and threw the torch across the line and they both ducked back out of sight of the cave mouth.

There was no sound or movement from the cave. When they peeked around the corner they could see the torch lying on the rough rock floor of the cavern, burning brightly.

The space revealed by the torchlight was perhaps three times Cormac's height and somewhat less than that wide, but it ran back into the mountain well beyond the circle of illumination. There was no sign of life or movement.

"The demon must only materialize when someone enters the cave," Shiara whispered.

"Well what now?" Cormac whispered back. "Are you satisfied with your view of the demon's empty home?"

"Wait," said Shiara, pointing inside the cavern. "What's that?"

Cormac followed her finger. There was something lodged in a crevice high on one wall of the cave. "A box, I think," he said.

Shiara eyed the thing speculatively. "I wonder . . . Cormac, have you a rope in your pack?"

"You know I do, Light. And a grapnel too."

Quickly Cormac retrieved the rope and hook from where they had dropped their packs.

"You want that box then?"

Shiara stood by him, her wand in hand. "I do. But be ready to run if we get more than we bargain for."

Cormac swung the grapnel and cast it expertly into the cave. There was a hollow "clang" as the hook connected with the box. Cormac tugged and it clattered out of the crevice and onto the cave floor.

In the torchlight Cormac saw that his prize was a bronze coffer, decorated in high relief and apparently bearing an inscription on the top. Another quick throw and Cormac dragged the box out of the cave and across the warding line.

"Don't touch it," Shiara warned. As Cormac recoiled his rope she bent to examine the coffer.

Shiara opened the box with a pass of her wand and

a whispered incantation. Nestled inside was a smoky gray globe about six inches in diameter.

"The heart of the demon!" Shiara exclaimed triumphantly. "Now we can truly control this creature."

She removed the ball from the coffer and held it in her hand. Another muttered spell and a dense cloud of smoke began to form within the cavern. Through the smoke loomed a great black shape.

The huge horned head swiveled toward them, but before the creature could do more, Shiara raised her wand and spoke another spell. The demon froze as it was, the only sign of life the fire burning deep in its eyes.

Shiara sighed and sagged. "That should hold it," she said. "Carefully, she replaced the sphere in the box and carried it back into the cave. The demon did not even twitch when she crossed the threshold.

The wizardess was still considering the coffer when Cormac came up to her.

"Do we take that with us?"

"I wish we dared. It is a dangerous thing to leave behind, but it would be a greater danger to carry it with us. There might be something above us which can undo what I have done and I do not wish to find a rampaging demon here when we return."

"Conceal it?"

"That is best." She cast about the cavern looking for a hiding place.

"Light, come look at this."

Cormac was standing over a head-high pile of bones.

"So our demon did clean the place deliberately."

"Not that. Look." Cormac shifted his torch and used his sword as a pointer. At one side of the bone pile lay the crushed and mutilated corpse of a man in a brown robe.

"An acolyte of the League! Then they are here before us."

"Yes, but why only one body? Surely they would not send a brown robe alone on such a mission?"

"Surely not. But they might use an acolyte as we used our mandrake homunculus."

Cormac nodded grimly. "Aye, that's just the kind of thing they would do. But then where are the rest? Did they scatter away at the sight of the demon?"

"Most likely they are somewhere up ahead of us. Once they knew the demon was here, they found a way to counteract it. I do not think they tampered with the box, so perhaps they had the password." She looked up the tunnel. "I think we face an interesting meeting."

"Best be on with it then," Cormac said, shifting his grip on his sword.

The passage sloped up, climbing steadily toward the summit. Cormac went first, naked sword in one hand and smoking torch in the other. Shiara followed with another torch.

"You're unusually pensive," Cormac told her when they had gone a small ways into the cavern. What bothers you, Light?"

"That demon."

"Well, it is trouble past and overcome. I am more concerned about what we might find above us."

"Yes, but it is how we overcame it. Why was the box where we could reach it? A few feet further back in the cave and the demon would have been safe from our efforts."

Cormac shrugged. "So our sorcerer made an error. Even the best magician can err through overconfidence."

"I know," Shiara said. "That is what troubles me."

Their way climbed steeply upward but the path was smoothed and widened. Either this had never been a natural cavern or it had been extensively reworked. The smooth black rock seemed to soak up the light of their torches and the darkness pressed in on them from all sides. Shiara hurried slightly to stay within touching distance of Cormac.

There was a low, distant rumble and the earth beneath them moved slightly.

"Earth magic," Shiara said. "Very potent and barely held in check here." She looked around. "Left to its own, I think this mountain would have erupted hundreds of years ago."

"A fitting lair for a sorcerer."

"More than that, perhaps."

"Light, will you stop being so gloomy? You're beginning to make me nervous."

She smiled. "You're right, my Sun. This place is affecting me, I am afraid."

They climbed and climbed until it seemed they would emerge at the very top of the mountain. Finally their way leveled out and there before them was a door.

The portal was of the deepest black granite, polished so smooth the burning brand in Cormac's hand threw back distorted reflections of the two adventurers. A gilt tracery ran along the lintel and down the doorposts. Runes, Shiara saw as she moved closer. Runes of purest gold beaten into the oily black surface of the granite.

Shiara formed the runes in her mind, not daring to move her lips. "It is a treasure indeed," she said at last. "A trove of magic of the sort seldom witnessed. This is the tomb of Amon-Set."

Cormac wrinkled his nose. "The name is somewhat familiar. A boggart to frighten children, I think."

"More than that," she told her beloved. "Before he was a night-fright, Amon-Set was mortal. A sorcerer. So powerful his name has lived after him and so evil he is a figure of nightmare."

"Aye," Cormac breathed. "The great dark one from the beginning of the World. And he lies here?"

"I would not take oath he is dead."

"I mislike rifling the tombs of sorcerers," Cormac said apprehensively.

"I like it even less than that. Such places are

mazes of traps and snares for the greedy or the careless." She sighed and straightened. "Fortunately we do not have to steal. Only keep what is here from being loosed upon the World."

"But before that we must enter."

"So we must, love." Shiara set down her pouch and knelt beside it. "Leave that to me."

The lock was a cunning blend of magic and mechanics. Slowly and deliberately, Shiara worked upon it, running her fingers over the surface to sense the mechanism within. Sometimes she operated upon it with cleverly constructed picks. Sometimes she used incantations. Finally she pushed against it gently and the door swung open. Motioning Cormac to remain outside, she entered cautiously.

The room was vast, so big the walls were lost in the gloom. The marble floor, tesselated in patterns of black and darkest green, stretched away in front of them. Shiara had the feeling that by stepping through the door she had become a piece on a gigantic game board.

The way was lit by witch-fires of pale yellow enclosed in great massively-carved lanterns, the light pouring out through the thin panels of alabaster or marble that formed their panes. The glow held an odd greenish tinge that gave an unhealthy pallor to everything it touched.

Here and there a censer smoked, emitting heavy fumes that curled and ran along the floor like snakes. The incense was pungent with hints of cinnamon and sandalwood, heady with the fumes of poppies and the sharp chemical tang of ether. It was neither pleasant nor offensive, just strange. It did not quite hide the musty odor of time long passed in a place undisturbed and the faint sweetish hint of corruption that hung in the air.

Worse than the incense to Shiara was the magic that closed around her as soon as she stepped over the threshold. It was as close and stifling as a heavy quilt on a hot summer's day. It pressed against her flesh and blocked her nostrils until she wanted to gasp for breath. It twisted and moved around her in odd directions and peculiar angles. She felt that if she stared into the air long enough the magic would become visible. She did not want to contemplate what might follow.

Shiara took one more step forward and did gasp. There on the floor of the chamber, like a flock of crows dropped in mid-flight, lay half a score of black-robed bodies, already decomposing in the strange atmosphere of the room. Obviously the League's sorcerers had found a trap that guarded the treasure.

In spite of the dead, Shiara's gaze was drawn to the objects scattered around the room. Each sat on its own pedestal like exhibits in a museum—or pieces on a game board—and each of the ones Shiara could see was different. There was no obvious pattern or order to their placement, but Shiara did not doubt there was some subtle design there.

"What lies within?" Cormac asked from just over the threshold.

"Danger and magic," Shiara told him. "Stay where you are a moment."

On the nearest pier of blue-white marble sat a jeweled crown. The golden band was made to curl snake-like around the wearer's brow. Gems covered its surface so thickly the gold would be scarce visible when it was worn. Blue sapphires, blood-red rubies, sea-green emeralds and lustrous pink pearls ran in twisted bands across the gold. Over each temple sat a smoky yellow topaz, golden as the eye of a dragon. In the center of the forehead was a blue-white gem the likes of which Shiara had never seen. Over all of it flashes of substanceless flame licked and leaped, clear as the fire of burning alcohol. Truly this was a thing designed to adorn the brow of a mighty sorcerer.

Awed, Shiara reached out to touch the crown.

Reached and then drew back. Some sense warned her that to touch it would be fatal.

"Cormac, come in," she called, not taking her eye off the glittering prize on the podium. "Move carefully and on your life, touch nothing!"

"Fortuna!" Cormac exclaimed when he saw the remains of the League's expedition. "What happened to them?"

"One of them touched something, I think. Help me search the room, but move carefully!"

As Shiara and Cormac passed from pedestal to pedestal the extent of the trove became apparent. Each pedestal held an item of magician's regalia. Here a great gold thumb ring with a strangely carved sardonyx cameo stood on a drape of leaf-green velvet. There a chest of scrolls stood open, each scroll bearing the name of the spell it recorded. Against one wall an elaborately embroidered robe, set with gems and so stiff with bullion it stood upright and ready to receive its wearer. Above another pedestal floated a pair of silken slippers decorated with pink-blushed pearls. There were flashing swords and black lacquered armor, chests of gold and heaps of jewels, amulets and talismans and silver-bound spellbooks galore. Every item reeked of powerful, subtle magic and ancient, ancient evil.

"Fortuna!" Cormac called from the shadows at the far end of the huge wall. "Light, come look at this."

Shiara followed the sound of Cormac's voice and gasped at what she saw. This was no mere treasure house or centopath. It was indeed the tomb of a mighty wizard!

The body lay beneath a clear crystal bell on a dais of milk-white crystal. Beneath the white silk shroud broidered round with blood red runes, the wizard's husk was as incorrupt and composed as if he were only sleeping. Amon-Set had been a man of no more than average height, Shiara saw, with pale skin given only a semblance of color by the stark whiteness of the sheet. The tracery of blue veins patterned his flesh in a manner disturbingly like the scales of a venomous reptile. The hands crossed on his chest were as long and slender as the hands of an artist. His hair was dark and shiny as polished jet and his brows were thin and dark, elegant against his skin. His lashes were long and dark as well. Shiara did not care to contemplate what the eyes beneath them must have been like.

"Back away from it!" she called to Cormac. "Do not get closer."

As Cormac edged off, Shiara approached. With shaking hands she passed her wand over the bier. Then she sighed and her shoulders slumped. Magic aplenty she found there, but not the smallest spark of life. Amon-Set was truly dead.

"The scroll did not lie," Cormac said awestruck. "There is treasure indeed here."

"The life's work of one of the most powerful wizards that ever lived," Shiara agreed grimly. "My Sun, can you imagine the havoc all this could wreak if it were loosed upon the World?"

"Well," said Cormac briskly, "that is what we are here to prevent, is it not?"

Shiara nodded and passed her wand over the closest pedestal. Then she frowned and drew back. She moved to the next pedestal and repeated the pass. The expression on her face showed that what she found was no more to her liking.

"Magic?" asked Cormac.

"Aye. What is on these stands is protected by the spells around them and cannot be touched. I will have to unravel this maze before we dare move any of it."

Again and again, Shiara tested the pedestals, until at last she had tried each of them.

"I see how it is now," she said at last. "The spells protecting these things are all interlocked like jackstraws. If you move them at random then the whole mass comes down upon you."

"Jackstraws have a key," Cormac pointed out.

"And so does this riddle. One of these objects is the key. It can be moved first and then the next and then the next."

"How long will it take you to sort out the pile then?"

"Hours. Perhaps days. This is no simple puzzle and I dare not make a mistake." Her eyes went to the bodies on the floor.

"Should you summon more of the Mighty to help?"

Shiara considered and then shook her head. "There is nothing others could do here that I could not. Involving others only means risking them as well."

Cormac shrugged acceptance and Shiara set to work on unravelling the puzzle. Three times she passed round the great gloomy chamber, testing each object.

"It is no good," she said at last. "All of the spells are interlinked and apparently none of them are the key."

"I thought you said there had to be a key."

"I thought so, but I can find no sign of one."

"Well, Light. Where does that leave us?"

Shiara frowned and tapped the wand against her jaw. "I do not know. It seems beyond reason that all this exists merely as a death trap for the unwary. There must be a key. Else why not destroy everything in the beginning and be done with it?"

"Malice?" Cormac suggested.

"A poor motive for all this work. Those of Amon-Set's skill seldom did things for such simple reasons."

"Well then?"

"There is one alternative. Rather than remove all these objects we could destroy them here."

"Wouldn't that scar the land?"

"Most probably," Shiara agreed. "It also means the loss of all the knowledge here. I do not want to do that unless I have to. But Cormac, we cannot allow what is here to fall to the wrong person. Even a hedge wizard could rise to bestride the World with what is in this place."

Cormac sighed. "Do as you think best, Light."

She nodded. "I think with the right spell I can destroy all of this at once."

"How do you propose to do that?"

"Earth magic. The forces are finely balanced here. They can be upset with but little effort—well, little enough in terms of the results. I believe I can fashion a spell to turn the magic against itself and so unbalance the flow."

"Earth magics are hardly a specialty of the Mighty," Cormac pointed out.

"Earth magics are uncontrollable. But all we want is destruction. It should be an easy matter to take the top of this mountain off."

"And take us up with it?"

"No. I will set the spell in motion through a counting demon. We will have time to get away."

Again Shiara knelt with her bag and set to work. She had nearly finished the spell when Cormac came over to her. He waited at a respectful distance until she paused.

"You know, Light, I have been thinking."

"And?"

"Well, curse my suspicious nature, but it occurs to me there may be more here than we see. We know that none of the visible things is the key to this pile of magical jackstraws, but did it occur to you that there might be something here that is not visible?"

"Cormac, you are brilliant! Of course the final key would be hidden! Why did I not think of that?"

"Because you're an honest thief, lass," Cormac grinned. "Now myself, I'm a bit of a rogue."

She leaned over and kissed him. "You are that."

He looked around the room. "Now if I were a

master sorcerer with a secret to hide, where would I hide it?"

"Someplace close, I think," Shiara said, looking around the great room. Either in this room or in a room off of it." She started toward one wall and then stopped.

"Cormac, I want you to examine the room carefully for anything strange or unusual."

"In this place? Fortuna! But what will you be doing?"

"I am going to finish my spell." She bit her lower lip. "Even once we find the key we may not want to use it. And I wish to finish this business and be away quickly."

"As you will, Light." He moved off.

"And Cormac, touch nothing!"

Again the grin. "Since it's you who ask, Light."

While Cormac searched, Shiara concentrated on completing her spell. She forced herself to think only of the technical aspects, blocking out the unease that almost stifled her. Only when the spell was complete and primed and her counting demon duly instructed did she look up.

"Have you found anything?" she called to Cormac across the gloomy expanse of the hall.

"Nothing I care to think overmuch on," he called, crossing the black-and-green floor. "The place is strangely proportioned, these pedestals seem strewn about at random and the pattern on this miserable floor makes my eyes ache." He looked down at the patterned marble at his feet.

"The floor," Shiara said reflectively. "Yes." She looked up. "There may be a message here." She stepped back to the entrance and looked out over the elaborate pattern formed by the squares of marble that floored the hall.

From the door the tiles made the floor seem to swoop away in a roller-coaster perspective, tilting and writhing off into the distance. There seemed to be no horizon line and no point of perspective save madness in the bizarre geometry of the tiles. And yet . . .

"Cormac, walk out that way," she said pointing toward one corner of the hall. The swordsman followed her pointing finger. "A little further. Now stop." Inexorably the pattern seemed to pull him to the right. It was somehow *wrong* to move to the left at that point.

"Now go left," she commanded. Cormac dubiously obeyed. "Further left. No, don't look down at the floor! Don't close your eyes. Just keep to your left." With his gaze locked at shoulder level Cormac moved more to his left and off into the gloom.

"Now what do you see?"

"Nothing much," Cormac called back. "I just bumped into a wall. Wait a moment, I seem to have company."

Shiara gasped.

"Nay lass, he's not dangerous now. But I think you will enjoy this."

"Stay where you are." Shiara moved away from the door and toward Cormac who was invisible in the vapor and gloom. "Talk to me. Anything, just so I can follow the sound of your voice."

"Well, it's dark over here, darker than any other part of the room. And our friend isn't much of a conversationalist."

"Fine," said Shiara coming up to him. "Don't look at that floor. It's both a trap and a hiding place. It is designed to draw you away from this spot and perhaps ensnare you if you are so foolish as to watch the floor as you walk."

She nodded to Cormac's silent companion. "I think that's what happened to him."

Standing almost next to Cormac with his eyes fixed on the floor was a black-robed wizard. He was obviously alive but equally obviously caught fast in the grip of a spell. He could neither move nor talk but his eyes burned with venomous hatred as he looked at the floor.

"Why it's Jul-Akkan isn't it?" Shiara said pleasantly. "I thought you might be along on this and of course you're too old a fox to be caught by the death spells around the hoard. What did you do, wait outside while the others rushed to the pedestals?"

She turned to Cormac. "Note him well, Cormac. Jul-Akkan is high in the Council of the League. Indeed he bid fair to become master of all the League, were he able to rid himself of one or two of his more troublesome colleagues. Now here he is, caught like a fly in a honey bowl."

Cormac shifted and raised his sword for the killing stroke.

"No," Shiara commanded. "I don't know what that would do to the spell and I doubt you could kill him so easily. No, best leave him while we attend to our main business." She stooped to examine the wall behind Cormac.

"Now let us see what is here."

A quick search of the wall revealed a thin narrow crack in the polished black stone of the wall. Carefully she ran her hand along it, feeling rather than seeing the unevenness that marked a panel in the otherwise solid stone.

She knelt down and pressed her hand against the panel. "It is locked and enchanted, but not guarded, I think."

"Don't bet your life on that, lass," Cormac warned. "This fellow was tricky enough for ten wizards."

"I will venture nothing on the chance. I merely make the observation."

Shiara looked up at him from where she knelt. "You do not have to be here for this."

Cormac shook his head. "You may need me." Then he laid his hand on hers. "Besides, a World without Light is not a World fit to live in."

"Thank you Cormac," she squeezed his hand. "Now stand out of my light while I unravel this puzzle."

Again working partly by magic and partly with her

picks and other tools, Shiara carefully pried the secrets from the lock. Cormac stood by nervously, fingering his sword hilt, his head turning this way and that as he searched for tangible manifestations of the danger he sensed here. Finally there was a click and the panel swung smoothly back.

Behind the panel lay another smaller room lit with the same balefire glow as the great hall. It took only a single lantern to light it. The stink of incense and the reek of magic was fully as strong here as it was beyond. But there were fewer pedestals bearing treasures.

"A puzzle within a puzzle," Cormac said as he surveyed their latest find.

Shiara pointed to a pier off to one side of the chamber. "There, I think."

Cautiously she approached and then sucked in her breath at what she saw.

Laying atop the pedestal was a magician's staff. But it was like no magician's staff Shiara had ever seen. It was perhaps four feet long and as thick as her wrist, but it was not wood or even metal. Instead it was made of a crystalline substance that seemed to show flickers of an amethyst light deep within itself. Tiny crabbed characters ran inscribed in bands around its surface, save for a space about a hand's breadth wide near the top. There was no knob or filial on either end. It was more a sceptre than a staff, she realized. A symbol of rule as well as a tool of magical power.

The wizardess passed her wand over the pedestal and smiled at the result.

"This is the key. If I neutralize the spell and move this, we can remove all else in this place."

"Be careful, Light."

"I will, my Sun."

Slowly and carefully Shiara began to unravel the spell binding the staff to the pedestal. She made a final sweeping gesture and the spell flickered and died.

In spite of removing the spell and in spite of her urgent desire to finish this business, Shiara was reluctant to touch the evilly-glinting object before her. She had handled staffs of other wizards before, but there was something about this one that awed and dismayed her.

Finally she placed her hand upon it and felt the waves of magic flow through her. It seemed as if a dark and vastly deep space opened up around her, inhabited by huge shadow things that pressed close, whispering offers of power, the fulfillment of all dreams and the slaking of all lusts. She had but to wield the staff and . . .

Quivering, Shiara fought the temptation. She lifted the staff and carried it across the chamber at arm's length as if it were a poisonous serpent.

The waves of magic beat stronger against her, calling to her more and more clearly. In a fit of panic Shiara tried to drop the staff and found she could not. Now it was the staff which was holding her.

All too late Shiara saw the deadly nature of the trap. The demon at the gate, the spells upon the common items were sufficient to ward off an ordinary thief or hedge magician. To penetrate those and unravel the maze of spells within the cavern and ultimately to possess the key would take someone truly skilled in magic. One of the Mighty, or a black-robe wizard of the League.

The whole cavern and all the magics within it existed simply to sort the untalented or the incompetent from the powerful and to lure the powerful to the sceptre. The sceptre was the last and deadliest trap of them all.

No, Amon-Set was not dead, not truly. Within the smoky purple depths of the sceptre he had waited out the ages, waiting for one whose body and skill he could use to live again. The snow-white corpse on the crystal bier was indeed dead. But his soul lived within the sceptre; lived, hungered and awaited its prey.

The wizard who was skilled enough to grasp the sceptre of Amon-Set was a suitable vehicle for his reincarnation. And that was the true purpose of everything here. To find such a one and put them in a position where Amon-Set could possess them and so live again.

Shiara could feel herself ebbing away as the alien presence intruded. She twisted and struggled in the grip of the long-dead sorcerer. She fought back with every bit of skill and knowledge at her command.

It was a hopelessly uneven fight. She felt the chamber's magics convulse and yield under her desperate thrusts, but the core of Amon-Set locked her in an ever tightening embrace.

"Now!" a strange creaking voice cried from the door of the chamber. Shiara realized vaguely that someone else had entered the fray.

Cormac whirled at the voice and saw Jul-Akkan stumble into the room. Shiara could not break Amon-Set's hold on her, but her struggles had loosed the grip of the guard spells.

Cormac's sword flickered at the wizard with the speed of a striking snake, but not fast enough; even weakened Jul-Akkan was faster still. His hand flicked out and Cormac screamed and dropped to the floor.

Without pausing, Jul-Akkan leaped across the room and grasped the sceptre with both hands.

For an instant three beings warred. Then with a final mighty effort Shiara was able to let go of the cursed thing. Jul-Akkan fell back with both hands planted on the sceptre and his eyes widening as Toth-Amon took him.

Shiara staggered and shook her head. Through pain-dimmed eyes she saw Cormac writhing in the final agonies of a death spell and the one who was Jul-Akkan writhing in the throes of rebirth. In seconds Cormac would be dead and Toth-Amon would be loosed upon the world again. Her Sun and her World both teetered on the brink of destruction.

Shiara eyes locked with Cormac's as he pleaded silently with her to do something to release him from the awful pain.

Without bothering with the timing demon, Shiara triggered the destruction spell. "Forgive me, love," she whispered as he slumped to the floor.

Magic after magic flared incandescent around the living, the dead and the reborn. The room shook under the force of the spells. The pedestals tottered and toppled. The lanterns crashed to the floor and went out.

Amon-Set struggled to rise, but he did not have full control. The sceptre slipped from his hands and dashed into pieces on the shaking floor. All around them the magic grew in violence as forces contained past their time burst free at last.

And then, in a mighty explosion of magic, the roof fell in. Shiara screamed as she saw Cormac's body crushed under a falling block. Waves of magic flayed her. Her last sight was of the brillant blue glow. The after-image burned itself into her brain. Reflexively and in shock, she stumbled from the room.

Above her the top of the mountain blew off. A column of angry orange fire shot high into the smoke-stained sky and bombs of flaming lava arced down into the forest, setting fires where they fell.

Toth-Ra examined the great still demon carefully. Obviously the guardian had been neutralized in some manner. *So far, so good* he thought. He had the word and sign to pass the demon, stolen from the crypt of the League, but he was satisfied not to use them.

Let us see if anything of use remains here. He walked past the thing and inspected the cavern carefully. It did not take him long to find the coffer. When he opened it, he gasped. The heart of the demon lay within.

Toth-Amon smiled. Here was an auspicious beginning. Obviously the Council's agents had beaten him here, but they were unlikely to know all the secrets of this place. There were still treasures to be gleaned while they attempted to unravel the mysteries.

Then the ground began to move under him. Toth-Ra ran to the mouth of the cave and reached it in time to see the mountain erupt, taking the treasures of Amon-Set with it.

Balked, he danced in fury. "Gone. Gone, ay, all gone," he shrieked.

No, he realized. Not *all* gone. There was still the guardian of the gate.

Heedless of the shaking earth or the erupting mountain he moved back across the magically marked threshold clutching the box tightly. Once safely outside, he released the demon.

"What is your name?" he asked sharply.

"Bale-Zur," the thing rumbled.

"And what is your virtue?" the wizard asked.

"To slay," the great deep voice boomed out again. "To rend and tear any whose true name has ever been spoken in the World."

Toth-Ra shivered. Here was power indeed! The treasure of Amon-Set might be consumed in fire, but at least one of his servants could be bound to his cause. He eyed the burning mountaintop carefully. Perhaps this one alone would be sufficient to make him the greatest in the League.

"And what is your desire?"

"To slay," the demon repeated. "To slay and slay again."

Toth-Ra placed both hands on the dusky globe. "Then I will bargain with you," the wizard said.

It was hours later when Ugo found Shiara wandering in the canyon above the boulder field.

"You live, Lady," the little wood goblin cried joyfully as he ran to her.

"Who?"

"Ugo, Lady. You set me to watch. Then bad things happen and I come to look." He stopped. "Where is other?"

"Gone," Shiara said dazedly. "Gone." Then she seemed to gather herself and held out her hand.

"Lead me, Ugo. Your senses are keen and between the night and the clouds I cannot see."

"Close to high noon, Lady," the little creature said sadly. "Sorry, Lady."

Shiara said nothing. Ugo approached her and gently took her hand in his.

"Famous victory," the wood-goblin said. "Bards will sing it long."

Shiara the Silver only laughed bitterly and let the goblin lead her down the smoldering mountain.

"And what happened afterwards?" Moira breathed at last.

Shiara the Silver raised her head from her breast and turned her blind, lined face to her questioner. "Afterwards?" she said simply. "There was no afterwards."

"Foolishness," grumbled Ugo, poking up the fire.

EIGHT

FORLORN HOPE

The long golden days of Indian Summer dragged by at Heart's Ease. Moira worked in the garden or the kitchen. Wiz chopped wood and mooned over Moira. If the tensions within the household did not ease, at least they did not grow significantly worse.

There was always work to be done and the time rolled forward with everyone except Wiz fully occupied. But for all of them, except perhaps Ugo, there was a sense of being suspended. Greater plans and long-range decisions were set aside awaiting word from Bal-Simba and the Council on what was to be done with Wiz.

For Wiz everything depended on what the Council found. If he did have some special ability then perhaps he could redeem himself with Moira. At least he would be able to make himself useful and stop feeling like a parasite.

In his more realistic moments, Wiz admitted he couldn't possibly imagine what that ability might be. The image of him standing before a boiling cauldron in a long robe and a pointed cap with stars was simply silly and the thought of himself as a warrior was even worse.

"Lady, may I ask you a question?" Wiz said to Shiara one day when Moira wasn't around. The former wizardess was sitting on a wooden bench on the sunny side of the keep, enjoying the warmth from the sun before her and the sun-warmed stones behind.

"Of course, Sparrow," she said kindly, turning her face to his voice.

"Patrius was a great Wizard wasn't he?"

"One of the greatest the North has ever seen." She smiled reminiscently. "He was not only skilled in magic, he—well—he *saw* things. Not by magic, but because he had the kind of mind that let him see what others' sight had passed over."

"But he didn't make mistakes very often?"

"Making mistakes is dangerous for a wizard, Sparrow. Magicians who are prone to them do not last."

Wiz took a deep breath and rushed on. "Then he couldn't have been wrong about me, could he?"

Shiara paused before answering. "I do not know, Sparrow. Certainly he was engaged in a dangerous, difficult business, performing a Great Summoning unaided. If he were to make a mistake it might be in a situation such as that.

"On the other hand," she went on as if she sensed Wiz's spirits fall, "Patrius could look deeper and see more subtlely than anyone I ever knew. It may well be that we cannot fathom his purposes in bringing you here."

"Do you think the Council will figure out what he was up to?"

Again Shiara paused. "I do not know, Sparrow. Patrius apparently confided in no one. The members of the Council are the wisest of the Mighty. I would think they would discover his aim. But I simply do not know." She smiled at him. "When the Council knows something they will send word. Best to wait until then."

In the event it was less than a week later when word came to Heart's Ease.

It was another of the mild cloudless days that seemed to mark the end of summer in the North. Wiz was up on the battlements, looking out over the Wild Wood—and down at Moira who was busy in the garden.

"Sparrow," Shiara's voice called softly behind him, "we have a visitor."

Wiz turned and there, standing next to Shiara was Bal-Simba himself.

"Lord," Wiz gasped. "I didn't see you arrive."

"Such is the nature of the Wizard's Way," the huge wizard said with a smile. "How are you, Sparrow?"

"I'm fine, Lord."

"I am happy to see that you made your journey here safely. Although not without peril, I am told."

"Well yes, Lord, that is . . ." Wiz trailed off, overawed by the wizard's size and appearance.

"I will leave you now, Lord," Shiara put in. "Doubtless you have things to discuss."

"Thank you, Lady," Bal-Simba rumbled.

"What did you find out?" Wiz demanded as soon as Shiara had closed the door.

"Very little, I am afraid," Bal-Simba said regretfully. "There is no trace of magic in you. You are not a wizard and have not the talent to become one. There is a trace of—something—but not the most cunning demons nor the most clever of the Mighty can discern ought of what it is."

Wiz took a deep, shuddering breath. "Which means—what?"

"It means," the wizard said gently, "that to all intents and purposes you are an ordinary mortal with nothing magic to make you special."

"Okay, so send me home then."

Bal-Simba shook his head. "I am truly sorry, Sparrow, but that we cannot do."

"Oh crap! You brought me here, you can send me home."

"It is not that simple, Sparrow."

"It is that simple! It is exactly that simple. If you can bring me here you can send me back."

"No it is not!" Bal-Simba said sharply. "Now heed me. I will explain to you a little of the magic that brought you here.

"Did you ever wonder why Patrius chose to Summon you at a place far removed from the Capital? No, why would you? He did it because he hoped to do alone what he and all the Mighty could not accomplish acting together.

"Normally a Great Summoning is done by several of the Mighty together. But such a gathering of magic would be immediately visible to the magicians of the Dark League. They would strive to interfere and we would have to use magic to protect it. Soon there would be so much magical energy tied up in thrust and parry that the circle could not hope to make the Great Summoning.

"Of us all, only Patrius had the knowledge and ability to perform a Great Summoning unaided. He knew he could not completely escape the League's attention, but he apparently hoped that they would not realize what was happening until he had completed the spell." Bal-Simba looked grim. "As it happened he was wrong and the gamble cost Patrius his life.

"Simply put, Sparrow, there is no hope of returning you to your world unless we can perform a Great Summoning unhindered and there is no hope of that with the League growing in power."

Wiz's face twisted. "Damn."

"Even non-magicians should not swear, Sparrow," Bal-Simba said sternly.

"Well, what am I supposed to do? You've just told me I'm nothing and I'll always be nothing. I'm supposed to be happy about it?"

"I did not say you were nothing. I said you have nothing of magic about you. You have a life to live and can make of it what you will."

"Fine," Wiz said bitterly. "I don't suppose you could use your magic to whip me up a VAX? Or even a crummy IBM PC?"

"I am afraid not, Sparrow. Besides, I do not think those things would work here."

Wiz leaned forward against the parapet and clasped his hands together. "So," he sighed. "What do I do now?"

"Survive," Bal-Simba said. "Live. That is the lot of most."

"That's not very enticing," Wiz growled. "I can't go home and there's nothing for me here."

Bal-Simba followed his gaze down into the garden where Moira was kneeling among the plants.

"Things change, Sparrow. Things change."

"Not much to hope for, is it?"

"Men have lived on the hope of less," Bal-Simba rumbled. "Do you have courage, Sparrow? The courage to hope?"

Wiz turned to face him and smiled bitterly. "I can't have much else, can I?"

They stood looking out over the battlements and to the forest beyond for a moment more.

"You can stay here for as long as you like," Bal-Simba said finally. "The Dark League still seeks you and it is not safe for you to wander abroad in the world."

"Thanks," Wiz mumbled. "I guess I can find some way to make myself useful."

"That will be your choice, Sparrow."

As he moved to go, Bal-Simba placed his left hand on Wiz's shoulder and made an odd gesture in front of his eyes with his right. A thrill ran through Wiz's body and he shivered involuntarily.

"What did you do?" he asked.

"A minor magic, Sparrow," the giant black wizard said. "It is for your own good, I assure you."

He left Wiz staring out over the forest and descended the stairs.

After Bal-Simba left, Wiz looked down at the flagged courtyard spread out below.

It's a long way, he thought. *It would take, what?, five, six seconds to fall that far.*

That was one out, anyway. Short and relatively painless. He could just swing a leg over and solve everyone's problems in an eyeblink. Moira could go back to her village, Shiara and Ugo would have peace again and him, well, he wouldn't care any more.

He drew back from the edge. *No dammit! I'll be damned if I'll let this beat me like that!* Besides, he thought wryly, with my luck I'd probably just cripple himself. *Oh to hell with it!* He went back to staring out at the forest.

Moira met Bal-Simba in the great hall.

"Forgive me, Lord. I do not mean to pry into what is not my affair, but what did you find out about Sparrow?"

Bal-Simba shrugged. "As we suspected Lady. He has no magic and none of the Council can imagine what use he might be to us."

Moira closed her eyes and sighed. "I had hoped . . ."

"So had we all, Lady," Bal-Simba rumbled. "But do you care so much for him?"

"Care for him?" Moira blazed. "I can't stand him! Lord, he is not competent to weed a garden! He can barely be trusted within these walls by himself and he needs a keeper if he goes abroad."

"You should not be so hard on him," Bal-Simba said. "He cannot help it that he is as he is. Would you fare better in his world?"

"You are right, Lord," Moira sighed. "But it is so terribly hard when he is making eyes at me constantly. And when I look at him I'm reminded of what he cost us. He cost us so much and he is worth so little."

"Do not presume to judge his worth," Bal-Simba rumbled. "True worth is often hidden, even from the Mighty."

"I know, but . . . Oh Lord, let me return to the Fringe and my people," she pleaded. "They need me and Shiara can look after him."

Bal-Simba shook his head. "Your people are looked after, little one. As for letting you go—do you so relish the trip back across the Wild Wood and through the Fringe alone?"

Moira thrust out her chin. "I did it before, and with Him in tow."

The black wizard shook his head. "And you made it only by luck and the grace of an elf duke. I do not think Aelric would be so accomodating a second time and you used more than your share of luck getting here."

"You mean I am trapped here?"

"For a time, little one. When the League's interest has died somewhat more, we can bring both of you back to the Capital by the Wizard's Way. From there you may go as you will. In the meantime, try to be kind to our lost Sparrow."

Moira sighed. "I will try, Lord. But it is not easy."

"Very little in life is," the wizard said.

Wiz stood at the top of Heart's Ease and looked west over the Wild Wood. The sun was going down and already the shadows had stretched across the clearing below. The swallows swooped and wheeled over the keep and Wiz heard the whoosh of their passage more often than he saw one flit by.

"Is it a beautiful sunset, Sparrow?" asked a soft voice behind him. Wiz turned and saw Shiara standing by the door.

Wiz swallowed his misery. "Yes Lady, it is a very pretty sunset."

Shiara moved unerringly to the parapet. "Describe it for me if you would."

"Well, there are a lot of clouds and they're all red and orange. The sun's almost down on the horizon, but it's still too bright to look at directly. The sunlight's only on the very tops of the trees, so they're bright green and everything else is a real dark green."

They stood together in silence for a bit.

"Before—before I used to love to watch the sunset," Shiara said.

"I never had much time for sunsets," Wiz told her. "I was always too busy."

"Too busy for the sun?" Shiara's face clouded slightly. "Too busy for the sun, Sparrow?"

Wiz sighed. "Yeh. Too busy for the sun and a lot of other things. There was always so much to do, so much to learn." He grinned wryly. "You may not believe this, but computer programming really is a discipline. You have to work and study and slave over it to be any good. I did and I was good. One of the best."

"These things sound like hard taskmasters."

"Sure, sometimes. But it was rewarding too. There were always new things to discover and new ways to apply what you knew. Someone was always coming up with a new hack or a user would find some kind of obscure bug—ah, problem."

"And you devoted your life to this. To the exclusion of everything else?"

"Yeah, I guess I did. Oh, I had friends. I was even engaged to be married once. But mostly it was computers. From when I was fourteen years old and my school got its first time-sharing terminal." He smiled. "I used to spend hours with that thing, trying to make it do stuff the designers never thought of."

"This girl you were promised to, what happened?"

Wiz shrugged. "We broke up. She had kind of a bad temper and I think she resented the time I spent with the machines."

"I'm sorry."

"Hey, don't be. She married someone else and the last I heard they were happy together."

"I meant for you."

Wiz shrugged again. "Don't be," he repeated. "I

wouldn't have been a very good husband and I had the computers." He turned to face her, away from the forest and the setting sun.

"You know the worst thing about this business? It's not being jerked out of my own world and plopped down here. It's not being chased by a bunch of monsters out of the Brothers Grimm's nightmares. It's that there are no computers. It's that I'll never again be able to do the thing I spent all my life learning to do. The thing I love most doesn't exist here at all. I can't have it ever again."

"I know, Sparrow," said Shiara the Silver softly, looking out toward the sunset with unseeing eyes. "Oh I know."

"I'm sorry Lady," said Wiz contritely. "I've been thinking of my own problems."

"We each of us dwell on our own lot," Shiara said briskly, "sometimes too much. The real question is what do we do to go beyond it."

They were silent for a bit as the clouds darkened from orange to purple and the shadows crept deeper across the yard below. The swallows were fewer now and a lone brave bat fluttered around the battlements, seeking the insects that had attracted the birds.

"Lady, may I ask you a kind of personal question?"

"You may ask," said Shiara in a tone that implied it might not be answered.

"How do you go about rebuilding a life? I mean I can't work with computers here and that's all I know. How do I become something else?"

"The same way you became a—ah, hacker? Yes, hacker. One day at a time. You learn and you try to grow." She smiled. "You will find compensation, I think."

Bal-Simba left them that evening, walking the Wizard's Way back to the Capital. For several days Wiz remained sunk in black depression, dividing his time between the battlements and his room and only coming down to eat a hasty and silent evening meal. Ugo took over the woodcutting chores again.

Finally, on the fifth day, Shiara asked for his help. "We have many things ripening in the garden," she explained. "Moira is busy in the kitchen preserving what she has picked, Ugo has so much else to do and I," she spread her hands helplessly, "I am not much good at harvesting, I am afraid."

Moira looked askance at Wiz when Shiara brought him to the kitchen for directions. But he had been so genuinely miserable since Bal-Simba's visit that she kept her reservations to herself. *Anything to get him out of himself*, she thought, *even if it means ruining half the crop*.

So Wiz took a large basket and set to work picking beans. He worked his way down the rows without thought, examining every vine methodically. The beans had been trained to tripods of sticks, making rows of leafy green tents. As instructed, he took only those pods which were tan and dry, meaning the beans within were fully ripe.

He filled the basket and two more like it before the afternoon was over. Then he sat down outside the kitchen and carefully shelled the beans he had picked.

He was nearly done with the shelling when Moira came out of the kitchen and saw him working.

"Why thank you, Sparrow," she said in genuine pleasure. "That is well done indeed."

Once it would have thrilled Wiz to hear her praise him like that. But that time was past. "Pretty good for someone who's worthless, huh?"

Moira sobered. "I'm sorry, Wiz. I should not have said that."

"Meaning it's all right to think it, but not to say it."

"It isn't right to hurt another person needlessly," she said earnestly. "I spoke in anger and loss. I hope you will forgive me."

The way she said it hurt Wiz even more. She was

sincerely sorry, he realized, but she was sorry for hurting his feelings, not for the thought. She was a queen, graciously asking pardon of one of her subjects.

"You know I can't refuse you anything, Moira."

Moira closed her eyes and sighed. "I know, Wiz. And I'm sorry."

"Well, that's the way it is. Anyway, here are your beans."

Wordlessly Moira took the basket of shelled beans and went back into the kitchen.

That day in the garden was a turning point for Wiz. From then on he largely took over the job of harvesting the rapidly ripening crops. He spent several hours a day working outdoors while Moira divided her time between the kitchen, pantry and stillroom. Most of the time Wiz picked without supervision, although Moira occasionally came out to instruct him in the finer points of gathering herbs and some of the more delicate vegetables.

A few times he went out into the Wild Wood with Ugo to gather fruits and berries. There were several ancient orchards in the quiet zone, their trees long unpruned and loaded with apples, pears and other fruits. The sight of the trees, so obviously planted and long unattended, made Wiz sad. He wondered if some long-ago Lothar had planted those saplings, full of hope for the future.

Ugo forbade Wiz to gather more than half the fruit on any tree. "Leave for forest folk," he admonished. Still they brought back basket upon basket of crisp pears and small flavorful apples which Moira set about processing in the kitchen or storing in the cellars.

Three of the four "cellars" were not under the keep or hall at all. They were root cellars, small underground rooms a few steps from the kitchen door. One day Moira asked Wiz to help her move several barrels of apples packed in oak leaves from the kitchen out to the furthest cellar.

Huffing and puffing, they tilted the heavy barrels and rolled them out to the place where they would be stored. It took both of them to carry each barrel down the steps into the cool twilight of the root cellar.

"Whoo!" Wiz gasped, standing upright after the last of the barrels had been shifted into place. "I wonder how they did this before we got here?"

"Ugo doubtless did it," panted Moira. "Wood goblins are stronger than they look and they can be very ingenious when needs be."

"Do you think we've got enough food here for the winter?"

Moira ran a practiced housewife's eye over the cellar. "That and then some, if I am any judge. It is the flour, salt and other staples that are the concern. The Mighty bring those to Heart's Ease over the Wizard's Way and they have not increased the supply since we came."

"Why not?"

"First because the Wizard's Way was chancy when the Dark League was in full cry for us. Secondly, because they dared not increase the amount of supplies brought through lest it reveal to the League that there are extra mouths here."

Moira looked around the cellar again and breathed deeply to take in the scent of the apples and other good things stored in the earth. Then she sighed.

"Penny," Wiz said.

"What?"

"A penny for your thoughts. I was wondering what you were thinking."

"What I was thinking was none of your concern, Sparrow," Moira said coldly. "And if you are through prying into my private thoughts, we still have work to do. Come!"

"No, I don't think I am done," Wiz said slowly. He moved in to block her way out. "There's still something I want to know and I think you owe it to me to tell me."

Moira stopped, suddenly unsure of herself. She'd seen Wiz bewildered, sullen, lovesick, awestruck, depressed and in the throes of a temper tantrum, but she had never seen him coldly angry as he was now.

"What is it I must tell you then?"

"Why are you so mad at me?"

"Crave pardon?" she said haughtily.

Wiz plowed ahead. "From the moment I met you you've disliked me. Fine, I'm not a magician, I don't know my way around this place and I'm a first-class klutz. *But why are you so bleeding mad at me?*"

The question brought Moira up short. Wiz had never spoken to her like that before and she had never really examined her feelings toward him deeply.

True, he was inept and he had nearly gotten them both killed repeatedly on the journey. But it was more than that. She had disliked him from the first meeting in the clearing.

"I had to leave people who needed me to bring you here."

"Not guilty," Wiz said. "That was Bal-Simba's idea, not mine." He paused. "Besides, I think there's something more to it than that."

"There is," she said bitterly. "Patrius died to bring you here." Her eyes flashed. "We lost the best and most powerful of the Mighty and got *you* in return."

Wiz nodded. "Yeah, so you've told me. But I wasn't looking to come here and I've suffered more from what Patrius did than you or any of the others. Again, not guilty."

Moira drew herself up. "If my feelings do not meet with your approval I am truly sorry! It is perhaps unreasonable of me, but that is the way I do feel."

"I doubt it," Wiz bit out. "Bal-Simba's loss was greater than yours and he doesn't hold me responsible. There's something a whole lot more personal here. Now what?"

"I don't . . ."

"Lady, I think the least, the very least, you owe me is a straight answer."

Moira didn't reply for a long time. "I think," she said finally, "it is because you remind me of my failure."

"What failure?"

"The death of Patrius." Moira's eyes filled with tears. Don't you see? I failed in my duty and Patrius died."

"What I see is you trying to take the whole bleeding world on your shoulders," Wiz snapped. "Look, I'm sorry for what happened to Patrius, all right? But *I* didn't make it happen. I was kidnapped. Remember?"

"You were involved," Moira shot back. "If he hadn't Summoned you, he wouldn't have died."

"Wrong. If he hadn't had gotten me he would have gotten someone else—maybe the super-wizard he wanted, I don't know. But the point is, I had nothing to do with it. He made the choice of his own free will. He knew the risks. *I am not responsible.*"

"No," Moira admitted slowly, "you are not."

"And I'll tell you something else, lady. *You* weren't responsible either."

"Little you know about it! An acolyte's job is to protect the master."

"You're not an acolyte. You're a hedge-witch Patrius stumbled across and roped into his scheme. From what you and the others tell me, there is no way you could have protected him."

"Thank you," Moira said tightly. "All I needed was to be reminded of my weakness."

"Yes, you do need to be reminded of it!" Wiz flared. "You're not all-powerful and you cannot be held responsible for something utterly beyond your control."

"Ohhh!" Moira gasped, turning from him.

"I'll tell you something else you're not responsible for," he said to her back. "You're not responsible for what happened to your family. You didn't do it and you can't undo it and feeling guilty about it is only going to make you miserable."

Moira spun on her heel and slapped him with all
the force of her body. Wiz's head snapped to the side
and he staggered back. Their eyes locked. Then
Moira's shoulders heaved and she began to sob silently, hugging herself and rocking back and forth on
her heels.

Wiz took a step toward her and stopped. "Look,
I'm sorry I said that. I shouldn't have, okay?

"But dammit," he added forcefully, "it's true!" and
he turned and left the cellar.

Moira took her dinner in her room that night,
making Ugo grumble and complain about the stairs
he had to climb to take it to her. Shiara made a point
of not noticing and Wiz picked at his food and
muttered.

The argument marked a change in their relation-
ship. Wiz still loved Moira, but he began to notice
things about her he hadn't seen before. She had a
temper, he realized, and a lot of the time the things
she said to him weren't justified. She was beautiful
but she wasn't really pretty by the conventional stan-
dard of either world. Most of all, he saw, she was
terribly involved with her work. She was as married
to being a hedge witch as Wiz had been to computers.

For her part, Moira seemed to warm slightly to
Wiz. She never spoke of their fight in the cellar and
Wiz could see she still resented the things he had
said, but she started to unbend a little. They could
hardly be called close, but Moira began to go a little
beyond common civility and Wiz's dreams were no
longer haunted by Moira.

NINE

MAGIC FOR IDIOTS AND ENGLISH MAJORS

Slowly summer came to an end. The air grew cooler and the trees began to change. Standing on the battlements Wiz could watch flocks of birds winging their way over the multicolor patchwork tapestry of the Wild Wood. The swallows no longer flitted about in the evenings and the nights bore a touch of frost.

The garden was harvested now and Moira and Shiara spent their days in the kitchen, salting, pickling, preserving and laying by. Wiz helped where he could in the kitchen or out in the garden where Ugo was preparing the earth for its winter's rest.

In some ways Wiz was more at home in the kitchen than Moira. The way of preserving that the hedge witch knew relied heavily on magic. But for Shiara's comfort there could be no magic in the kitchen at Heart's Ease.

"These will not be as good as if they were kept by a spell, but we will relish them in deep winter nonetheless," Moira said one afternoon as they chopped vegetables to be pickled in brine.

"Yeah," said Wiz, who had never particularly liked sauerkraut. "You know on my world we would can most of this stuff. Or freeze it."

"Freezing I understand, but what is canning?"

"We'd cook the vegetables in their containers in a boiling water bath and then seal them while they were still very hot. They'd keep for years like that."

"Why cook them before you sealed them?"

"To kill the bugs." He caught the look on her face. "Germs, bacteria, tiny animals that make food spoil."

"You know about those too?" Moira asked.

"Sure. But I'm surprised you don't think disease is caused by evil spells."

"I told you that there is no such thing as an evil spell," Moira said, nettled. "And some ills are caused by spells. But most of them are the result of tiny creatures which can infest larger living things. What I do not understand is how you can sense them without magic."

"We can see them with the aid of our instruments. We have optical and electron microscopes that let us watch even viruses—those are the really tiny ones."

"You actually see them?" Moira shook her head. "I do not know, Sparrow. Sometimes I think your people must be wizards."

"I'm not."

Moira bit her lip and turned back to her cutting.

As evenings lengthened the three of them took to sitting around the fireplace in the hall enjoying the heat from the wood Wiz had cut. Usually Moira would mend while Wiz and Shiara talked.

"Lady, could you tell me about magic?" Wiz asked one evening.

"I don't know many of the tales of wonders," Shiara said. She smiled ruefully. "The stories are the work of bards, not the people who lived them."

"I don't mean that. What I'm interested in is how magic works. How you get the effects you produce."

Moira looked up from her mending and glared. Shiara said nothing for a space.

"Why do you want to know?" She asked finally.

Wiz shrugged. "No reason. We don't have magic where I come from and I'm curious."

"Magic is not taught save to those duly apprenticed to the Craft," Moira scolded. "You are too old to become an apprentice."

"Hey, I don't want to make magic, I just want to know how it works, okay?" They both looked at Shiara.

"You do not intend to practice magic?" she asked.

"No, Lady." Wiz said. Then he added: "I don't have the talent for it anyway."

Shiara stroked the line of her jaw with her index finger, as she often did when she was thinking.

"Normally it is as Moira says," she said at last. "However there is nothing that forbids merely discussing magic in a general fashion with an outsider—so long as there is no attempt to use the knowledge. If you will promise me never to try to practice magic, I will attempt to answer your questions."

"Thank you, Lady. Yes, I will promise."

Shiara nodded. Moira sniffed and bent to her mending.

After that Wiz and Shiara talked almost every night. Moira usually went to bed earlier than they did and out of deference to her feelings they waited until she had retired. Then Wiz would try to explain his world and computers to Shiara and the former wizardess would tell Wiz about the ways of magic. While Shiara learned about video games and multi-user operating systems, Wiz learned about initiation rites and spell weaving.

"You know, I still don't understand why that fire spell worked the second time," Wiz said one evening shortly after the first hard frost.

"Why is that, Sparrow?" Shiara asked.

"Well, according to what Moira told me I shouldn't have been able to reproduce it accurately enough to work. She said you needed to get everything from the angle of your hand to the phase of the moon just right and no one but a trained magician could do that."

Shiara smiled. "Our hedge witch exaggerates slightly. It is true that most spells are impossible for anyone but a trained magician to repeat, but there are some which are insensitive to most—variables?—yes, variables. The coarse outlines of word and gesture are sufficient to invoke them. Apparently you stumbled across such a spell. Although I doubt a spell to start forest fires would be generally useful."

Wiz laughed. "Probably not. But it saved our bacon."

"You know, Sparrow, sometimes I wonder if your talent isn't luck."

Wiz sobered. "I'm not all that lucky, Lady."

The former sorceress reached out and laid her hand on his. "Forgive me, Sparrow," she said gently.

Wiz moved to change the subject.

"I can see why it takes a magician to discover a spell, but why can't a non-magician use a spell once it's known?"

"That is not the way magic works, Sparrow."

"I know that. I just don't understand why."

"Well, some spells, the very simple ones, can be used by anyone—although the Mighty discourage it lest the ignorant be tempted. But Moira was basically correct. A major spell is too complex to be learned properly by a non-magician. A mispronounced word, an incorrect gesture and the spell becomes something else, often something deadly." Her brow wrinkled.

"Great spells often take months to learn. You must study them in parts so you can master them without invoking them. Even then it is hard. Many apprentices cannot master the great spells."

"What happens to them?"

"The wise ones, like Moira, settle for a lesser order. Those who are not so wise or perhaps more

driven persevere until they make a serious mistake."
She smiled slightly. "In magic that is usually fatal."

Wiz thought about what it would be like to work
with a computer that killed the programmer every
time it crashed and shuddered.

"But can't you teach people the insensitive spells?"
he asked. "The ones that are safe to learn?"

Shiara shrugged. "We could, I suppose, but it
would be pointless. Safe spells are almost always
weak spells. They do little and not much of it is
useful. Your forest fire spell was unusual in that it
was apparently both insensitive and powerful.

"There are a very few exceptions but in general
the spells that are easy to learn do so little that no
one bothers to learn them, save by accident."

"Well, yeah, but couldn't you build on that? I
mean start from the easy spells and work up to the
harder ones that do something useful?"

Shiara shook her head. "Once again, magic does
not work that way. Mark you, Sparrow, each spell is
different. Learning one spell teaches you little about
others. Wizardry is a life's work, not something one
can practice as a side craft. You must start very
young and train your memory and your body before
you begin to learn the great magics."

"I see the problem," Wiz said.

"That is only the beginning. Even if ordinary folk
could learn the great spells, we would be cautious
about teaching them lest they be misused. A wizard
has power, Sparrow. More power than any other
mortal. By its very nature that power cannot be
easily checked or controlled by others. Few have the
kind of restraint required to do more good than
harm."

"But people are dying because only wizards can
use the really powerful spells," Wiz protested, thinking of Lothar and his cottage in the Wild Wood.

"More would die if those who are not wizards tried
to use them. Life is not fair, Sparrow. As you know."

Wiz didn't pursue the matter and their talk went on to other things. But it troubled him for the rest of the evening.

Shiara's right, he thought as he drifted off to sleep that night. *You can't have just anyone working magic here. It would be like giving every user on the system supervisor privileges and making them all write their own programs in machine language. Not even assembler, just good old ones and zeroes.* He sleepily turned the notion over in his mind, imagining the chaos that would cause in a computer center. *You can't trust users with that kind of power. God, you don't even want most programmers writing in assembler. You make them use high-level languages.*

A vagrant thought tugged at the edge of Wiz's sleep-fogged brain. A computer language for magic? *My God! I'll bet you could really do that!*

He sat bolt upright. Well why not? A computer language is simply a formalism for expressing algorithms and what's a magic spell but an algorithm?

If it did really work that way the possibilities were mind-boggling. You'd need the right language, of course, but God what you could do with it!

These people were the original unstructured programmers. They were so unstructured they didn't even know they were programming. They just blundered around until they found something that worked. It was like learning to program by pounding randomly on the keyboard.

They never seemed to generalize from one spell to another. They needed some kind of language, something to let them structure their magic.

It would have to be something simple, Wiz decided. A language and an operating system all in one. Probably a very simple internal compiler and a threaded interpreted structure. And modular, yes, very modular.

Forth with object-oriented features? Yep, that made

sense. All thought of sleep vanished as Wiz got out of bed. His mind was full of structural considerations.

He dug a chunk of charcoal out of the fireplace and started sketching on the hearth by the wan moonlight. Just a basic box diagram, but as he sketched, he became more and more excited.

A Forth-like language was about the simplest kind to write. Essentially it was nothing but a loop which would read a command, execute it and go on to read the next command. The thing that made such languages so powerful was that the command could be built up out of previously defined commands. MOBY could be defined as command FOO followed by command BAR. When you gave the loop, the interpreter, the command MOBY, it looked up the definition in its dictionary, found the command FOO, executed it, went on to the command BAR and executed it, thus executing the command MOBY.

At the top of a program was nothing but a single word, but that word was defined by other words, which were defined by other words, all the way back to the most basic definitions in terms of machine language—or whatever passed for machine language when the machine was the real world.

The more Wiz thought about that, the better he liked it. Forth, the best-known example of the genre, had been originally written to control telescopes and Forth was a common language in robotics. It had the kind of flexibility he needed and it was simple enough that one person could do the entire project.

That Forth is considered, at best, decidedly odd by most programmers didn't bother Wiz in the slightest.

The critical question was whether or not a spell could call other spells. The way Shiara had used a counting demon to trigger the destruction spell in her final adventure implied that it could, but the idea seemed foreign to her.

He sat on the hearth, sketching in the pale moonlight until the moon sank below the horizon and it became too dark to see. Reluctantly he made his way back to bed and crawled under the covers, his excitement fighting his body's insistence on sleep.

Nothing fancy, he told himself. He would have to limit his basic elements to those safe, insensitive spells Shiara had mentioned. So what if they didn't do much on their own? Most assembler commands didn't do much either. The thing that made them powerful was you could string them together quickly and effectively under the structure of the language.

Oh yes, debugging features. It would need a moby debugger. Bugs in a magic program could crash more than the system.

It's a pity the universe doesn't use segmented architecture with a protected mode, Wiz thought to himself as he drifted off.

As he was slipping into unconsciousness, he remembered one of his friend Jerry's favorite bull session raps. He used to maintain that the world was nothing but an elaborate computer simulation. "All I want is a few minutes with the source code and a quick recompile," his friend used to tell him.

He fell asleep wondering if he would get what Jerry had wanted.

All through the next day Wiz's mind was boiling. As he chopped wood or worked in the kitchen he was mentally miles away with dictionaries and compiler/interpreters. He didn't tell Moira because he knew she wouldn't like the notion. For that matter, he wasn't sure Shiara would approve. So when they were sitting alone that evening he broached the subject obliquely.

"Lady, do you have to construct a spell all at once?"

"I am not sure I know what you mean, Sparrow."

"Can't you put parts of simple spells together to make a bigger one?"

Shiara frowned. "Well, you can link some spells together, but . . ."

"No, I mean modularize your spells. Take a part of a spell that produces one effect and couple it to part of a spell that has another effect and make a bigger spell."

"That is not the way spells work, Sparrow."

"Why not?" Wiz asked. "I mean couldn't they work that way?"

"I have never heard of a spell that did," the former wizardess said.

"Wouldn't it be easier that way?" he persisted.

"There are no shortcuts in magic. Spells must be won through hard work and discipline."

"But you said . . ."

"And what I said was true," Shiara cut him off. "But there are things which cannot be put into words. A spell is one, indivisible. You cannot break it apart and put it back together in a new guise any more than you can take a frog apart and turn it into a bird."

"In my world we used to do things like that all the time."

Shiara smiled. "Things work differently in this world, Sparrow."

"I don't see why," Wiz said stubbornly.

Shiara sighed. "Doubtless not, Sparrow. You are not a magician. You do not know what it is like to actually cast spells, much less weave them. If you did it would be obvious."

Wiz wasn't sure who had said "be sure you're right and then go ahead," but that had been his motto ever since childhood. The stubborn willingness to go against common opinion, and sometimes against direct orders, had gotten him the reputation for being hard to manage, but it had also made him an outstanding programmer. He was used to people telling him his ideas wouldn't work. Most of the time they were wrong and Wiz had always enjoyed proving that. In this case he knew he was right and he was going to prove it.

All the same, he didn't want anyone to know what he was up to until he was sure he could make it work. The thought of Moira laughing at him was more than he could bear.

Just inside the Wild Wood, perhaps 200 yards from the keep of Heart's Ease, was a small log hut. From the stuff on the floor Wiz suspected it had been used to stable horses at one time. But there were no horses here now and the hut was long deserted. Wiz cleared out the debris and dragged a rude plank bench which lay in a corner under the window. There was a mouse nest in another corner, but he didn't disturb that.

The next problem was writing materials. This world apparently wasn't big on writing, at least there weren't any books in Heart's Ease. The usual material was parchment, but he didn't have any. Finally he settled on shakes of wood split from the logs in the woodpile and wrote on them with charcoal.

Fundamentally, a computer language depended on three things. It had to have some method for storing and recalling data and instructions, instructions had to be able to call other instructions and it had to be able to test conditions and shift the flow of control in response to the results. Given those three very simple requirements, Wiz knew he could create a language.

His first experiment would just be to store and recall numbers, he decided. He wanted something useful, but he also wanted something that would be small enough not to be noticed, even here in the quiet zone. Besides, if magic hurt Shiara he did not want to make detectable magic.

Drawing on what Shiara had told him, he put

together something very simple, even simpler than the fire spell he had discovered by accident.

Although the spell was simple, he labored over it for an entire day, checking and rechecking like a first-year computer science student on his first day in the computer lab.

Late that afternoon he picked up a clean slab and a piece of charcoal. His hand was shaking as he wrote 1 2 3 in large irregular characters on the wood. Then he very carefully erased the numbers leaving only a black smear.

"Remember," he said and passed his hand over the board. There was a stirring shifting in the charcoal and the individual particles danced on the surface like an army of microscopic fleas. There, stark against the white of newly split wood, appeared 1 2 3.

"Son of a bitch!" Wiz breathed. "It worked."

He stared at the reconstituted numbers for a long time, not quite believing what he had done. He repeated the experiment twice more and each time the characters or designs he scrawled on the board and erased reappeared on command.

Okay, the next step is a compare spell. An IF-THEN. For that I'll need . . . Then he started as he realized how late it had gotten. He still hadn't cut wood for the next day and it was almost time for dinner.

For a moment the old fascination and new sense of responsibility warred in his breast. Then he reluctantly put down the board and started back to the keep. *If I don't show up soon someone is likely to come looking for me,* he thought. *Besides, they'll need wood for tomorrow.*

No one seemed to notice his absence or made any comment when he disappeared the next day after his stint at the woodpile. The comparison spell also proved to be straightforward. The final step was the calling spell, the spell that would call other spells. That was the key, Wiz knew. If it worked he had the beginnings of his language.

Again Wiz worked slowly and carefully, polishing his ideas until he was sure he had something that would work. It took nearly three days before he felt confident enough to try it.

Once more he wrote a series of numbers on a clean slab of wood. Then he erased them. Then he readied the new spell.

"Call remember," he commanded.

There was a faint "pop" and a tiny figure appeared on the workbench. He was about a foot high with dark slick hair parted in the middle and a silly waxed mustache. He wore white duck trousers, a ruffled shirt and a black bow tie. Without looking at Wiz, he passed his hand over the board and once again the bits of charcoal rearranged themselves into the numbers Wiz had written. Then with another "pop" the figure disappeared.

Wiz goggled. *A demon! I just created a demon.* Shiara had said that once a spell grew to a certain level of complexity it took the form of a demon but he had never expected to make one himself.

He had never considered what a command would look like from within the computer. *I never had to worry about that,* he thought, bemused.

This particular command looked darned familiar. Wiz didn't know for sure, but he doubted that bow ties and waxed mustaches were worn anywhere on this world. After wracking his brains for a couple of minutes he remembered where he had seen the little man before. He was the cartoon character used to represent the interpreter in *Starting Forth,* Leo Brodie's basic book on the Forth language.

That made a crazy kind of sense, Wiz told himself. What he had just written functionally was very close to a Forth interpreter. And he was basing his language in part on Forth. Apparently the shape of a demon was influenced by the mental image the magician has of the process.

I wonder if he speaks with a lisp?

Then he sobered. More to the point, how could he be sure that his language's commands would respond only to the explicit spells that defined them and not to some chance idea or mental image? Wiz made his way back to the castle in deep thought.

It wasn't at all as easy as that. The first thing Wiz discovered was that the universe was not orthogonal. The rules of magic were about as regular as the instruction set on a Z80. Some things worked in some combinations and not in others. Murphy said "constants aren't" and Murphy was apparently one of the gods of this universe.

He was uncomfortably aware that he didn't really understand the rules of magic. He deliberately limited his language to the simplest, most robust spells, counting on the power of the compiler to execute many of them in rapid succession to give him his power. But even that turned out to be not so simple.

There were some things which seemed to work and which were very useful, but which didn't work consistently or wouldn't work well when called from other spells. Wiz suspected the problem was that they were complex entities composed of several fundamental pieces. He deliberately left them out of the code. *After all*, he rationalized, *this is only version 1.0. I can go back and add them later*.

He benchmarked his compiler at about 300 MOPS (Magical Operations Per Second). Not at all fast for someone used to working on a 3 MIPS (Million Instructions per Second) workstation, but he wanted reliability, not speed. *Besides, my benchmarks are for real*, he told himself, *not some vapor wafting out of the marketing department*.

There were other problems he hadn't anticipated. Once he tried to write down a simple definition using a combination of mathematical notation and the runes of this world's alphabet. He gave up when the characters started to glow blue and crawl off the board. After that he was careful never to put a full definition on a single piece of anything. He split his boards into strips and wrote parts of code on each board.

The clean, spare structure of his original began to disappear under a profusion of error checking and warning messages. To keep side effects to a minimum he adopted a packaging approach, hiding as much information as possible in each module and minimizing interfaces.

Wiz spent more and more time at the hut poring over his tablets and testing commands. Sometimes the mice would come out and watch him work at the rude plank bench under the window. Wiz took to eating his lunch in the hut and he left crumbs for the mice. Winter was a hard time for the poor little things, he thought.

Moira noticed the change in Wiz, but said nothing at first. Part of her was relieved that he was no longer constantly underfoot, but part of her missed the ego boost that had given her. Deep down there was a part of her which missed seeing Wiz constantly, she finally admitted to herself.

If Shiara noticed, she said nothing. She and Wiz still talked magic, but now it was no longer an everyday occurrence.

What Ugo noticed was anyone's guess. Probably a great deal, but the goblin kept his counsel and grumbled about his chores as always.

Like a small boy with a guilty secret, Wiz went well beyond Heart's Ease for the first test of his new system. He found a sheltered glade surrounded on all sides by trees and bushes. There he set to work on his first real spell.

There was a jay's tail feather lying on the leaves,

slate blue and barred with black. Wiz picked it up, held it by the quill and slowly and carefully recited his spell.

Nothing happened. The spell had failed! Wiz sighed in disappointment and dropped the feather. But instead of fluttering to the ground, the feather rose. It rotated and twisted, but it ever so gently fell upward from his hand.

Wiz watched transfixed as the feather wafted itself gently into the air.

It wasn't much of a spell, just enough to produce a gentle current of air which could barely be felt against the outstretched palm. But Wiz was elated by its success. He had actually commanded magic!

They marked Mid-Winter's Day with a feast and celebrations. Ugo cut a large log for the fire. They had mulled wine flavored with spices, nuts, dried fruits and delicacies. With the nuts, fruit and spices Moira whipped up what she called a Winter Bread. It reminded Wiz of a fruitcake.

"In my country it is the custom to give gifts at this time of the year," Wiz told them. "So I have some things for you."

Wiz was not very good with his hands, but from a long-ago summer at camp, he had dredged up the memory of how to whittle. He reached into his pouch and produced two packages, neatly tied in clean napkins for want of wrapping paper.

"Lady," he said, holding the first one out to Shiara. She took it and untied the knot by feel, fumbling slightly as she folded back the cloth. Inside lay a wooden heart carved from dark sapwood, laboriously scraped smooth and polished with beewax until it glowed softly. A leather thong threaded through a painstakingly bored hole provided a way to wear it.

"Why, thank you Sparrow," Shiara said, running her fingertips over the surface of the wood.

"This is for you," he said holding the second package out to Moira. Inside was a wooden chain ending in a wooden ball in a cage.

"Thank you, Sparrow." Moira examined her present. Then his head snapped up. "This is made from a single piece of wood," she said accusingly.

Wiz nodded. "Yep."

She stared at him gimlet-eyed. "Did you use magic to get the ball into the cage?"

"Huh? No! I carved it in there." Briefly he explained how the trick was done.

Moira softened. "Oh. I'm sorry, Sparrow. It's just that when I see something like that I naturally think of magic."

"It's a good thing I didn't make you a model ship in a bottle."

"No," she said contritely. "I'm sorry for believing you had gone back on your promise not to practice magic."

"It's all right," he mumbled uncomfortably.

In spite of that, the holiday passed very well. For perhaps the first time since he had been summoned, Wiz enjoyed himself. Part of that was the holiday, part of it was that he now had real work to do and part of it—a big part of it—was that Moira seemed to be warming to him.

Wiz was chopping wood the next morning when Ugo came out to see him. "More wood!" the goblin commanded, eyeing the pile Wiz had already chopped.

"That's plenty for one day," Wiz told him.

"Not one day. Many day," the goblin said. "Big storm come soon. Need much, much wood."

Wiz looked up and saw the sky was a clear luminous blue without a cloud in sight. The air was cold, but no colder than it had been.

"Big storm. More wood!" Ugo repeated imperiously and went on his way.

Well, thought Wiz, *it's his world*. He turned back to the woodpile to lay in more.

All day the sky stayed fair and the winds calm, but during the night a heavy gray blanket of clouds rolled in. Dawn was rosy and sullen with the sun blushing the mass of dirty gray clouds with pink. By mid-morning the temperature had dropped ominously and the wind had picked up. Ugo, Moira and Wiz all scurried about last-minute tasks.

It started to snow that afternoon. Large white flakes swirled down out of the clouds, driven by an increasing wind. Thanks to the clouds and the weak winter sun, dusk came early. By full dark the wind was howling around Heart's Ease, whistling down the chimneys and tugging at the shutters and roof slates.

For three days and three nights the wind howled and the snow fell. The inhabitants warmed themselves with the wood Wiz had cut and amused themselves as they might in the pale grayish daylight that penetrated through the clouds and snow. They went to bed early and stayed abed late, for there was little else to do.

Then on the fourth day the storm was gone. They awoke to find the air still and the sky a brilliant Kodachrome blue. Awakened by the bright light through the cracks in the shutters, Wiz jumped out of bed, ran to the window and threw the shutters wide.

Below everything was white. The snow sparkled in the mild winter's sun. Tree branches bore their load of white. Down in the courtyard of the keep, the outbuildings were shapeless mounds buried under the snowdrifts. The whole world looked clean and bright and new that morning from Wiz's window.

After a quick breakfast Wiz and Moira went outside.

"It appears no damage was done," Moira said as she looked over the buildings in the compound. "The roofs all seem to be secure and the snow does not lie too heavily on them." Her cheeks and the tip of her nose were rosy with the cold, almost hiding her freckles. "We will have to shovel paths, of course."

"Yeah, and make snowmen," Wiz said, sucking the cold crisp air deep into his lungs and exhaling in a huge cloud.

Moira turned to him. "What is a snowman?"

"You've never made a snowman?" Wiz asked in astonishment. "Hey, I'm a California boy, but even I know how to do that. Here, I'll show you."

Under Wiz's instruction, they rolled the snow into three large balls and stacked them carefully. There was no coal, so stones had to serve as eyes and buttons, while Moira procured a carrot from the kitchen to act as the nose.

"What does he do?" Moira asked when they finished building him."

"Do?" said Wiz blankly.

"Yes."

"It doesn't do anything. It's just fun to make."

"Oh," said Moira, somewhat disappointed. "I thought perhaps it came to life or something."

"That's not usually part of the game," Wiz told her, remembering *Frosty the Snowman*. "It's something done only for enjoyment."

"I suppose I ought to do more things just for enjoyment," Moira sighed. "But there was never time, you see." She looked over at Wiz and smiled shyly. "Thank you for showing me how to make a snowman."

"My pleasure," Wiz told her. Suddenly life was very, very good.

He spent most of the rest of the day helping Ugo shovel paths through the drifts to reach the outbuildings. For part of the afternoon he cut firewood to replace the quantities that had been burned during the blizzard. But with that done, they were at loose ends again. The snow was still too deep to do much outside work and most of the inside work was completed. So Wiz suggested a walk in the woods to Moira.

"If it's not too dangerous, I mean."

"It should not be. The storm probably affected all kinds of beings equally." She smiled. "So yes, Wiz, I would like to walk in the woods."

They had to push through waist-high drifts to reach the gate, but once in the Wild Wood the going was easier. The trees had caught and held much of the snow, so there was only a few inches on the ground in the forest.

Although the weak winter's sun was bright in the sky it was really too cold for walking. But it was too beautiful to go back. The snow from the storm lay fresh and white and fluffy all around them. Here and there icicles glittered like diamonds on the bare branches of the trees. Occasionally they would find a line of tracks like heiroglyphics traced across the whiteness where some bird or animal had made its way through the new snow.

"We had a song about walking in a winter wonderland," Wiz told Moira as they crunched their way along.

"It is a lovely phrase," Moira said. "Did they have storms like this in your world?"

"In some places worse," Wiz grinned. "But it never snowed in the place where I lived. People used to move there to get away from the snow."

Moira looked around the clean whiteness and cathedral stillness of the Wild Wood. "I'm not sure I'd want to be away from snow forever," she said.

"I had a friend who moved out from—well, from a place where it snowed a lot and I asked him if he moved because he didn't like snow. You know what he told me? I like snow just fine, he said, it's the slush I can't stand."

Moira chuckled, a wonderful bell-like sound. "There is that," she said.

They had come into a clearing where the sun

played brighter on the new snow. Wiz moved to a stump in the center and wiped the cap of snow off with the sleeve of his tunic.

"Would my lady care to sit?" he asked, bowing low.

Moira returned the bow with a curtsey and sat on the cleared stump. "You have your moments, Sparrow," she said, unconciously echoing the words she had said to Shiara on their arrival at the castle.

"I try, Lady," Wiz said lightly.

Sitting there with her cheeks rosy from the cold and her hair hanging free she was beautiful, Wiz thought. So achingly beautiful. *I haven't felt this way about her since I first came to Heart's Ease.*

"But not as hard as you used to." She smiled. "I like you the better for that."

Wiz shrugged.

"Tell me, where do you go when you disappear all day?"

"I didn't think you'd noticed," he said, embarrassed.

"There have been one or two times when I have gone looking for you and you have been nowhere to be found."

"Well, it's kind of a secret."

"Oh? A tryst with a wood nymph perhaps?" she said archly.

"Nothing like that. I've been working on a project." He took a deep breath. *It's now or never, I guess.*

"Actually I've been working out some theories I have on magic. You see . . ."

Moira's mouth fell open. "Magic? You've been practicing *magic*?"

"No, not really. I've been developing a spell-writing language, like those computer languages I told you about."

"But you promised!" Moira said, aghast.

"Yes, but I've got it pretty well worked out now. Look," he said, "I'll show you." He reached into his pocket and pulled out the jay's feather he had used in his experiment. "I'll use a spell to make this feather rise."

"I want nothing to do with this!"

"Just hold up a minute will you? I know I can make this work. I've been doing it in secret for weeks."

"*Weeks?*" Moira screeched. "Fortuna! Haven't you listened to *anything* you've been told since you got here?"

"I'm telling you it works and I've been doing it for a long time," Wiz said heatedly. "You haven't seen any ill effects have you? In fact you didn't even know I was working magic until I told you."

Moira let out an exasperated sigh. "Listen. It is possible, *just possible*, that you have been able to do parlor tricks without hurting anything. But that doesn't make you a magician! The first time you try something bigger there's going to be trouble."

"I tell you I *can* control it."

"Those words are graved on many an apprentice's tomb."

"All right. Here, give me your shawl."

"No. I'm going to tell Shiara."

"Moira, please."

Dubiously, Moira got off the stump and unwound the roughly woven square of cloth she wore around her neck under her cloak.

The shawl was bigger than anything Wiz had ever worked with, but he set it down on the stump confidently. Mentally he ran over the rising spell, making a couple of quick changes to adapt it for a heavier object. He muttered the alterations quickly and then thrust his hands upward dramatically.

"Rise!" he commanded.

The edges of the shawl rippled and stirred as a puff of air blew out from under the fabric. Then the cloth billowed and surged taut as the air pressure grew. Then the shawl leaped into the air borne on a stiff breeze rising from the stump. The wind began to gently ruffle Wiz's hair as the air around the stump pushed in to replace what was forced aloft by the spell.

"See," he said triumphantly. "I told you I could make it work."

"Shut it off!" Moira's green eyes were wide and her freckles stood out vividly against her suddenly pallid skin. "Please shut it off."

The wind was stronger now, a stiff force against Wiz's back. Wisps of snow and leaves on the forest floor began to stir and move toward the rising air. Even as Wiz started the spell the wind rose ever higher. Moira's shawl was long gone in the uprushing gale.

The wind grabbed leaves and twigs off the ground and hurled them into the sky. The trees around the clearing bowed inward and their branches clattered as they were forced toward the column of air rising out of the clearing.

"Do something!" Moira shouted over the force of the wind.

"I'm trying," Wiz shouted back. He recited the counter spell, inaudible in the howling wind. Nothing happened. The gale grew stronger and Wiz backed up against a stout tree to keep from being pushed forward.

He realized he had made a mistake in the wording and swore under his breath. Again he tried the counter spell. Again nothing.

In designing the spell Wiz had made a serious error. The only way to undo it was to reverse the process of creating it. There was no word which could shut the flow of air off quickly.

Meanwhile the wind was picking up, gaining even more force. Now the leaves and twigs were supplemented by small branches torn from the trees around them. With a tremendous CRACK and a thunderous

CRASH, a nearby forest giant, rotten in its core, blew over and toppled halfway into the clearing.

The wind was so great Wiz was forced to cling to the tree trunk to keep from being swept up in the raging vortex of air. Moira was invisible through the mass of dirt, leaves, snow and debris being pulled into the air. Desperately Wiz tried the counterspell again. Again nothing.

The vertical hurricane carried denser ground air aloft. As it rose the pressure lessened and the water vapor in the air condensed out. Heart's Ease was marked by a boiling, towering mushroom cloud that could be seen for a hundred miles.

In the heart of a raging hurricane Wiz forced himself to think calmly. Again he reviewed the spell, going through it step by step as if he were back in front of his terminal. Taking a deep breath and ignoring the howling in his ears, he recited the spell again, slowly and deliberately.

The wind cut off as if by a switch.

The clearing was quiet save for the sound of branches falling back to earth and crashing through the trees around them. Moira was wet and disheveled, her red hair a tangled mess from the buffetting it had received from the wind.

"Of course there are still a few bugs in the system," Wiz said lamely.

"Ohhh," Moira hissed. "I don't want to talk to you." She spun away from him.

"All right. So it wasn't perfect. But it worked didn't it? And I shut it off didn't I?"

Moira shuddered with barely suppressed rage. But when she turned to face him she was icy calm.

"What you have done is less than any new-entered apprentice could do, were his master so foolish as to allow it," she said coldly. "Not only have you proved that you have no aptitude for the Craft, you have shown you have no honor as well."

"Now wait a minute . . ."

"No!" Moira held up a hand to silence him. "You gave your word that you would not attempt to reduce the things Shiara told you to practice. Now you boast of having violated that oath almost from the beginning and with no shred of excuse. You were not driven to forswear yourself by need. You did so only for your own amusement."

"Shiara didn't teach me . . ."

"Shiara taught you far more than was good for either of you," Moira snapped. "You have proven yourself unworthy of her teaching and of her trust." She paused and considered. "Normally a matter such as this would be handled by your master. But you," she sneered, "have no master."

The way she looked at him made Wiz feel as if he had crawled out from under some forest rock.

"Doubtless this matter will be placed before the Council and they will decide your fate. In the meantime you must be kept close and watched since it is obvious you cannot be trusted and your word cannot be relied upon."

She turned and stalked out of the clearing and back toward Heart's Ease. Wiz opened his mouth to call after her, then trudged up the path in her wake, fuming.

TEN

STORM STRIKE

"Moira, wait!" Wiz ran up the path after her. She kept walking, eyes straight ahead.

"Okay," Wiz said defensively, as he trotted along beside her. "So it got a little out of hand."

"A *little* out of hand?" Moira screamed. "A *LITTLE* out of hand. Ohhh . . . This is beyond all your stupidity. Not only do you learn nothing, you cannot even be trusted to keep your word."

"Now wait a minute . . ." Wiz started.

"Get back to the keep. You must be kept mewed for your own safety and ours as well." She threw him a contemptuous glance. "Tomorrow I will destroy your tools before they wreak more mischief."

"Destroy it? But I was right!"

"Go!" Moira commanded with a hefty shove in the small of his back. Wiz stumbled forward and gave his beloved a wounded look.

"Must I take you by the ear?" she demanded. "Now go!"

Shiara was collapsed in a chair with Ugo hovering about her. Her skin was ghastly pale and she was breathing in quick shallow pants."

"Magic," Ugo said. "Big magic and close pain her."

Wiz started guiltily. *Of course. That much magic must have hurt her terribly.* Seeing Shiara was even worse than Moira's anger.

"It seems that our Sparrow adds untrustworthiness to his other accomplishments," Moira said tightly. "He has been using your 'purely theoretical discussions' to learn to practice magic."

Ugo threw Wiz a look of poisonous hate.

Shiara clenched her fists on the chair arms so hard her knuckles turned white and levered herself erect. "Go to your room and remain there," she commanded. "We will decide what is to be done with you tomorrow."

"I'm getting damned tired of being ordered around," Wiz said.

"Your feelings and the state of your soul are of very little concern to me right now," Shiara said. "Now go. Or must Ugo escort you?"

"Look, I'm sorry . . ."

"That too is of no concern to me. Ugo!"

"Okay, okay," Wiz backed off hastily as the wood goblin came toward him with fire in his eye. "I'm going." He spun and started for the stairs.

"What was that?" The voice of Toth-Set-Ra boomed out in the head of the new Master of the Sea of Scrying.

"I do not know, Dread Master. Something to the North . . ."

"Imbecile! I know that already." Toth-Set-Ra's mental "voice" settled back into normal tones.

"It appears to come from a quiet zone in the Wild Wood."

There was a thoughtful pause. "Yessss. I know of the place. Send word that it is to be investigated. I want to know what caused that."

Toth-Set Ra turned back to the grimore he had been perusing. His hand caressed the elaborately illuminated parchment made from human skin but his eyes would not focus on the glowing runes that squirmed wormlike across the page. *The end to you and all yours* the demon's voice echoed tinnily, mockingly, in his ears. *A bane, a curse a plague upon the race of wizards. Magic beyond magics.*

He slammed the book shut and stalked out of his chamber. "Send Atros to me by the Sea of Scrying," he flung over his shoulder to the goblin guards.

The watchers around the rim of the great copper bowl bowed low as he swept into the vaulted stone chamber and fell back respectfully as he approached the edge. Toth-Set-Ra ignored them and stared deep into the sea.

The waters within were stained the color of weak tea by the blood of virgin sacrifices but the map graved on the bottom was easy to read. Glowing gems marked the cities of the World. A blood-red ruby, pulsing fitfully with inner light, represented the City of Night on the southern shore of the Freshened Sea. To the north and inland was the blazing blue sapphire which represented the headquarters of the Council. Here and there other gems winked green or blue or red or orange, their depth of hue marking the strength of the magics to be found there.

The effect was breathtaking, like a handful of gemstones strewn carelessly across the bottom of a rocky pool. But Toth-Set-Ra paid no heed. His trained senses searched for bright spots not marked with precious stones. Those were places of new or unexpected magic.

There, well within the line setting the Wild Wood off from the Fringe was a glowing white pustule on the reddish copper surface. It was fading, the wizard saw as he bent his full attention to the spot, but it had been strong. Very strong and uncontrolled while it lasted. In the center of one of the quietest places in the Wild Wood, too.

He scowled again and reached out, weighing and

savoring the magic that marked this place. It was powerful, that he knew almost without bothering to look. He sensed the disturbance in the weather, but he could see no purpose in it. There had been a mighty wind, but nothing seemed to have been accomplished.

His scowl deepened. Strange. Great spells were almost always supposed to accomplish great purposes. The spell itself was strange as well. It was as if a mass of minor spells had suddenly worked in the same direction.

Toth-Set-Ra was reminded of a marching column of army ants. Individually insignificant, they assumed enormous power because they all moved together. He savored the image and decided he didn't like it at all.

Behind the wizard, the door opened and Atros entered quietly. He spoke no word and Toth-Set-Ra paid him no heed. Heart's Ease. Yes. That was the place. Heart's Ease.

Then Toth-Set-Ra's fist smashed to the rim of the bowl, making the waters within quiver and the magical indications dissolve. He whirled to face his lieutenant. "Storm that place," he commanded, his brows dark and knit. "Bring me the magician responsible for that magic."

"Dread Master . . ." Atros began.

"Do it!" Toth-Set-Ra commanded. "Do not argue, do not scruple the cost. Do it!"

The big dark man bowed. "Thy will, Lord."

"Alive, Atros. I want that magician alive."

"Thy will, Lord."

Toth-Set-Ra turned back to the Sea of Scrying, searching it with his eyes, trying to pry more meaning from it. Atros bowed again and backed from the room, considering the ways and means of accomplishing the task.

A purely magical strike was clearly impossible. The Quiet Zone lay well beyond the barriers set up by the Northerners. Magical assault would be detected immediately and countered quickly. If he was willing to spend his strength recklessly he could undoubtedly penetrate the Northern defenses, but he might not have time to find and seize the magician before the counterassault.

Fortunately, thought the big wizard, *I have minions in place*. The old crow thought always of magic, but there are other ways to accomplish things. This time magic would be the mask, the shield, the cloak flourished in the opponent's face. The dagger behind that cloak would use no magic at all.

Even as he strode down the corridor, he began issuing orders into a bit of crystal set in his cloak clasp. Before he had reached the end of the hall those orders were being carried out.

As Wiz was making his sullen way up the stairs at Heart's Ease, the City of Night erupted into a hive of activity. Lines of slave porters toiled down the gloomy narrow streets, bent under the burden of provisions and weapons. Apprentices, wizards and artisans all jostled each other and the slaves as they rushed to carry out Toth-Set-Ra's commands.

In the bay, ships were hurriedly rigged and loaded. In the mountain caves where the dragons and flying beasts were kept, animals were groomed, harnesses checked and packs were loaded.

Within minutes of Toth-Set-Ra's order, the first flights of dragons were away from their cave aeries high on the mountain that loomed over the City of Night. They issued from their caverns like flights of huge, misshapen black bats. Their great dark wings beat the air as they climbed for altitude and sorted themselves into squadrons under the direction of their riders.

In a tower overlooking the bay, the busiest men of all were the black-robed master magicians who would coordinate the attack and make the magical thrusts.

Down in the great chantry beneath the tower, brown-robed acolytes and gray-robed apprentices turned from their magical work and set to preparing the spells the black robes commanded. Astrologers updated and recast horoscopes to find the most propitious influences for the League and those which would be most detrimental to the Council.

Further below, in the reeking pits where the slaves were stabled, slavemasters moved among their charges, selecting this one and that to be dragged out struggling and screaming. Whatever the spells, they would require sacrifices.

Far to the North, a spark appeared in a crystal

"Lord, we are getting something," the Watcher called out as the pinpoint of light caught his attention.

The Watch Master hurried to his side. "Can you make it out yet?"

The Watcher, a lean blonde young man stared deep into his scrying stone. "No Lord, there is too much background, or . . . Wait a minute! I think we're being jammed."

"A single source?" The Watch Master bent over to peer into the crystal.

The Watcher frowned. "No Lord, it is spread too wide." The Watch Master straightened up with a jerk.

"Sound the alarm. Quickly!"

On a cliff overlooking the Freshened Sea, the Captain of the Shadow Warriors reviewed his troops' dispositions and permitted himself a tiny smile of satisfaction.

For months he and his men had camped undetected on the enemy's doorstep. They used no magic in camp, save for the communications crystal the commander wore about his neck. Even their great flying beasts were controlled, cared for and fed without magic. Instead their magicians had spent their time listening intently to the world-murmurs of magic from the Northerners.

For months the men had subsisted mostly on cold food. Cooking was limited so the smoke might not betray them. In twos and threes they had penetrated miles inland, observing and sometimes reporting back to their masters in the City of Night.

Thinking on that, the Captain frowned. This was not supposed to be an assault mission. But now his patrols had been hastily consolidated into a strike force and ordered to penetrate a Quiet Zone to assault a castle and capture the magicians laired there.

The message he received was as short as it could be so the Watchers of the North would not intercept it. *Burn the keep called Heart's Ease and bring the magicians there alive and unharmed to the City of Night.* That was all, but for his well-trained band that was enough.

He had no doubt his men could do it. The castle defenses were minimal and although his men did not normally use magic, they had it at their call.

In the forest clearing three flying beasts waited. Their gray wrinkled skin bore neither hair nor scales. Their long necks and huge blunt heads thrust aloft as their great nostrils quivered in the wind. The huge bat-like wings were unfurled to their full 300-foot span and the animals moved them gently up and down at the command of their mahouts. Unlike dragons, these creatures were cold-blooded. They must warm themselves up before they could fly. Even from this distance the captain could smell the carrion stench of the animals.

Ritually, the Captain checked his weapons. The long, single-edged slashing sword was over his back with the scabbard muffled with oiled leather at the mouth. His dagger and axe hung at his waist. The contents of the pouches and pockets scattered about his harness: poisons, powders of blindness, flash powders and pots of burning. A blowgun lay alongside his sword and the needles were sheathed in their special pouch. Everything was muffled and dull. There was nothing on him or his men to shine, clink or clatter and almost nothing of magic.

Their enemies might see the Shadow Warriors but even the Mightiest of the Mighty would be hard-put to sniff them out by magic.

The Captain moved to his flying beast and an aide formed a stirrup so he could mount. Behind him the five Warriors of his troop had settled themselves onto the beast's broad back, their feet firmly placed in the harness.

The animal shifted slightly as the Captain settled in and opened its gaping mouth to honk complaint. But without a sound. Its vocal cords had been cut long ago so it might not betray itself in the presence of the enemy.

The Captain looked over his shoulders. Three other beasts were visible with their warriors aboard and their mahouts holding the reins without slack. To the side one of his sergeants signaled that the beasts out of his sight were also ready. The Captain nodded and raised his arm in signal.

In unison great leathery wings beat the air, raising flurries of dead leaves and dust as the animals clawed for purchase in the sky. Once, twice, three times the animals' mighty wings smote the air and then they were away, rocking unsteadily at first as each animal adjusted its balance, and then climbing swiftly into a sky only touched by the rising moon. From other clearings on the forested top beasts rose by twos and threes to soar into the clouds. As they climbed they sorted themselves out into four formations of threes. They might have appeared to be on a mass mating flight, save that not even these creatures mated so deep in winter.

The long, snake-like necks stretched forth and the animals squinted to protect their eyes from the searing cold.

The cold bit sharp and fierce at the Captain despite his gloves and the muffler-like veil wound around his face. He flexed his fingers to keep them supple and otherwise ignored it. Cold, hunger and hardship were always the lot of the Shadow Warriors and they were trained from childhood to bear them. Again he considered the plan and nodded to himself.

A glance behind him showed the Captain that the other warriors on his beast were flat against the animal's back, partly to cut the air resistance and partly to stay out of the wind.

As the gaggle of flying beasts scudded through the sky, the Captain kept a close watch for landmarks. With the force under a strict ban on magic, he could not use more reliable methods. His trained senses told him there was little magic below or around him to conceal any use of magic by the Shadow Warriors.

Far below a lone, lost woodsman caught a glimpse of the horde as it hunted across the sky. With a whimper he thrust himself back into a bramble thicket and hid his eyes from the sight.

As the Shadow Warriors flew east the other parts of the operation fell into place.

The stone hall was boiling with activity. All along the line Watchers called out as new magic appeared in their crystals. Reserve Watchers rushed to their stations. Magicians whispered into communications crystals. Wizards took their stations, ready to repel magical attacks and to add their abilities to those of the Watchers. Finally, from their laboratories and lodgings, the Mighty began to arrive. The room filled with the nose-burning tang of ozone and shimmers of magical force.

Bal-Simba entered with Arianne at his side. He stood in the doorway for a moment, surveying the organized chaos, and then moved to the great chair on the platform overlooking the room.

On the wall opposite a map sprang into existence

showing the Lands of the North and much of the Freshened Sea. Already there were six arrowheads of red fire approaching the Southern Coast. Six strikes coming in at widely spaced points, two of them obviously directed at the Capital. Here and there nebulous patches of gray and dirty green glowed on the map where the Sight would not reach.

Bal-Simba leaned forward in the chair to study the pattern of the attack.

"What do you make of it?" he asked his apprentice.

"If half of that is real," she said, gesturing to the colors on the map, "it is the biggest attack the League has ever mounted. Do you suppose that has something to do with the great disturbance in the Wild Wood this afternoon?"

"No, that was something else."

"This is powerful, but it seems—disorganized—as if it was hastily put together. Also, we have had no reports from the South to suggest an attack was being readied."

Bal-Simba waved her to silence. "Let us watch and see if we can find the underlying pattern."

Down in the pit three sweating magicians worked to keep the map updated. To the right of Bal-Simba's great chair on the platform five of the Mighty sat in a tight ring around a glowing brazier, mumbling spells. Now and then one or the other of them would throw something on the fire and the smoke and the reek would rise up to fill the chamber. Down in the earth and up in the towers, others of the Mighty worked alone, weaving and casting their own spells to aid the defense.

"Seventh group coming in," sang out one of the Watchers. "Airborne. Probably dragons."

Bal-Simba studied the configuration written in lambent script on the wall.

"Launch dragons to intercept. Tell them not to stray over the water."

"Dragons away, Lord."

"Time to intercept seventeen minutes," another talker reported. Others huddled over crystals keeping contact with the dragon force.

"Porpoises report three krakens moving toward the Hook. Formation suggests they are screening something else."

Around the room crystals glowed green, red and yellow as the talkers contacted the forces of the North and prepared for the struggle. From the most battle-ready guard troops to the hedge-witches in the villages the word went out. All the North braced to receive the assault.

But no one thought to tell the inhabitants of a small keep hidden away in the Wild Wood.

High above the Capital the Dragon Leader climbed for altitude. Reflexively he checked the great bow carried in a quiver by his steed's neck. The fight was unlikely to close to a range where arrows would do any good, but it gave him a sense of security to know they were there. Outside the freezing wind tore and whistled about him, but inside his magically generated cocoon a warming spell kept him comfortable. He would have to turn that off as he approached intercept to present minimal magical signature and to make his detectors more sensitive, he knew, and he hated that more than he feared dying.

Echeloned out below and behind him were the seven other dragons of his squadron. He spared them a glance as he checked his communications with the other dragon flights and with the Watchers back in the high hall of the keep.

His dragon's wings beat air as the beast clawed for height. With each stroke the Dragon Leader felt muscles pulse and jump beneath his thighs. With gentle leg pressure he turned his mount south, toward the Freshened Sea and the swiftly moving misty patch on the magic detectors that might indicate an air attack coming in. Reflexively his head swiveled, seeking any sign of his foes.

The moon was bright and just beginning to wane. The silvery light picked out the surface of the clouds, creating a wonderland of tops and towers, nubbly fields and high streaming pennons beneath him. Here and there the contorted fields of clouds were marked by pools of inky black where an opening let the light stream through to the ground below.

The Dragon Leader took it all in as he scanned the surface. He was less interested in the beauty than in what the clouds might conceal. As the first group off, his troop had drawn high cover—flying above the clouds to seek out the League's agents. Other troops were at work beneath the clouds while the clouds themselves were searched magically. Somewhere ahead of him was the enemy—or what appeared to be the enemy, he corrected himself. It was not unknown for the League to enhance a bat or a raven to make it look like a ridden dragon. The Dragon Leader bit his lips and kept scanning the cloud tops.

"Time to intercept twelve minutes," a voice said soundlessly inside his skull. He did not reply.

One of his men waved and pointed below. There, silhouetted against the pale cloudtops, were four dragons skulking north. The Dragon Leader did not need to call the Capital to know they were not in the Council's service.

He rose in his stirrups and looked behind him. The rest of his troop had seen the enemy too and were waiting expectantly for his signal.

The Dragon Leader switched off his warming spell, gestured down at the other dragons and patted the top of his head in the time-honored signal to dive on the enemy. A gentle nudge with the knees, a slight pressure on the reins and his mount winged over to dive on the invading force.

The Dragon Leader was well into his dive when the four dragons below him winged over and scattered into the clouds. The leader swore under his breath and signalled his squadron to break off the attack. *We'll never find them in that*, he thought. *Sharp eyes in that patrol. It was almost as if they had been warned.*

As if they had been warned . . . !

"Break! Break!" he screamed into his communications crystal. But it was already too late. The hurtling shapes plummeting down from the moon-haze were upon them and two of his dragons had already fallen to the ambush.

Abstractedly, the Dragon Leader realized he had been suckered. A flight of enemy dragons had snuck in earlier, perhaps laying silent and magicless on the ground until it was time to climb high above the chosen ambush site. Then they had waited until the flight committed to the attack on the decoys. Another part of his mind told him that if they succeeded in eliminating the top cover the lower squadrons would be horribly vulnerable to dragons diving out of the clouds.

But that was all abstract. The reality was the twisting, plunging battle all about him. In the distance he saw the flare of dragon fire. Another circle and he saw a ball of guttering flame dropping into the clouds. A dragon and probably a rider gone. He could not tell whose.

The Dragon Leader leaned forward against the neck of his mount and pressed his body close to cut air resistance. His dragon was diving with wings folded for maximum velocity. Now it was a simple speed contest. If he could plummet fast enough he had a chance of reaching the dubious safety of the clouds. If not, man and beast would be incinerated in a blast of dragon fire or dashed to pieces on the cold earth below.

The clouds reached out for him, first in wisps and tendrils and then as a solid, gray mass. He was in them now and hidden from sight. Magic could find him, but unless the searcher was a wizard, he would need to scan the clouds actively. He doubted his enemies would try. Dragon riders had a saying: "He who lights up first gets smoked." The Dragon Leader had no intention of using active magic.

Enough hiding, he thought, and turned his mount in a wide, climbing arc. His attackers had not followed him into the clouds, which meant they had probably gone hunting other prey. Even if they had not, they would be loitering on the cloud tops, without a speed or height advantage. Fine with him. The Dragon Leader had lost his wingman in the first stoop and he was spoiling for a fight.

His mount was tiring, but the Dragon Leader urged her up out of the clouds, trying for enough altitude to rejoin the battle.

His magic detector screamed in his ear and he jerked under the impact of the searching spell. Too late he saw his mistake. The enemy dragon had been laying for him, not down on the clouds but well above with no magic showing. Now he was trapped. The other was too close and had too much maneuvering ability to lose in the clouds again and there was no time to turn into the attack.

In desperation the Dragon Leader threw his mount into a tight spiral dive and clawed his bow and a heavy iron arrow free from his quiver. Over his shoulder he could see his opponent hurtling down on him, with speed, altitude and position all on his side.

At the last instant he kneed his mount and jerked the reins hard over and down. The dragon dropped her inside wing and dived even more steeply. A brilliant burst of dragon-fire destroyed his night vision and bathed his face with heat. Then his first opponent hurtled past, so close they could almost have touched, and was lost in the pearly clouds.

His opponent's wing man had more time to react. He had slowed his dragon, great wings beating mightily to brake his dive and he had used the time to line up. Worse, the Dragon Leader was in the process of recovering from the sideslip and could not maneuver.

But shooting dragon fire is not an easy matter and the wing man was not as skilled as his leader. The blast of blinding, scorching heat only touched the Dragon Leader and his mount. He smelled burned hair and knew it was his. His dragon bucked and roared in pain, but both of them were still in the air. Meanwhile the wing man was diving past, still trying to slow and turn on his opponent.

It was a fatal combination. The Dragon Leader loosed a shaft as the enemy swept by. It was nearly a right-angle deflection shot and the mechanics worked against him as much as they did against the enemy. But he felt a tingle in his hands as the arrow lept from the bow and he knew the arrow had seen its target.

The shaft sensed the enemy dragon and adjusted its trajectory accordingly. The tiny crystal eyes on either side of the broad barbed head both acquired the dragon and guided the arrow unerringly. The range was so close that the wing man's magic detector barely had time to begin to sound and he had no time at all to maneuver out of the way.

The shaft struck deep into the dragon's neck with force that drove it through scales and muscle until it struck bone. The beast arched its neck back and screamed in mortal agony while its rider clung desperately and despairingly to its back. Then the arrow's spell took hold and the dragon went limp.

Below him the Dragon Leader saw the shape of the other dragon twisting dark against the gray-white clouds. As it disappeared into the cloud bank there was a faint pinkish glow marking the dragon's last feeble gout of flame.

The Dragon Leader craned his neck, swiveling and searching for others in the night sky. There were none and no sign of battle anywhere. The moonlit cloud field was as quiet and serene as if nothing had happened here.

But it had happened, the Dragon Leader knew. His own scorched skin told him that. Soon there would be pain as the nerves started to complain of destroyed tissue. Now it was merely heat. The wheezy breathing and weary movement of his mount's great wings told him she too had suffered from the other dragon's fire. And worst, there would be at least three empty roosts back at the aerie tonight. That hurt more than the burns ever would.

"There will be other days," the Dragon Leader promised through cracked and blistered lips as he looked to the south. "There will other days."

It was late and the fire in Wiz's chamber had long since burned to cold, gray ash. He sat by the fireside, now lit only by the silver moonlight pouring in through the window, watching cloud shadows make patterns on the pier glass.

Damn fools, he thought for the tenth time. *Can't they see how valuable all this is. All right, so I made a mistake. But don't they see its worth?*

"We've had this conversation before," the mirror told him.

"But they're wrong," Wiz said. "Damn it, they are wrong and I'm right. I know it."

All evening he had alternated between anger, chagrin and self-pity. Each cycle was less satisfying than the one before and by now he was just going through the motions.

"That's not really the issue, is it?" the mirror spoke quietly in Wiz's mind. "If it was you wouldn't be telling me all this again, would you?"

"Can't they see . . . ?"

"Can you? What is really eating at you?"

"They were wrong!" Wiz protested tiredly. They were wrong and he was right and that was all there was to it.

"Is it?" the mirror asked. "Is that all there is to it?"

Wiz didn't answer. Magic or no, the damn mirror was right. There was more than that.

He had been convinced he was right and he had done what he always did when he believed that: he went ahead without worrying about what others thought.

"And this time?" the mirror prompted him.

This time others had been involved, he realized. There was no way they could not be.

Working magic wasn't like sneaking some extra time on the computer to try a new hack. If this barfed, the results were a lot worse than crashing the system. It wasn't just his life he was messing with, but theirs as well, and not surprisingly they resented it bitterly.

"Well, wouldn't you?" the mirror asked. "Do you like having people mess with your life?"

"All right," Wiz said tiredly. "You're right. I was right too, but I was wrong in the way I went about it. I should have tried to work with them rather than ignoring them. Maybe I should have convinced them, won them over, before proceeding. But dammit! They didn't have to make such a big deal of it."

"But you promised," the mirror said soundlessly.

That stopped him. To these people promises were something important. You kept your promises here because they had a force more binding than contracts on his home world.

People were so much more *sincere*, so much more *real* here. Surrounded by magic and the stuff of fantasy the people were more intensely human than the people he had known at home.

Or was it just that he cared more about them? He did, he realized. Not just Moira, but Shiara and Ugo, too. Even the tiny unseen folk of the forest.

He'd hurt them by betraying their trust and that, in turn, had hurt him. He was unhappy here so he'd tried to do what he always did—take refuge in technical things, to bury himself in not-people. Only this time it had only involved him more closely with the people around him.

Slowly, slowly, William Irving Zumwalt began to
think about what it meant to consider other people's
feelings.

Perhaps he was right about the magic language.
But that didn't make what he had done right. Magic
wasn't a computer system where he had the exper-
tise to follow up his idea.

What was it one of his professors used to say?
*Always use the right tool for the job. The right tool
to repair a television set is a television repairman.*
The right tool for this job was a wizard. He should
have talked to Bal-Simba or one of the other Mighty
and let them follow through. But he had wanted to
be somebody here so he had charged ahead like
some damn user with a bright idea. And very pre-
dictably he had screwed things up and caused a lot of
people trouble.

*Let's face it. I'm not a magician and I never will
be. I can't be anything special here. I'm just me and
I have to live with that and make the best of it.*

Bal-Simba had said that too. The black giant was
wise in ways more than magic.

So no more magic, Wiz resolved firmly. *I'll explain
my idea and that will be the end of it. Then I'll chop
the wood and learn to live as best I can. Perhaps
some day they'll forgive me for what I did. In the
meantime . . .*

He grinned. *In the meantime I accept being a
sparrow and quit trying to be an eagle.*

He looked at the mirror. But all he saw was the
dim reflection of a moonlit window and he heard
nothing at all.

Wiz rose from his chair, drained, exhausted and
his knees aching from sitting in one place too long.
Time for bed, he thought. *Way past time. You've got
a life to build tomorrow.*

There was a "whoosh" overhead followed by several bumps on the roof.

A confused bat? He hesitated, then picked his

cloak off the chair and went into the hall. It was doubtful anyone else had heard and he wanted to see what the noise was.

His shoes padded lightly on the stone corridor. All the castle was deathly still. He heard no more thumps. At the end of the corridor was a short flight of stone steps to the roof door. Wiz put his foot on the first step up.

The door burst inward with a crash and black-clad warriors poured down on him. Too stunned to shout, Wiz flinched back from the black apparitions.

He found himself staring into merciless dark eyes and felt the prick of a dagger at his throat. He was forced back roughly against the wall and held as the rest of the storming party rushed by, but otherwise he was unharmed.

The Shadow Warriors' orders were explicit: seize the magicians and burn the castle. Whether the other inhabitants lived or died was not in their orders and was thus of little concern to them. Wiz was subdued and silent, so he lived.

The Shadow Captain spared a long searching glance for the prisoner as he went by. The man so expertly pinned against the wall was peculiar, but he was clearly not a magician. There was neither trace nor taint of magic about him.

It never occurred to the Shadow Captain that someone might be working magic second hand or that there was no more reason to expect a magic sign on such a one than to expect machine oil on the clothes of a programmer who wrote control software for industrial robots. The notion was so utterly alien that Toth-Set-Ra himself had not considered it. The captain's orders covered only magicians.

Swiftly and silently, the assault force padded down the stairs. In teams of two and three, warriors checked every room on every level, but the vanguard never slowed. Wiz was dragged along by a knot of Shadow Warriors to the rear of the party.

They were down to the second level when they met their first opposition. It was Ugo, coming up the stairs with a tray balanced on one hand and a branch of candles in a candelabra in the other.

The Shadow Warriors flattened against the wall as the flickering light preceeded the wood goblin onto the landing. When he reached the top of the stairs the warriors closed in.

Unlike the human, Ugo did not freeze when the black shapes came out at him out of the shadows. With a roar he threw the tray at the closest men and rushed the others brandishing the heavy brass candelabra. He made three steps before a blade lashed out. The wood goblin gasped, staggered and took two more steps toward the Shadow Warriors. This time three blades licked evilly in the candlelight and Ugo shuddered and fell. The candles flickered out on the cold stone floor.

The door on the landing flew open and Shiara and Moira appeared, outlined by the hearth fire in the room behind them.

"Ugo. What . . . ?" Moira gasped at the sight of armed men in the hall and tried to slam the door, but the warriors bounded foward, pushing the women back into the room.

Instinctively Wiz tried to break free of the warriors holding him.

"Wiz!" Moira screamed as she saw a knife flash high and then descend at his back, but the warrior had flipped the blade so he struck only with the heavy pommel. Wiz collapsed instantly, held up only by the warriors.

The Captain's gaze flicked about the room. The one on the floor was not a magician. He knew of the white-haired one and confirmed that she was not practicing magic. That left the shorter red-haired woman and she was definitely a magician. He gestured and his men closed in on her.

If it had been in the Shadow Captain's nature to question orders he might well have questioned this one. However Shadow Warriors exist to obey, not question.

"Sparrow? Wiz?" Shiara asked plaintively. "Moira, what have they done to Sparrow?"

But Moira did not answer. Three warriors closed in on her and Moira screamed and struggled in their grasp. Wiz lay like a sack on the floor and Shiara stood helpless, groping about her. Then one of the warriors broke a seed pod under Moira's nose. She inhaled the dark, flour-like dust and sagged unconscious.

At a gesture from their leader, the Shadow Warriors turned and filed out of the room. Two of them carried Moira and two more stood in the door menacing the unconscious man and the blind woman lest they should try to follow. Then they too turned and ran fleetly down the stairs.

As they passed through the great hall, the last of the Shadow Warriors tossed small earthen pots in behind them. The pots shattered against the walls and floor and burst into searing, blazing flame that clung and clawed its way up the wooden beams.

The wood was dry and well-seasoned. The flames ran across the painted rafters and leaped into the shingles. The hangings caught and flared up as well.

"Lord, they're pulling back!" the Watcher sang out. Bal-Simba scowled and shifted on his high seat. To his left the magicians continued their mumbling and gestures.

The runes of fire on the wall told the tale. The League forces were veering off, turning away to the south. Here and there the skirmishes continued as forces too closely engaged to break off fought it out. A few northerners pursued, but cautiously, aware that every league to the south strengthened their opponents' magics and weakened their own.

Even the clouding magic was ebbing away.

"What damage?" Bal-Simba asked. Down in the

pit a talker passed her hands over her crystal again and her lips moved silently.

"Three villages burned, Lord. Alton, Marshmere and Willow-by-the-Sea. A hard fight at Wildflower Meadows where a band of trolls gained the wall and torched some houses. There are others but I cannot see clearly yet. And the battle casualties, of course." She shrugged. The last were not her concern.

Bal-Simba frowned. "Little. Surprisingly little for such an effort."

Arianne looked up tiredly. "We were too strong for them," she said.

"Or they did not push too strongly," the High Lord said half to himself. He turned quickly to his talker.

"Get reports from all the land. I want to know what else has happened."

"Isn't this enough Lord?" asked Arianne.

"No," Bal-Simba told his apprentice grimly. "It is not nearly enough. I would learn the rest of the price we paid this night.

"Sparrow? Sparrow." Dimly and faintly Wiz heard Moira's voice calling from a great distance. He stirred, but his head hurt terribly and he just wanted to sleep.

"Sparrow, wake up, please." Moira's voice? No, Shiara's. He was laying on the floor and there was smoke in the air. He pushed himself to his hands and knees. His head spun from the effort.

Shiara helped him stand. "Quickly" she said. "We must leave."

"Moira?" Wiz asked weakly.

"Outside! Hurry."

"I won't leave Moira."

"She's not here. Now outside." Wiz clasped her hand in his and started for the door.

As he led the way down the stairs he stumbled on a small limp form in front of the stairway.

"It's Ugo," he said, bending down. He gasped as he saw the horrible gaping wound that nearly severed the goblin's head from his shoulders.

Shiara knelt and moved between him and the body. She gently cradled it in her arms and the ends of her long silver hair turned dark and sodden where they touched the goblin's breast.

"Oh Ugo, Ugo," she crooned. "I brought you so far and for so little." By the flickering orange light Wiz could see the tears streak her face.

"He's dead, Lady." A fierce, hot gust brought choking gray strawsmoke and the pungent odor of burning pine up the stairwell. "Come, Lady," Wiz tugged at her sleeve. "Come on. We've got to get out of here."

Shiara raised her head. "Yes," she said. "Yes we must." She picked up Ugo's body, supporting the nearly severed head with one hand, cradling him as if he were a baby. For the first time Wiz realized how small the goblin had been.

With Wiz leading, they groped down the stairs, gasping in the heat and blinking from the thick smoke. Wiz guided Shiara through the blazing Great Hall, past the overturned furniture and patches where the floor burned fiercely. As they skirted along one wall, they passed the window seat. Wiz saw that the chair he had moved so long ago lay on its side roughly where he had dragged it.

They picked their way over the shattered remains of the door and out into the courtyard. The cold night air was like balm on their faces and they sucked great, gasping lungfuls, coughing and hacking up dark mucus that reeked of smoke.

Behind them the flames consumed Heart's Ease and shot high into the sky, grasping for the pitiless stars.

ELEVEN

HACKING BACK

Heart's Ease burned the whole night through. Far into the bleak winter morning sudden tongues of flame leapt from the ruins as the rubble shifted and the embers found fresh fuel. The walls stood, black and grim, but a little before dawn the roof crashed in, carrying with it what was left of the floors. There was nothing to do but stand aside and watch the flames. There was no help for Heart's Ease.

Shiara buried Ugo, refusing Wiz's offer of aid. Wiz didn't press. He sat alone, wrapped in Shiara's smoke-stained blue velvet cloak, utterly filled with pain and misery. Not even the chill of the stone beneath him penetrated.

It was mid-morning when Bal-Simba arrived. He came upon the Wizard's Way, accompanied by a party of armed and armored guardsmen who quickly spread out to search for any of the League's servants who might remain. The wizard closeted himself with Shiara for the rest of the day.

Wiz barely noticed. About noon he got up from his rock and returned to the tiny stable workroom in the clearing outside the palisade. It was almost evening when Bal-Simba found him there.

236

"You will be leaving Heart's Ease," he told Wiz gently. "There is nothing left worth staying for. The Lady Shiara has agreed to accept accomodation closer to the Capital and you will live in the Wizards' Keep itself. There is no longer any point in trying to hide you, it seems."

Wiz just nodded mutely.

"Shiara has told me what happened yesterday," he went on. "I hope you learned from it." He paused. "I am sorry the lesson had to be taught at such great cost," he said more gently.

Wiz said nothing. There was nothing to say. Bal-Simba waited, as if expecting some reply.

"What about Moira?" Wiz asked at last.

"Most likely she was stolen away for questioning in the City of Night. The raid here was masked by a whole series of attacks all along our southern perimeter. It seems the League has a powerful interest in your kind of magic so I would expect she will be taken to their citadel for interrogation."

"Shiara said it was me they were after," Wiz said miserably.

"Most likely. The League has been tearing the North apart seeking knowledge of you ever since you were Summoned. When your actions drew their attention here they came looking for a magician and Moira was the only one they could find.

"What will they do with Moira?"

Bal-Simba hesitated. "For now, nothing. The Shadow Warriors are fierce and cruel, but they are disciplined. Doubtless their orders are to bring her alive and unhurt to their master."

"And then?"

Bal-Simba looked grave and sad. "Then they will find out what they wish to know. You do not want the details."

"We've got to get her back!"

"We are searching," Bal-Simba said. "The Watchers have been scouring the plenum for trace of her.

Our dragon riders patrol as far south as they dare. We have sent word to all the villages of the North and searchers have gone out."

"Can they find her?"

Bal-Simba hesitated. "I will not lie to you, Sparrow. It will be difficult. The Shadow Warriors use little magic and they are masters of stealth. We are doing everything we can."

"But you don't think they'll find her." It was a statement not a question.

"I said it would be difficult," Bal-Simba sighed. "The Shadow Warriors may already be upon the Freshened Sea, or even back in the City of Night itself. If that is so, she is lost. We only know they did not transport her magically."

"We'll have to go get her! We can't let them have her."

Bal-Simba sighed again and for the first time since Wiz had known him he appeared mortal—tired and defeated.

"I'm sorry Sparrow. Even if she is already upon the sea there is nothing we can do."

Rage rose up in Wiz, burning away the guilt and grief. "Maybe there's nothing you can do, but there's something *I* can do."

"What is that?"

Wiz interlaced his fingers and cracked his knuckles. "I'm gonna hack the system," he said smiling in a manner that was not at all pleasant.

"Eh?"

"Those sons-of-bitches want magic? All right. I'll *give* them magic. I'll give them magic like they've never seen before!"

"It is a little late to start your apprenticeship, Sparrow," Bal-Simba said gravely.

"Apprenticeship be damned!" said Wiz, taking slight satisfaction at the way the wizard started at the blasphemy. "I've spent the last five months building tools. I've got an interpreter, an editor, a cross-reference generator and even a syntax checker. They're kludgier than shit, but I can make them do what I need. They didn't call me Wiz for nothing!"

"Remember what happened the last time you tried."

Wiz's face twisted. "You think I'm likely to forget?" He shook his head. "No, I know now what I did wrong. I knew it then, really. The next time I call up a hurricane it will be on purpose."

"Will you then compound your folly?" Bal-Simba asked sternly. "Will you add fresh scars to the land just to satisfy your anger?"

"Will you get Moira back any other way?" Wiz countered.

The Wizard was silent and Wiz turned back to the wooden tablets scattered over the rude table.

"Hurting us further would be an ill way to repay our hospitality to you," Bal-Simba said.

Wiz whirled to face him. "Look," he snapped. "So far your 'hospitality' has consisted of kidnapping me, making me fall in love with someone who hates me, getting me chased by more damn monsters than I ever imagined and nearly getting me killed I don't know how many times. When you get right down to it I don't see that I owe you much of anything."

He glared at Bal-Simba, challenging him to deny it. But the huge black Wizard said nothing.

"There's another thing," he went on. "You're so damn worried about the effects of magic on your world. Well, your world is dying! Every year you're pushed further back. It's not just the League. There's Wild Wood too. How long do you think you have before the whole North is gone? Do you really have anything to lose?

"All right, maybe I'll screw it up again." He blinked back the tears that were welling up in his eyes. "I've done nothing but screw things up since I got here. Maybe I'll make that scar on the land you keep talking about. But Dammit! At least I'll go out trying."

"There is no maybe about it," Bal-Simba said sharply.

"You will 'screw it up.' You have no magical aptitude and no training. At best you can destroy uncontrolled."

"Patrius didn't think so," Wiz shot back. He turned to his tablets again.

"I could forbid you," Bal-Simba said in a measuring tone.

"You could," Wiz said neutrally. "But you'd have to enforce it."

Bal-Simba looked at him and Wiz stayed hunched over the tablets.

"I will do this much," he said finally. "I will not forbid you. I will not commit the resources of the North to this madness but I will send word to watch and be ready. If by some chance you do discomfit the League, we will make what use of it seems appropriate."

Wiz didn't turn around. "Okay. Thanks."

"I will arrange for some protection for you in case the Shadow Warriors return. I will also pass word for everyone to avoid this place. I think you will scar the land and kill yourself unpleasantly in the process."

"Probably."

Bal-Simba sighed. "Losing a loved one is a terrible thing."

Wiz grinned mirthlessly, not looking up. "Even that wasn't a free choice."

"Love is always a free choice, Sparrow. Even where there's magic."

Wiz shrugged and Bal-Simba strode to the door of the hut. The black giant paused with his hand on the doorjamb.

"You've changed, Sparrow,"

"Yeah. Well, that happens."

Wiz did not see Bal-Simba leave. He stayed in the hut most of the day, scrawling on wooden tablets with bits of charcoal. Twice he had to go out to split logs into shingles for more tablets.

The second time he went to the woodpile Shiara approached him.

"They tell me you will make magic against the League," Shiara said.

Wiz selected a length of log and stood it upright on the chopping stump. "Yep."

"It is lunacy. You will only bring your ruin."

Wiz said nothing. He raised the axe and brought it down hard. The log cleaved smoothly under the blade's bite.

"Where will you work?"

Wiz rested the axe and turned to her. "Here, Lady. I figure it's safe enough and it seems appropriate."

"You will need help."

He hefted the axe and turned to the billet. "I can manage alone."

He raised the axe above his head and Shiara spoke again. "Would it go better if I were here for—ah—a core dump?"

Wiz started, the axe wobbled and the log went flying. "You'd do that? After what happened?"

"I would."

"Why? I mean, uh . . ."

"Why? Simple. You mean to strike at the League for what they did here when even Bal-Simba himself tells us we can do nothing. I owe the League much, and I would hazard much to repay a small part of that debt."

"It will be dangerous, Lady. Most of what you said about this thing is true. It's a kludge and it's full of bugs. I could kill us both."

For the first time since Wiz had known her, Shiara the Silver laughed. Not a smile or a chuckle, but a rich full-throated laugh, as bright and shining as her name.

"My innocent, I died a long time ago. My life passed with my magic, my sight and Cormac. The chance of dying against the chance of striking at the League is no hazard at all."

She glowed as bright and bold as the full moon on

Mid-Summer Eve and held out her hand to Wiz.
"Come Sparrow. We go to war."

Donal and Kenneth entered Bal-Simba's study quietly, respectfully and with not a little trepidation. It
was not every day that the Mightiest of the North
summoned two ordinary guardsmen and even Donal's naturally sanguine disposition didn't lead him to
believe that the wizard wanted to discuss the weather.

"I have a service it would please me to have done,"
Bal-Simba rumbled.

"Command us, Lord," said Kenneth, mentally brac-
ing for it.

"That I cannot do," Bal-Simba told them. "This
service carries a risk I would not order assumed."

Oh Fortuna, we're in for it now! thought Kenneth. Out of the corner of his eye he saw that Donal
looked unusually serious.

"May we ask the nature of this service?"

"There is a Sparrow whose nest needs guarding,"
Bal-Simba told them.

"Have you got any tea?" Wiz asked Shiara. They
were sitting by the fire in the hut which had been
the kitchen and was now their home. Both of them
were hoarse from talking and Wiz was surrounded by
a litter of wooden shingles with marks scrawled on
them in charcoal.

"Herbs steeped in hot water? Are you ill?"

"No, I mean a drink that gives you a lift, helps you
stay awake."

Shiara's brow furrowed. "There is blackmoss tea. I
used to use it when I was standing vigil. But it is vile
stuff."

"Do you have any?"

"In the larder, if it was not burned," she told him.

The tea was in a round birchbark box which had
been scorched but not consumed. Wiz put a pot to

boil on the hearth and watched as Shiara skillfully measured several spoonsful of the dried mixture into the hot water. The stuff looked like stable sweepings but he said nothing.

Shiara proferred the cup and Wiz took a gulp. It was brown as swamp water, so pungent it stung the nose and bitter enough to curl the tongue even with the honey Shiara had added.

"Gaaahhh" Wiz said, squinching his eyes tight shut and shaking his head.

"I told you it was vile," Shiara said sympathetically.

Wiz shook his head again, opened his eyes and exhaled a long breath. "Whooo! Now that's programmer fuel! Lady, if we could get this stuff back to my world, we'd make a fortune. Jolt Cola's for woosies!"

"That is what you wanted?" Shiara said in surprise.

"That's exactly what I wanted. Now let's let it steep some more and get back to work."

Bal-Simba's guardsmen showed up the next day. They were a matched set: Dark-haired, blue-eyed and tough enough to bite the heads off nails for breakfast. Kenneth, the taller of the pair, carried a six-foot bow everywhere he went and Donal, the shorter, less morose one, was never far from his two-handed sword. In another world Wiz would have crossed the street to avoid either of them, but here they were very comforting to have around.

With their help Wiz moved his things out of the old stable and into one of the buildings in the compound. The accomodations were not much of an improvement, but it was closer to the huts where they now lived and Shiara could come to it more easily to advise him.

"What do you think of this Sparrow?" Donal asked Kenneth one night in the hut they shared. Kenneth looked up from the boot knife he was whetting. "I think he's going to get us all killed—or worse."

"The Lady trusts him."

"The Lady, honor to her name, hasn't been right in the head since Cormac died," Kenneth said. "That's why she's been living out here. Even for a magician she's odd."

"Not half as odd as the Sparrow," said Donal. "I don't think he's slept in three days. He sits in there swilling that foul brew and muttering to himself."

"He's a wizard," pronounced Kenneth as if that explained everything. "All wizards are cracked."

"They say he's not a wizard," said Donal. "They say he's something else."

"That's all the world needs," Kenneth said. "Something else that works magic. I say he's a wizard and I'll be damned surprised if we come out of this one whole."

"Well," said Donal as he stretched out on the straw tick. "At least he keeps things interesting."

"So does plague, pox and an infestation of trolls," said Kenneth, replacing the knife in his boot.

Toth-Set-Ra sat on his raised seat in the League's chantry and heard the reports of his underlings. The great mullioned windows let in the weak winter's light to puddle on the floor. Magical lanterns hung from the walls provided most of the light that glinted off apparatus on the workbenches. Seated at a long table at his feet were the dozen most powerful scorcerers of the Dark League. Atros sat at his right. The Keeper of the Sea of Scrying was just finishing his report.

"And what else?" asked Toth-Set-Ra.

"Lord, there are signs of magical activity at Heart's Ease. It is possible the Shadow Warriors missed the magician."

Atros scowled at the man. The Shadow Warriors were his special preserve.

"Our magic detectors are excellent," Toth-Set-Ra said. "If there was another magician there, we would have found him."

"As you will, Lord. But we still show signs of magic in what was once a dead zone."

"Strong magic? Like before?

The black robe shrugged. "Not strong, Lord, but the taste is much like before. The magician is . . . odd."

A thrill went down Toth-Set-Ra's spine as he remembered the demon's words.

"Perhaps our magician had an apprentice who was absent when the attack came," Atros suggested.

"You say not as strong as before?" Toth-Set-Ra asked. The black-robed one nodded. "Then watch closely," he ordered. "I wish to know all which happens at that place."

"Thy will, Lord," the black robe replied. "But it will not be easy. The northerners are screening it and we cannot get clear readings."

"Keep trying," he snapped.

"Thy will, Lord. Perhaps however the Shadow Warriors should return."

Toth-Set-Ra shook his head. "No, that is a trick which only works once. Bal-Simba—may the fat melt from his miserable bones!—will not be caught napping again." He frowned and sunk his head to his chest for a moment. "But I am not without resources in this matter. I will see what my other servants can do."

Night and day, Wiz drove himself mercilessly. Writing, thinking, rewriting and conducting occasional experiments—usually in the forest with only Donal or Kenneth for company. He slept little and only when exhaustion forced him to. Twice he nearly slipped because of fatigue. After that he made a point of getting a little rest before trying an experiment.

The blackmoss tea numbed his tongue and made his bowels run, but it kept him awake, so he kept drinking it by the mugful.

Wiz wasn't the only one getting little or no sleep. Shiara wasn't sleeping much either and there was no blackmoss tea to ease her. Once Wiz passed her hut late at night and heard her sobbing softly from pain. The lines in her face etched themselves deep around her mouth and down her forehead, but she never complained.

"Lady, you are suffering from all this magic," Wiz said to her one afternoon as they waited for a spell to finish setting up.

"I have suffered for years, Sparrow."

"Do you need a rest?"

A haggard ghost of a smile flitted across her face. "Would *you* rest, Sparrow?"

"You know the answer to that, Lady."

"Well then," she said and returned to her work.

And the work seemed to go so slowly. Often Wiz would get well into a spell only to have to divert to build a new tool or modify the interpreter. It was like writing a C compiler from scratch, libraries and all, when all you wanted was an application. Once he had to stop work on the spells entirely for three precious days while he tore apart a goodly chunk of the interpreter and rewrote it from the ground up. He knew the result would be more efficient and faster, but he gritted his teeth and swore at the delay.

Wiz took to talking to the guards, one of whom was with him constantly when he worked. Neither Kenneth or Donal said much as he favored them with his stream of chatter. Donal just leaned on his two-handed sword and watched and Kenneth simply watched.

Worst of all, he had to be painstakingly careful in constructing his spells. A bug here wouldn't just crash a program, it could kill him.

There was no one to help him. Shiara had no aptitude for the sort of thinking programming demanded and there was no time to teach her. Besides, even being around this much magic was an agony for her. Actually trying to work some, even second-hand might kill her.

But somehow, slowly, agonizingly, the work got done.

"Behold, my first project," Wiz said with a flourish. He had been without sleep so long he was giddy and the effects of the tea had his eyes propped open and his brain wired. Conciously he knew that he desperately needed sleep, but his body was reinforcing the tea with an adrenaline rush and it would be some time before he could make himself crash.

Shiara held out her hand toward the silky transparent thing on the table. It moved uneasily like a very fine handkerchief on a zephyr.

"What is it?"

"It's a detector. You can send it over an area and it will detect magic and report back what it—uh—senses. 'Sees' would be too strong a word. It doesn't really see, it just senses and it sends back a signal." He realized he was speed-rapping and shut up.

Shiara moved her fingers through the thing's substance, feeling for the magic. The detector continued to flutter undisturbed by the intrusion into its body. "That is not much use," she said doubtfully. "It sees so little and can tell so little of what it sees." She drew her hand back sharply and the gesture reminded Wiz how much it cost her to have anything to do with magic.

"One of them is almost no good at all. But I'm going to produce them by the hundreds. I'll flood the Freshened Sea with them. I'll even send them over the League lands—who knows?—perhaps the City of Night itself."

Shiara frowned even more deeply. "How long did it take you to produce this 'detector'?"

"Separate from the tools? I don't know. Maybe three days."

"And you will make hundreds of them? In your spare time, perhaps. Impractical, Sparrow. Or do you plan to teach the craft to a corps of apprentices?"

"Oh, no. When I say three days, I mean the time it took me to write the program to make them. Once I run some tests and make sure it's up to spec, I'll start cranking them out automatically."

"You will not need to watch them made? Isn't that dangerous?"

Wiz shook his head. "Not if I do it right. That's the whole point of the interpreter, you see. It lets you spawn child processes and controls their output."

It was Shiara's turn to shake her head. "Magic without a magician. A true wonder, Sparrow."

"Yeah," said Wiz uncomfortably, "well, let's make sure it works."

Silent, dumb and near invisible as a smear of smoke, the thing floated above the Freshened Sea. Sunlight poured down upon it. Waves glittered and danced below. Occasionally birds and other flying creatures wheeled or dove above the tops of the waves within its view. Once a splash bloomed white as a sea creature leaped to snare a skimming seabird.

A human might have been entranced by the beauty, opressed by the bleakness or bored to inattention by the unchanging panorama below. The wisp of near-nothingness was none of these things. It saw all and understood nothing. It soaked in the impressions and sent them to a bigger and more solid thing riding the air currents further north. That thing, a dirty brown blanket perhaps large enough for a child, flapped and quivered in the sea winds as it sucked up sense messages from the wisp and hundreds of its fellows. Mindlessly it concentrated them, sorted them by content and squirted them back to a crag overlooking the Freshened Sea where three gargoyles crouched, staring constantly south.

The gargoyles too soaked in the messages. But unlike the things lower in the heirarchy and further south, they understood what they saw. Or at least they were capable of interpreting the images, sounds and smells, sorting according to the criteria they had been given and acting on the results.

Most of what came their way, the sun on the waves, the fish-and-mud smell of the sea, the wheel of the seabirds, they simply discarded. Some, such as the splash and foam of a leaping predator, they stored for future correlation. A very few events they forwarded immediately to a glittering thing atop a ruined tower in a charred stockade deep in the Wild Wood.

Thus it was that a certain small fishing boat seemed bound to pass beneath the cloud of wisps which was gradually blanketing the Freshened Sea. But no net is perfect and no weave is perfectly fine. Scant hours before the last of the insubstantial detectors wafted into position in that area, the boat sailed placidly through the unseen gap in the unsensed net.

Her name was the *Tiger Moth*. Her sails and rigging were neat and well cared for but not new. Her hull was weathered but sturdy with lines of dark tar along the weatherbeaten planks where she had been caulked for the winter's work. In every way and to every appearance she was a typical small fisher, plying a risky trade on the stormy winter waters of the Freshened Sea. If you looked you could find perhaps a hundred such boats upon the length and breadth of the sea at this season.

On the deck of the *Tiger Moth*, the captain of the Shadow Warriors looked at the clouds and scowled. There was another storm in the offing and naturally it would come from the south, blowing the vessel and its precious cargo away from League waters and

safety. One more delay in a long series of delays.
The Shadow Captain swore to himself.

His orders were strict. Bring the captured magician back at all costs. Do not fly. Use no magic which
might attract attention, not even the sort of simple
weather spells a fisherman with a mite of magical
ability could be reasonably expected to possess.

When the flying beasts brought the raiders back to
their seashore camp, he had bundled his captive
aboard the waiting boat and set out at once for the
League's citadel in the City of Night. The other
raiders had rested the day and then flown off on their
great gray steeds after sunset. They had been back at
the City of Night for days now, while the Shadow
Captain and his crew of disguised fishermen faced
days more of sailing to reach the same destination. It
was much safer to sneak his prize south like this at
the pace of an arthritic snail, but it tried even the
legendary patience of a Shadow Warrior.

The sea was against them. That was to be expected
at this time of the year, when what winds there were
blew up from the south and the frequent storms
came from the south was well. It was not a time for
swift travel upon the Freshened Sea.

The Shadow Captain knew too that the Council
was searching strongly for him and his prisoner. Several patrols of dragon riders had flapped overhead,
gliding down to mast-top height to check him and his
boat. The Shadow Captain had stood on the poop
and waved to them as any good Northerner would,
never hinting that what the dragon riders sought lay
in a secret cubby in the bow of his vessel.

For two days his ship had been trailed by an
albatross which floated lazily just off the wavetops as
if searching for fish in the *Tiger Moth's* wake. It had
not escaped the Shadow Captain's notice that the
bird never came within bowshot.

While the albatross was with them, the Shadow

Warriors had acted the part of fishermen, casting their nets and pulling in a reasonable catch, which they gutted and salted down on the deck. Thus they kept their cover, but it slowed them even more.

And now a storm, the Shadow Captain thought, *Fortuna!*

The object quivered gossamer and insubstantial in the magic field which held it, fluttering weakly against the invisible walls.

"What is it?" Atros asked.

"We do not know, Lord," the apprentice told him. "One of our fliers found it in the air above the city."

"What does it do?"

"We do not know."

"Well, what do you know?" the magician snapped.

"Only that we have never seen its like before," the apprentice said hastily.

"Hmmm," Atros rubbed his chin. "Might it be natural?"

The apprentice shrugged. "Quite possibly, Lord. Or perhaps the work of a hedge magician. No wizard would waste his substance making such a bagatelle."

The magician regarded the caged thing on the table again. He extended his senses and found only a slight magic—passive magic at that. "Very well. Return to your watch. Inform me if any more of these are found."

"Thy will, Lord. But they are very hard to find or see."

"Wretch! If I need instruction from apprentices I will ask for it. Now begone before I give you duty in the dung pits.

"What does this do?" Shiara asked, tracing the slick surface of Wiz's latest creation dubiously.

"It's a Rapid Reconnaissance Directional Demon—R-squared D-squared for short." He grinned.

"Eh?"

"It's an automatic searcher. It transports to a place, searches for objects which match the pattern it's been given and if it doesn't find such an object, it transports again. When it does find the object, it reports back. It has a tree-traversing algorithm to find the most efficient search pattern."

"I doubt you'll find what you want in a tree," Shiara said doubtfully.

"No, that's just an expression. It's a way of searching. You see, you pick a point as the root and . . ."

"Enough, Sparrow, enough," said Shiara holding up her hand. "I will trust you in this." She frowned. "But why did you make it in this shape?"

"To match its name," Wiz grinned.

"You see, Kenneth, names are very important," Wiz said seriously. "Picking the right ones is vital."

Wiz sucked another lungful of cold clear air and exhaled a breath that was almost visible. Overhead the sun shone wanly in a cloudless pale blue sky. The weak winter's light gave the unsullied snow a golden tinge.

"Yes, Lord," replied Kenneth noncomittally from where he lounged against a tree, his long bow beside him.

Wiz paid no heed to the response. He continued to pace the little clearing as he talked, not really looking at Kenneth at all. The crusted snow crunched under his boots as he circled the open space among the leafless trees yet again.

"The wizards are right," Wiz went on. "Names are critical. You need a name that you can remember, that you can pronounce easily and that you aren't likely to use in conversation." He smiled. "It wouldn't do to ask someone to pass the salt and summon up a demon, would it?"

"No, Lord," said Kenneth tonelessly.

Wiz never stopped talking, even though Kenneth

was behind him now. "And most importantly, Kenneth, most importantly I need names that easily distinguish the named routine, uh, demon. I can't afford to get mixed up."

"Yes, Lord."

"It's a common problem in programming. There's a trick to naming routines meaningfully without violating the conventions of the language or getting things confused." Wiz altered his stride slightly to avoid a spot where a dark rock had melted the snow into a dirty brown puddle. "Here I'm using a mixture of names of Unix utilities for routines that have cognates in Unix and made-up names for the entities that aren't similar to anything. So I have to pick the names carefully."

"Yes Lord." Kenneth shifted slightly against the tree and squinted at the pale sun, which was almost touching the treetops. Fingers of shadow were reaching into the clearing, throwing a tangled net of blue across the golden snow and dirty slush alike.

"It's especially important that I keep the differences in the similar routines straight," Wiz said. "I have to remember that "**find**" doesn't work like "**find**" in Unix. In Unix . . ."

"Lord . . ." said Kenneth craning his neck toward the lowering sun.

". . . the way you search a file is completely different. You . . ."

"Lord, get . . ."

A harsh metallic screech stopped Wiz in his tracks. He looked over his shoulder and glimpsed something huge and spiky outlined against the sun.

"*Down!*" Wiz dropped into the dirty slush as the thing barrelled over him. The wind of its passing stirred his hair and one of its great hooked talons slashed the hem of his cloak.

Open-mouthed, he looked up from the freezing mud in time to see a scaly bat-winged form of glitter-

ing gold zooming up from the clearing, one wing
dropping to turn again even as its momentum carried
it upward.

From across the clearing Kenneth's bowstring sang
and a tiny patch of pale blue daylight appeared in the
membrane of the thing's left wing close to the body.
The creature craned its snaky golden neck over its
shoulder and hissed gape-fanged at its tormentor.

Then it was diving on them again.

Wiz rolled and rolled toward the edge of the clearing, heedless of the snow and mud. Kenneth's bow
thrummed again and Wiz heard the whine of the
arrow as it passed close to his right. Then the beast
shrieked and there was a heavy thud as it struck
earth. Wiz looked up to see the golden dragon-thing
on the ground not five yards from him. The wings
were still spread and the animal was using a wickedly-
taloned hind leg to claw at the arrow protruding from
its breast. There was a spreading scarlet stain on the
glowing golden scales and the creature roared again
in rage and pain.

Suddenly a second arrow sprouted a hand's span
from the first. The animal stopped pawing at the
arrow in its chest and brought its head up to look
across the clearing. There was a disquieting intelli-
gence in its eyes. Its head snaked around and it
caught sight of Wiz. Without hesitating the beast
dropped its leg and started toward him.

Kenneth's great bow sang yet again and another
arrow appeared in the thing, in the shoulder this
time. But the beast paid it no heed. It advanced on
Wiz with a terrible evil hunger in its eyes.

Wiz whimpered and scrambled backward, but his
heavy cloak had wrapped itself around his legs and it
tripped him as he tried to rise.

The creature craned its neck forward eagerly and
the huge fanged mouth gaped shocking red against
the golden body. The arrows in the chest wobbled in

time with its labored breathing and the dark red blood ran in rivulets down its body to stain the snow carmine.

Again an arrow planted itself in the thing's body and again it jerked convulsively. But still it came on, neck craning forward and jaws slavering open as it struggled to reach Wiz.

The great eyes were golden, Wiz saw, with slit pupils closed down to mere lines. The fangs were white as fresh bone, so close Wiz could have reached out and touched them could he have freed an arm from the cloak.

Suddenly the beast's head jerked up and away from its prey and it screamed a high wavering note like a steamwhistle gone berserk.

Wiz looked up and saw Kenneth, legs wide apart and his broadsword clasped in both hands as he raised it high for the second stroke against the long neck. The guardsman brought the blade down again and then again, slicing through the neck scales and into the corded muscle beneath with a meat ax thunk.

The beast twisted its neck almost into a loop, shuddered convulsively, and was suddenly still.

The silence of the clearing was absolute, save for the beathing of the two men, one of them panting in terror and the other breathing hard from exertion.

"Lord, are you all right?"

"Ye . . . yes," Wiz told him shakily. "I'll be . . ." He drew a deep breath of cold air and went into a coughing fit. "What was that thing?"

"One of the League's creatures," Kenneth said somberly. "Now you see why you must not walk alone, Lord."

Wiz goggled at the golden corpse pouring steaming scarlet blood from the rents in the neck. "That was for me?"

"I doubt it came here by accident," Kenneth said drily.

Wiz tried to stand, but the cloak still tangled him. He settled for rolling over onto his hands and knees and then working the entangling folds of cloth out of the way before rising.

"You saved my life. Thank you."

The guardsman shrugged. "It was Bal-Simba's command that you be protected," he said simply. "Can you walk, Lord?"

"Yes. I can walk."

"Then we had best get you back to the compound. You'll catch cold, wet as you are."

Wiz looked down at his soaked and muddy cloak and for the first time felt the icy chill of his wet garments. He shivered reflexively.

"Besides," Kenneth said thoughtfully, "it is beginning to get dark and mayhap there are more of the League's creatures about."

Wiz shivered again and this time it had nothing to do with the cold.

Back at the compound, Shiara was concerned but not surprised at the attack.

"We could hardly expect to keep ourselves secret forever," she sighed. "Still, it will be inconvenient to have to be much on our guard. I think it would be best if you discontinued your walks in the woods, Sparrow."

"I was thinking the same thing myself, Lady," Wiz said fervently from the stool in front of the fire where he huddled. Save for a clean cloak he was naked and the fire beat ruddy and hot on his pale skin as he held the garment open to catch as much warmth as possible.

"Uh, Lady . . . I thought we were supposed to be protected against attacks like that."

Shiara frowned. "Sparrow, in the Wild Wood there is no absolute safety. Even with all the powers of the North arrayed about us we would not be completely safe. With Bal-Simba's protection we are fairly immune to magic attack and the forest folk will warn of any large non-magical party that approaches. But a single non-magical creature can slip through our watchers and wards all too easily."

"What about a single magical creature?" Wiz asked.

Shiara smiled thinly, her lips pressed together in a tight line. "Believe me, Sparrow, I would know instantly of the approach of any magic."

From the corner where he had been listening, Kenneth snorted. "If all they can send against us are single non-magical beings then they stand a poor chance of getting either of you." He tugged the string of his great bow significantly. "Lady, I own the fault today was mine. I was not properly alert. But rest assured it will not happen again!"

"It would be well if it were so," Shiara said. "But I am not certain they expected to get anyone in today's attack."

"They came darned close," Wiz said.

"Oh, had they killed or injured one of us the League would have been happy indeed, but I think they had little real expectation of it."

"Then what is the point?" asked Kenneth.

"In a duel of magics you seek at first to unbalance your opponent. To break his concentration and unsettle his mind and so lay him open to failure. I think the League's purpose in such attacks is to upset us and hinder our work."

"Then they failed twice over," Wiz said firmly and stood up. "I'm dry enough and I've got work to do tonight. Kenneth, will you hand me my tunic?"

Another day, near evening this time, and Wiz had another creation to demonstrate to Shiara.

"Here, let me show you." Wiz made a quick pass and a foot-tall homunculus popped into existence. It eyed Wiz speculatively and then started to gabble in a high, squeaky voice. "ABCDEFGHIJKLMNOPQRSTUV WXYZ1234567890," the creature got out before Wiz could raise his hand again. At the second gesture it froze, mouth open.

"What good is that thing?" Shiara asked.

"You told me wizards protect their inner secrets with passwords? Well, this is a password guesser. When it gets up to speed it can run through thousands of combinations a second." He frowned. "I'm going to have to do some code tweaking to get the speed up, I think."

"What makes you think you can guess a password even with such a thing as that?" Shiara said.

Wiz grinned. "Because humans are creatures of habit. That includes wizards. The thing doesn't guess at random. It uses the most likely words and syllables."

"Ridiculous," Shiara snorted. "A competent wizard chooses passwords to be hard to guess."

"I'll bet even good wizards get careless. You remember I told you we used passwords on computer accounts back home? There was a list of about 100 of them which were so common they could get you into nearly any computer in existence. Just run the list for any computer and the chances were at least one person had used one of them.

"Look, a password has to be remembered. I mean no one but an idiot writes one down, right?" Shiara nodded reluctantly. "And you've got to be able to say them, don't you?" Again Shiara nodded.

"Well then, those are major limits right there. You need combinations of consonants and vowels that are pronounceable and easy to remember. You also can't make them too long and you probably don't want to make them too short. Right? Okay, this little baby," he gestured to the demon on the table, "has been given a bunch of rules that help guess passwords. It's not a random search."

"But even so, Sparrow, there are so many possible combinations."

"That's why he talks so fast, Lady."

They brought Moira on deck the day the *Tiger Moth* raised the southern coast.

With no one at her oars and no wind behind her, the *Tiger Moth* ghosted between the great black towers that guarded the harbor. From the headlands of the bay mighty breakwaters reached out to clasp the harbor in their grasp. Where the breakwaters almost touched, two towers of the black basalt rose to overlook the harbor entrance. Great walls of dark rhyolite enclosed the city with its tall towers and narrow stinking streets snaking up the sides of an ancient volcano.

Everywhere the southland was bleak and blasted. The earth had been ripped open repeatedly by magic and nature and had bled great flows of lava. Now it was dark and scabbed over as if the wounds had festered rather than healed. The sky was dark and lowering, lead gray and filled with a fine gritty ash that settled on everything. In the distance dull red glows reflected off the clouds where still-active volcanoes rumbled and belched. The chill south wind brought the stink of sulfur with it. Nothing lived in this land save by magic.

Moira was hustled off the ship and hurried up the street by a dozen of the false fishermen. After days in the cramped cubby it was agony for her to walk. But her captors forced the pace cruelly even when she cried into her gag in pain.

The street ended suddenly in a great wall composed of massive blocks of dark red lava. The party turned right at the wall and there, in a shallow dead-end alley, was a tiny door sheathed in black iron. The Shadow Captain knocked a signal on the door and a peephole slid back, revealing a hideously tusked unhuman face. Quickly the door opened and Moira was thrust through into the midst of a group of heavily armored goblins. The goblins closed in and bore her off without a word or backward glance.

"Only one magician, you say?" Toth-Set-Ra asked the Shadow Captain harshly.

"Only the woman, Dread Master. There were two other humans within the walls, the former witch they call Shiara and a man called Sparrow. She called him Wiz."

"And they were not magicians?"

"I would stake my soul upon it."

Toth-Set-Ra eyed him. "You have, captain. Oh, you have."

The Shadow Captain blanched under the wizard's gaze. "I found no other sign of a magician there," he repeated as firmly as he could manage.

"There should have been at least one other magician, a man. You're sure this Wiz or Sparrow was not a magician?"

"He had not the slightest trace of magic about him," said the Shadow Captain. He was not about to tell Toth-Set-Ra there had been something strange about that man.

"We shall see," Toth-Set-Ra said and waved dismissal. "Now return to your ship and await my pleasure." The Shadow Captain abased himself and backed from the room.

Toth-Set-Ra watched him go and drummed his fingers on the inlaid table. He was frantically anxious to know what this new prisoner could tell him, but he was skilled enough in the ways of interrogation to know that a day or two of isolation in his dungeons would do much to break her spirit. Question a magician too soon and she was likely to resist to the point of death. First you must shake her, wear away her confidence. Then she would be more pliable to magical assaults and more susceptible to pain.

Tomorrow would be soon enough. Let her lie a

while in the dungeons. Then let five or six of the goblins use her. And then, then it would be easy to find out what she knew.

He smiled and his face looked more like a skull than ever. Yes, it would take a little time. But then, he had the time.

"(defun replace—variables (demon))" Wiz muttered, sketching on a clean plank with a bit of charcoal. "(let((!bindings nil)))"

"Lord."

"(replace—variables-with-bindings(demon))"

Wiz turned from the spell he was constructing to see Donal standing in the door, near blocking out the light.

"You made me lose my place," he said accusingly.

"Sorry Lord, but it's Kenneth. He's asked for you and the Lady."

Reluctantly Wiz put down the stick of charcoal and stood up, feeling his back creak and his thighs ache from sitting in one position on the hard bench too long. "What is it?" he asked. "More trouble?"

Donal regarded Wiz seriously. "I think he wants to sing a song," he said.

"A song?" Wiz asked incredulously. "He takes me away from my work to sing a song?"

Donal's face did not change. "Please, Lord. It is important."

As they stepped out of the hut, Wiz realized it was mid-morning. The air was still chill, but no longer iron-hard. The sun was warm even as the earth was cold. Spring was on its way, Wiz thought idly as Donal led him to the courtyard. Shiara was already there, sitting on the stump used to chop firewood, her stained and worn blue cloak wrapped firm around her, but the hood thrown back and her hair falling like a silver waterfall down her back.

Kenneth stood facing her. He was holding a small

iron-stringed harp Wiz had never seen before. From time to time he would pluck a string and listen distractedly to the tone.

Music, Wiz thought. *In all the time I've been here I've never heard human music.* His resentment dulled slightly and he pulled a small log next to Shiara for a seat.

Shiara reached a hand out of her cloak and clasped Wiz's hand briefly.

"You may begin Kenneth," she said.

Kenneth's expression did not change. He struck a chord and a silvery peal floated across the court and up to the smokestained peak of Heart's Ease.

> *Now Heart's Ease it is fallen*
> *for all the North to weep*
> *And the hedge witch with the copper curls*
> *lies fast in prison deep*

His voice was a clear pure tenor and the sound sent chills down Wiz's spine. There was loss and sadness in the music and the pain Wiz had felt since that terrible night Heart's Ease fell came rushing back with full vigor. Instinctively he moved closer to Shiara.

> *And none can find or follow*
> *for there's none to show the way*
> *and magic might and wizards ranked*
> *stand fast in grim array*
>
> *There's neither hope nor succor*
> *for the witch with copper hair*
> *for the Mighty may not aid her plight*
> *deep in the Dark League's lair*
>
> *Where the Mighty dare not venture*
> *the meek must go instead*
> *for shattered hearth and stolen love*
> *and companion's blood run red*

There's the Lady called Shiara
with blue, unseeing eyes
whose magic's but a memory
but still among the wise

There's a Sparrow who's left nestless now
bereft by loss of love
whose land lies far beyond his reach
past even dreaming of

With neither might nor magic
their wit must serve in place
and wizard's lore and foreign forms
twine in a strange embrace

But the fruit of that embracing
is nothing to be scorned
and the hedge witch with the copper curls
may yet be kept from harm

And if there's no returning
the witch with flame-bright hair
the price of a Sparrow's mourning
be more than the League can bear

Kenneth's voice belled up over the harp and the song rang strong off the ruined stone walls behind.

For there will be a weregeld
for life and hearth and love
though worlds may shake and wizards quake
and skies crash down above

Aye, there will be a ransom
and the ransom will be high
for the blood-debt to a Sparrow
the League cannot deny.

He stopped then, lowered the harp and bowed his head.

"Thank you, Kenneth," said Shiara. And wiz stepped forward to embrace the soldier roughly.

"The mood was upon me, Lady," Kenneth said simply. "When the mood is upon me, I must."

"And well done," said Shiara, standing up. "Thank you for the omen."

"So, Sparrow," she sighed. "We go soon. Do we go tomorrow?"

"I don't know Lady," Wiz protested. "I've still got some spells to tune and . . ." Unbidden a quotation from his other life rose in his mind. *There comes a time in the course of any project to shoot the engineers and put the damn thing into production.* He raised his chin firmly.

"Tomorrow, Lady. Tomorrow we strike."

TWELVE

THE NAME IS DEATH

Moira didn't know how far they had come. The flagged corridors twisted and turned in a way that made her head spin. The floor was uneven and the tunnels that led off usually sloped up or down.

The trickle of water down the center of the tunnel made footing treacherous, but she stayed to the middle nonetheless. To step out of the trail of slime was to risk ramming into a rough stone or dirt wall.

Worst of all, she could not see. There was no light and her magic senses were blocked everywhere by the coarse, suffocating pressure of counter-spells. The magic was almost as nauseating as the stink of her goblin guards.

The dark was no hinderance to the goblins. They took crude amusement from her plight, forcing her along at a pace that kept her on the verge of stumbling. Finally, after she had fallen or run into the walls too often, they grabbed her arms and half-pushed, half-dragged her along.

By the time the goblins threw her in a small, mean cell and slammed the door, Moira was bruised, filthy and scraped and bleeding in a dozen places. Her palms were raw from falling and there was a cut on

her head which turned her hair damp with blood.
Her knees and shins ached.

She pulled herself into a sitting position and dabbed
at the cut on her head with the least-dirty part of the
hem of her skirt. She tried to ignore the small skit-
tering sounds in the dark around her and refused to
think about the future.

"Well, Sparrow?" Shiara asked as she ducked to
enter the low door of Wiz's workroom.

"I think we're about there, Lady." For the first
time in days the crude plank table was clear. The
rough wooden tablets which had been piled on it to
toppling were now stacked more or less neatly in the
corners of the room. The table had been pushed
away from the small window and a bench had been
drawn underneath it. A brazier in the center of the
room made a feeble attempt to take the late-winter
chill out of the air but neither Wiz nor Shiara doffed
their cloaks. The door was open to let in more light.

"Are you sure you want to be here?" Wiz asked. "I
mean it isn't necessary and it may be dangerous."

The blind woman shrugged. "It is dangerous everywhere and I would rather be at the center of
events."

Shiara came into the hut and almost bumped into
the table in its new and unfamilar position. With a
quick apology, Wiz took her hand and guided her to
the bench.

"When do you begin?"

"I'll let you know in a minute. Emac!"

"Yes, master?" A small brown creature scuttled
out of the shadows. It was man-like, perhaps three
feet tall, with a huge bald head and square wire-
rimmed glasses balanced on its great beak of a nose.
A green eyeshade was pushed back on its domed
forehead and a quill pen was stuck behind one flap-
like ear.

"Are we ready?"

"I'll check again, master." The gnome-like being disappeared with a faint "pop." Shiara winced involuntarily at the strong magic so close to her.

"I'm sorry, my Lady. I'll tell them to walk from now on."

"What was that?" Shiara asked.

"An Emac. A kind of a magic clerk. They help me organize things and translate simple commands into complex sets of instructions. I have several of them now."

"Emacs," Shiara said, wrinkling her nose. "I see—so to speak."

There was another "pop" and the Emac was back before Wiz. "We are all ready, Master."

Wiz looked at Shiara, who sat with her head turned in his direction, beautiful and impassive. The pale, soft winter light caught her in profile, making her look more regal than ever.

Wiz took a deep, shuddering breath. "Very well," he said and raised his hands above his head. **"backslash"** he intoned.

"$" replied the Emac.

"class drone grep moira"

"$" said the Emac again.

"exe" Wiz said and the Emac's lips moved soundlessly as he transmitted the order, expanding it into a series of commands to each of the drones.

Far to the South, in a dozen places along the frozen shores of the Freshened Sea, stubby white shapes popped into existence, scanned their surroundings and disappeared again.

"running" *said the Emac.*

Wiz was silent for an instant. *Please God, let them find her.* "All right," he said briskly. "Now let's see how much Hell we can raise with the League. **backslash!"**

It started as a tiny spark deep in the Sea of Scrying, a pinpoint of light on the graven copper likeness of the World. The acolyte peered deeper into the Sea and rubbed his eyes. Was there something . . .? Yes, there it was again, stronger and sharper. And another, equally sharp and growing stronger. He raised his hand to summon the black-robed Master. When he returned his attention to the murky water there were four bright spots apparently scattered at random through his sector. Then the four doubled and there were eight, and sixteen, and thirty-two.

In the time it took the black-robed wizard to cross the room over a thousand points of bright magic light had bloomed on the bottom of the bowl. By the time the word was passed to Toth-Set-Ra, the Sea of Scrying glowed with a uniform milky luminescence and all sight of things magic in the World had been lost.

With a small "pop" an apparition materialized in Moira's cell.

She clenched her jaw until her teeth ached. *I will be brave* she told herself. *I will not scream.*

But her visitor was the most unlikely demon she had ever seen. It was a squat, white cylinder with a rounded, gray top and two stubby legs beneath.

The dome-shaped head rotated and Moira saw it had a single glowing blue eye. As the eye pointed at her, the thing emitted a series of squeaks and beeps. Then it vanished, leaving Moira awake and wondering.

Deep beneath the bowels of the City of Night three demons guarded the portal to the Pits of Fire. The first of the demons bore the form of an immense dragon who coiled in front of the gate. The second demon was shaped as a gigantic slug, whose skin oozed pungent acid and whose passage left smoking grooves burned into the rock. The third and mightiest of the demons appeared as an enormously fat old man with three faces seated on the back of a great black toad.

Ceaselessly, tirelessly and sleeplessly the three

watched, holding the sole entrance to the lake of boiling incandescent lava and well of earth magic that was the League's greatest resource.

Their vigil was broken by a "pop" and a tiny brown manniken stood before the three awesome sentries. Three heads and four faces swiveled toward him but the little man-thing made no move to approach the gate. Instead he opened his mouth and began to gabble in a voice so fast and high as to be inaudible to human ears. The three demons watched impassively until the little brown creature spoke a certain word. Then the dragon demon rose and crept away from the door, the slug demon heaved its acid-slimed bulk to the side of the corridor and the man demon spoke.

"Pass on," it said in basso profundo three-part harmony.

Without another word the little creature skipped through the now unguarded gate.

Beyond the great iron portal other demons reached deep into the roiling white-hot lava to sift out the magic welling up from the center of the World and turn it to their masters' uses. Feeding like hogs at a trough, they ignored the little brown creature who pranced in among their mighty legs. They paid no attention when the newcomer drew a pallid wriggling little grub from his pouch and cast it into the blazing pit.

As soon as it touched the flow of magic the grub began to swell. It grew and grew until it was as large as the demons, soaking up magic like a dry sponge soaks up water. The demons shifted and jostled as magic was diverted away from them. They tried futilely to regain their share. But now there were two full-sized worms in the pit and a dozen more growing rapidly. Unable to shoulder the worms away, the demons milled about in frustration and the flow of magic from the Pit to the city above dwindled to nothing.

*   *   *

Bal-Simba paced the great stone hall like a restless bear. Now and again he paused to peer over the shoulder of one of the Watchers.

"Anything?" he asked the head of the Watch for the dozenth time that morning.

"Nothing, Lord. No sign of anything out of the ordinary."

"Thank you." The wizard resumed pacing. The watcher stared into the crystal again and then frowned.

"Wait, Lord! There is something now." Bal-Simba whirled and rushed to his side.

"It's faint. Very faint, but there is something around the edges . . . No, now it's getting stronger." The Watcher looked up at Bal-Simba, awed. "Lord, there are indications of new magic in the City of Night itself!"

"What is it?"

"I do not know, Lord. Considering the distance and the masking spells it's a wonder that we can pick up anything at all. Whatever is happening there must be extremely strong."

"Hai Sparrow!" Bal-Simba roared. "You spread your wings, eh? Well fly, Sparrow, fly. And we will do some flying of our own." He motioned to Arianne who was sitting nearby. "Sound the alert. We will make what use we can of the opportunity our Sparrow gives us."

Again the dragons rose from their roosts in the Capital, formed into echelons and climbed away to the south. Again the Dragon Leader reviewed his instructions. A reconnaissance in force over the Freshened Sea, they told him. Scout to the South until you meet resistance. *Well,* he thought *We'll see just how far South we can go. And then perhaps we'll go a little further.* He tested his bowstring grimly.

In their dark towers above the City of Night, the

magicans of the League flew to arms. Spells pushed upon them from a hundred directions, elemental and relentless. In the harbor ships stirred uneasily as the waters tossed them.

"Get underway immediately," the Shadow Captain ordered, scowling at the sky. Most of the crew was still aboard the *Tiger Moth* and a mooring is the worst place for a ship to be in a time of danger.

Under the lash of the captain's voice the crew rushed to their stations. Hawsers were quickly cast off and two hands scrambled for the rigging. The oars were broken out and fitted into the locks. The crew hastily arranged themselves with an even number on each side. The captain saw the result and scowled again. Half the benches were empty, but it would have to do. With the mate beating time and the Shadow Warriors pulling for all they were worth, the *Tiger Moth* threaded its way through the clutter of ships and made for the breakwater gate and the open sea.

High in the watchtower overlooking the sea gate, a brown-robed mage threw back his arms and began his incantation. As the spell took shape in the plenum beyond human senses, a certain configuration of forces appeared. It was only a small part of the spell, but a lurking worm sensed it and battened onto that configuration. The worm's own spell twisted the conjuration out of its intended shape and the wizard screamed as he felt the spell writhe away from him and into a new and dangerous direction. The last thing he saw was a blinding, searing flash as the room exploded around him. His fellows, those who were not too close, saw the top of a black tower disappear in an incandescent blast.

The rest of the tower slumped like a child's sand castle built over-high and toppled into the bay. A huge block of hewed basalt crashed through the *Tiger Moth* just aft of the mast, breaking her back and bringing a tangle of rigging down on the poop where the Shadow Captain stood.

Impelled by the force of the block the *Tiger Moth* plunged beneath the cold black water. Only a few pieces of wood and rigging floated up.

The worm fed on the new power and spawned several copies of itself to lurk in the unimaginable spaces of magic and feed in turn when the opportunity arose.

"Master, our spells weaken!" the sweating wizard cried. With a curse Toth-Set-Ra strode to the lectern where the man had been conjuring and shoved him roughly aside. Quickly he scanned the grimore's page, creating the spell anew, and scowled at the result. What should have been bright and shining was wan and gray. Angrily he reached out for more power, but instead of the expected strong, steady flow he found only a wavering rivulet.

"To the Pit!" he roared at the shaking Wizard. "Something interferes with the flow."

As wizards and acolytes alike hurried to do his bidding, Toth-Set-Ra stared unseeing at the awful runes inscribed on human parchment before him.

Was the Council attacking in retaliation for the raid on the North? He dismissed the idea even as the thought formed. He knew Northern magic and there was none of it here. The Council might have a new spell or two, but everything the League faced was new. Besides, he knew the work of every one of the Mighty and this was unlike any of them.

An attack from within, aimed at himself? He considered that somewhat longer. It would explain how someone had gotten into the Pit to interfere with the flow of magic. Had he given Atros too much power? That too he discarded. If Atros or any of the others had half this much power they would have struck long before. And again, he knew the magics of the League even better than he knew those of the Council.

Then who? As the City of Night shook and towers toppled Toth-Set-Ra racked his brains trying to find the source of the attack.

A doom. A plague. A bane upon all wizards. The demon's words came back to him and the mightiest wizard in all the World shivered.

The alien wizard! The stranger from beyond the world. This mass of army-ant spells pressing in on them must be his work.

It was as well for the Shadow Captain that he was already dead, for the wizard's next oath would have blasted him where he stood. *He had the wrong magician!* Somehow this other one, this Wiz, the one they called Sparrow, had fooled the Shadow Warriors. The hedge-witch was a pawn to be sacrificed to protect the Council's king.

And he had fallen for it. By all the demons in the nine netherhells, he had been duped!

For a moment chill panic shook Toth-Set-Ra. Then he stopped short and laughed aloud. The other wizards in the chantry paused involuntarily at the sound. The Master of the Dark League seldom laughed and when he did it boded something truly horrible for someone. They turned back to their spells and incantations with renewed vigor.

Toth-Set-Ra was still chuckling when he reached the door of the chantry. *Fool me, will you? We shall see who is the fool in the end. For I tell you Wiz, or Sparrow, or whatever your true name is, you are as much in my power as if it were you and not that red-haired bitch I hold fast.*

Far to the north on a crag above the shores of the Freshened Sea three gargoyles stared forever South, testing the wind, sifting the whispers borne to them and sending on what they heard.

"It goes well, Sparrow." It was a not a question. Shiara sat on the bench, pale and calm as a winter's dawn while Wiz paced the room, muttering in a way that had nothing to do with magic. He paused to glance once more into the bowl of water on the rude table between them.

"We're shaking them good and proper," he confirmed. "I can't interpret everything, but there are fires and earthquakes all over the area. Part of the City of Night's wall is down and a couple of towers have already slid into the harbor." He smiled. "We've just about ruined their whole day. Now if only . . ."

Shiara nodded. "I know, Sparrow. Fortuna grant us this one final boon."

The crystal contrivance atop the ruined tower sparkled and flashed with the magical force of the messages arriving from the south.

Deep in her cell, Moira didn't know what was going on, but she was increasingly certain it wasn't being done to frighten her. Even this far under the earth she could hear occasional explosions, faint and muffled but audible nonetheless. Twice, groups of goblin soldiers tore by her cell in clattering, shouting masses. Once something huge and foul and slithering whuffled up the corridor while she pressed against the slimy rock wall and prayed to the depths of her soul that the thing would not notice her. Even the vermin seemed to have gone into hiding in the crannies and under the piles of rotting straw.

First the demon with the glowing blue eye and now this. What could it possibly mean?

Moira didn't hope, for hope had long since burned out of her. But she felt a stirring. Whatever was going on couldn't be good for her captors and misfortune to them was as much as she dared wish for.

With a faint "pop" an Emac appeared in front of Wiz, so close he almost stumbled over the demon in his pacing.

"We have found her, Master! RDsquaresquare has found her."

"Thank God! Where?"

"Underground master, far and deep underground. The coordinates are . . ."

Wiz waved the small brown demon to silence. "Show me in the bowl!"

The demon removed the quill pen from behind his ear and dipped the point in the water. Ink flowed from the pen, turning the clear water black and then shimmering as the image formed. Wiz looked intently at it and breathed a sigh of relief.

"Have we got a good enough fix?"

The Emac cocked his bald brown head and his huge ears quivered as he listened to something unhearable. "Yes, Master. We can come within a few cubits of the place."

"Then come with me." Wiz strode to the door, grabbing his oak staff and wrapping his cloak tighter as he stepped into the outdoor chill.

"Wait, Lord."

Wiz turned and saw Donal and Kenneth arrayed for battle. Their mail hauberks hung to their knees and their greaves and vambraces were secure to their limbs. Donal's great sword was over his shoulder and Kenneth's bow was slung across his back. Both wore their open-faced helms and their mail coifs were laced tight.

"You're not going," Kenneth said. "Not alone."

"I have to," Wiz told him.

"Bal-Simba told us to guard you and guard you we shall," said Donal.

Wiz shook his head. "It's too dangerous. Look, I appreciate the idea, but you can't come."

"Stubborn," said Donal.

"Too stubborn," said Kenneth. "You look, Sparrow. Someone has to keep your back while you're making magic."

"My magic can do that for me."

"Unlikely," said Kenneth.

"Take them, Sparrow," Shiara put in from the hut's door. "You may need them."

"It's dangerous," Wiz warned again. "You might get . . ." He cast his eyes over their well-used armor and weapons and trailed off. Both men looked at him in grim amusement. "Uh . . . right."

"It is Bal-Simba's wish," said Kenneth simply.

Wiz sighed. "Very well. Stand close to me and I'll see if I can make this thing work."

Donal and Kenneth pressed in against his back and he shifted his grip on the staff.

Wiz drew a deep, shuddering breath, filling his lungs with the cold, sweet air of Heart's Ease. He looked around slowly at the place he had come to call home. Then he tightened his grip on the staff and began.

"**backslash**" he said to the Emac. "**$**" the Emac responded, now ready and waiting for orders. "**transport**" he said and the Emac began to gabble silently, translating the predefined macro spell into the words of power. "**arg moira**" He raised the staff high over his head as the air began to waver and twist around him. "**EXE**" he shouted.

And the world went dark.

Something's gone wrong! Wiz thought frantically. *It's not supposed to be like this!* His arms quivered from the strain of holding the heavy staff high. He could feel Donal and Kenneth pressing hard against his back and hear their breathing, but still the darkness did not lift. Then he shifted slightly and his staff scraped against something overhead, showering him with noisome dirt. He nearly laughed aloud as he realized that this darkness was simply the absence of light.

He pointed with his staff. "**backslash light exe**" he said, and a blue glow lit the world around him. All three blinked and looked about.

They were in a tunnel so narrow they could not pass abreast. The rough flagged floor was slippery with condensation and the air was close and foul with the odors of earth and decay. About ten yards in either direction the tunnel twisted away, hiding what was beyond. Wiz could see four or five low wooden doors bound strongly with iron set into the walls along this section of the corridor.

"Moira!" Wiz called "Moira!" But ringing echoes and the distant sound of dripping water were the only replies. Donal and Kenneth quickly moved up and down the corridor, checking the cells.

"They are empty, Lord," Donal said, as they returned to where Wiz stood fidgeting. He forbore to mention that some of the cells were merely empty of life.

"Damn! She's got to be here someplace. The Emac said they had her located to within cubits."

The two guardsmen exchanged looks. They knew how unreliable magic could be, how susceptible to counterspells or the blurring effects of other magics, and how magicians could use magic to trap other magicians. What better place for a threat to the League than the dungeons under the League's own stronghold? As unobtrusively as they could they shifted their stances and loosened their weapons.

Unheeding, Wiz reached into his pouch and pulled out a shiny silver sphere. He cupped it in his palm. **"backslash cd slash grep moira"** he said to the marble. It pulsed with a golden glow, flashing brighter and fainter to acknowledge the order. **"exe"** Wiz said and the light from the sphere steadied into a warm yellow illumination that highlighted his face. The marble grew into a ball of light the size of his fist and floated to the top of the tunnel.

"She's above us," Wiz told the other two. "We'll have to go up to the next level."

"Carefully, Lord," Donal said in a near whisper.

"These tunnels are chancy at best and there are enemies about."

Wiz nodded and stepped under the glowing ball bobbing against the ceiling. "**backslash**" he said softly. "**in here moira**" Again the warm light pulsated. "**exe**" Wiz whispered and the ball drifted off to the left, glowing steadily as it travelled up the tunnel. Wiz moved to follow it and Donal stepped in front of him, his great sword at the ready. Kenneth fell in behind with his bow in hand and the flap open on his belt quiver.

There was no need to renew the light spell. The golden ball suffused the tunnel with an even glow, warmer and more natural than the weird blue light of the staff.

Donal and Kenneth were not comforted. The light would be a beacon to anyone or anything guarding the tunnels. Wiz didn't notice. His eyes were fixed on the glowing ball.

They saw no one as they moved up the tunnel, but twice they heard movement behind one of the stout, low doors set in the wall at irregular intervals. In neither case was the sound the sort that made them want to stop and investigate even if they had the time. Once there was an explosion that shook dirt down on them. Donal and Kenneth looked apprehensive, as if the passage might collapse, but Wiz only smiled and pressed forward.

The tunnel twisted and turned, it wandered and wobbled, it branched and joined, it doubled back and redoubled on itself and it dipped and it rose. But it rose more than it dipped and always the sphere of light led them on.

Kenneth and Donal kept swivelling their heads, their eyes scanning everywhere for signs of danger. Wiz kept his attention on the sphere, with just enough on his surroundings so he didn't trip on the miserable footing. Thus when Donal stopped dead at a corner, Wiz walked into him.

"Oh shit," Donal breathed silently.

"Oh shit!" Wiz whispered, peering over his shoulder.

"Oh shit?" mouthed Kenneth, bringing up the rear.

Around the corner the tunnel widened into a room, its stone floor worn smoother and more even than the corridor. The seeking ball was not the main source of light, for on one side of the room logs burned brightly in a cavernous fireplace. Along the other walls rush torches flared in wrought iron holders. Sturdy tables and benches were scattered about. And in the center, clustered around the glowing golden intruder, were twenty goblins, all armored, armed and very much on the alert.

They were staring up at the light and muttering among themselves in their coarse goblin speech. A very large goblin poked at the seeker with a halberd.

One of the goblins turned from the light to look back the way it had come. His piggy little eyes widened at the sight of three human heads peeking around the corner and he opened his tusked mouth to yell to his comrades.

"Fortuna!" Donal said under his breath, making the word a curse. Then he brandished his great sword and leaped into the open shouting a war cry. Kenneth was instantly at his back and Wiz stumbled in behind them.

Now goblins are powerful creatures, crafty, patient and fierce. But they are also excitable and given to panic if things go wrong. Goblin attacks are legendary, but so are goblin routs.

These goblins were already in a bad way. Their citadel was beseiged by powerful magic. Their last orders were to stay on guard, but those had come hours ago and they had had no word from their officers or the wizards they served since. They were on edge from hours of waiting and when three screaming humans burst into their guardroom in the wake of a mysterious light, they did what came naturally to their goblin natures. They panicked and ran.

"Son of a bitch," Wiz breathed as the clatter and shouting of the departing goblins died away.

"I told you you would need us, Lord," Donal said as he looked up the tunnel after the goblins.

Kenneth merely scowled. "They will be back soon enough. And others with them. Let us not be here when they return."

"Right," Wiz said. Already the golden ball was disappearing out the door the goblins had taken. "Come on then."

If the tunnel had been convoluted before, now it became positively mazy. Every few yards there was another branching and never were there fewer than four ways to go. At times even the seeker hesitated before plunging off down one or the other of the passages. Wiz's sense of direction, never his strong point, was completely befuddled. It seemed they had walked for a mile at least, all of it over rough, slippery ground that always sloped up, down or to the side, and sometimes several ways together.

Finally they came to a place where a fresh fall of dirt and rocks blocked most of the passage. The ball did not hesitate. It floated to the top of the tunnel and vanished in the crevice between the debris and the ceiling. That left Wiz and his companions in darkness except for the faint glow coming through the crack.

"It doesn't look very big," Donal said, eyeing the crack doubtfully.

"The spell does know enough not to go where a man may not follow?" Kenneth asked.

"Well, ah . . ." Wiz realized he hadn't thought of that. "Come on, let's see if we can get through."

He scrambled up the mound of loose earth and tried to wedge his body through. His arms and head went in easily enough, but his torso went only halfway. He tried to back out but with his arms extended in front, he couldn't get any purchase. He kicked his legs and tried to writhe his body from side to side, but only suceeded in getting a mouthful of the fetid dirt.

"Help me out of here," he called as he twisted his head to one side and spat out the foul-tasting earth.

Donal and Kenneth each grabbed a leg and tugged strongly. Wiz slid out, still spitting dirt.

"Gah!" he wiped his tongue on the inside of his tunic. "No good. We'll have to dig."

Kenneth muttered a comment about half-something spells. Wiz ignored him and picked up his staff. "backslash light exe" he commanded, pointing the staff down the corridor. At once everything lit up with eerie blue light. Then Wiz turned to work on the blockage.

They had no shovel, so at first Wiz threw dirt back between his legs like a dog. Then Kenneth took off his helm and passed it up to use as a scoop. When they came to rocks too large for Wiz to move by himself, Donal squeezed into the tunnel beside him to help. All the while Kenneth stood guard with his bow at the ready, looking nervously down the way they had come.

"I think it's big enough," Wiz said at last, panting from the exercise. "Let me check."

As he moved to climb back up the dirt pile, Donal caught his arm and shook his head. "Bal-Simba said to take care of you, Lord. I'll go first."

"I wish you'd remembered that while I was digging," Wiz said as Kenneth knocked the dirt out of his helm and laced it tight to his mail coif.

"Bal-Simba did not say to do your work for you," Donal replied. Then he scrambled up the dirt pile and squeezed into the crack, dragging his great sword behind him.

"All clear," he called after a moment from the other side and Wiz slithered through after him with Kenneth close behind.

Amazingly, the seeker's golden light was still visible, reflected off the wall at the end of the corridor.

Wiz and his companions hurried on, turned a corner and there, about twenty-five yards in front of them, was the seeker, bobbing up and down gently in front of a stout oaken door.

"Moira? Moira?" Wiz called as they came down the corridor.

A pale tear-stained face appeared in the tiny barred window set in the door.

"Wiz? Oh, Wiz!"

Wiz rushed ahead of his companions and pressed against the door. "Oh my God! Darling, are you all right?"

"Oh Wiz, Wiz. I've been so . . . Oh Wiz!" and Moira started to cry.

"Come on, we'll get you of there. Stand away from the door, now."

Moira backed from the window, as if reluctant to lose sight of him.

"Get as far away as you can and cover yourself," Wiz instructed her. "Tell me when you're ready."

"I'm . . . I'm ready" Moira called tentatively from within the cell.

Wiz raised his staff.

"What was that?" Atros growled.

"Vig noisss. Egplhossion." The goblin commander's human speech was slurred by his great tusks.

"I know that, idiot! But what caused it?"

The goblin merely shrugged, which only increased the wizard's ire. For over two hours Atros had been searching the dungeons based on the report of a troop of goblins who had been attacked in their guardroom by a strong force of human warriors and wizards. At least that was *their* story, Atros thought sourly. So far he had seen nothing to prove it.

"Well, where did it come from?" he snapped.

"That way, Master. Where special prisoner is." Atros's ears pricked up. What was the old crow hiding down here? "Well, let's check. Quickly."

With nearly fifty heavily armed and armored goblins behind them Atros and the goblin commander set off down the tunnel at a trot.

The dungeons were a difficult labyrinth in the best of times, but with the incredible attack going on above, the maze of twisty little passages was almost impenetratable. The magic which usually guided the knowledgable wasn't working and Atros was forced to rely on the memory and navigating skill of the goblins. He had a sneaking suspicion they had spent most of their time down here lost and wandering in circles—if a circle wasn't too regular a figure to describe their movements.

But something had obviously happened to those guards and Atros was encouraged by the report of humans in the dungeons—apparently Northern guardsmen at that. What was going on over their heads was unbelievably powerful, but it was also all strange. None of the familiar magic or non-magical forces of the North had been encountered. Atros had perforce learned a grudging respect for the Northerners, not only for developing so many mighty new spells but for keeping everything so secret that the League's spies had gotten only the vaguest of hints.

However that left the League's more conventional resources uncommitted and Atros had a shrewd suspicion that they would be thrown in at a critical point. When that happened, he vowed as he jogged along grimly, he would be there and there would be such a duel of wizards as the World had never seen.

Wiz charged through the smoldering ruins of the door and swept Moira into his arms. She was dazed and weeping. She was filthy and her long red hair was matted with dirt, but she was still the most beautiful woman Wiz had ever seen.

"Oh my God, Moira, I thought I had lost you forever."

"Wiz, Oh Wiz," Moira sobbed into his chest. Then he reached down, lifted her chin and kissed her.

"Now what?" Atros demanded of his hulking companion as they came around the bend. Ahead of them was a faint golden glow, the likes of which Atros had never seen down here.

The head goblin only shrugged and signalled his men to advance cautiously. As they moved down the tunnel cautiously the light grew brighter and steadier. They came around another bend and there, at the end of the tunnel was a shattered door with a golden light emanating from it and the sound of voices. Human voices. Atros stepped aside as the goblin captain and his soldiers advanced.

At the cell door, Kenneth stared down the corridor and fretted. It was bad enough that the Sparrow hadn't turned off his seeker ball now that they had found the hedge-witch. Worse he was clinched with her and he wasn't making any effort to get them away. Kenneth's well-developed sense of danger had been nagging ever since they entered the dungeons and now the nagging had grown to a full scream. If they stayed here much longer they were going to run into something they could not handle. Kenneth had no doubt at all these passages were full of things like that.

He frowned and squinted down the way they had come, careful not to expose his body with the light behind him. Was it his imagination or had he just heard a scuffling sound, like something heavy trying to move quietly?

Well, one way to find out," he thought to himself. Silently he nocked the arrow he was carrying in his bow hand. Then he drew and loosed a shaft down the corridor.

He was rewarded with a shout and the sound of running feet.

"*Attackers!*" Kenneth yelled, and fired another arrow. Donal was at his side instantly, his sword at the ready.

"Lord, light the corridor and douse that globe!"

Wiz jerked his head up at Kenneth's cry. "Right," he said and snatched up his staff. "**backslash light exe**" he yelled, pointing the staff down the corridor. Moira gaped at him. Instantly the whole corridor lit up blue, revealing a packed mass of goblins thundering down on them.

"For-tuna," Donal breathed and grasped his sword more tightly.

Kenneth's bowstring thrummed twice more and two more goblins fell. The last one to go down was the goblin commander who dropped kicking and writhing with an arrow in his eye. His momentum carried him nearly two paces further.

The combination of the light and the loss of their commander was too much for the goblins. They broke and fled back down the tunnel. Kenneth got one more as they rounded the bend.

"Magic, Master! We must have magic!" The goblin soldier was breathing hard and foam slavered down his chin as he knelt before Atros.

"Fools! Buffoons!" roared Atros. "Must I do your work for you? There is no magic here. Only two humans. Finish them. Now."

"Magic, Master!" the goblin soldier begged.

"Idiot!" Atros kicked the creature in the face, sending him sprawling. The other goblins shifted and muttered. Atros realized he was dangerously close to overplaying his hand with these servants.

"Attack again," he ordered. "Attack now. If they use magic *then* I will loose my powers against them."

The goblins muttered more but they began to sort themselves out for an attack.

Atros watched, frowning. He still wasn't sure the alien wizard was with this group and he didn't want

to use his magic unnecessarily. Whatever was going
on in the City of Night was nullifying or weakening
spells. Demons were not responding reliably to his
call, so he could not learn the identity of his adver-
sary. He did not know his strengths or weaknesses
and the feel of the magic was maddeningly unfamiliar.
Worse, he could not establish contact with his fellow
wizards. He was on his own and deprived of his most
reliable weapons.

If the wizard was in that room, then he would
crush him. But there was no sign of great power and
if the wizard was not there, Atros would rather sacri-
fice this band of goblins than reveal and weaken
himself.

He stood aside as the goblins formed up, ignoring
their sidelong glances and their mutterings. One more
attack and he would have those humans. Then he
would know.

"Lord, we have to get out of here," Kenneth said
over his shoulder. "They're reforming just around
the bend."

"Uh? Oh, right. Let's get going. Gather round
close everybody. He put an arm around Moira's waist
and drew her to him. Donal stepped in close behind
and at the last second Kenneth spun away from the
door and raced to them. Wiz lifted his staff. **backslash
transport** . . . he began and then stopped.

"Damn," Wiz said under his breath.

"What is it?" Moira asked.

"I don't have enough power to make the transport.
I can't make the spell work with all those worms
active."

"I would suggest, Lord, that you come up with an
alternative," said Kenneth quietly, nocking an arrow,
"and do so quickly." He returned to the door and
stared down the weirdly lit corridor.

"I'll have to shut down the worms. It'll just take a
few minutes."

"We may not have them," Kenneth replied, drawing his bow and stepping quickly into the corridor to loose a shaft. There was a roar of pain and then other roars and yells as the attackers charged.

Again, Kenneth brought down two more before they closed. By the time he laid his bow aside and drew his sword, Donal's two-handed sword was cleaving a glittering arc of death in the air before them. The leading goblin charged unheeding and died twitching and flopping at the guardsman's feet, his arm and shoulder nearly shorn from his body.

The other goblins hesitated for a fraction. Experienced fighters all, they knew that their situation was not as favorable as it looked to Moira gaping from the doorway. True, they had the humans outnumbered 20 to 1, but the tunnel was so narrow they could only come on three abreast, and a tightly packed three abreast at that. Their armor was good, but their weapons were for guard work, not a battle with armored men at close quarters. They had no archers, only a few pole arms and no shields.

Still, they were seasoned warriors and if the effects of the magical assault on the City of Night had unnerved them, they had no doubt they could win *this* fight. They dressed their lines and advanced in a packed mass. Barbed spears and cruelly hooked halberds reached out from the back ranks toward the two men.

Donal skipped forward, beating the pole arms aside and down with an overhead sweep of his blade. The goblins to his right were tied up by the tangle of weapons but the one to his left raised his sword for a killing stroke.

Before the blow could land Kenneth thrust home into the creature's exposed armpit. The light mail under the arm popped and snapped and the goblin went down shrieking. Donal gave ground, parrying with his great sword as the weapons of the back ranks thrust at him. Donal took advantage of the gap created by the falling goblin to slash the face of his rank mate and then leapt away so that the swords of the goblins cut empty air.

The goblins pressed forward as the humans retreated, the ones on the left stumbling on the bodies of their fallen comrades. Kenneth reached to his belt and drew a small war axe with his left hand. Donal parried a spear thrust from the rear ranks and riposted with a quick thrust to the head of the right-most goblin. The blade slid off the creature's knobbed helmet, but the force of the blow jarred the goblin and made him break step. The middle goblin aimed a whistling low cut at Kenneth's leg and gave Donal the opening he had been waiting for.

Kenneth stepped in and thrust to the goblin's neck. At the same time he brought the hatchet up and caught the left-most goblin's sword stroke between the haft and bit. A twist of his wrist and the sword was levered out of its owner's grasp and flying across the tunnel. The creature gaped in tusked amazement and then his eyes glazed in death as Kenneth's sword found his vitals.

But before Kenneth could skip out of range, a halberd licked out from among the goblins' legs. With a vicious jerk the hook on the back of the blade sank into the unprotected rear of Kenneth's calf. The guardsman hissed in pain and dropped. Donal slashed mightily with his great sword to cover his fallen companion, but the goblins pressed forward inexorably. Goblin blades flashed out, three and four at once. Rings popped on Donal's mail and a bright red gash opened in his side.

Wiz turned from his half-built spell at Moira's gasp in time to see Donal reel backward from the blows.

"cancel!" he shouted and pointed his staff at the packed mass. "for 1 to 10 flash do"he shouted. "exe!"

Instantly the corridor went from a bluish gloom to a light more brilliant than the brightest summer noon. Then it went pitch dark and then the light again and again and again. The goblins howled in pain from the blasts of light. In the strobe of the bolts Wiz could see them weirdly frozen, trying to shield their eyes and ignoring the two helpless men on the floor.

Wiz pointed his staff at the goblins and muttered another command. "bibbity boppity boo!"

A ravening lance of flame shot from the end of the staff and struck the foremost goblin squarely. The creature shrieked, a high, almost womanish sound, as the fire took it. Another bolt shot from Wiz's staff and another goblin turned into a living torch. Again and again Wiz's staff shot fire and more goblins burned.

That was too much. The goblins broke and fled, the ones in the fore trampling their fellows behind them in their haste to escape.

Wiz closed his eyes and breathed a silent prayer. Moira dashed out into the corridor to the wounded men.

Kenneth had an ugly wound in his calf but he could limp back with only a little assistance. Donal was in a worse way, conscious but groggy and bleeding heavily from the wound in his side. Moira and Wiz got the two inside and laid them on the dirty straw.

"My bow," Kenneth commanded and Wiz rushed back to get it. When he returned he found the guardsman had dragged himself to the door and was standing propped against the jamb.

"Thank you, Lord," he said as Wiz handed him the bow. "I will keep watch from here. But we need to be gone quickly."

"I'm trying," Wiz told him, "but this is more complicated than I bargained for. I don't think those damned worms were such a hot idea after all."

"Make haste Lord," Kenneth panted. "They have not gone far and they will come again soon."

"Likely with others who are not so flighty," said

Donal, who came limping up in spite of Moira's efforts to keep him lying down.

Wiz took a deep breath and returned to the job of shutting down a worm.

It was an intricate process. The worms were under the control of the Emacs back at Heart's Ease and Wiz had no direct communication with them. He could not simply neutralize the worms, he had to shut at least some of them off completely. The entities had been busy reproducing themselves since they first appeared, so that was difficult.

"**backslash, class worm suspend . . .**" He shook his head. No, that wouldn't work! "**cancel**" He tried again. "**backslash . . .**"

"Lord, you'd better get out here quickly," Kenneth said quietly. "We have a new problem."

The dragons rose from their shaking caverns as their riders fought to keep them under control. They formed into a group of ragged Vs as they swept once around the peak and then turned toward the sea. There was no attack warning, no battle plan, not even any orders. It was simply better to sortie blindly than to wait.

High above, the Dragon Leader watched them come. He had barely two squadrons behind him and the entire dragon cavalry of the City of Night was on the wing below. But he had height and position and the climbing ranks were confused and hesitant. He raised his hand over his head and pointed down. Then he nudged his mount and the entire force hurtled earthward in formation.

In the midst of a hurricane of sorcery there was no magic to aid either side. Magic detectors screamed constantly, useless in the boil of spells. Even the psychic link between dragon and rider weakened and wavered in the maelstrom of magics that enveloped the City of Night.

Freed from close control, the dragons fought by

instinct. Formations dissolved into whirling, flaming chaos as the two groups collided. Great winged bodies hurtled into each other, ripping and tearing and unseating riders. Dragon fire flew in all directions without discipline or guidance.

The Dragon Leader got one good pass out of his mount and saw his target go down smoking. Then he was through the League formation and the dragon was climbing on powerful beats of leathery wings. He tried to pull clear of the milling swarm to get altitude for another pass, but his dragon had other ideas. Still climbing, they charged into the thick of the fight.

The dragon caught one opponent by climbing underneath him and blasting him before the hapless beast even knew they were there. But now they were in the thick of the fight with hostile dragons on all sides.

True to his instinct the dragon raised her head and bellowed out a challenge. Answering roars came from all around them. The Dragon Leader gave up trying to control his mount. Instead, he drew his bow and swiveled, looking for the nearest opponent.

The attack came from behind. A League dragon swooped down on them before either dragon or rider knew he was there. The dragon must have exhausted its fire because it made no attempt to flame them as it went past. Instead the Dragon Leader had a glimpse of the figure on its back drawing his bow and twisting to track them as he swept by. The swarthy face, slitted eyes and scalplock of the enemy rider burned themselves into his brain.

There was no room to maneuver and no time to turn. The League rider fired and the iron shaft buried itself in his dragon's neck.

But the dragon barely noticed. She dropped one wing and flicked her tail to turn more tightly on her tormentor. Almost as an afterthought she reached up with a forelimb and plucked the shaft free.

What the . . . ? Somewhere in the back of his mind the Dragon Leader was amazed he wasn't plummeting out of the sky on a dead dragon. Meanwhile he was turning inside his foe and closing rapidly.

The Dragon Leader fitted an iron arrow to his own bow, but there was no tingle of recognition from the seeker head. The spells on death arrows were being overwhelmed by the competing magics. Swearing, he shifted his aim and fired. If magic would not work, perhaps skill would.

It did. The shaft flew straight and true and pierced the rider through the back. The man threw up his arms and crumpled into his saddle. The dragon turned to take on another opponent, still bearing the dead man on its back.

The Dragon Leader looked around and urged his mount forward for another foe.

Eventually it was all too much. The League dragons, outfought, disorganized and only under rudimentary control, broke and fled south in a confused gaggle. Some dove and dashed for safety scant feet off the earth. Others concentrated on making the best possible speed no matter what their altitude. A few fell to the flames of their attackers as they ran.

As soon as they were well clear of the City of Night, the Dragon Leader signaled his men to break off and re-form. The squadrons were tattered and several of the dragons were riderless, but his force was intact. There was no question who had won this day.

Counting his men, the Dragon Leader ordered one more sweep over the City of Night before they turned to the north and home.

With shaking hands, Toth-Set-Ra removed the globe from the cabinet and set it in the middle of the floor. There was a muffled roar and the palace shook, showering a sprinkle of mortar on the wizard's dark robe. He paid no attention.

Quickly but carefully he checked the pentagram, brushing away dust or debris that might breach it. Bale-Zur was not to be invoked lightly nor without scrupulous attention to the proper precautions. He could be counted upon to take advantage of any loophole in the bargain.

Toth-Set-Ra shook back the sleeves of his robe, picked up the silver wand off the lectern and began his chant.

A cloud of stinking, reeking sulphurous smoke billowed up, hiding the walls of the chamber and making Toth-Set-Ra's eyes water and his lungs burn. He paid no notice but continued chanting as a dull red glow coalesced and grew in the heart of the smoke cloud.

"Bale-Zur. Bale-Zur. Bale-Zur. By the power of your true name and the force of our bargain I call you, I summon you, I command you to make yourself manifest."

As the wizard gestured, the smoke billowed even thicker and the glow grew fiercer and larger. And then the smoke wafted away as though on a breeze, leaving the mightiest of demons revealed.

The huge black creature squatted toadlike in the chamber, nearly filling the pentagram and almost brushing the stone vaulting of the ceiling. His horned and warty head swivelled slowly and continually from side to side, as if seeking prey. The great claws clenched and relaxed against the stone.

"My due," the demon's voice boomed out, so low that the undertones made the wizard's bones quiver. "I will have my due."

"I give you one" hissed Toth-Set Ra. "I give you the one known to men as Sparrow, called Wiz. By the power of his true name I give him to you."

The monster paused and considered. The huge mouth opened, showing rows of teeth like daggers, and the beast ran a surprisingly pink tongue over its black scaly lips.

"Sparrow is not his true name," the creature rumbled. "Nor is Wiz."

"By the power of his true name I give him to you!" Toth-Set-Ra repeated, more shrilly.

Again the demon Bale-zur considered. At last the massive head stopped moving and the glowing red eyes focused on the wizard.

"This one's true name is not written upon the wind," the demon said at last.

Toth-Set-Ra licked his lips, suddenly gone dry. "But he has a true name," he insisted desperately. "All men have a true name."

"Then it has never been spoken within the World," said the demon, hopping cumbersomely forward. "Our bargain is broken and I will have my due."

Toth-Set-Ra screamed and backed away as the demon crossed the now-useless pentagram. He scuttled toward the door, but the great creature was too quick for him. A huge clawed foot caught him squarely in the back as his hand touched the door handle.

In the riot and confusion of the shuddering palace no one noticed the screams. But they went on for a long, long time.

Blinded, burned and screeching, the goblins fell back around the bend in the tunnel. Atros paid them no heed.

So, breathed the wizard, now unknowingly the Mightiest in the League. *So he is here after all.* He spared a quick glance for his companions. Of the fifty or so who had accompanied Atros into the dungeons perhaps a dozen remained. No soldiers here, this would be a duel of wizardry.

The auspices were not ideal, but Atros meant to have this wizard and if his goblin soldiers could not take him, then he would do so himself. He flipped back his great fur cloak, baring his thickly muscled arms, and muttered a protective incantation before he stepped around the corner.

*   *   *

"What is it?" Wiz asked as the hulking skin-clad figure strode down the tunnel toward them.

"A wizard," Kenneth told him. "I'm sorry, Lord, but we cannot help you now. You must meet magic with magic in a duel of wizards."

Wiz licked his lips and took a deep, shuddering breath. Then he stepped into the blue-lit corridor, staff in hand.

Atros did not check his stride as Wiz came through the broken door. Stepping around the broken burned bodies of his goblin bodyguard he bored straight toward the slight dark-haired figure holding his oak staff as if it were a baseball bat.

As Atros came on Wiz pointed his staff at him. "bippity boppity boo," he said and again the roaring lance of flame shot from the staff's tip. But the big wizard made a dismissing gesture with a flip of his wrist and the flame veered to one side, splashing off the wall and dissipating harmlessly.

Atros raised his hand and balls of fire flew from his fingertips; one after the other they caromed down the hall at Wiz. Wiz reached into his pouch and threw a tiny, pallid grub at his attacker. Grub and fireballs met in mid-tunnel and the flames were sucked away, leaving only a medium-sized worm behind.

Quickly Wiz muttered another spell. Suddenly Atros found his progress slowed, as if he were walking through molasses. The more he pushed, the slower he moved until by exerting all his mighty strength he was barely able to move at all.

Atros paused for a second, examining the spell, tasting it. Experimentally he tried moving a hand slowly and found it moved normally. The resistance built higher the faster he tried to move. The southern wizard smiled slightly and spoke a counter-incantation. Then he strode forward unhindered.

His next step was nearly his last. His foot landed on a patch of something as slippery as the slickest ice over polished marble. He could get no purchase and his feet shot out from under him. Instinctively Atros used a spell to stay upright. Again a pause while he analyzed the magic and again Wiz's best effort was nullified by a counterspell.

Atros assayed a transformation spell. But Wiz just stood there, unchanged and unharmed. A disorientation spell, a sleep spell and an earthquake spell followed in quick succession. Still his slender opponent stood unscathed.

Atros was baffled. He had never seen its like before. Normally a barrage of spells had some effect, but this was as if they weren't even reaching their target. A bit tentatively, Atros hurled a bolt of lightning down the corridor. It reached the worm and vanished.

Aha! The worm had grown noticeably larger. The thing was actually soaking up magic. Again Atros smiled and shaped a spell carefully.

The Southern wizard raised his staff, an inky blob of darkness formed on the end of it and wobbled down the corridor. It was black beyond black, blacker than night and it floated toward Wiz like a balloon wafted on a breeze.

Wiz watched as the sphere of darkness passed over the now-fattened worm. The worm reached out greedily for the magic just as the sphere bobbed to the floor of the corridor to meet it, bending toward the worm like a lover bending toward a kiss.

The pair touched. Suddenly the worm faded and shrunk as the black sphere of negation drained the magic it had hoarded. As the worm grew smaller so did the sphere, until at last there was again a tiny writhing grub and the sphere closed in on itself and vanished.

Atros ground the worm under his heel as he stepped forward to confront Wiz.

Wiz hit Atros with everything but the kitchen sink. A hundred lightning bolts flashed toward him so fast the corridor was lit by a constant blinding glare and the air reeked of ozone. The tunnel roof caved in with a roar and a huge cloud of dust. Thirty sharp knives flew at Atros from all directions. His bearskin tried to crawl off his back. A hurricane swept down the corridor blowing with a force no man could withstand.

Still Atros came on. The lightning struck all about him but never touched him. The falling rocks bounced off an invisible shield over his head. His skin garment convulsed and lay still. The wind did not move a hair on his head.

Wiz's spells had raw power, but they lacked the carefully crafted subtlety of a truly great wizard. And Atros, for all his braggado, was one of the great wizards of the World. More, he had the hard-won experience that comes from fighting and winning a score of magical duels. But most of all, Atros was a killer. Wiz simply was not.

Now Atros raised his staff and it was Wiz's turn to endure.

"New magic in the City of Night, Lord. Strong and strange."

Bal-Simba rushed to the Watcher's side. "Is it Sparrow? Can you locate him?"

"It appears to be and, yes Lord, we have it very precisely. He is in the dungeons beneath the city." The Watcher peered deeply into the crystal again. "There is other magic close by, Lord. Very strong and . . . Atros! Lord, your Sparrow is locked in a magical duel with Atros!"

"Fortuna!" Bal-Simba swore. "How is the Sparrow doing?"

"I can't tell, Lord. His spells are so peculiar. But there is a lot of magic loose in those tunnels." Another pause and the Watcher tore his eyes from the crystal to face Bal-Simba. "He seems to be holding his own, but I don't think he is winning, Lord."

"A Sparrow against a bear. That is not an even match."

"I fear not, Lord."

Bal-Simba bowed his mighty head and frowned into the crystal. Then he snapped his head up and slapped his palm on his thigh with a crack like a pistol shot.

"A circle!" he bellowed to the assembled Mighty. "Quickly to me! I must have a circle!"

Magic constricted around Wiz like a vise. As quickly as he erected a barrier against the onrushing spells, it was torn away and magic wound ever tighter around him. Again and again Atros thrust with his staff and Wiz was driven back toward the door of the cell where Moira and the two wounded guardsmen cowered, blinded and deafened by the effects of the duel and choked by the dust and magic thick in the air.

Suddenly Atros took his staff in both hands, raised it high over his head and brought it down with a vicious chopping motion. Wiz raised his staff to ward it off, but he was driven to his knees by the force of the blow. Blindly he raised his staff and gestured again. But the stroke was weak and ill-judged and Atros thrust it aside contemptuously. He stepped forward again and raised his staff for a final, killing spell.

From the cell door a blazing ball flew over Wiz's head and straight at Atros's face. The wizard dropped his staff and flinched aside from the burning sphere. He gestured and it swerved off to splatter in a flaming gout on the tunnel wall behind him.

Atros looked over Wiz and saw Moira standing in the door with her eyes blazing and her hands extended clawlike.

"Witch!" he said contemptuously and made a shooing motion with both hands. Moira screamed and flew back into the cell as if pushed by an unseen hand. Then the skin-clad giant stooped to pick up his staff.

Inside the cell an explosion blasted out. A choking cloud of dirt billowed from the shattered door and a reddish light like a new-kindled fire burned within. Atros frowned and made a warding move with his staff. Wiz shook his head and climbed half to his feet.

Within the cell, obscured by the dust and lighted by the fire behind, a huge misshapen thing moved. Atros took a step back and a firmer grasp on his staff. What new sort of demon was this?

The light grew brighter as the fire took hold of the straw. Through the smoke and reddish backlight the thing resolved itself into a vaguely man-like figure. It groped through the smoke and dust, narrowing and resolving as it moved toward the door as though coalescing into something solid. Atros shifted uneasily. There was something familar about that figure . . .

Then it came through the door and out of the smoke. "So," it rumbled in a familar voice. "A bear chasing a sparrow, eh? Not very edifying Atros. Not very edifying at all."

"Bal-Simba!" Atros spat the name like a curse.

"Bal-Simba indeed," the great wizard agreed. He was disheveled and his hair and skin were powdered gray with dirt and dust, but his teeth showed white as milk and sharp as daggers as he smiled. "A worthier opponent than yon sparrow, mayhap?

"Sparrow," Bal-Simba said without taking his eyes off the southern wizard, "please put out the fire in the cell. Atros and I have wizard's business to discuss."

"We discuss it on my ground, Northerner," Atros said with an evil smile.

"Oh, I think no one's ground." Bal-Simba's smile was no less evil. "Your protective spells are neutralized, your brother wizards are, ah, occupied elsewhere and Toth-Set-Ra is dead." He raised his eyebrows. "What? You did not know? Demon trou-

ble, I believe. Troublesome things, demons. Almost
as much trouble as sparrows."

Their eyes locked and neither moved while Wiz
scrambled on his hands and knees behind Bal-Simba's
trunk-like legs and through the cell door. Moira was
waiting and they clung together like frightened children, heedless of the smoldering straw.

Finally Atros snarled and thrust his staff at the
black giant. Wiz saw the air between them twist and
contort into a half-sensed shape that flew straight at
Bal-Simba's chest. Bal-Simba turned his staff side-
ways and the thing disappeared in a shimmer of air.

He took a step forward. Atros gestured again and
the bloody green slime in the center of the corridor
massed and grew and rose up in a foul dripping wave
in front of Bal-Simba.

Again Bal-Simba gestured and the slime hung back.
It recoiled, gathered itself and thrust forward like a
striking snake. With an easy grace Bal-Simba pirou-
etted to one side. The slime thing missed and fell
into the center of the corridor with a hollow "splat."
Before it could gather itself again the Northerner
pressed his staff into the slime's "back." It quivered
for a moment and then lay still.

The giant turned to face his giant assailant. Atros's
lips were working as he prepared another spell. But
Bal-Simba didn't give him the change to use it.

"And now." Bal-Simba tapped his staff on the flag-
ging and stepped forward. Atros gave ground, pawing the air frantically with his staff.

"And now." Bal-Simba stepped and struck the pave-
ment a ringing blow as Atros blanched and flinched.

"*And now,*" he bellowed and smote the floor so
hard his staff shattered into three pieces. Atros
screamed as a great chasm opened beneath him. He
teetered on the crumbling brink for an instant and
then toppled forward. He was still screaming ever
fainter and further away when the earth closed with
a clap of thunder, cutting off his screams forever.

The black giant sagged and put a hand on the tunnel wall to stay upright. "Whoo," he gasped and shook his head. "Whoo."

"Lord, am I glad to see you!" Wiz stepped out of the cell, leaning on Moira for support.

"Sparrow," Bal-Simba rumbled, "you are a great deal of trouble."

Wiz just laughed and hugged him.

"Lord," Moira hugged him from the other side. "Lord, I had lost hope."

"Always unwise, Lady," said Bal-Simba. He frowned. "My two guardsmen? Donal and Kenneth?"

"Here, Lord," croaked Kenneth, pulling himself erect on the frame of the cell door. "Donal is with me, but he is in a sore way."

"Then I suggest we take him someplace more comfortable," Bal-Simba said. "Sparrow, will you do the honors? I'm not sure I am up to walking the Wizard's Way just yet."

"With pleasure," Wiz grinned. "Uh, it may take me four or five tries to get the spell right."

It actually took six.

THIRTEEN
THE BEGINNING

Spring was returning to Heart's Ease.

Except for the spots in deepest shade the snow was melting, exposing the wet black earth beneath. Here and there the hardiest plants thrust forth brave green shoots and the branches of the trees swelled with the promise of buds. The ground was soggy and chill, and there was still a skin of ice on the puddles in the morning, but the afternoon air was soft and the sun shone more brightly onto the warming land.

Wiz and Moira stood together in the door of his hut, sharing a cloak and looking out over the Wild Wood.

Heart's Ease was still a gaunt blackened thumb against the blue sky, but the burned parts of the stockade were already down, removed by the forest folk. As soon as the paths through the Wild Wood dried out men would arrive, masons and carpenters who would begin rebuilding Heart's Ease. As before there would be no magic in its construction.

"We don't have to stay here, love," Wiz told Moira. "It will take time to make the place habitable and there's no reason you should live in a log cabin. We could go someplace more civilized. Even the Capital if you prefer."

"I want to stay here, I think," Moira said, snuggling to him under the cloak. "Oh, I'd like to go visit my village after things thaw and dry. But I like it here." She turned her face to his for a kiss and Wiz responded enthusastically.

"Besides," she went on after a bit, "I think Shiara likes having us." She turned to him. "But where do you want to live?"

"Anywhere you are," Wiz told her. "I'd be happy anywhere with you."

Moira bit her lip and dropped her gaze. "We need to talk about that."

"Fine," Wiz agreed, "but not now. We've got company."

Moira looked up and saw Bal-Simba picking his way across the muddy court.

"Merry met, Lord," Moira said as he came up to them.

"Merry met, Lady, Lord," the great black wizard replied as he came puffing up, his bone necklace jangling. "Merry met indeed."

"What's happening at the Capital?" Wiz asked once they were seated around the log table in the tiny cabin. Wiz and Moira sat holding hands on one side and Bal-Simba seemed to fill the rest of the dwelling.

Bal-Simba smiled. "Ah, they are still as roiled as ants whose hill has been kicked over. From the ditherings of the Council you would think it was the Capital which had been destroyed, not the City of Night." Then he sobered.

"But that is not why I am here, Lord. I came to tell you that with the Dark League's power broken, we may be able to send you home again."

Wiz frowned. "I thought that was impossible."

"With the League in ruins many things are possible. Their wizards are scattered and cannot interfere if the Mighty band together for a Great Summoning. I have consulted the Council and we are willing to perform a Great Summoning to return you to your world."

Wiz felt Moira's hand tighten in his and caught his breath.

Home! A place with pizza, books, movies, records and music. A place where someone or something wasn't trying to kill him all the time. A place where he didn't have to be dirty or cold or frightened. And computers again.

But a place with no Moira. He saw she was staring intently at the table top. Was all the rest of it worth that?

There was something else too. He could help people here. Back home it didn't matter if he worked on a project or not, not really anyway. There were other programmers who could do what he did, although maybe not as well. Here he *did* matter. He could make a big difference. And that was worth a lot.

"I will not lie to you, Sparrow," Bal-Simba said. "There will be an element of danger. It will be hard to locate your world out of the multitude and even with all of us working together we are not sure we can send you back. But we believe the chances are very good."

"I don't think I want to go," he said firmly and drew Moira to him. "Not now." The hedge-witch came close, but he could still feel the tension in her body.

Bal-Simba grinned. "I thought that would be your answer. But I had to make the offer. And remember Sparrow, you can change your mind. The North owes you a great debt."

"You owe a greater debt to Patrius," Wiz said. "It was his idea."

The wizard nodded. "I wish Patrius had been here to see it,"

"I wish he had too," Wiz said gravely. "He should have been here to see it. It really was his victory. Besides, I would liked to have known him."

"But you made it happen," Moria insisted. "You did the work. And Patrius made a mistake. He said you were not a wizard."

Wiz sighed. "You still don't get it, do you? I'm *not* a wizard. Most likely I never will be."

"There are those among the League who would dispute that—were they still alive to do so," Bal-Simba said, showing all his pointed teeth.

"They'd be wrong." Wiz sighed again. "As wrong as you are. Look, you still don't appreciate what Patrius did. It wasn't that he found me and brought me here—and I'm not unique, by the way. In fact I was probably a poor choice if things had gone as Patrius intended them. But he wasn't looking for a wizard at all."

"I did not know you had added necromancy to your talents, Sparrow."

"No magic, just logic. Although I didn't work it out until everything was all over." Wiz took his arm from around Moira's waist and leaned both elbows on the table.

"Your real problem was that you had a magical problem that couldn't be solved by magic. Every great spell was vulnerable to an even greater counter-spell and as the League waxed you inevitably waned. Individually, the League's magicians were stronger than the Council's, they *had* to be because they didn't care about the consequences of their actions. Patrius knew that a conventional solution, a bigger magician, would only make matters worse in a generation or so when the League learned the techniques."

"That is common knowledge in the Council," Bal-Simba rumbled. "Indeed one of the reasons it was so easy to get agreement to attempt to return you is there is a strong faction which wishes to be rid of you. Go on, Sparrow."

"Okay, take it one step further. Patrius must have. He realized what you needed was a completely new approach. He had the genius to see that despite everything you believed, everything your experience showed you somewhere behind all your magic there had to be some kind of regular structure. He realized that if he could find that formalism you could control magic."

"Eh?" said Bal-Simba. "Forgive a fat old wizard, but I was under the impression that we do control magic."

"No," Wiz said emphatically and then caught himself. "Forgive me Lord, but it is true. Each magician can use the spells or demons he or she stumbles upon and masters, but none of you—Council or League—controls magic. You don't deal with magic as a whole. You have no coherent theory of magic and you usually can't generalize from what you do know to what you don't. That was the root of your problem. The League and the Wild Wood were just symptoms."

Wiz could see Bal-Simba rolling that idea around in his mind. Obviously he didn't like it, but he was not going to reject it out of hand. "Go on," he said neutrally.

"In my world we have a saying that Man is a creature who controls his environment. You're in trouble because there's an important part of your environment you can't control: Magic. Patrius didn't go looking for a wizard to beat the League. He wanted someone who understood abstract formalisms and how to apply them to complex problems in the hope he *could* learn to control magic. He needed a computer programmer or a mathematician. Magical ability wasn't in the job description."

"It appears that he got more than he bargained for," Bal-Simba said.

Wiz shook his head. "No. He got exactly what he bargained for. I'm not a magician in the way you mean.

"I've told you about computers, the non-living thinking machines I used to work with? Well, back when they were very new we worked with them the way you work your spells. Every new program was written by cut-and-try and every program was unique.

Anyone who wanted to use a computer had to be an expert and it took years of work and study to master a machine.

"Later we realized it didn't have to be that way. We found the computer could do a lot of the work. We could write programs that would take care of the tiresome, repetitive parts and we could design programs whose parts could be used over and over in many different programs.

"Finally we figured out that you didn't even have to have a programmer for every computer. You could write programs that anyone could use to do common jobs like word processing or accounting.

"So today anyone can use a computer. Even children use them regularly. You still need programmers, but we work at a higher level, on more difficult or unusual problems—or on writing the programs that those children use."

Bal-Simba frowned. "Well and good for your world, Sparrow, but I am not sure I see what use it is to us."

"Patrius did," Wiz told him. "He hoped he could do the same thing with magic we do with computers. And he was right.

"In the long run the important thing wasn't that I beat the League with magic. It wasn't even that I was able to rescue Moira." *Although I'll be damned if I'll take that long a view,* he thought. "The important thing was programs—ah, the 'structure'—I had to build to do it." He learned forward intensely.

"Don't you see? With my system you don't need to be a wizard to work spells. You need programmer-wizards to create the spells, but once they are set up anyone can use them. All you have to do is understand how those spells work and anyone can make magic. Good, controllable magic."

"Magic in the wrong hands is dangerous," Bal-Simba said dubiously.

Wiz smiled. "Don't worry. Where I come from we

have a lot of experience in keeping our systems secure and users' fingers out of the gears. If the spells are properly designed just about anyone can use them safely.

"And it goes beyond that. I can teach someone to do what I do. It's not hard, really. It takes an organized mind and a knack for thinking logically, but just about anyone can learn it. If your magicians have the knack I can show them the tools and teach them how to use them.

"Don't you see?" he repeated. "It means humans don't have to walk in fear any more." He thought of a small cabin deep in the Wild Wood and the four carefully tended graves behind it. Of a burned farm near the Fringe and the mound of raw earth among the cabbages. "People don't have to be afraid."

Bal-Simba sat silent for a long time. "This will require thought," he said at last. "The Council must consider it carefully. No doubt you will be asked to come to the Capital to explain to them." He chuckled. "Oh, we're in for some rare debates in the Council chantry, I can see that."

The wizard pushed away from the table and rose. "But it will be soonest over if it is soonest started. And I should carry the news to them quickly. For that I will leave you now." He turned toward the door.

"No, wait!" Moira rose from the table. "There is one more thing you must do."

Baal-Simba cocked an eyebrow and waited.

Moira clasped her hands in front of her, took a deep breath and closed her eyes.

"Lord, I want you to remove the infatuation spell from Wiz," she said in a trembling voice.

"Eh?"

"Uh, never mind," Wiz told him. "I'm not sure I want it removed. Not now." He put his hands on Moira's shoulders but she shook them off with an angry gesture.

"Please, Lord. It is not fair to Wiz that I hold him in thrall thus."

"Now wait a minute . . ." Wiz began, but Moira cut him off. "It is his right, Lord."

"Now how is this?" asked Bal-Simba with a twinkle in his eye. "You wish to be rid of this troublesome Sparrow?"

"No, Lord, I do not. But I love him and I cannot . . ." she took a deep ragged breath and rushed on. "I cannot accept what is constrained from him. I love him too much to hold him by magic."

"Don't I have anything to say in this?" Wiz interjected.

Moira turned to him. "No, Wiz you do not. Not now. After the spell is removed, perhaps then. But don't you see? You feel what you must because of the spell."

"He may not love you once the spell is removed," Bal-Simba said gravely.

"Yes, I will!" Wiz shouted but neither paid any attention to him.

"I know that, Lord." Moira looked as if she would cry. "I know that. But I cannot take by magic what is not mine by right."

"You have treated him very badly, you know."

"Lord, please."

Bal-Simba steepled his hands and rested them on his great belly. "Lady, you ask a thing which is impossible."

"Lord!" Moira gasped, her face white. "But you said . . ."

"I know, but there have been changes since then. Your Sparrow is now the mightiest of the Mighty. His method of magic will likely spread throughout the World and he bids to outshine us all from hedge-witch to master sorcerer. And he does not want the spell removed.

"You on the other hand bid to become the Lady to the mightiest of the Mighty and that raises you high indeed. A poor old fat wizard who wishes to live out his days in peace would be well advised to stay in your good graces."

The black giant smiled, showing all his filed, pointed teeth, looking for all the world like an avuncular shark.

"More to the point Lady, I cannot remove what is not there."

"Huh?" said Wiz brilliantly.

"Lord, I saw Patrius cast the spell."

"And I removed it on my visit some months back," Bal-Simba said, still smiling. "It no longer seemed necessary."

Moira dropped her hands to her sides. "Then . . ."

"Oh yes, your Sparrow has been free for some little time." He cocked his head and eyed Wiz. "Although he seems to show no great interest in leaving his cage."

In response William Irving Zumwalt, the Sparrow grown large as a roc, spun Moira the hedge witch around and clasped her to him. She melted into his arms and their lips met again.

Over her shoulder and through a haze of coppery red hair, Wiz saw the Mightiest of the Mighty ease through the door and close it softly after him.

He moved amazingly quietly for one so large.

ANNE McCAFFREY
ELIZABETH MOON

Sassinak was twelve when the raiders came. That made her just the right age: old enough to be used, young enough to be broken. Or so the slavers thought. But Sassy turned out to be a little different from your typical slave girl. Maybe it was her unusual physical strength. Maybe it was her friendship with the captured Fleet crewman. Maybe it was her spirit. Whatever it was, it wouldn't let her resign herself to the life of a slave. She bided her time, watched for her moment. Finally it came, and she escaped. But that was only the beginning for Sassinak. Now she's a Fleet captain with a pirate-chasing ship of her own, and only one regret in her life: not enough pirates.

SASSINAK
You're going to love her!

Coming in March, from
BAEN BOOKS

Paksenarrion, a simple sheepfarmer's daughter, yearns for a life of adventure and glory, such as the heroes in songs and story. At age seventeen she runs away from home to join a mercenary company, and begins her epic life . . .

ELIZABETH MOON

THE DEED OF PAKSENARRION

"This is the first work of high heroic fantasy I've seen, that has taken the work of Tolkien, assimilated it totally and deeply and absolutely, and produced something altogether new and yet incontestably based on the master. . . . This is the real thing. Worldbuilding in the grand tradition, background thought out to the last detail, by someone who knows absolutely whereof she speaks. . . . Her military knowledge is impressive, her picture of life in a mercenary company most convincing."—**Judith Tarr**

About the author: Elizabeth Moon joined the U.S. Marine Corps in 1968 and completed both Officers Candidate School and Basic School, reaching the rank of 1st Lieutenant during active duty. Her background in military training and discipline imbue The Deed of Paksenarrion with a gritty realism that is all too rare in most current fantasy.

"I thoroughly enjoyed *Deed of Paksenarrion*. A most engrossing, highly readable work."
—Anne McCaffrey

"For once the promises are borne out. *Sheepfarmer's Daughter* is an advance in realism. . . . I can only say that I eagerly await whatever Elizabeth Moon chooses to write next."
—Taras Wolansky, *Lan's Lantern*

* * * * *

Volume One: Sheepfarmer's Daughter—Paks is trained as a mercenary, blooded, and introduced to the life of a soldier . . . and to the followers of Gird, the soldier's god.

Volume Two: Divided Allegiance—Paks leaves the Duke's company to follow the path of Gird alone—and on her lonely quests encounters the other sentient races of her world.

Volume Three: Oath of Gold—Paks the warrior must learn to live with Paks the human. She undertakes a holy quest for a lost eleven prince that brings the gods' wrath down on her and tests her very limits.

* * * * *

These books are available at your local bookstore, or you can fill out the coupon and return it to Baen Books, at the address below.

All three books of The Deed of Paksenarrion ____
SHEEPFARMER'S
 DAUGHTER   65416-0 • 506 pages • $3.95 ____
DIVIDED
 ALLEGIANCE   69786-2 • 528 pages • $3.95 ____
OATH OF GOLD 69798-6 • 528 pages • $3.95 ____

Please send the cover price to: Baen Books, Dept. B, 260 Fifth Avenue, New York, NY 10001.
Name_____
Address_____
City_____ State_____ Zip_____